The Belle of Oyster Bay

Angela Moody

To Aunt Jennie
Because you waited…

Also by Angela Moody

No Safe Haven

1

Saddlebags overflowing with Osnaburg linen, sugar cones, tea, and a quire of paper, Sally Townsend set off for Daniel and Susannah Youngs' farm on Cove Road.

Such a beautiful morning with a hint of building summer heat. The salty ocean breeze rustled through the trees and blew soft on her brow, teasing her hair. She lifted her face to the sun as she swayed to the movement of Farmer Girl beneath her. Chores waited for her at home, but she rode at a slow and steady pace, enjoying her rare solitude.

As she turned onto Cove Road, a strident scream startled her out of her languid mood. She straightened, bringing Farmer Girl to a stop. But after surveying the countryside, she found nothing except trees to her right and small waves caressing an empty shore on her left. A small dinghy sat forgotten on the beach.

Heart pounding, she slid the rein through her gloved hand. Shouts rent the air, echoing, and blending with the wind and waves breaking on the shore. She couldn't discern where they came from. Twisting her head from side to side, she tried to discover what and where the danger lay.

A sudden rustling in the trees focused her attention. Sally laid a gentle hand on Farmer Girl's neck, letting the strong muscle beneath her palm calm her. She ignored the warning to turn back. Susannah needed the goods, and since she made an issue of delivering them, Father would be annoyed if she didn't fulfill her duties.

Farmer Girl tossed her mane as if asking why they stopped. More rustling convinced Sally someone startled an animal, and itself startled, now tried to escape. She drew in a deep breath and willed herself to relax.

Sally tapped Farmer Girl with the heel of her riding boot. "Come on, girl," but Farmer Girl refused to move, tossing her head and snorting. "What's wrong with you?"

A group of men burst from the trees, dragging a struggling family with them.

Farmer Girl neighed and pranced to the side, kicking out. Sally gasped at the sudden move and struggled to regain control.

A man, a woman, and two small children fought their adversaries. The children cried while their mother struggled to protect them, and their father fought to protect his family.

Six men drew away and surrounded Sally. All twelve men carried flintlock pistols or muskets.

As her horse whinnied and tried to rear, she struggled to stay on. Speaking soothing words, she soon calmed the mare, though the poor animal's skin shivered. Wait! Cousin George? Heat coursed through her veins.

"What do you think you're doing?"

She grabbed her riding crop, keeping her arm lowered but ready to whip anyone who made a threatening gesture. She may not be able to hit them all, but a few lashes might do some damage.

"Sally! Where are you bound?" He sounded pleased to see her, but a rising flush stained his sunburned cheeks. He crossed his arms and widened his stance.

"My task is none of your concern. However, since you ask—," she allowed sarcasm to sour her voice he was just Cousin George— "I'm making a delivery to Daniel Youngs," she said, pointing with her crop. "Who are they? Why do you treat them so?"

The children were no more than five or six years old. The girl fisted her little hands into wads of her linsey-woolsey dress. Bare, dirty legs and toes dug into the dirt.

The boy thrust himself between her and the men. Clods of dirt stuck between his toes as if stitching them together like the patches on his shirt and breeches.

The poor dirt farmers must've proved an easy target for George's marauding band. As Sally and the woman made brief eye contact, she tried to reassure her through her expression that she would do her best to help.

"Weel now, missy..." A man said, sauntering forward and planting his hands on his hips, the rough gesture almost loosening one poorly mended patch from his white cotton shirt. His gravelly voice sent shivers down her spine. "These people are not your concern," he said, his upper lip curled, and his brown eyes glinted with something dark and dangerous.

She recoiled as he reached for Farmer Girl's bridle. Remembering her crop, she drew her arm back, ready.

Cousin George gripped his wrist. "None of that, John Kirk. She's the daughter of my cousin. They're our people."

"She asks too many questions." John Kirk spat in the mud, but he allowed George to lower his arm. "Fancy folk. They all think they're better'n us."

Sally gasped. *Filthy swine.* The words shot through her brain, but she possessed the sense not to utter them.

George ignored him, tapping Sally's elbow to regain her attention. "You familiar with the Tory Act?"

"Yes." She never took her eyes from Kirk. "Father read it to us from the paper yesterday. A stupid law if you ask me."

Kirk averted his eyes. She smirked.

"Good thing nobody asked you," George said, and his men grumbled laughter. He grinned at his companions as though encouraging them. He jerked his thumb at the family. "These people are Tory scum. We're taking them to Connecticut."

His chin rose. He gave her a self-satisfied grin, dropped his hands on his hips, and drew back his shoulders, thrusting his chest forward.

"We're gonna go to their house and take us a look-see," Kirk said. "If we find somep'n we like, well, we'll confiscate same in the name of the Sons o' Liberty."

Sally stiffened her spine as she drew the reins close to her chest. Farmer Girl gave a nervous step to the side and Sally laid a calming hand on her, praying she hid how her own hand shook.

"Who gave you the right?"

Her words constricted in her throat, forcing her to draw a deep breath. Sally glanced at the woman again and the terror in her eyes steadied her. She must do something.

"Leave these people be. Go home to your pitiful farm. I doubt the Sons of Liberty want your thievery—or you—on their side. Not if this is how you intend to behave. They'll brand you as nothing more than the thieves you are."

Kirk reached for the bridle again. "And you, missy, should ride on to Mr. Youngs's while he still lives there, drop your goodies, and go home."

His fingers closed around the leather on Farmer Girl's cheek.

"I'll do as I please." She drew herself straighter on Farmer Girl's back. "Which includes telling my father about you two!" The sight of his hand on her filly's tack angered her more. An expert flick of her wrist sent the crop snapping across the back of Kirk's knuckles. He jerked his hand away.

Farmer Girl tossed her head and Sally imagined her laughing.

George chuckled. "Just like your father, ain't you?"

He, too, grabbed the bridle, almost daring her to hit him, but Sally remained still.

"Kirk's right, Sally. Make your deliveries, mind your business, and return home posthaste. Many of us are out, following the letter of the Tory Act. You don't want to be accosted by someone without a family connection."

Sally adjusted her grip as she tried to assess his threat. She slid a soothing hand down Farmer Girl's neck and patted her shoulder. To gather her thoughts, she stared at the hostages before shifting her gaze back to George. "You should be ashamed of yourselves. This is wrong. The Tory Act is wrong if this is how people like you plan to carry it out. You're nothing but a bunch of thieves."

Being an expert equestrian, she booted Farmer Girl, who jumped forward, jerking the bridle out of George's hand.

John Kirk growled and slapped her horse on the rump. Farmer Girl squealed and shot forward. The momentum jolted Sally backward, but she kept her seat. After calming the mare, she turned, intending to give John Kirk a scolding the likes of which he would never forget.

4

But they were at the beach pushing the family toward the water. Helpless rage shook her to her toes as Kirk thrust the family into the dinghy. She gasped when he pulled his pistol on the father who tried to rise in defense of his wife and children.

The man sat down and gathered his children close as two men pushed the boat off the sand. They set off across the Sound.

Cousin George and John Kirk walked back toward the road, laughing, and clapping each other on the back. Kirk glanced at her, and despite the distance between them, his malevolence flowed over her like a wave.

Sally kicked Farmer Girl into a gallop. After riding hard for a quarter of a mile, she only slowed when the safety of Daniel and Susannah's home swung into view. Why didn't she ask for the family's identity? She failed to defend them well, but what might she do against a group of twelve armed men?

In front of the white farmhouse, Sally slumped in her seat, breathing hard. Farmer Girl snorted and shook her head, throwing off thick ropes of foam as Sally patted her neck in a gesture of thanks. The front door opened.

"Sally!" Daniel said with a wave before trotting down the walk. His smile of greeting changed to concern. "What happened to you?"

Sally didn't answer, gasping for breath.

He seized her waist and helped her from the saddle.

"Something...on the way over... I must tell you..."

She squeezed his arms to hold herself upright after he set her on her feet. When her muscles stopped quivering, she let go and undid the strap holding her saddlebags in place.

He took them from her. "Come inside and we'll talk."

Susannah gave her a cup of cool cider and put out a plate of biscuits. Sally plunked into a chair and recounted her story.

She crumbled a biscuit on her plate, her whole body still shaking as another fear coursed through her. "John Kirk told me to come here and make my deliveries while you still live here," she said. "They wouldn't do you harm, would they, Daniel?"

"No, my dear. I doubt they'll try to do us harm."

"But you're the head of the loyalist militia. If they're rounding up Tories, wouldn't they include you?"

5

Daniel sat back exchanging a glance with Susannah. He pursed his lips before shaking his head and grasping her hand. "They won't do me harm. As you said, I'm the head of the loyalist militia. I can call more important men to my aid than they can call to arrest me. Don't worry. We're safe."

"I pray so," she said and swirled her cider, her thoughts as shaken up, letting the sweetness soothe her throat, set the cup down, and scooted out of her chair. "I best go home before Father wonders what happened to me."

Daniel rose. "Stay here and chat with Susannah for a bit. We'll let Farmer Girl cool down before I escort you home," he said with a smile. "I'll see how Seth is doing with her care."

After the back door shut behind him, Sally resumed her seat and clasped Susannah's hand. "In truth, will you be all right?"

"If Daniel says so, I will accept he has things under control," Susannah said, squeezing her hand, then refilled her cider cup. "You needn't worry, though I thank you for your concern."

Sally twisted the cup in her hand. "Life is so Topsy-turvy nowadays," she said and shivered. "If that family is indeed loyalist, the Connecticut Whigs might kill them. It isn't right!" Sally shook her head as guilt over her lack of effort tried to erode her confidence. "I don't know what to think anymore."

Wood creaked as Susannah sat forward in her chair. "No. You're right. But relationships are deteriorating ever faster these days. How do you recognize who to trust anymore?"

So deep in her head, Sally frowned into her cup, her reflection wobbling on the cider's surface, she missed Susannah's reply.

She shrugged a shoulder as though throwing off her ugly imaginings. Maybe the best thing was to change the subject. She faked a laugh. "Well, it's too much for me to fathom." Rubbing the chill from her arms, she grinned at Susannah. "When do you think my cousin, Robert Stoddard, will work up the nerve to ask for Sarah Coles' hand?"

Susannah didn't answer right away, and Sally squirmed under the speculative stare her friend leveled on her. Susannah's lips twisted, and she waved a hand, as if in silent acceptance of Sally's reluctance.

"I understand his mother's side of the family objects, though I can't think how anyone can. Sarah is such a sweet person, and she loves Robert dearly."

Sally rose in indignant defense of their friend. They discussed the possible betrothal, laces, and ribbons for her dress until Daniel returned.

"Are you ready, Sally?"

She stood and hugged Susannah. "I am. Thank you and thank you for the cider. I hope I can come back soon and visit again."

Susannah hugged her back and whispered in her ear. "Whatever happens, my dear, you're welcome in our home any time. I hope you understand."

Sally kissed her cheek, before following Daniel to the front walk. "Thank you for riding home with me. I must admit I'm afraid of running into more bandits like Cousin George."

"Be sure and tell your father. He can put a stop to George and his band of miscreants."

He helped her mount, and they rode down Cove Road.

"Daniel?" she asked, unable to let go of her anxiety for them. "Susannah says you two will be fine, but what if the Tory hunters come for you? You won't be safe."

"Don't worry. My friends are more important than theirs."

"Who are your friends?" The question flew out of her mouth, unable to stop herself. She cringed at the demand in her question, but Daniel didn't respond with anger.

With a lazy roll of his head, he smiled at her. "Well, I like to think you're a friend."

"Of course." Sally couldn't hide a note of impatience. "But if anything should happen to you or Susannah, I'm afraid my friendship wouldn't amount to much."

He dipped his head, conceding the point. "Perhaps no," he said.

They picked up the pace and rode the rest of the way in silence.

2

If Lucifer claimed a home, Captain John Graves Simcoe was positive Staten Island was the place. Surrounded by water, the saturated air suffocated like steaming wet wool. Not only stifling during the day and cold and foggy at night, but the place stank from Manhattan City's rubbish. He couldn't decide which reeked worse, the pigs rooting in the refuse or the constant stench from the heap called Pig Hill.

And the biting insects were so much bigger than those in England. He would die before admitting he feared stings and bites.

When dark clouds formed in the west and thunder muttered, he and his men shared the same fate. In the torrential rains, their shelters flooded and poorly set up tents collapsed. He lost two men who drowned in the fast-moving mud.

But this was his situation for now. His job—to train his troops—well downwind of Pig Hill whenever possible. Someday, he might leave this deplorable piece of rock and do some real soldiering. But, for now, he trained his men and did his best not to take his frustrations out on them. His men had no choice either.

He removed his hat and, using his arm, wiped his brow before dropping his cap on his sweat-matted head. "Let's try again, shall we?"

He hollered orders, pacing up and down the rank. "This time, in unison!"

Facing his troops, he drew in a huge breath, pushing out his chest. "Attention!"

The 40th Foot snapped to attention, ramrod straight, chests out, shoulders back, heels two inches apart. Their heads faced to the right. John paced the line looking for incorrect posture, fidgeting, a man out of position.

"Captain Simcoe!"

John's name floated across the parade ground but ignoring the call, he drew in breath for another command.

The man called again, insistent this time. "Captain Simcoe!"

John spun, ready to berate his intruder, but the utterance died on his lips. He jogged a few steps, remembered his men standing at attention, and shouted "At-rest!"

He cringed at the uneven snap of his men. "Lieutenant Percival, they're all yours. Make them repeat At-Rest until they can do so in their sleep."

Percival's face fell, but he snapped a sharp salute. "Yes, sir," he said before John jogged away.

He held out his hand to greet his old friend. "John Andre, what are you doing on this vile-smelling rock?"

They shook hands with a strong grip of welcome.

"I came to visit you."

Andre tapped John on his jacket front, blue eyes crinkled and shining beneath the bushy brows shadowing his warm face. His sharp nose ended above full lips always stretched into a smile.

John's brows quirked. "I thought you were attached to General Lord Cornwallis. Are you reassigned?" He didn't hide his hope. Life here would be much more pleasant in the company of friends. Selective about those with whom he spent time John didn't claim many friends. Unlike Andre, a reserve in his personality did not permit him an open way with people.

"No," Andre said, clamping a hand on John's shoulder. "I'm still Lord Cornwallis' aide-de-camp. We arrived earlier for a meeting."

Andre's gaze wandered past John's shoulder. Amusement shone in his blue eyes and twisted his lips as John's men repeated the At-Rest command.

John turned as well. He wanted to excuse them, but what might he say that wouldn't sound defensive?

Andre chuckled. "Why don't you dismiss your men so we can go somewhere and catch up?"

"Lieutenant Percival will continue their training," John said. "Believe me, they need the practice."

Seated at a table in Billops's Tavern, John ordered himself and Andre a mug of ale. The pine plank floor covered in sawdust stank of old vomit, turning John's stomach. Mr. Billops and his sons bustled about serving men, while his wife and daughters cooked in the back.

"So, have you thought about the assignment?" Andre's eyebrows lifted with his question.

"What assignment?" John asked, searching Andre's face for some sign.

Just as he feared when General Howe set up his headquarters in Manhattan City. The distance would leave him without current news. His assessment was correct. He missed a possible assignment. He cursed fate and General Howe.

"The commission, of course," Andre said.

They stopped talking when Mr. Billops appeared and placed tankards of ale before them, scooped up the coins John left, and sauntered back to the bar.

After taking a sip, Andre made an unpleasant face and set the tankard down. "Sour ale. That's going to wreak havoc with my stomach."

He leaned toward John again, bracing an elbow on the table. "A man as ambitious as you cannot be interested in training raw recruits for the remainder of the war."

Of course not, but a commission? A real commission, not playing nursemaid to a bunch of raw recruits! His heart began to pound. "What commission? What are you talking about?"

Andre's brows creased, reminding John of an untidy lawn in need of several sheep. The sudden thought almost made him smile. He hid the urge by taking a drink.

"Ugh! Nasty!"

John plunked his tankard onto the roughhewn pine table and shuddered as some of the liquid splashed onto his hand. "Now, explain yourself."

Sitting back in his chair, Andre dropped his arm into his lap. "I thought you knew. Of course, you might not want the assignment as you'll lead a regiment of irregulars, made up of provincial soldiers. I quite understand," he said with a sneer wrinkling his nose and curling his lip. "Provincials!"

"Are you teasing me?" John asked gripping his tankard with both hands. "I wanted to command an irregular force ever since Boston."

Andre leaned his elbow on the table, a conspiratorial gleam in his eye. "Would I tease you? Generals Cornwallis and Howe met this morning to discuss a suitable candidate to relieve Robert Rogers from the Queen's Rangers. He received a wound in their last campaign."

John heard—and dared not hope. This was what he wanted, what he needed, and Andre came to serve it up almost on a silver platter. Tightening his grip on his tankard, John kept his expression neutral.

"I couldn't speak," Andre said, "so I listened, and thought to myself, I know the perfect candidate to take Rogers's place. Which is why I sought you out. You need to meet with General Howe, today, if possible, and obtain your commission."

Andre waved a hand, his white lace cuff flowing beneath his red tunic, showing off well-manicured fingers.

John hid his hands in his lap to hide his rough chapped fingers and ragged nails. What kind of life did Andre lead?

"You can't be happy drilling and training every day."

John's scowl confirmed Andre's assessment of his situation.

From the kitchen, a metallic crash rent the air.

Mrs. Billops appeared gesticulating and shouting at a young girl, down on her knees, scooping up the mess she made and making no attempt to fend off the blows now raining down on her head.

Frantic, she scooped the contents back into the pot before gathering it up and disappearing, Mrs. Billops following her, still berating her in a shrill manner.

When the ruckus died away, John and Andre continued their

conversation as though nothing happened.

John lifted his tankard and gathered his thoughts, scowling at the frothy liquid. He saw his coveted opportunity slipping. "General Howe is on Manhattan Island. I cannot arrange to arrive today, but if I wait, someone else might receive the assignment."

"No, he isn't," Andre said, rocking his chair back, and lifting the front legs off the floor. He laced his long fingers across his belly. "He's here."

John's jaw clenched. How much did he not know? And why didn't he? He stared at his friend, assessing him, trying to figure out why he had more information than him. "No, his headquarters are on Manhattan."

"Were on Manhattan," Andre said correcting him and dropping the chair legs with a thunk. "But with so much to do in the way of preparations, the general moved his headquarters to a place called Rossville on the other side of Staten Island. He's been there for two days."

"Two days!"

John slammed the table. Why didn't anyone tell him? It didn't matter why. The fact remained and being testy wouldn't help him obtain his command. He raised his tankard. "I shall speak to General Howe. Today, if I can arrange it."

He and Andre clinked their tankards and John choked the liquid down.

Andre shuddered and put his tankard aside before removing a timepiece and noting the time. "I must go. I promised General Lord Cornwallis to return by five," he said, picking up his tankard, and peering within, he shook his head, pushing the foul drink away.

John rose, leaving his half-filled cup. As they meandered toward the parade field, Andre's shadow stretched out before them, further accentuating his extra inches in height.

John glanced askance at Andre. "What's your opinion of the colonies?"

Andre peered toward New Jersey his full lips creeping upward. "I like this country. So vast. Full of possibility and industry. Manhattan is an exciting place." He laid a hand on John's shoulder and leaned in close with a wink. "All sorts of vices, temptations, and adventures."

John glanced away and rolled his eyes. Someday his friend's

cavalier nature might come back to haunt him.

Andre slapped him hard on the back. "Dour John. Always so careful, which is why I like you. You're my perfect foil."

"Don't say such things," John's words rushed from his lips. He held out his hands in apology at Andre's annoyed expression. "I'm sorry. I didn't mean to snarl. But foils have the misfortune of seeing their protagonist come to a bad end."

3

John tucked his white trousers into thigh-high, shining black leather boots. He found no blemish on his spotlessly clean red coat. The ample white belt crossed his chest from left shoulder to right hip and showed no sign of wear or dirt. If this didn't impress General Howe, nothing would.

Lieutenant Bamford moved about him, adjusting, and smoothing, his fingers tracing over John's uniform. He ran the bristles of a small brush over his shoulders. "You're smashing, Captain."

The night before, John laid out his plan to Bamford, the only man he trusted other than Andre.

John straightened and rolled his shoulders within the confines of his coat. "Thank goodness I'm not going on patrol dressed like a lighthouse beacon." He said, twisting each way, trying to examine his backside, but detected no wrinkle or spot.

The bright red and white uniforms of the British Army never made sense to John. The soldier was too easy to see.

He offered his aide a nervous grin. "Well done. I thank you. Well, Bamford, wish me luck."

"You won't need luck, sir. I'm sure."

14

John set out for General Howe's headquarters, hoping his friend was right.

He arrived before mid-morning, his uniform still immaculate, despite the beads of sweat beginning to run down his back. Swallowing hard, he approached the general's tent.

"Greetings, Captain Simcoe. How may I help you?" Major Gordon said, holding papers in his left hand and reading from a page in front of him, he dipped a quill and made a notation, but never glanced at John.

John peered down at the supercilious aide-de-camp and straightened his shoulders, to throw off his negative thoughts. "I have an appointment with General Howe."

Major Gordon deigned to glance at him.

John shifted his cap from one arm to the other.

The major smirked, and with a languid movement of his hand, he indicated a camp chair. "Please, make yourself comfortable. I'll ask if the general can entertain you."

Ignoring the camp chair as Major Gordon walked away, John read the sheets in front of him, to learn if they contained information on troop activity, but the letter from Lord Cornwallis contained nothing impacting John or the 40th Foot.

"Captain Simcoe," General Howe said from within. "Enter."

John pushed aside the tent flap and bent to step inside. He straightened and saluted. Major Gordon forced him to step to the side by passing in front of him on his way out of the tent.

"What can I do for you, Captain?" Howe rose from behind a small table. His tall, broad-shouldered frame unfolded and for a moment John almost regretted this meeting, but then the general smiled.

John shifted his gaze to the parchment and quill on the writing desk and back to his commanding officer. "Sir, I came to speak to you about the Queen's Rangers. I understand Colonel Rogers—."

General Howe held up a hand, palm out. "Say no more, Captain. Robert Rogers returned with full assurances he is willing and able to perform his duties." Howe laid that hand on John's shoulder.

Disappointment crushed him like a load of rocks. "I understand, General. My apologies for making a nuisance of myself. I shall leave you to your work."

When John started to salute, General Howe once again raised a hand. "One thing I would discuss with you." Howe went back to his desk. He picked up a quill, which he twirled between his fingers before laying it back down, as though gathering his thoughts. "You're a fine officer, John," Howe said, speaking to the quill. "Don't mistake me, but if I needed to replace Colonel Rogers, you are not my first choice."

Hands fisted at his sides, John's nostrils flared, and his eyes grew round. He opened his mouth to protest, but his brain went blank. "I—I, Sir, I don't understand."

Ugh! He sounded like a fool so clamped his lips together.

"Let me explain." Howe's smile disappeared and his thin upper lip folded itself within a full lower lip. Stern brown eyes pinned John beneath arched eyebrows.

The general's resemblance to the king was startling. The fact his mother, and the king's grandfather, were illegitimate siblings was an open secret in London society.

Howe continued. "You are a captain in my service since Boston. You do fine work for me. I must say, exceptional work, but you lack the requisite experience. Colonel French is my first choice. He's a fine man and a more than competent leader." Howe's tone suggested he expected a positive response from John, who pulled air into his lungs, determined to make the effort.

He pursed his lips and exhaled through his nose. "I quite agree, General."

Howe arched a brow, his skepticism obvious. "Buying a commission does not, in my opinion, make a quality officer," he said, waving a dismissive hand. "I'm not denigrating you for buying your captaincy," he went on with relentless cruelty. "Many men buy their commissions, and I do not condemn the practice, but I believe rank is something one earns, not buys. You will earn your rank, assuring me I can trust you."

A dagger to his heart couldn't hurt him more. Not knowing what to say, John shifted his gaze over Howe's shoulder and stared at a spot on the canvas, concentrating all his anger on that spot. He couldn't think, let alone speak. Rage made him shake, and he prayed General Howe was unaware.

Howe placed his hands behind his back. He inclined his head toward John, a sympathetic gleam in his brown eyes. "I put you in charge of the 40th Foot for a reason, Captain. I appreciate the frustration of doing nothing but training, but when the action starts, your training will prove important. You must be willing to work your way up the ranks, Captain Simcoe."

General Howe shifted in his seat. Lifting a sheet of parchment, he said, "now, sir, if you'll excuse me. I must return to my work."

Between clenched teeth, John uttered, "yes, sir. Thank you, sir."

He lifted his right hand to his eyebrow, though General Howe didn't acknowledge the salute. He went back outside and ignored the major's snickers. Placing his cap on his head, he threw his shoulders back, and head held high, he returned to duty. General Howe wanted him to earn a command. Fine. He prayed his men could take the punishment.

The 40th drilled in full packs around Bentley Mano. Any man who dropped from heatstroke repeated the drill once recovered. His men grumbled. Some grew to hate him, others feared him.

Not knowing when the British Army would move, John trained his men in all weather conditions heedless of what they thought.

July rolled into August, each day hotter and steamier than the one before. On the second of August, he received orders to move the 40th Regiment of Foot to Prince's Bay. He gave word to decamp, and his men struck their tents in less than an hour. They packed and stacked their equipment for transport, keeping only one blanket, their haversacks, and a three-day provision, and were ready to move out before the other regiments broke camp. John pulsed with pride over how well his training paid off.

While August drew on, he relaxed their training, but his standing order to remain vigilant and ready to move remained in force, drawing jeers and sneers from other regiments and camp commanders. He ignored them, believing his men would receive more opportunities in their constant state of readiness.

Bounded on three sides, Staten Island stank of water and marine life that overwhelmed the senses and left one in a constant state of dampness. Guns rusted faster and food spoiled from the moisture-laden air. John hated the place but loved the days when massive swarms of gigantic marine life passed by. No wonder the fishing industry thrived here. One only had to reach out and almost pluck life from the sea.

To his delight this morning, as he awaited breakfast, a pod of whales breached the surface. His breath caught when a giant humpback flung himself from the sea, arced, and twisted before splashing back, a giant geyser of water showing where he submerged. On its heels, a smaller leviathan followed suit. Smiling at the show, John stretched, buttoned his summer tunic, and returned to his camp desk where correspondence and dispatches waited.

Captain Bamford entered with a tray laden with food and a cup of Bohea tea. The woody aroma wafted to John's nose evoking memories of home. Outside the sound of John's men preparing for another day of training reached his ears.

"Good morning, Bamford."

"Good morning, Captain," Bamford said, setting down the tray and pouring tea.

"How soon before the men will be ready?"

"They're preparing now, Captain. You should be able to finish your breakfast." Bamford left.

John picked up his cup for a sip and set it back down. Another court-martial for rape. The generals discouraged the behavior, but their laughably light protestations made his blood boil. He calculated fifty-seven charges in two months, and those were the ones he recalled.

John pushed away images of his mother or his betrothed, Elizabeth. He would kill any man who put his hands on them in such a way. He set the parchment down and called in Captain Bamford. Breakfast would wait. This was too important.

Bamford saluted. "Yes, sir."

"Assemble the men into line, Captain."

John pushed the chair back to rise. "I wish to address them before their march."

"Your breakfast will grow cold, sir."

"This is too important."

The drummer's beats vibrated in his ears. John pulled his coat off the back of his chair and drew it on, allowing his men time to assemble. Picking up the parchment he went to review his men. His critical eye roamed over the 40th Foot standing ramrod straight, eyes front, shoulders back, heels two inches apart. He marched to the forefront and without preamble, read the dispatch. Then he lowered the sheet, locked his hands behind his back, and scanned his men.

"Gentlemen, this conduct is outrageous and unbecoming for soldiers of the British Army. I do not blame the soldier as much as I blame their commanding officers, however—," he said, raising a finger for emphasis—"if I find out you committed such heinous acts. If any of you force yourself upon a young woman without her consent—." He stopped and shook his head. "No, let me rephrase that."

He stalked up and down the ranks. "You will not find yourself in such a position. I forbid any of you to go any closer to the women on this continent than needs be for polite conversation. If word comes to me of a dalliance, and I don't care if she's willing—in fact, I don't care if she's a woman of the evening—you will experience the lash before I send you home in disgrace. Do I make myself clear?"

Their resounding "Yes, sir!" skipped across the parade ground and echoed back. John nodded once and dismissed his troops.

While reading a missive in his sweltering tent, someone scratched at the flap. "Enter."

Captain Bamford entered and placed a tray of fresh food along with a packet of envelopes in front of John. "Inspiring words, sir."

John picked up the packet. "You think my stand foolish?"

"Not at all, sir, but I do wonder. I mean, men will be men, sir. If you take my meaning, sir."

"I do."

Setting the packet down, he studied his aide. "But I think by now my men realize I mean what I say when I say it."

"Yes sir, they do." Bamford's face reddened, and he dropped his gaze to the ground.

John's eyes narrowed. "Do you wish to confess something, Captain Bamford?"

"Well, sir...That is...no sir...well...."

Bamford sighed and shrugged finding great interest in his spotless boots.

"End it." John stood. "End it or find another regiment. The officers must lead by example."

Bamford saluted. "Yes, sir."

"Dismissed."

Captain Bamford turned to leave, but John stopped him. "Who else is in your predicament?"

When Bamford opened his mouth to answer, John held up a hand. "Never mind. Tell them the same thing I told you. All relationships will cease before the end of the week."

All afternoon John endured a parade of officers asking permission to leave camp for a few hours.

4

Before five o'clock on the morning of August twenty-first, Admiral Howe's ships arrived to ferry the Army, including Captain John Graves Simcoe and his 40th Regiment of Foot to Gravesend, across the Sound on Long Island. Within three hours, the 40th, along with four thousand other troops landed, and by the end of the week, more than fifteen thousand troops arrived.

The five-day delay irked John. On the fourth day, accompanied by Captains Bamford and Cooke, he rode out of camp determined to discover the location and strength of the enemy. They returned before sundown, hot, tired, and hungry.

As he changed out of his filthy uniform, Captain Bamford spoke through the tent flap. "A message from General Howe, Captain."

"Come in, Bamford." John made the last few adjustments to his uniform before sitting sat at his desk chair, when his aide-de-camp entered, clicked his heels, and made a short quarter bow. Right arm stiff, he held out a folded sheet of parchment.

"What's in the note?" John asked picking up a quill, which he twiddled between his fingers.

"I'm ignorant, Captain," Bamford said as he focused his gaze on the tent behind John's head.

Liar. John stabbed the pen into the ink pot. "What does the missive say, Andrew?"

The muscles in Bamford's face shifted. He did well to keep the grin off his lips, but the humor in his blue eyes gave him away. He shrugged and laid the folded note beside John's left hand. "General Howe requests the presence of your person in a war council as soon as you return to camp, sir."

John eyed the parchment. "Anything else?"

Bamford stood at the ready position, hands behind his back and feet placed shoulder-width staring at the back of the tent. He read all the missives the minute they came into his hands, but they played this charade to fill the time.

When John slapped his hand on the note and unfolded the parchment, Captain Bamford pulled his lips between his teeth, but a chuckle escaped him.

"Ha! Got you." John pointed at his aide. Even in war, laughter where they found some, was still the best medicine. He rose and unfolded the note.

My Dear Captain Simcoe, a council will convene at 6:00 p.m. Be ready to report—W. Howe, Major Gen'l.

John fumbled in his pocket for his father's timepiece, given to him by his father before going off to sea as an ensign. He traced his finger over the gold filigree around which a shield with an ornate S gleamed. He popped open the piece and the long hands pointed to the Roman numerals. A smaller circle showed the sweep of the second hand. Noting the time, he snapped it closed.

He recalled how his heart swelled with pride when his grandfather gave him the timepiece before leaving for the colonies. He read the etched writing on the back: To my son, John Simcoe, Ensign 1740.

Owning the timepiece was a connection to the father he lost when a youth of eight. Not wanting to wallow in nostalgia—and dare he admit—homesickness, he shoved the piece back into its special pocket.

He fingered his way up the front of his jacket, to ensure his buttons were straight. "I was going to go eat some food, but I better make my way over to the general's headquarters, instead."

He ran a hand over his uniform, then to his face and smooth

cheek. Excellent. No need to shave. Tugging on his coat hem, he left for headquarters.

When John arrived, he announced himself to a minor aide who left him waiting outside General Howe's tent. Major Gordon approached, and John straightened and saluted him. "Captain Simcoe reporting. General Howe requested my presence."

The major rubbed his chin, eying him. "Yes, quite," he said. "I sent word several hours ago. Thank you for saving me from going through a great deal of trouble looking for you. General Howe is convening a war council."

John crossed his arms and drew a long breath in through his nose. "So, your note said, and the meeting is at six o'clock. The time is five forty-five. I'm here."

Major Gordon raised an eyebrow. "Well, you left camp without permission and disappeared for several hours. One couldn't surmise if you would return in time or how to find you."

He slapped some pages down on a small table. "We are at present awaiting General Grant, among others, so please, take a seat."

The major indicated a chair by the tent opening. John sat bouncing his knee until he became conscious of the movement. He set his foot flat to keep still.

When the other officers arrived, propriety dictated, as a junior officer, John enter the tent last. The presence of so many men forced him to remain inside the tent flap, well away from the center of activity.

Having no use for small talk, he didn't engage with the other officers of his rank who congregated on the opposite side from Generals Grant, Clinton, and Howe. Surreptitiously, he removed his timepiece. A quarter past the hour and General Howe still had not called the men to order, although the generals all gathered around a map spread out on an oversized table.

Rain began spattering on the canvas. He wedged deeper into the tent, gaining annoyed glances from others.

General Howe locked his hands behind his back. "Captain Simcoe, I understand you and two of your aides left camp earlier today."

Despite his resolve, John fumbled. Under everyone's focus, heat rose in his neck and suffused his face.

Was he in trouble? Howe's expression gave nothing away.

"Yes, General. I... well, I thought..." He drew in a deep breath and exhaled as he straightened his shoulders and squared up.

"Yes, General. Captain Bamford, Captain Cooke, and I went out this morning to scout the enemy position. I was curious to discover where the continentals are and what their strength is. I desired to gain an understanding of the topography as well." Now would be the time to demote him to lieutenant.

"And what did you find?"

John's hopes rose a little, which he prayed didn't show in his voice. He gestured to the table. "If I may?"

When Howe stepped back, the officers opened a path for him to proceed. He braced his hands on the table, leaning over the map, gathering his thoughts.

"A road to Brooklyn, with a marshy swamp on either side, separates us from the town and is the only route through the bog. I believe Mr. Washington posted about twelve thousand men in the area."

He shifted his feet and hovered a finger above the map. "This swamp, the locals call the Gowanus Marsh, is a land choked with trees, thickets, and water. Impossible to march an army through without using the road."

"Yes, we surmised the same," General Clinton said, sounding bored. When General Howe scoffed, Clinton glowered at Howe and clamped his lips together.

Ignoring the animosity between the two, John dropped his finger along a series of gaps marked on the diagram. "However, four major passes in the landscape may offer a way around. This first one—," he said, tapping the first pass— "has the road leading straight through to Brooklyn. But this is where Mr. Washington concentrated most of his force. The next, a mile and a half away, is Flatbush Pass. A mile from Flatbush is Bedford Pass. Three miles further is Jamaica Pass. Each subsequent gap guarded with about four to five hundred or so men."

He traced Jamaica Pass. "Except for this one. No one occupies the position, which means Mr. Washington either doesn't have sufficient troops to guard here, is unaware the pass exists, or believes we would never find it. I believe he's ignorant of its existence."

"Or" General Grant said, "he thinks, having found the pass, we wouldn't want to go so far out of our way."

"Possible," John said.

"Another option," Clinton spoke up. "He's left the Jamaica Pass unguarded as a ruse to draw us. After having gone through like a pack of lemmings, he attacks."

A general murmur followed Clinton's assessment.

All these options were possible, but John was confident Washington didn't possess enough men to guard the pass. More important, according to a loyalist farmer in the area, the continentals consisted of men from Massachusetts and Virginia, who likely remained unaware the pass existed. John expressed this.

General Howe shouldered him aside. "We can keep a regiment or two in front of the rebels, make them think we're going to attack along the road to Brooklyn. At which time, we can swing a larger force around to Jamaica Pass behind the enemy. They will have no choice but to flee into the swamp where we can defeat them."

John slid his hands behind his back. He sidled out of the way while the generals leaned over the map nodding, talking over each other, and at times pointing for emphasis.

He stood at rigid attention and stared out at the pouring rain as his heart banged against his ribs. Behind his back, his hands clenched into fists. What had he expected? A well done. Perhaps a thank you?

Rain drummed above him as they talked. General Howe caught John's eye. "Well done, Captain Simcoe. Now, if you'll excuse us, we must plan."

John pursed his lips and saluted. He did his best. The rest was up to them.

John drove his men hard amid a flurry of anxious orders. They drilled and marched all day, every day, stopping only to eat and clean their equipment. He ordered them to remain in full dress, even when sleeping, for a constant state of readiness, and his hard work paid off. General Howe requested the 40th Foot join his regiment, rather than remain with General Grant, with the understanding they would be in reserve. That didn't matter. He had the chance to prove his leadership skills.

At dusk on August twenty-sixth, they moved out and marched under a full moon, casting a yellow glow over the ocean. General Howe fell back, allowing Clinton to take the lead with Cornwallis behind him. Howe, with John's 40th regiment, now brought up the rear with six battalions and fourteen artillery pieces rumbling behind.

At least ten thousand men stretched over two miles. Mr. Washington couldn't possibly have enough men to counter. Riding alongside General Howe, John said as much. The general acknowledged him with a grunt, prompting John to fall back. He should leave the man to his thoughts.

They left their campfires burning to deceive the Colonials into thinking all was well. The ruse worked for they encountered no one on their travels.

The column headed northeast before turning north toward Gowanus Heights. Beyond should be the Jamaica Pass. Clinton's and Cornwallis's armies broke off for their designated positions.

Near the Jamaica Pass, General Howe stopped at a small tavern marked "Howard's Half-way House".

Halfway to where? Hell? Though the building was dark and shuttered, Howe ordered his men to dismount. John and Captain Bamford approached the front door. Withdrawing his sword from its scabbard, Howe used the hilt to pound on the wood.

A light went on in an upstairs window, prompting him to pound harder. Footsteps echoed on the stairs, and the door latch rattled. A crack appeared wide enough for an eyeball to peek out. A candle held waist-high illuminated the man inside.

"Who's there?"

"Open the door!" Howe demanded.

"Identify yourselves."

When General Howe gestured, John and Bamford each raised a booted foot and kicked the door in. A shout rang out as the wood panel crashed inward.

The man, still bellowing, sprawled on the floor, his bloody hands covering his nose.

John and his men surrounded him, muskets at the ready, bayonets fixed. Major Gordon walked to the fallen candle and using the toe of his boot, snuffed out the small flame growing on the planked floor.

General Howe sauntered into the room and peered down at the man, unconcerned about his pain. "We are His Majesty's troops. Need you any more identification? You, sir, will accompany us to the Rockaway Foot Path skirting the Jamaica Pass to the west."

Howe glanced at his men. "Search the house."

They fanned out. Two went upstairs and returned moments later dragging a struggling boy no more than thirteen years old, by the elbows. When the boy saw his father, fear contorted his features, and he struggled harder, earning a punch in the gut.

His breath left him with an oof followed by a ragged gasp for air.

Howe faced the commotion. "Whom have we here?"

The boy glared, but when the man who hit him made another fist, he relented. "My name is William Howard, Jr."

"My name is William Howard, Jr. *sir*," Howe said leaning close, a smile creasing his lips. "Bring me a glass of whiskey, William Howard, Jr."

Young Howard yanked his arms free. "Yes, sir."

At the bar, he slammed a glass down and poured two fingers of whiskey.

General Howe meandered over and in one gulp, drained the contents. He gestured with the glass before setting it down in front of the boy, who poured another. Howe lifted the drink, and this time savored the liquid.

"Capital."

He set the glass down, fitting it perfectly to a round stain on the wood. "Now, go dress. You and your father will be our guides and escorts tonight. You will show us the way to the Rockaway Foot Path."

Before the boy answered, his father spoke up. "We belog to de odder side, ged'ral. We cannot serve you again't our duty." His nose was swelling, and his eyes turned a delightful shade of purple.

General Howe reached into a pouch and produced a small cloth, which he held out. "Clean yourself up, Howard. You look a fright."

The men, including John, grumbled laughter.

Mr. Howard accepted the handkerchief, which he pressed to his bleeding nose. "Doh, sir. S'a matter of pridciple. We will not help you."

"A matter of principle," Howe said creasing his brow, as though giving the matter due consideration. Then he shrugged. "Fine, Howard. Stick to your country or stick to your principle, but you are my prisoner. You must guide my men over the hill."

"Why should he?" Young Howard asked in a shout. He started toward his father, but General Howe pivoted fast, stopping the boy in mid-stride.

"Because you have no alternative," Howe said raising a hand as if explaining to a simpleton. "You are my prisoner. If you refuse, I shall shoot your father through the head."

5

They found the Rockaway Foot Path and by nine o'clock in the morning, Howe fired his guns, signaling the Hessians to begin their attack. Then Howe advanced his army to catch the continentals from the rear.

Despite their lack of experience, the enemy showed gumption and John, held in reserve, was desperate to take part, but he had strict orders. If Howe required the 40th, he would send for them.

As the fighting continued, they were at long last, drawn into battle. Lining his men in the marsh's tight confines, he gave the order to fire at will. The unit before him from Maryland refused to give way, and the day dragged on as men died. Grudging respect for their tenacity grew and he regretted their loss, but if they continued to fight, so would he.

The Continental left collapsed. Desperate Americans swung their muskets like clubs hoping to save their pathetic lives. When the Marylanders surrendered, John gave quarter.

Captain Bamford walked to the water's edge and extended a hand to a sodden, weeping man who took his hand.

With a shout Bamford was jerked off his feet, disappearing into the green scum.

"Andrew!" John froze, his terrified gaze fixed on the spot where his friend vanished. Horror struck he was transported back to the day his younger brother drowned. And he did nothing.

Percy pretended distress over and over, laughing each time John jumped into Grandfather's pond to rescue him. When Percy truly needed his help, John stomped back to the house, ignoring his pleas.

Andrew bobbed to the surface with a great gasping breath. Lieutenants Carmichael and Percival jumped in to help him.

John dropped to his knees and gripped his friend's face. "Andrew are you alright?" His voice shook but he didn't care, cursing himself for his inaction.

Bamford coughed then spat. He started to wipe his mouth on his sleeve, but at the sight of the filthy garment, he put his arm down.

John fumbled in his pocket and produced a handkerchief, offering it with a shaking hand.

Smiling his thanks, Bamford wiped his face and mouth then stood. John examined him from head to foot, almost weeping with relief.

Perplexed stares brought John back to himself. If his reaction made the rounds, he'd have to rebuild his reputation. He glanced around as if assessing what needed doing next.

Shaking his arms to rid them of excess moisture, Bamford strode to where three privates beat the man who tried to drown him. "Enough! Release the poor fellow."

John took over. His men captured a major, two lieutenants, and fifteen privates whom he rounded up to present to General Howe.

Disturbing whispers insinuated the Hessians bayoneted their surrendering foes. Hessians were uncouth, coarse people who behaved like the barbarians they descended from. If the wayward Colonials were to return to the king's good graces, committing atrocities on them was foolish.

Once at camp, John gave his prisoners to Major Loring, the provost marshal. Exhausted, sweaty, soot-covered, and famished, he wanted nothing more than a bath, a meal, clean clothes, and sleep.

Ducking inside his tent, John stopped short at the sight of a young boy, no older than seventeen or eighteen years old, skin the color of ebony, holding one of his riding boots and polishing the toe as though he tried to rub a hole in the leather.

The young man was powerfully built with strong arms, broad shoulders, and a thick neck. He sat on the floor his long legs stretched out in front of him.

Cranky and in no mood for jokes, John was about to accost the young man when Captain Bamford spoke from behind.

"He arrived about an hour ago, sir looking for work, so I gave him some tasks."

"You're well, Bamford?"

"Yes, sir." Bamford exited the tent and John again regarded the young man who now clutched the boot to his breast and shrank away.

"What's your name?"

"Israel, suh."

"Israel what?" John asked, kneeling, and studying Israel's tattered and patched clothing.

Israel's frown deepened and he shrugged. "Just Israel, suh."

John nodded. "Well, 'Just Israel', where are you from? Not the famed biblical land for which you're named, I'm sure." His comment was met with a blank stare.

"Maryland, suh. My massa was kilt this afternoon so I run away. I want my freedom. I can work. I come here looking for freedom, and that man yonder," he gestured to the tent flap, "said I might stay if'n I work." He gulped, then remembered himself. "Suh."

"I don't hold with slavery, Israel. If you work here, we will pay you for your services. How does one shilling, six pence per day sound to you?"

Israel bobbed his head. "Tha's fine, suh. One shilling six pence be fine."

"Captain Bamford!" John rose to his feet as his aide entered.

"It appears we have a new member of our troop."

"Excellent, sir," Bamford said. "I thought you might like a personal attendant, which is why he's polishing your boots."

John pursed his lips. He glanced down at Israel who still clutched his boot. "What do you say, Israel? You'll still be paid, mind you."

"Yes, suh. I'd like that, suh."

"Good." John laid a hand on his shoulder. The linsey-woolsey shirt was rough under his palm, but the warmth from Israel's body surprised him. John assumed because of his dark skin; he might be cold to the touch. He removed his hand.

"Captain Bamford will acquaint you with the job of personal attendant."

Bamford nodded.

"For now, your first task is to find me some food. I am done for. I require a bath and sleep."

Israel's head bobbed with each directive, as though he committed to memory every order John gave, but he made no effort to move. John snorted. "Well, don't stand idle. You have your instructions."

"Yassuh," Israel said, placing the boot in his arms next to its companion and rushing out of the tent.

The two-story stone mansion around which John fought the Marylanders was now General Howe's headquarters. In the great room, he waited near the hearth, tamping down impatience. When it came to meetings, the man was notoriously late.

Lightning lit the room in a bright, brief flash, followed by a rolling drumbeat of thunder. Daylight dimmed and a strong gust of wind blew the storm in. Heavy raindrops splashed against the windows as another flash burned into John's retinas, leaving a window-shaped impression when he closed his eyes.

His mind was still full of Bamford's near drowning, but neither John nor Andrew spoke of the incident. He was so lost in his thoughts John didn't hear the general enter the room.

"So, what do you think, Captain Simcoe?"

John blinked. "I'm sorry, sir? What do I think about what?"

"Siege trenches. If we catch Washington in a siege, he will have no choice but to surrender. Would your men like to take charge?"

John struggled for something to say. Siege was the last word he expected from General Howe.

"Captain Simcoe?" Howe's voice took on a menacing tone.

John stepped forward. "My apologies, sir. I'm flattered you want to give me the opportunity."

Howe smiled, placated. "Well, your information proved so accurate we had no trouble winning the battle. I believe some reward is in order."

Doing his best not to let the insult sting, John gestured to the map on the table. "Permission to approach, sir?"

"Of course." Howe stepped aside his chest puffed out with his largess.

John studied the map, noting the lines and arrows crisscrossing the map.

"Sir, why not engage Washington in one decisive battle? A siege takes months."

Stark lines appeared around the general's mouth and his brown eyes hardened. "We can't," he said. "My brother was to sail up the East River and bombard Brooklyn yesterday, but he faced unfavorable winds and an ebb tide. I will not move without his assistance. Which means a siege."

"But sir, you cannot allow Mr. Washington to escape."

Howe uttered a short bark, silencing John.

His voice rose along with the color in his cheeks. "Escape? To where? His back is to the East River, and if Richard cannot sail upriver, Mr. Washington cannot escape."

John locked his hands behind his back and cast his gaze past General Howe's shoulder. "Yes, sir."

Howe eyed him. "Speak out, Colonel."

John hesitated. "Well, sir," he said, sweeping a feeble hand across the table. "I fear you may be overestimating him. One decisive battle while his back is to the river would leave him no choice but to surrender. We mauled him yesterday. One more good fight might do him in."

As the general fixed his gaze on the map, John shifted his feet and prayed his next words didn't destroy his argument. "We can proceed without your brother." His heart pounded while he studied his superior's face. The man's countenance gave nothing away.

"General, we're here to restore the king's rule of law." Hearing his impatience, he stopped to gather himself. "Our mission is to punish those in rebellion and restore loyalty to the king. We can do so with one smashing victory." John pounded his fist on the table, as a way to emphasize his point, but unfortunately, it had the opposite effect.

General Howe straightened as though the blow hit him square in the sternum. He leveled hard brown eyes on John. "You didn't fight at Breed's Hill, did you, Captain?"

"No, sir," John said, his brows lowering in confusion. "I arrived in Boston a week later."

Howe walked to the hearth and stretched his hands toward the fire as he stared into the flames.

"Those colonials built six-foot redoubts around the entire circumference of Breed's Hill in one night."

Impressive. John had built his share of redoubts. The massive earthen trenches with high walls made from the dugout earth reinforced with logs and sharpened branches were formidable forms of defense. Hard to build under the best of conditions but to do so in one night was unheard of.

Howe sighed and his tone conveyed his awe. "They did more work in one night than my army would have done in a month."

Praying the point of the story came soon, John held back a sigh.

"We advanced up the hill, and they shot my men down. I sent them back up only to have them decimated again. We retreated again. Reinforcements arrived, so I sent them up for a third time. Luckily the continentals ran out of ammunition. I hate to contemplate the fate of my men otherwise. I lost two hundred and twenty-six men killed, eight hundred and thirty or so wounded. Are you aware of how many they lost?"

John shook his head.

The general thrust a finger in his face. "They lost four hundred fifty killed and wounded, while our side sustained almost one thousand, one hundred fifty killed and wounded. A high price to pay when, to be honest, the only thing we accomplished was boosting their confidence."

"Forgive my impertinence, General, but might I inquire as to the point?" John didn't know how he dared ask such a question and prayed a demotion was not forthcoming.

The general lowered his hand, smoothing it over his jacket front before straightening his white powdered wig. He leveled John with a hard stare.

"We had success...too dearly bought. I won't do such a thing again. That is my point. You will gather your men, and tonight, begin work on siege trenches."

Resigned, John straightened his shoulders and saluted. As he walked to his horse, he kicked at a stone in his path. Siege trenches.

Might as well build redoubts for the Colonials to hide behind.

In the darkness and torrential rain, his men dug and grunted their way to within one mile of the Continental line. When dawn approached, the rain finally let up, but a cold northwesterly wind buffeted his men who shivered in their soaked clothing.

Heavy labor and burning resentment kept John warm enough. They wouldn't have to do this ridiculous work if General Howe had done his job in Boston, but the good General spent his time at the gaming tables or in bed with Mrs. Loring.

General Grant sent over a regiment to man the trenches. Exhausted, John returned to his tent where Israel stripped him of his filthy clothes.

He fell into an exhausted slumber until Mr. Washington poked John in the shoulder, calling Cap'n. He couldn't figure out why or what the man wanted but he continued to poke until his body jerked, and John's eyes flew open.

Israel's concerned and frightened brown eyes stared down at him. "I'm sorry, Cap'n. Time for you to git up. I been trying to rouse you for some time."

John uttered a sleepy growl. "What time is it?"

Israel shrugged. "Time to git up, suh."

Rising, he rubbed a hand over his forehead and down his face. "I need my shaving kit."

"Yassuh, right here and ready for you, suh."

Israel laid out a washed and pressed uniform with bright white trousers. Handing the shaving brush to Israel, he gestured toward his trousers. "Did you clean my uniform?"

"Yassuh. Whilst you was sleeping, I cleaned off the mud and muck, and Lieutint Carmichael showed me how to paint your trousers," he said, teeth flashing in a quick smile. "Funny thing, paintin' your pants, if'n I do say, suh."

John grinned through the lather. "If you stay here long enough, you'll discover many ridiculous things about the British Army."

Like digging siege trenches when a battle would be the better move.

John stretched his neck as Israel drew the razor toward his chin. Best not to let those thoughts fester. They would erupt one day.

Relaxing under the shave, he appreciated Israel's presence.

How much earlier would he have had to rise to be ready?

Israel dropped the razor and held a warm, wet towel to John's face before handing him another to dry his cheeks.

"So, how do you like being here, Israel?"

Israel's eyes grew guarded. "Fine, suh."

"I'm glad. I like it fine as well."

"Yassuh, thank ye, suh," Israel said, bobbing his head.

"You'll tidy up while I'm gone?"

"Yassuh."

John's breath puffed white clouds and his muddy clothes stuck to his body. The shovel hung slack in his hand. Sweat and rainwater dripped off his nose and chin and his hair was matted to his head from the constant downpour. The seething rain voiced his fury.

Staring toward the East River, he watched helplessly as a tall, wet man in a blue coat and buff breeches jumped into a vessel and vanished into the soupy gloom.

All night, John and his men had worked despite torrential rain and wind. Getting to within a mile of the American lines. Lightning killed a man from another unit.

The slap of oars in the water, muffled by the dense fog, grew fainter with each pull. John's heart sank. The wily fox melted away like a wraith.

The fog grew whiter and thickened and the black lines of trees took on definition, as growing daylight cut through the gloom.

Flinging his shovel into the mud, he turned away from the river, drawing deep calming breaths hoping to control the tremors in his arms and legs.

When John turned back, he found General Howe beside him gazing out over the fog-blanketed water, his features inscrutable. His only sign of agitation was the rapid tapping of his eyeglass against his trouser leg.

Howe's expression acknowledged his mistake, and with a bowed head he returned to mount his horse, then he stared hard at the fog-shrouded river as if, by sheer dint of will, he might persuade Mr. Washington to return.

The slap of the oars faded, replaced by muted early morning birdsong, the crick-crick of tree frogs, and the cheeping of marsh insects. Howe tugged the reins and his horse turned away.

Like witch's brew, the mist hovered inches from the East River, swirling and eddying as the current directed its movements.

"Someone needs to teach that country bumpkin about the rules of warfare," Bamford said, coming to stand beside John. "Mr. Washington should recognize defeat and behave accordingly."

John couldn't agree more.

6

Refugees streamed into Oyster Bay, their worldly possessions piled high in pushcarts and oxcarts, carrying tales of woe wrought by the British Army. In all her sixteen years, nothing saddened Sally as this sight.

"Sally." She turned to find Father in the hallway. Sadness etched deep lines in his face and sloped his shoulders. "Close the door, Poppet."

Obeying, she strode to him, arms outstretched.

Wrapping herself in his warm embrace, Father kissed the top of her red head. "I need you to stay in the house for a few days. Until things settle down."

Nestling against his soft linen shirt, she nodded. "Will that happen to us, Father? Will the British make us leave?" She raised her tear-streaked face to him.

Removing a handkerchief from his pocket, Father smiled at her while he wiped her eyes. "No, Poppet."

She closed her lids, smiling as he wiped her cheeks with gentle strokes.

"How would you like to help me inventory the shop?" He asked.

"Of course."

Wrapping an arm around his waist, they entered the front parlor. Sally went to the cupboard in which Father kept the inventory and began counting the bolts of Osnaburg linen, lace, linsey-woolsey, and ribbons.

Father wrote down her amounts in his ledger.

"Am I imagining things, Father or does it seem we have less and less in the store to count these days?"

Father's grim smile confirmed her suspicion. "We are sheep these days, my dear and the wolves are running rampant. But not to worry. Robert still manages my store in Manhattan."

Perched on a ladder, Sally continued counting a case of ribbons when the hallway clock bonged out twelve times.

On the last chime, Mother entered. "Dinner is ready, you two."

Father glanced at Sally. "Do you wish to stop and eat?"

Her stomach grumbled making Father chuckle.

"Despite what my belly says, I want to finish," she said.

"I can't let you faint away with hunger," he said with a mischievous glance at Mother. "Your mother would never forgive me."

Mother swatted a hand as if giving Father a good-natured slap from the doorway. "I declare, you two," she said, wagging a teasing finger at them. "I'll make a tray for you."

She soon returned with a platter of cheese, roast beef, bread, blueberries, and some donuts. Behind her, Audrey carried a pitcher of cider and two cups.

After Mother and Audrey left, Sally stood behind her chair and bowed her head as he intoned a blessing.

He set a plate of cold roast beef, bread, and cheese in front of her while she helped herself to some berries before pouring each cider.

The sweet scent of fermented apple drifted to her nose as the golden liquid filled her cup. Then she reached for a donut, which she balanced on the rim of her dish.

"Father, may I ask something of a personal nature?" Sally gripped her cup. The question burned in her mind since her encounter with Cousin George, but she feared offending or angering him. Father had strict personal boundaries and she never crossed them without care.

He sliced meat, but his hand stopped midway. His gaze, blue and guarded, flicked to her face and back to his task. The knife sawed back and forth. "Ask your question, and I'll decide if I want to answer."

Swallowing hard, she forged ahead. "You posted an article in Mr. Cooper's newspaper condemning Cousin George for what he did to me."

Father arranged meat and cheese on a slice of bread, which he covered with a second slice, while Sally licked her lips. Her heart started beating faster.

"I was wondering why Mother said she feared something bad might happen, 'like before.'" Brow furrowed she cocked her head to one side. "What happened before?"

Father set down his knife and fork and sat back with a grimace. "I suppose you're old enough to learn the story."

Talking while he arranged his sandwich, he told her a story she'd never heard before.

"During the last war, about a year before your birth, in fact, the British government evicted thousands of French citizens from their homes. They were a gentle, hardworking people for all I discerned of them.

"But they cultivated the best farmland in Nova Scotia, which the government wanted for its own. So, they rounded up these people, Acadians, put them on ships, and dispersed those ships up and down the eastern seaboard. Thousands ended up here on Long Island, though most made their way to the French colony of Louisiana."

He formed his hands into fists as his face blotched with a dull red mottling. Sally didn't take her eyes off him.

"Our neighbors shunned and drove them out." When his voice shook, he stopped, closed his eyes, and drew in a deep breath. "Our own good citizenry responded, out of a fear of strangers, I suppose. And because the Acadians are French Papists."

"Oh," Sally said, and sipped her cider, almost sorry she asked. She set the cup down and fingered her sandwich. "So, what I said this morning is true? The British can evict us?"

"No!" His stern gaze fell on her. "The Acadians are French. England's traditional enemy. We are not enemies."

Not yet. She kept the words hidden behind a clenched jaw.

His smile was reassuring, and Sally wanted reassurance. But doubt lingered. She took a bite and tucked the food into her cheek. "You still didn't explain what Mother meant when she asked if you recalled what happened before."

His lips puckered into an approximation of a smile. "In my anger, I wrote a severe letter to His Majesty's government and to the New York General Assembly defending the Acadians. I told the King his actions were wrong, criminal, in fact, and sought to warn His Majesty, that one day he might come to regret them."

Sally's eyes widened. Father? Her father? Reprimanded the king? That took nerve. Could she do something so brave? At that moment, she saw not her father, but a man willing to seek justice, even when unpopular to do so. She chewed and swallowed her food to let this new image sink in and rearrange her mental portrait of him. "What happened then?"

Father kept his eyes averted. "I was incarcerated for a week. I paid a heavy fine to the New York General Assembly, who considered my letter as high treason, a misdemeanor, and a most daring insult to the honor, justice, and authority of the General Assembly and to His Majesty."

She cleared her throat to rid the huskiness. "I think you did a brave thing," she said, squeezing his arm to communicate how much she loved him. "Not everyone would go to such lengths for their beliefs."

But he shook his head. "I was foolhardy and self-righteous in my youth. Which is why your mother would prefer I keep my mouth shut and go about my business. But my nature won't allow me to remain quiet when the less fortunate are trod upon."

His gaze appraised her. "I grew up Baptist but never paid much heed to my religion in my younger days. While in prison, I repented of my sins, renewed my faith in the Lord, and never glanced back."

His blue eyes softening, he raised her hand to his lips. "I never said how proud I am of your encounter with Cousin George. You defended that family, though you had no cause to."

She avoided his gaze, "I didn't help them." Regret furrowed her brow. "They took them away."

"Yes, you did. You tried and you reported George so we could put a stop to him and others. It may not seem like much, but it is."

Smiling, she arched a brow affecting a surprised tone. "He said

I'm like you. I think he meant to insult me."

Silent laughter shook Father's shoulders. "He is a devil, isn't he?"

They laughed together, and when they sobered, Sally sat up straight. "Father, may I ask one more question?"

He braced his elbows and tented his fingers as his gaze held hers. "Of course."

"What happened...was seventeen years ago. The redcoats wouldn't remember one man after so much time, would they?"

Father's sad smile communicated his regret. His words, though soft, stung. "The British are like elephants, my dear. They forget nothing."

Sally's apron sagged with apples from their orchard. The trees were full of ripening fruit, and she wanted to make some pies.

A regiment of mounted, red-coated soldiers clattered toward her, but she only gave them a quick glance, as she continued toward the house. Since Brooklyn, they paraded past the house regularly.

But when they rode into the yard, they swarmed her, crowding and squeezing her against the animals and booted men. Apples tumbled from her apron, as she tried to protect herself.

Sally pushed ineffectually at the rump of a horse eating her fruit.

"We are searching for the home of the traitor Samuel Townsend," he said in a clipped British accent. His blue-eyed leer lifted from her bosom to her face. "Do you know of him?"

Sally opened her mouth to speak, but she could only utter a small squeak.

"Sally," Mother called from the kitchen door.

Sally squeezed through the throng and ran to her.

"Who are they?"

"The officer says they're looking for the traitor, Samuel Townsend." Tears filled her eyes. "They made me drop my apples, Mother."

Mother patted her arm. "Don't worry, dear. Go inside. I'll deal with them," she said and stepped into the yard.

Sally ran through the kitchen, intent on finding Father. At the sitting room door, she found Phebe hunched over her sampler. "Where's Father?" Sally's hands wound themselves in her apron.

"Redcoats are outside looking for him."

Phebe gawked. "I heard them ride by. They're here? Looking for Father? Why?"

"I don't know. Where is he?"

"In the parlor," Phebe said, pointing with her sampler.

At the front window, Father turned at the sound of her entrance. He extended an arm to her.

"I don't need to tell you," she said slipping into his embrace.

"No, you don't."

Tucking herself in she wrapped her arms around his waist.

"Remember what I told you about these men. Give them no reason to mistreat you."

"I'll be discreet, Father," she said, as a shiver rocked her body. Recalling the way the soldier stared at her, she didn't need a reason.

The parlor door banged open, rebounded against the wall, and jarred to a stop by the palm of a hand.

A half-gasp, half-scream escaped her. Father's arm tightened around her shoulders.

The arrogant officer stopped before them, one foot in front of the other, knee cocked in an arrogant pose as he let his gaze roam the room. When he spied the fowling piece hanging over the mantel, he uttered a deep growl and strode toward the gun.

Thinking he was going to shoot them, Sally flinched when the officer yanked the gun off its pegs. Instead, using an overhand motion, he slammed the gun against the floor, shattering the stock and gouging the planks. As the stock flew to pieces, he put his foot on the barrel and twisted, leaving useless pieces on the floor.

Panting, he glared at them. "No one disloyal to the Crown may own a weapon. King's orders." Turning back to the hearth he studied the portrait of Sally's oldest brother, Solomon who had gone to sea as a cabin boy a year after her birth. He was a stranger to her and, if not for the portrait, would not know what he looked like.

"Where did you obtain this?" The officer demanded. "Who did you steal it from? I am duty-bound to smash this."

Sally's body stiffened as a gasp escaped her.

Father squeezed her hard, a signal to keep silent. He'd held her close to protect her from flying gun pieces, but now he pushed her toward Mother. David opened his arms, and Sally went to him.

Father strode to the hearth as the man reached for the painting.

"Please." Father made a grand gesture toward the mantel. "Destroy my son's portrait. After doing so, you can supply me with your name and rank, so His Majesty may learn who ruined the portrait of the man ferrying his troops from England to the colonies."

Suddenly uncertain, the officer yanked his hands back.

"Yes." Father crossed his arms and widened his stance. "That is my son, Captain Solomon Townsend, of His Majesty's ship, *The Glasgow*. If I'm not mistaken, she left a sizable number of troops in Halifax and heads back to London for more."

"Sir," a young private spoke up. "Lieutenant, if you'll recall, we came to America on *The Glasgow*."

The lieutenant swung his body around. "Did I require a comment from you, Private?"

The private retreated, Adam's apple bobbing and his face flaming.

"I shall inform you when I require a comment from you. Until such time, you will be silent."

The lieutenant pointed a finger at Father, almost jabbing him in the chest. "You, sir, are under arrest. Ready yourself to accompany me and my men to the Provost in Jericho."

Sally gasped. David shouted a protest. Mother and Phebe cried out and clasped each other.

"On what charge?" Father asked, ignoring his family's cries and pleas.

The officer ignored Father and leered at Sally.

David straightened his spine and drew his shoulders back. Sally edged behind him. Grasping his shoulders, she tried to make herself as small as possible.

The officer smirked at Father. "Fine-looking girls."

Father's face went beet-colored, and the vein in his forehead pulsed, but he remained silent, locked in a stare-down battle of wills.

The officer broke away first. "Follow me." As he strode toward the door, David swung a protective arm around Sally and shifted so he blocked her and Phebe with his body as he passed.

Following, the private cast a shamefaced glance at Sally, who tipped her nose up and followed her mother and siblings outside.

Father shuffled past his family to the middle of the yard where his friends and neighbors might have a clear view of him.

David patted Sally's arm, then went to stand beside Father.

The lieutenant surveyed the crowd. A smirk twisted his thin lips as he withdrew a sheet of parchment from his tunic. With pompous motions, he unfolded the sheet and placed a monocle in his right eye before shouting the words, "hear ye, hear ye, Samuel Townsend of Oyster Bay, Long Island, of New York Colony, is hereby under arrest, by order of His Royal Majesty, King George the Third. Long live the King."

He shouted the last four words, paused for the requisite response, and scowled when met with an uneasy silence. "The list of crimes is numerous and follows thus: participation in the Continental Correspondence Committees of New York; planned attendance of the so-called Continental Assembly of Fishkill, New York."

Sally and Phebe exchanged frightened glances. How did he know that? They had spent last evening packing his clothes. At his next words, the blood drained from Sally's face.

"Looting and pillaging of loyalist households; aiding and abetting the enemy French..."

Father turned and met Sally's eye. His expression said, "what did I tell you? They forget nothing."

She steeled herself not to cry.

"You have the wrong man." Mother's terrified voice jolted Sally, and Phebe made a mewling noise.

Sally grasped her sister's hand as Mother approached the lieutenant. "You're thinking of his cousin, George Townsend. He did those things, not my husband. Sam put a stop to it. You can ask anyone here," she said, sweeping a hand to indicate her neighbors.

But their neighbors remained in frightened silence. Someone had to do something!

The lieutenant released a wicked chuckle and dangled the parchment between two fingers. "And yet, they all remain...silent. A pity."

"He's the wrong man." Mother advanced on him. "I'm telling you—you're wrong!"

Father grasped her elbow and pulled her back to the front porch. With both hands on her arms, he planted her there before returning to his position in the yard where he listened to the rest of the charges.

Anger roiled Sally's insides. Why did their friends remain silent now? If Father wasn't scared, why should they be? Why wouldn't they help him?

Glancing around, she realized she and Phebe were closest to the house and everyone, including the redcoats, paid no attention to them.

She let go of Phebe's hand and at her questioning stare, Sally put a finger to her lips and took a step backward.

Phebe shifted her stance to shield her as Sally inched her way to the front door. Once within the hallway, she lifted her skirts and ran to the back door.

Yanking open the door Sally had the presence of mind to check for idling soldiers. Finding the yard empty, Sally scampered to the barn.

Their slave, Peter, waited inside. His body shook, and he gripped a pitchfork, as though ready for battle. "Miss Sally, what's happening?"

"Quick, Peter, no time for explanations. Father's under arrest. Saddle Farmer Girl for me fast as you can."

He flung the pitchfork, which clanged against the wall and dropped in the hay. Within minutes, the horse was ready. Peter cupped his hands together and when she slipped her foot into the cradle of his palms, he hoisted her up.

Sally settled herself and stared into his frightened brown eyes. "If anyone asks, you saw nothing."

He nodded.

She bolted out of the barn and raced to a stretch of trees at the edge of their property. She didn't breathe easy until she gained the tree line where she turned back to discover if anyone noticed.

Peter's father, Hiram, worked with Luke and Joseph in the flax field nearby. Hiram glanced at the house and back to her. He held a sheaf of flax in one hand, which he flicked at her as if shooing her away, before going back to work.

She disappeared into the woods. Her only thought: Find Uncle Thomas.

7

Who defeated whom? The question reverberated through John's head as he stomped toward the Grey Goose Tavern. Did General Howe defeat Washington? Would the man concede defeat? What if he didn't? What would happen if the British Army roundly beat the continentals in every engagement, but Mr. Washington refused to acknowledge their superiority? How long would this conflict last?

John found a seat in the far corner, away from the hearth and fire. He ordered rum. The tavern owner nodded, wiped his hands on his apron, and hurried to fill a tankard.

The room was almost empty with a few patrons eating breakfast or talking among themselves. Near the hearth, a group of old men sat at a table, coffee cups and pastry untouched in front of them. Occasional laughter rang out. Why did they laugh? Were they mocking him? The Army?

At John's baleful glare, the man facing him stopped laughing and his brows lowered. He reached out to his companions on either side of him and laid a hand on their arms. John turned his back. After a moment, their talk resumed, but subdued and sober. Excellent. He wanted to drink his questions and doubts into submission without anyone laughing at him. He wanted silence. As he raised his tankard, footsteps stopped near his chair.

Knuckles pressed into the back of his shoulder. John slammed his tankard down, ignoring the wave of rum splashing over his wrist. Andre peered down at him his mouth twisted in a weak smile.

John's shoulders slumped, and his facial muscles relaxed. He motioned to the chair across from him and raised two fingers to the barkeep who came over to take his order. Andre ordered a tankard of flip, a mixture of ale, rum, beaten eggs, and molasses sprinkled with nutmeg.

When the barkeep left, he leaned on his elbows and studied John, then sat back as the barkeep placed the tankard on the table, scooped up the coins Andre put down, and walked away.

John tilted his chin at the concoction. "How can you drink that vile stuff?"

Andre hoisted his stein. "Flip is a bit like drinking liquefied earth, but when in Rome..."

John didn't clink with him.

Andre lowered the cup. "I understand you had a rough couple of days."

Rage made John tremble and he gripped his stein so hard; he glanced down to see if he left dents on the metal.

"I don't want to talk about it," he said slamming his fist down. Guests glanced over in alarm. "I told him he should attack. I told him not to lay siege lines. Like Boston all over again."

Andre sipped and made a face but listened without interruption. "I'm sorry, Simcoe. Truly I am."

Minutes passed before John came out of himself. "What are you doing here?"

Andre laughed. A hearty, joyful sound that coaxed a chagrined smile out of John. "Well hello to you too. Do you mean what am I doing here in this tavern or what am I doing here on Long Island?"

John's body shook with a humorless chuckle. "Both, I guess."

His friend lifted a hand, which he let drop as if his presence were of no consequence. "General Lord Cornwallis attached General Clinton's army before marching on the Jamaica Pass. I'm sorry I didn't tell you I was in the area, but I had no time. As for what I'm doing here," he said, pointing at the floor with both index fingers, "I learned what happened."

"Well, I'm glad you're here now," John said raising his

tankard. They clinked and drank. "I'm certain Washington is laughing at us from the other side of the river."

"I doubt that" Andre said. "He may be safe across the river now, but he realizes the tenuous position he's in. Once Admiral Howe moves his fleet upriver, he will trap Washington."

John shook his head. "Siege trenches! With Washington's back to the river, he had nowhere to go. He would've surrendered. He wouldn't have had any other choice."

He grasped his mug again. "What do you think he'll do?"

Andre's forehead scrunched up. "Howe? or Washington?"

"Howe. Washington. Either." John couldn't make up his mind. Howe couldn't either, but Washington—that fox had a plan—and they needed to find out what.

Andre shrugged. "If we're smart, we can trap him in Manhattan. If not, he'll slip away to New Jersey, or Pennsylvania. Winter is coming. He'll need a place to hide and regroup if we don't catch him first."

"And what if we don't catch him first? What will General Howe do?"

Stiffening, Andre averted his face, his posture guarded. He took a drink as his eyes roamed the room. "I can't presume to understand another man's mind." He spoke in quiet tones. "But I would hope he pursues Mr. Washington with the utmost vigor and ends this disgraceful misunderstanding before it becomes a full-blown civil war."

John snorted. "Come on, Andre! Tell me honestly. What do you think he'll do?"

Andre slouched back in his chair. When he leaned forward, John closed the gap, in case anyone tried to overhear them.

"He'll let him escape again. I don't comprehend what Howe's end game is but capturing Mr. Washington doesn't appear to be it."

John gawked at Andre; aghast his friend spoke the words he tried to hide from himself. All morning, John tried to drink away the horrible idea he dug siege trenches to give Washington time to remove his forces.

Sally rode through the trees, hoping to arrive at Spring Street. Even then, she wouldn't be out of danger. Spring Street intersected Main Street, and she would be forced to cross the road in front of the house. If the redcoats caught her, might they arrest her? She should consider her actions more but now was too late for regrets.

As she neared the intersection, Sally puffed out her cheeks. Only the Buchanan's home stood between her and discovery. She straightened her back and guided the horse around the back of the crowd, keeping her face averted, determined to ride as if nothing was out of the ordinary.

Halfway through the intersection, she glanced left. A crowd milled about the house, but Sally's family, along with the arrogant officer, disappeared from the front lawn. Where was Father? Had they left so soon? If so, she had no hope of helping. Would they execute him on the spot?

Forcing herself to ride at a sedate pace, she headed for Orchard Street. No one stopped her or called out to her, but she dared not relax yet.

At the end of Orchard Street, she turned right on South Street, stifling the urge to kick her mount into a ground-eating gallop.

The Coles' house marked the edge of town, and once past it, Sally hawed and urged Farmer Girl into a wild gallop, hoping to avoid more redcoats, yet somehow intercept her uncle.

After gaining some distance, she brought her horse to a stop and listened hard for marching feet, the rumble of horses' hooves, Uncle's carriage, or Audrey's bay mare, Starlight. She stared down the road, but the thoroughfare remained empty.

Audrey and the Buchanan's spent the night at a spinning party in Jericho. She had no idea when they were due home, but they had to take this route.

"Oh," she said, the word slipping from her lips as her brows lowered toward her slim nose. Strands of red hair escaped her mobcap, fluttered in the breeze, and drifted across her nose and eyes. She faced into the wind to whip her hair back.

"Where are they?" Gazing back the way she came, she wasn't sure if she meant the soldiers and her father, or Uncle Thomas.

The road from Oyster Bay remained empty. Sally tapped Farmer Girl, and they rode to the top of a rise. She couldn't go home, but what if she missed Uncle Thomas? What if she had to ride all the way to Jericho?

While her mind whirled, she stroked the horse's neck. Sally bit down hard on her lip, forehead puckered. She checked back toward home. The road remained empty. The only sounds to reach her ears were the wind, birdsong, and crickets.

Behind her, a faint horse's whinny floated on the summer breeze. She spun toward the sound. Did a shadow emerge and disappear into a hollow? She sat up straight, eyes focused. The shadow reemerged, and Sally started breathing again. A horse and rider.

Farmer Girl's ears pricked forward, and she let out a sudden loud whinny. Sally clutched a hand to her hammering heart.

"Please be Audrey," she said aloud, urging Farmer Girl into another gallop. Sally held on tight, leaning over the horse's neck for maximum speed.

Farmer Girl bounded down the incline and raced to the top of another before Sally pulled her to a stop and locked her gaze on the rise.

Audrey appeared.

Sally kicked, and Farmer Girl took off running.

"Audrey!" Sally called above the din of her horse's hooves pounding on the hard-packed dirt road.

Audrey, looking smart in her peacock blue riding habit, black top hat with fluttering feathers, and form-fitting kid gloves, lifted a hand.

Farmer Girl skidded to a stop, making Starlight shy from fright. "Where's...Uncle...Thomas?"

Audrey waved a hand behind her. "He's coming. I rode ahead a bit."

Her gaze roamed up and down Sally's disheveled frame, disgust and annoyance fighting for control of her face.

"Honestly, Sally, I declare. Riding without gloves, or crop. Your hair is falling out of your mobcap. Where's your riding habit? I wager you're not wearing your stays either. When will you learn?"

The Buchanan's carriage rattled up, saving Sally from further scolding, and preventing a stinging reply to her bossy older sister. Instead, she settled for an irritated, "I haven't time for that."

She faced her aunt and uncle, bright smiles on their faces, but Sally gave them no time for pleasantries. "Uncle, you must come quickly!"

"Whoa there." Uncle Thomas said, stopping the carriage. "What goes, Sarah, dear?"

51

He always called her Sarah, unlike the rest of the family who called her Sally to distinguish her from their mother. His jolly greeting and constant upbeat nature broke through her reserve, and she fought back threatening tears.

"The redcoats came to the house this morning and arrested Father. They're taking him to Jericho," Sally said, in an emotion-clogged choke.

Audrey gasped.

Aunt Almy clutched her husband's arm.

The smile disappeared from his face as he thrust the reins into his wife's hands and jumped from his carriage. Reaching up, he almost yanked Audrey from the saddle.

"Audrey, ride home with Aunt. Sarah, ride beside them. If you encounter the soldiers, hide in the woods in case someone saw you leave. I'll see about your father."

As Audrey climbed into the carriage, he turned Starlight back toward Jericho. "Don't worry, girls," he said, jerking his lips into a bleak smile before galloping back the way he'd come.

Sally rode beside her aunt and sister and struggled to maintain a sedate pace, despite her pounding heart and shaking hands. The sisters exchanged frightened glances. Audrey gripped the side of the carriage, and Sally sensed her desire to rip the reins from Aunt Almy's grasp and race for home.

After an interminable ride, they pulled into the yard. Sally dismounted and left Farmer Girl with Peter. She arched a questioning brow, but Peter shook his head. She grasped his arm in thanks.

He took the horse to the barn as Isaac and Luke unhitched the Buchanan's horses and led them away.

The three women hurried toward the kitchen door where David waited. He pecked Aunt Almy's proffered cheek. "Mother's worried sick," he said.

She swept into the house. "Let me by, boy. I'll go to her."

After she disappeared, he turned to his sisters. "Is Uncle going to help or will he do us harm?"

They glanced at each other. An excellent question.

8

It was nearing dark, and Father and Uncle Thomas still had not returned. Aunt Almy went home hours ago, distraught over the possible arrest of her brother and worry over whether her husband put himself in danger by defending him.

Sally long suspected Aunt Almy was as much a Whig as Father, but to appease her loyalist husband, never let her true feelings show.

While her family waited in the sitting room, Sally cooked to work off the nervous energy which would only irritate the others. She rewarmed the stew and baked fresh biscuits before heating water for tea.

Isaac, Hiram, Peter, and Luke's whooping in the yard sent Sally to the window. Father and Uncle Thomas arrived.

Isaac and Peter each took the reins and led the horses to the barn while her father and uncle approached the house.

As the front door opened and closed, Sally prepared each a plate. Her family's exclamations reached her ears, and she pictured them embracing and speaking words of praise and gratitude.

"Where is she?" Father's voice boomed through the house. "Where's my Poppet?"

When she rushed to greet him, he drew her into a tight embrace before kissing her cheek.

"Ah, my bravest of brave girls." He drew her back and smiled down at her. "When they allowed me to say goodbye, I saw I was one child short but chose not to mention it. I decided if anyone might come up with a plan, my quick-witted daughter would. Uncle tells me I was right."

Heat rose into her face. Father was home! Her legs wobbled and relief sang in her heart.

"I made plates for you both," she said easing from his arms. "Please come. You must be hungry, and we're all dying to learn what happened."

They gathered in the kitchen while the men ate, and Mother fussed after Father.

Without warning, the back door flew open. The women uttered soft cries and Phebe cowered against Audrey.

Robert stood inside the door, disheveled and breathing hard as though he ran the fifty miles from Manhattan.

"I received...a note...from Aunt Almy. I... came...straightaway. Father, are you well?"

Father embraced him. "Sit down, son. Thomas is about to explain what happened."

He took a seat while Sally brought him food.

Uncle Thomas popped a forkful of stew into his mouth, chewed, and swallowed. He waved the utensil about.

"I had no difficulties at all," he said through a mouthful. "I rode to the magistrate's office and reminded them of your father's standing in this town. Who would handle the land records if he's imprisoned, how would they obtain their tea and the fine Wedgwood China in which to drink said tea, if unable to conduct his business?"

Another bite, chew, swallow. "I also stressed George and John Kirk are responsible for the rash of offenses against the loyalists. Sam held a meeting in his home, which I attended, and made them stop. Many in town would corroborate the fact."

He offered Father a pointed smile. "If that isn't a Loyalist..."

Another bite of stew disappeared into his mouth.

Father didn't smile back. "You paid an exorbitant amount for my bail, which didn't hurt your cause any."

Uncle Thomas shrugged as if the matter was of no consequence, but Father closed his eyes and bowed his head before leveling him with a pained glare.

"How am I going to repay you?" Father asked, concern deepening the lines around his mouth and eyes. "I will if it takes a lifetime."

Again, the fork made swirls above Uncle Thomas's head. "Nonsense, Sam. Almy and I are in your debt. I remember what you did for me when I first came to this country. I simply took the opportunity to repay a few past-due accounts."

Father flicked a hand, brushing away his argument, but said no more. The hard set of his jaw indicated how much the obligation galled.

David changed the subject. "I'm glad Sally's such a quick, cool thinker."

Again, her face warmed. "I didn't do any more than any of you would."

"What happens now?" Robert asked bringing the conversation back around to Father. "Are you safe, Father?"

Father pushed his food around on his plate. "Not yet. Next week I must stand trial for sedition."

"No, Sam," Mother said, laying a protective hand on his elbow. Her brown eyes shone with consternation.

"I'm afraid so, my love," he said, patting her hand. "I'm still too much of a patriot for their liking and past imprudence remains unforgotten," he said with a quick glance at Sally.

Tears filled her eyes, so she turned away.

Mother's face darkened. "But that was so long ago."

Phebe burst into tears, stopping the conversation. When Father moved to rise, Audrey wrapped her arms around her and led her from the kitchen. Her sobs receded as they made their way upstairs.

When her anguish died away, Uncle Thomas spoke up. "Sarah dear, all the Brits understand is in a time of war, your noble husband protected the French. They don't care they were helpless civilians."

He leveled an accusatory eye on Father. "Your work with the New York Convention as a delegate doesn't help matters, Sam. You intended to go to Fishkill to join the Committee. They were aware of your activities."

"I tried to find a replacement, Thomas, but no one stepped up," Father said waving a hand as if to encompass the town. His angry glare challenged his brother-in-law. "Someone must be present at the proceedings, to record what is happening. To protect this town's interests. I don't believe I did anything wrong."

"You're a fair-minded man, Sam. But sometimes fairness is misconstrued."

Uncle Thomas drew in a deep breath. "Ah, well," he said on the exhale.

Putting down his utensil, he wiped his mouth. "A lovely meal. Thank you. I'm afraid my own dear Almy must be frantic wondering what became of me."

He leaned across the table. "Think over what I said, Sam. You and your family are in a decided minority. You must cooperate with these people."

Father stared at his brother-in-law but remained silent.

Uncle Thomas pushed back his chair and tugged on his waistcoat as if to make room in his belly for the food he ate.

"Wish my sister a pleasant night," Father said. "Sally, show Uncle out."

When they reached the front door, Sally rose on her toes and kissed his cheek. "Thank you for bringing Father home."

"You're quite the resourceful young lady," he said, patting her shoulder. "I should like to have you around if ever I'm in a crisis." Then, pinching her cheek, he left.

Sally returned to the kitchen eager for more of Father's story.

"I can't tell you my relief when I arrived to find Thomas waiting for me."

"Father," Sally said as she resumed her seat. "How did we not encounter you? I was positive we would run into you."

"We stopped first for John Kirk and Cousin George. Thomas tried to speak for them too, but they will go to a prison ship for the foreseeable future."

Sally sat up straight and squared her shoulders. A prison ship! Terrifying stories of prison ships circulated and despite their actions, she hated for them to be confined to one. Would they come out alive?

Father's brow furrowed, and he ran a tired hand over his face before dropping his chin into his palm. "Thomas paid one thousand pounds to secure my release. One...thousand...pounds." He shook his head. "How will I ever repay him?"

September tenth dawned cool and cloudy. A perfect match for Sally's emotions because today Father must appear in court.

What should she wear? Because of her fast thinking, Father invited her to come along, and she wanted to appear her absolute best. Two nights ago, Father asked Mother to prepare his suit of Manchester velvet, remarking the British only respected wealth and position.

Standing in front of her armoire, she pressed her lips tight and tried to decide on a dress to show her off as a well-to-do daughter of a successful businessman. She took down her sapphire Lutestring silk and her emerald-green satin and held each in front of her, unable to decide which to wear.

"Go with the blue."

Sally whirled to find Liss, their new servant girl, standing at the bedroom door. With the girls getting older, Mother decided they needed a personal attendant. Besides, Liss was an excellent seamstress, and Mother needed help with sewing.

"You startled me," Sally said, still unused to the dark-skinned girl maybe three years older than herself.

"Your mother sent me to help you."

Sally cocked her head and held the blue dress against her body. "You think so?"

"Mm-hmm."

Liss held the gown under Sally's chin. "Your eyes and hair are set off beautifully and your cheeks pink right up."

Liss set aside the blue silk. "Now," she said holding the green dress against Sally in the same way.

"This one changes your eye color more to green and sharpens your red hair but fades your natural skin tone."

Sally took the Lutestring. "You know best."

Sliding her left hand along the banister, Sally descended the stairs. In her right hand, she gathered her skirts so she wouldn't trip. She never gave a thought to racing up and down the stairs before, but dressed like a grown-up, she moved with care.

Liss completed her outfit with ruffles attached to the ends of her three-quarter sleeves and a flat-crowned, wide-brimmed straw hat with blue ribbons tied next to her left cheek. Beneath her hat, Liss styled her hair with a top knot and a shower of red curls brushing her shoulders and the nape of her neck.

Her parent's voices drifted to her from the parlor, so she headed to the door.

"This is an important occasion, Sam and I'm sure she wants to appear her best for you. Don't be impatient. Sally will be down soon. I hope."

Mother stood with her back to the door, her head moving back and forth, following her husband's trail across the room.

"Well, if she doesn't come down soon, I'll be forced to leave her behind." Father's gaze traveled over his wife's head and a smile stretched his lips.

Mother's expression changed to nostalgic admiration. She went to Sally and clasped her arms before offering her a kiss on the cheek. "You're lovely."

She beckoned to Father and moved past Sally. "Breakfast is waiting."

How handsome Father was in his brown Manchester velvet, white silk shirt and cravat, yellow satin waistcoat, and white stockings! He wore brown leather shoes adorned with silver buckles, and a velvet tricorn hat lay on the parlor table. He cleared his throat and knuckled an eye before extending a hand to her. "Aren't you fine, Poppet! Perhaps I shouldn't call you Poppet anymore."

She went to him, clasped his hand, and squeezed. When did his hair begin to gray? "You're quite handsome yourself," she said, then hugged him. "And I'll always be your Poppet," she said, whispering in his ear.

Robert emerged from his bedroom wearing a plum suit, a white silk shirt and cravat, and white stockings. He too wore silver-buckled shoes.

His eyebrows shot up and he did a double take at Sally as his gaze roamed her from her straw bonnet and ended at her blue satin slippers peeping from beneath her silk petticoat. When he met her eye again, a smile lifted a corner of his mouth.

"Were you not my sister," he said, advancing into the room, a teasing grin stretching his lips. "I would seek out your father and ask permission to court you."

58

A giggle escaped her, and she pressed her fingers to her lips. As her face heated, she brushed a hand over her skirt. Her bottom lip tucked under her teeth she offered a shy smile. "Mother says breakfast is waiting."

Robert offered her his arm. Father chuckled as Sally took hold and let him lead her to the kitchen.

The carriage jolted along, and Sally clung to the strap hanging from the ceiling, lest she bounced to the floor.

"They're going to require you to sign the Loyalty Oath, Father," Robert said.

"I'll do no such thing. Honesty and integrity are inviolate qualities to me. I cannot swear allegiance to a government I consider unjust."

"But, Father, if you don't—."

Father slashed his hand through the air, cutting him off. "No, Son. I will not sign a pledge. I will not go against God's law."

"But. If. You. Don't," Robert said stressing each word and half turning in his seat, intent on getting his point across. He tapped Father's knee for emphasis in time to his words. "You endanger the entire family and the Buchanan's as well. They'll send you to a prison ship. Do you want to die of starvation or disease on a prison hulk?"

Father glared at Robert, blinked, and relaxed his face. "I shall pray on it."

When Father said nothing more, Robert sat back against the cushions and flung his arm across the back of the seat. He stared out his window for a moment before making a mute appeal to Sally, but what might she say to change Father's mind? She shrugged.

They rode in silence. The jingling of the harness, the creak of the wheels, and Hiram hawing to the horses speaking for them.

"You know," Father said to the window, "I considered escaping to Connecticut."

Sally and Robert turned shocked gazes to him.

"But I couldn't face what would happen to Thomas. He would lose his money and I'd implicate him if I escaped. Most likely they would imprison him in my place. Heaven forbid what would happen to my sister, your mother, and you children."

The carriage stopped, and Hiram jumped down. The door

swung open.

"We're at the ferry stop, sir, but we have to wait for it to return."

"Thank you, Hiram," Father said.

Hiram closed the door. The conveyance tilted as he climbed back to his seat.

Robert half turned again and laid a hand on his arm. "Father, please, I implore you——."

Father raised a hand silencing him again.

"Father." Sally sat forward. "May I ask a question?"

"Of course."

"You said you can't swear allegiance to an unjust government."

"Correct."

She creased her brow. "But when an unjust government forces you, is not such an oath given under duress? And if so, is your oath not recognized in the eyes of God?"

Robert's appreciative glance melted her heart, but she fought to keep her expression neutral. She clenched her fists and waited.

Father stared out the window. The ferry advanced ever closer. He scratched his nose. "You're quite right, Sally, I never considered the matter in such a light. Thank you."

He uttered a heavy sigh that sounded like a monstrous weight left his body.

Smiling at her, Robert mouthed the same words. To Father, he said, "Of course, she's right. I wish I'd thought of it."

9

John trained his men at Gravesend while Howe allowed Washington's army to sit in Manhattan where the rebel commander took refuge at Harlem Heights.

Admiral Howe attempted to dislodge him with a naval barrage meant to demonstrate not only Washington's weak defenses but the British as the dominant force. The lesson went unlearned.

Training siphoned off John's frustrations. In the sultry heat of early September, he put his men through several drills, after which he intended for them to embark on a twenty-mile march in full gear.

To John's surprise, Major Gordon waited on the far side of the parade ground. Halting his men, he approached General Howe's aide, stopped in front of the major, and saluted. Gordon saluted back and without a word, handed him a note, pivoted on his heel, and marched away.

One of Dr. Franklin's electricity bolts couldn't shock him more. Where was Bamford? He jogged back to his men and dismissed them, choosing to ignore their groans and cries of relief.

Israel perched at his station outside John's tent polishing his shining riding boots. At John's approach, he jumped to his feet.

"Find Captain Bamford for me," John said, snatching back the tent flap. He stopped in front of his desk but didn't sit. Instead, he remained on his feet, rereading the unbelievable note.

My dear Captain Simcoe. In humble thanks for your actions on August 29--30 inst. I wish your presence, along with a small detachment of men, to accompany me to Staten Island where we shall discuss terms of peace with Mr. Washington. Said meeting will take place on September 10 at two o'clock. Your most humble, servant, W. Howe, Gen'l.

When Bamford entered, John handed him the note, making no attempt to hide his glee.

Bamford's eyebrows rose ever higher on his forehead and when he finished reading, his brown eyes shone. "Captain, if this is true, or successful, does this mean the war might end soon?"

"One can hope, Andrew." John took the note back. "September 10, at two. Tomorrow. Tell Israel to clean my dress uniform. Yours too. You will accompany me."

Bamford straightened his shoulders. "Sir!"

John clapped a hand on his friend's shoulder. "You do excellent work, Andrew. I wouldn't bestow this honor on anyone else. Select a small group to accompany us."

Bamford saluted. "Yes, sir, thank you, sir."

Moments later, Israel entered to receive instructions. After giving them, he picked up the note again and sat down. A peace settlement. Did that mean Admiral Howe's bombardment scared Washington into realizing he had no other recourse? Facing mass desertion from a humiliating defeat, combined with an inability to recruit more men, must have convinced him.

The last time John visited Billops Tavern Andre told him Howe was looking for an officer to take over the Queen's Rangers. Face heating over the outcome, John pushed the unpleasant thoughts away while he scanned the room for his friend. A few inquiries told him, that Lord Cornwallis, was busy chasing Washington the length and width of Manhattan, and Andre was with him.

Mrs. Billops swept and mopped the pine plank floor and cleaned the massive stone hearth. A fire now popped and crackled within. The Howes commandeered the tavern, so no other patrons were present.

Two center tables pushed together created one long enough for the envoy to sit in comfort. Three chairs remained vacant. Viscount Admiral Richard Howe sat next to his brother, one leg crossed, an elbow resting on the edge of the table, as they chatted. An aide sat on the general's other side armed with parchment and quill to record the meeting.

The brothers waited for the men who represented the colonial peace envoy. The admiral's men clustered together near the bar while the general's men, including John, gathered close to the hearth.

Simcoe Bamford, Cooke, Lieutenant Carmichael, and Lieutenant Graham faced the door, wanting to be among the first to glimpse Mr. Washington.

Three-quarters of an hour passed, and the murmuring in the room began to grow, along with speculation about when or if the Colonials planned to arrive.

"Where are they?" Bamford asked fisting his tankard and peering within before lowering it again. He raised two fingers to the barkeep who brought another round for them all.

"Perhaps the Colonials—," Bamford said, using the approved name since Admiral Howe forbade calling them Americans— "decided against this meeting."

The door opened and the room went silent, except for the scraping of chairs across the wooden floor as the men rose to greet the envoys.

Thinking back, John remembered a tall man jumping into the last boat. He later learned that man was Mr. Washington. John was six feet tall. Mr. Washington had at least two inches on him and none of these men matched his height.

The brothers' Howe rose from their chairs and, with grave ceremony, and perfect synchronization, swept off their hats and bent double, one leg out, toe pointed, presenting a most elegant bow. They remained for the precise three seconds, straightened up, and with the same graceful movement, placed their hats back on their powdered wigs.

The three Colonials offered curt bows and head bobs, but at least each man removed his hat.

The general's ire showed in squared shoulders and stiffened back, but he swept a gracious hand to the chairs in front of the three. "Gentlemen, please, sit down. May we offer refreshments?"

John's admiration for General Howe rose. Keeping his voice at a pleasant modulation, he remained a most elegant host, despite the obvious insult.

When the three sat, the admiral lowered himself to his chair. He pointed at one man. "You're Mr. John Adams, are you not?"

He addressed a short, broad-shouldered man with what appeared like massive tufts of wool on either side of his head while the center was bald as an egg.

Mr. Adams offered a humorless smile, his demeanor cold as a New England winter. He inclined his head. "Your humble servant, Admiral Howe."

John scowled. Mr. Adams's tone sounded anything but humble.

"May I present my colleagues?" Adams swept a hand toward his companions. "Mr. Edward Rutledge of the Commonwealth of Pennsylvania, and I'm sure you are all acquainted with Dr. Franklin, also of the Commonwealth of Pennsylvania."

With a slow incline of his head to his right shoulder, Dr. Franklin acknowledged the slow murmur. He was famous in England. Regarded as a premier scientist. No doubt most of the men here would write to their families back home about their experience.

John released a breath, a little in awe of the short, squat man with longish hair and odd squared-off spectacles perched near the tip of his nose.

Dr. Franklin's sardonic gaze landed on him, giving John the impression, everything interested the man, yet he mocked it all. Like a puppet unable to control his body, John's head dipped when their eyes met. Dr. Franklin smiled and responded in kind.

Under his men's gawking, John raised his mug to hide behind.

Mr. Adams's rigid body stance announced he came prepared for battle, while Mr. Rutledge sat back and crossed his arms.

"Well, gentlemen," Admiral Howe said. "We are here to discuss terms of peace with our colonial brethren—."

Dr. Franklin lifted a hand and the admiral's shoulders stiffened. A murmur filled the room. How dare the man interrupt Lord Admiral Howe?

"Americans." Dr. Franklin said in a friendly tone that brooked no opposition. He gripped a cane, his fingers squeezing and flexing on the gold-tipped head. His lips stretched in a bland smile.

John shifted. Were they so impervious to the shocked outrage?

Admiral Howe squared up and glanced at his brother as if seeking reassurance. He cleared his throat. "We are here to discuss terms of peace...."

"We are here to discuss our independence," Adams said, leaning close, his eyes cold and full of disdain, piercing the admiral with loathing. "Nothing more. Nothing less, gentlemen." He put an ugly emphasis on the last word.

John sucked in his breath, ready to defend the admiral's honor, but Dr. Franklin reached across Rutledge and laid a restraining hand on his companion's arm. He turned his bland smile full on the admiral.

The general rested his elbows on the table and laced his fingers. "Our emissary sent a note to Mr. Washington requesting his presence today. We're saddened he was unable to attend."

Franklin's sardonic expression shot through the pretense. "General—" Franklin put a strong emphasis on the title— "Washington's duties elsewhere prevented, as I'm certain you understand," he said, gesturing at his companions. "We are here to act in the general's stead."

Mr. Adams slammed his palm down. Tankards rattled. The Howes jumped.

A slap across the face couldn't surprise John more.

"We had the impression, you and the admiral," he swept a hand toward the man sitting opposite him, "wanted to discuss terms for securing our independence. Is this true or not?"

As the brothers again exchanged glances, John's brows furrowed. This meeting was going awry with astonishing speed.

Admiral Howe shook his head. "King George gave us no such authorization. We are here to discuss the terms of your surrender to His Majesty's forces and to agree to return as loyal subjects of King George the Third."

"And why would we do that?" Mr. Rutledge spoke for the first time, peering down his long nose at the brothers. His round double chin bobbed as he spoke. "Why would we reduce ourselves to the status of the Irish?"

General Howe took a long drink and set the tankard down in a slow, deliberate movement while the admiral played with the brim of his hat.

Dr. Franklin played with the tip of his cane. "This is distressing news, gentlemen," he said. "We came here to discuss terms for ending the war and securing American independence. Nothing else will do. We would be most saddened to discover our invitation arrived under false pretenses."

Again, the false, flat smile appeared and disappeared, and his hard blue eyes pierced the two officers to their seats. "Now, we have strict orders from Congress. We hoped to pass glad tidings to General Washington."

Lord Howe rubbed a hand over his lips as he contemplated his arrogant guests. He dropped his hand. "I cannot view you as anything but British subjects."

Mr. Adams huffed so hard his shoulders shook. "Your lordship," he said, narrowing his blue eyes. "May consider me in what light you please... except that of a British subject."

Audible gasps spread through the room. Admiral Lord Howe sought to cool the situation by making light of the man's words. He turned to Franklin and Rutledge. "Mr. Adams appears to be a decided character."

Neither man replied.

Howe's pleasant smile disappeared into an angry frown. He pushed his hat aside in a swift movement. It teetered on the edge. An aide stepped forward, grabbed, and tucked it under his elbow before stepping back.

"Gentlemen, we cannot recognize any such organization as a Congress. The King does not recognize such a body, so neither do we. Likewise, we do not recognize any declarations or documents decreed by such body, as the King also does not recognize such declarations or documents."

The admiral stopped short of naming the vile declaration of colonial independence, masterfully playing their game of diplomacy.

Inclining his head, Mr. Franklin took on the tone of a patient father explaining to an errant child. "Surely your King understands it would be economically beneficial for him to deal with an independent United States than with a group of sulky colonies."

John bristled. *Your King? Your King?* Did Mr. Franklin

repudiate the king? He glanced around, his body heated, and he fought to remain seated, but the same dark anger tautened the faces of his friends.

Mr. Franklin waved a hand around the room, taking in all who witnessed the exchange. "You must realize to submit now solves nothing. Within a few years, we would be right back here, at war once again," Franklin said tugging the ruffled cuff at his wrist as he gave one sharp shake of his head. "No, gentlemen. Your King must accept our independence now rather than put off the inevitable."

Franklin sat back, crossing one leg over the other and allowing his foot to swing gently. The cat, having got the canary, now awaited the next move. Once again, he allowed his fingers to play with the head of his cane.

General Howe lifted a hand, seeming at a loss for words. He dropped his hand with a thunk.

"We are sorry you take this position," he said. "We, ah, we wrote to Mr. Washington, asking him to attend this meeting. Does he have a message he would like to convey to us?"

From his pocket, Mr. Adams withdrew a folded note, bearing the Howe coat of arms. The wax seal was unbroken. Washington never opened it.

Adams laid the note down and slid it across the table. The chair creaked as he resettled himself, crossing his arms. "Nothing, sir, but his compliments to you both."

The three men rose and, with short bows, stepped out into the pouring rain.

10

Sally allowed Robert to guide her into the courthouse. White marble columns supported the upper walkway and graced the walls halfway up giving way to creamy yellow rising to a vaulted marble ceiling. Black metal lanterns hung at intervals along the walls. The spotless white marble floors gleamed and clicked to the rhythm of a multitude of steps.

The domed ceiling high above her allowed sunlight to stream into the interior and reflect off the marble. A balustrade encircled the upper floor and important-looking men strode along, on the way to their jobs.

Sally gawked. Father prodded her. "Come, Sally. I mustn't be late."

Never in her life had she seen such beauty all contained in one place. A marvel to behold. When she found her voice, she uttered only a whisper, for the opulence demanded respectful modulation.

Staring up at the light streaming far above her head, Sally exclaimed, "oh, Father, how lovely!"

An amused smile softened his features. "Robert will take you up to the gallery. This is a moment when I expect my children to be seen and not heard. Do I make myself clear?"

Eyes still on the move, she nodded, unable to utter a word if she wanted to.

Robert's hand on her back propelled her forward. "Come, O amazed one." He teased as he led her toward a massive marble staircase. At the top, Sally gazed down to the floor below and gripped the railing. The height made her stomach make a fearful lurch. She stepped back and grabbed her skirt. "I've never seen such...such..." she broke off, unable to find a suitable word.

"Opulence?" He snorted as he took her elbow and escorted her along. "Yes. All very useful if your aim is to intimidate."

Her brow creased at the sarcasm that pulled his lips down and furrowed his forehead. She fell silent as they entered a door above where Father had disappeared, coming upon a gallery of seats.

Uncle Thomas rose near the front and waved them over. Aunt Almy sat beside him, and beside her sat Aunt Mercy Townsend.

"I didn't expect Aunt Mercy here," Robert said close to Sally's ear. "I hope she doesn't cause problems. She's become quite caustic since Uncle Jacob's death and Father's in enough trouble."

Uncle Thomas put a hand on Robert's shoulder, as though reading Robert's mind. "Don't worry, son. She assures me she's here for moral support and nothing more."

Robert lifted a dubious eyebrow. "I hope so," he said as they took their seats.

"I am in full support of my brother," Aunt Almy said. "I can't let them take him. Not without a fight. Of course, if he ceased and desisted earlier, perhaps he wouldn't be in this predicament."

Aunt Mercy crossed her arms over her ample bosom and jutted out her sharp chin. "Humpf," she said. "He doesn't go far enough."

Aunt Almy patted her sister-in-law's elbow. "Now, now, Mercy,"

Sitting back down, Uncle Thomas squeezed his wife's knee. "None of that, my dears. Sam is a high-minded and decent man. He does what he believes is right, and no one can fault him."

Aunt Mercy harrumphed again. This time, the sound echoed off the walls and drew several eyes in their direction.

Over his shoulder, Father stared up at them.

Heat flowed up Sally's neck and suffused her cheeks. She shook her head, proclaiming her innocence.

Father resettled in his seat, alone at the table, back straight, hands clasped, rubbing his thumb up and down the inside of his palm. Sally wished she could sit beside him. He appeared so small by himself.

Judge Whitehead Hicks took the bench, his long, white curly wig a sharp contrast to his flowing black judicial robe swaying with his steps. With a curt gesture, he summoned Father to the witness box.

"Mr. Townsend, explain your activities with the so-called Correspondence Committee formed by this rabble calling themselves the Continental Congress."

Father pulled at his cravat with his index finger. "Your Honor, the Correspondence Committee is a group of gentlemen who write to one another, reporting the goings-on in each town."

"But not," Judge Hicks cut in, "an organization of espionage designed to inform the rebels of the movements of our men?"

Father jerked back. "No, sir. We formed the Committee last year, following incidents in Concord and Lexington, Massachusetts Colony. Patriotic fervor erupted in Oyster Bay as strident Whig elements began persecuting our Loyalist neighbors. Vandalism, arson, and personal attacks grew in frequency, and violence against long-time friends, alarmed me, so I wrote to the Committee, which is how I ended up representing Oyster Bay."

Judge Hicks tapped a finger against his bench. "But you didn't quit your post as a correspondent. Why?"

Father made a gesture as though to say, what could I do? "Soon after the Tory Act became law, these so-called patriots imprisoned several loyalists for no reason than their loyalty to the King. I wrote to Congress describing the vengeance and score-settling. Soon after, Congress revoked the act. If I quit, the abominable law might still be in place. Who can say how many other loyalists would possibly be harmed by it."

With one hand on the railing, Sally licked her lips taking in every word. So many things she didn't understand before. She squeezed the wooden railing until it pinched her fingers as the lengths Father went to protect his family.

Raising a hand, Father gestured toward the gallery. "In August, these men accosted my daughter."

Straightening her spine, Sally lifted her chin and met the judge's eye before he returned his focus to Father.

"The man is my cousin, I'm ashamed to say, but fortunate for her, as he did her no harm," he said, shifting his feet. He tugged at his coattails, ire strengthening his voice.

Judge Hicks shuffled papers. "I'm in possession of affidavits signed by Mr. Amos Cooper, Mr. Thomas Buchanan, Mr. Wright, and Mr. Coles stating you held a meeting at your home in which you threatened to deport Mr. Kirk and Mr. George Townsend, your cousin, I assume, to Connecticut unless they stopped their harassment. Correct?"

"Correct, Your Honor."

Dropping the pages to the bench, Judge Hicks leaned across and peered down with narrowed eyes. "You gave aid and comfort to the enemy French," he said framing his words more as a statement than a question.

Sally squeezed her lips between her teeth as she awaited Father's answer.

Father drew in a breath and exhaled. "Yes, I did."

Judge Hicks picked up the papers and tapped them on the bench before setting them down. "A long time ago, Mr. Townsend, and from what I've learned, quite in keeping with your character. We'll say no more on that subject."

Blinking back happy tears, Sally leaned against Robert as Uncle Thomas slapped him on the back.

Judge Hicks's voice rose in timber. "Mr. Samuel Townsend, I hereby order you to sign the Oath of Allegiance to His Majesty, King George the Third, after which you will be declared a loyal subject." He held out a long piece of parchment, which Father took without comment. He walked to the table where a quill and inkpot stood. The quill shook in his hand as he penned his signature.

Robert rose from his seat. "Your honor."

"Yes, who are you?" Judge Hicks asked, squinting up at Robert.

"Your honor," Robert said again, moderating his voice in response to its echo. "My name is Robert Townsend, the third son of Samuel Townsend, and I also wish to sign the Oath of Allegiance."

Sally gasped, then pursed her lips, comprehending fast. She jumped to her feet. "Your honor, my name is Sarah Townsend, and I also wish to sign the oath in support of my father."

A rumble of laughter surged around her. Sally glanced around, confused. She saw no cause for amusement.

A grinning Judge Hicks pounded his gavel. "Thank you, Miss Townsend. I'm sure your father is most honored by your support. However, an Oath of Allegiance is not required from one so comely as you."

Heat flowed up her face, she sank to her seat, wondering what her appearance had to do with the situation.

Uncle Thomas chuckled as he squeezed her knee and for the first time, she wanted to slap her beloved uncle's hand away. She formed a fist, which she hid within the folds of her skirt.

Robert grasped her elbow. "Come, Sally. We must go downstairs now," Robert said leading her to the hallway.

Walking with her head low, he gave her a one-armed hug. "Interesting isn't it, that because you're a female men dismiss you out of hand. Something to think about, eh?"

She was halfway down the stairs before she realized the implications of his words. His smile held a message, though she didn't understand what. "Yes," she said, "interesting."

When they entered the courtroom she rushed to Father, arms outstretched. He embraced her and kissed the top of her head.

A man stepped up to Father and grasped his hand. "Such a thing to behold when your children offer their support in such a loving way. You must be proud."

Father shook the man's hand. His eyes shone as they rested on her. "I am."

"I'm sorry, Father," she said in a whisper. "You told me to be quiet."

Father squeezed her shoulder as Robert signed his name on the document. "I'm honored you would go to such lengths for me, Poppet. You never cease to amaze me."

The horses clip-clopped along the cobblestoned street, taking a right turn and continuing along a street with a stone wall running alongside. Father pointed. "The Dutch built the wall about one hundred and fifty years ago to protect them from Indians."

Was he teasing her? "That wall isn't high enough to protect your knees. What happened?"

The men laughed, alleviating her leftover anxiety.

"Over the years, as the threat diminished, people used the stones to build homes and shops, so now it isn't much more than a boundary wall, like the ones we use at home. It gave this street its name, though."

The carriage tilted over cobblestones and when they passed the ferry landing, Sally blinked. "We passed the landing."

Robert nodded. "We'll eat lunch before going home."

Hiram drove them three more blocks before halting in front of a narrow, three-story brick building facing the East River. Oakman and Townsend Mercantile graced the front door.

Across the road, a wharf jutted into the East River like a long finger where a three-masted ship swayed in the gentle swells. Men bustled about loading cargo into its hold. The overpowering odor of salt water and dead fish made Sally pinch her nostrils and draw shallow breaths.

Father clapped his hands together once as a smile lit his face. "When did the *Sally* come into port?"

"Yesterday," Robert said rocking up on the balls of his feet, a pleased grin lighting his face. "She should be ready to leave tomorrow or the next day at the latest. We're loading new cargo now."

Sally rolled her eyes. Robert spoke as if *Sally's* presence was his own doing. From the wharf, men rolled barrels up the gangplank.

Their words floating on the chill September breeze made her ears flame. Father owned four such ships: *Sarah*, *Audrey*, *Sally*, and *Phebe*. Her ship being in port today of all days was a propitious sign.

Rain began to fall, as Robert led the way to a side entrance and unlocked a small door. A narrow hallway with a stair led to the second floor. Upstairs, Louis XIV furniture and teakwood tables decorated the rooms. Wall sconces and candle boxes provided light, as did the massive hearth on the opposite wall. Natural light flooded in from the window overlooking the waterfront. Dense clouds cast a gloom the burning candles did little to eradicate.

Sally walked to the window edging a straight-backed chair aside so she might crowd in beside the rolltop desk. Rain darkened the wharf and street below. People hurried past, but the dockworkers ignored the weather.

Robert joined her. "When the weather is clear, you can see Long Island."

She lifted her gaze to gray clouds and mist.

"Come," he said, guiding her across the hall and into the dining room where a long, massive oak table gleamed from lit candles reflecting their light against the polished surface. Steaming platters of pork, potatoes, asparagus, bread, coffee, tea, and dessert awaited them.

"I entertain," Robert said, shrugging off the concern on Father's face. "I'm cultivating business relationships."

"You're spending a great deal of money, son," Father said glancing at the abundance of food and running his hand over the upholstered seat at the table. He peered into the living room at the French furniture before turning a questioning gaze to his son.

Robert lifted his chin and squared his shoulders. "I don't live above my means."

Father's eyebrows rose, but Robert didn't elaborate as he walked Sally to a chair near the head of the table. Father stood behind the head chair, as he took his place across from Sally.

She bowed her head as Father said the blessing, and at his amen, she sat, craning her neck for a glimpse of the servants who laid out their meal.

Robert chuckled. "You won't see them. I hired them to come, and when we pulled up, they left out the back way."

"Oh." Sally's shoulders sloped, disappointed she couldn't thank them, but the enticing aroma drew her in as she filled her plate.

The raised pork pie steamed as potatoes and carrots slid onto her plate with the gravy when she cut into the pastry. Sally ate with enthusiasm but stopped when she spied her father pushing his food around on his plate.

"Are you all right, Father?"

He dropped his fork and folded his hands in his lap, scowling.

Robert lowered his drink. "Father?"

Coughing into his napkin, Father used the gesture to wipe his nose and eyes. "I signed an oath swearing loyalty to a crown I lost faith in almost twenty years ago. God will condemn me for the lie."

"That's not true. There is no shame in protecting your family," Robert said. "You did what you must."

Sally laid her fork down and placed her hands on her lap. "You always say one earns loyalty, not demands it, the same as respect. Is that not true in your case?"

Father acknowledged their comments with a slight tilt of his head.

Robert leaned forward, and in a conspiratorial tone said, "Father, I know how to fight back without appearing involved in the conflict."

He speared some pork and ate, chewing with slow deliberation, watching for his words to sink in.

Sally ate in silence, hoping they might forget her presence.

It took a few minutes until Father's brows creased and he jolted as though Robert had thrown wet snow in his face.

Robert clasped his hands. "Since the Battle of Brooklyn, General Washington has been hard-pressed to remain in Manhattan. The Howe's are planning a move against him, and he must escape. With the loss of Long Island, what Washington needs now, more than ever, is information on the British, their plans, and so forth."

Father's hand shot up. "Don't say anymore," he said, casting a significant glance at Sally, whose heart sank. Though she didn't understand how passing information to General Washington worked, the exciting idea intrigued her.

Robert lifted his glass and saluted her. "If Audrey or Phebe were here, I would cut out my tongue before being so candid, but Sally's different."

She sat up straight, and for Father's sake, did her best to keep a happy grin off her face, but she let her love and gratitude for her brother shine in her eyes. *Believe it, brother. I am different.*

"For two years I helped the Sons of Liberty with their finances. Through this store."

Sally's fork froze midway to her mouth.

Father choked. "You did what?"

"From seventeen seventy-two until seventeen seventy-four, I assisted the New York Sons of Liberty filter their money. They made quite a profit too, which would smack of bragging if I said how much. Let me only say, they can continue to finance the war another ten years if necessary."

Robert's finger shot out, straight at Sally's nose. "You can never tell! Never!"

"Of course," she said and at this moment, she loved her brother more.

Folding his arms on the table, he caught and held Father's eye. "Those contacts are gone now, with the British tucked in tight here, but I have a friend who is close to Washington. I can contact him with any information you discover at home."

Father jumped from his chair. "No!"

Sally pushed her plate away, no longer interested in food when the conversation was so much better. "How would you obtain that from us?"

Father snarled at her. "It doesn't matter how," he said. "We're not doing it, it's too dangerous," he said, turning to Robert and jabbing his finger at his son.

"You listen to me, young man. Giving food and supplies to the Continental Army is one thing, and I'm happy to continue, but what you're asking is...is...." He shook his head, unable to finish the thought.

Sally stared at Father, aghast. Father? Providing food and supplies to the Continental Army? Was that why their supplies were always so depleted? He'd said it was red-coated wolves. She'd had no idea the sheep were so cunning.

"What you're advocating is dangerous. Deadly," Father said slamming a fist and rattling his plate. "I won't allow it. You might be killed."

"Only if I'm caught." Robert draped his arm across the back of his chair. "And I don't intend to be caught."

Father scoffed. "No one ever does."

11

November 1778

"Miz Townsend."

Patty worked at the table boiling bayberries for the Christmas candles. "Don't forget a soldier is to billet here. He should arrive anytime."

Sally, twisting lines of tow for candlewicks, set them into frames. "I wonder what manner of lobster back he will prove to be."

Dozens of racks of dangling wicks waited for the tallow pot. At the kitchen table, Audrey poured hot wax from a small copper cauldron into candle molds.

"Heavens!" Mother pushed her hair off her face, and with the tips of her greasy fingers, tucked the strands back under her mobcap. "I'd forgotten. I hope he doesn't choose to arrive today. With all this work there isn't time to entertain a soldier."

It was nearing noon and the women began making candles just after breakfast. To stop the process now would be disastrous.

"No one asked if we wanted to billet another redcoat," Sally said, hating the thought of another British Officer living in their home. Last winter Major Joseph Green arrived and stole her cousin Hannah's heart. Sally liked Joseph, but he would take Hannah back to England. One more thing the red coats would steal from her.

Patty gestured toward Liss. "After we're done here, we'll make sure Mr. Robert's room is in order."

Mother wiped her hands on her apron before adjusting her short coat and woolen skirt. "That would be so helpful, Patty, thank you."

The two servants murmured a response. Patty smiled at Mother's appreciation, but a scowl crossed Liss's face as she presented her back to the room and picked up a rack of half-made candles.

"I declare," Sally blew on her frozen fingers and shivered as a blast of wind bustled in, scurried across the floor, and wrapped icy tentacles around her. "What if Officer Lobster Back proves as unchristian and ungentlemanly as Major Hewlitt last year? Life shall be a dismal affair. I think I'll decide now to dislike him and save myself the disappointment of having to change my opinion."

Audrey laughed. "Come now. Major Green proved a gentleman and a friend, and now he's part of the family. Perhaps this new man will be the same."

"Ha!" Sally said, walking the rack over to Phebe, who shivered from an errant draft. "Perhaps, but Joseph is one man and things are different now. The Brits have changed. They were once friendly and willing to meet halfway, but now, they seem—I don't know—hard. They no longer care if you're loyal or not."

She glanced around the room. "Recall, in August, poor Mr. Weekes. A man truer hearted to the Crown you're unlikely to find, but Major Hewlett had him whipped," she said, pointing toward the front of the house. "Right outside our dooryard, because he broke curfew to find a doctor for Mrs. Weekes."

"God rest the poor woman's soul," Mother said when Sally stopped to draw in a steadying breath.

Sally and her sisters wept from their bedroom window as the sixty-three-year-old man endured twenty-five lashes without uttering a sound, while his children and wife begged for mercy. "Even now, the thought breaks my heart. Such a kind man didn't deserve a whipping."

She handed a completed rack to Liss. "No. I shall decide to hate this new lobster back on princi—."

Sally's gasp was audible as she turned toward the door where stood a tall stern-looking man, dressed in a black woolen cloak, under which he wore a green woolen coat.

He removed a high-topped bearskin hat. His dark hair, matted beneath the brim, curled where wet. Droplets gathered at the tips. A gob of snow splatted to the pine floor.

Did he comprehend how he appeared, standing in the doorway as though the carpenter built the frame around him? The gray backdrop of a blizzard swirling behind framed him to perfection.

When he spoke, Sally's heart melted. His rich baritone sent a shiver down her spine and left a strange ache in the pit of her belly.

"'Make thine own candle. Spare penny to handle,'" he quoted from an old English tale, raising one eyebrow, and challenging her to complete the poem.

"'Provide for thy tallow ere frost cometh in,'" Phebe piped up in a cheerful voice from the hearth.

The man's gaze flicked over Sally's head to Phebe and returned to Sally.

Fine. She met his bold stare with one of her own. Lifting her chin, she responded in what she hoped sounded cold and disinterested. "'And make thine own candle ere winter begin.'"

His other eyebrow went up and his regard made Sally tremble as her heart recognized his acknowledgment of her as a young, desirable woman. Sally was often told she was beautiful, but she had no patience with such blather. Her beauty was nothing she earned so was nothing to be proud of, but this man's gaze shouted to her they were not mere words. Her heart pounded in her chest and echoed in her temples.

Mother stepped between them, breaking their eye contact. "I'm Mrs. Townsend. May I help you?"

A curtain dropped in his blue eyes. "I beg your pardon, Mrs. Townsend. Lieutenant Colonel John Graves Simcoe, at your service. I'm to billet in your home for the winter." He said, then entered and closed the door. "It is quite cold outside."

Audrey tsked. "Please open the door. We're making candles."

Both Sally and the colonel gawked. "I beg your pardon," he said, reopening the door.

"Of course, Colonel." Mother said. She gestured to the work going on around them. "You caught us on a busy day. We are unprepared."

His gaze traveled back to Sally. "My apologies."

79

Did her hair fall from her mobcap? She played with the ruffled edge, surreptitiously tucking away an errant strand. Perhaps he disdained her gray woolen work dress. Not her best, but making candles was a hard, dirty task. Maybe he didn't understand and thought her an uncouth American.

Unable to withstand his scrutiny, she redirected her attention to tying new wicks, yet her pulse quickened, and her heart pounded at the way he stared at her. She must run to Aunt Mercy's and talk to Hannah. Today, if possible. Snowstorm or not.

"Please follow me, Colonel," Mother spoke up, "and I'll show you to your room." She left the kitchen, leaving Colonel Simcoe to weave past the candle racks.

Spellbound, Sally's gaze followed him across the room as he navigated through the maze without touching them.

At the door to the hallway, he smiled at her, swept his hat, and bowed from the waist. "Good day, ladies." His solemn blue eyes found her again.

He nodded, and her head bobbed of its own volition. Her lower lip caught between her upper teeth as he disappeared behind Mother.

Phebe walked over. "He's handsome," she said when he disappeared. "His voice is like...watered silk."

Marshaling her senses, Sally scoffed and dismissed him with a flippant wave of her hand. "He's a British Officer."

Audrey scowled.

"What's the matter?" Sally asked but her sister huffed.

"Nothing."

"Your tone doesn't sound like nothing. Have I offended you?"

Jutting her chin, Audrey pointed toward the door where the colonel disappeared. "You may well have angered him by calling him a lobster back and announcing to the world you're going to hate him on principle."

She snatched up a rack of candles. "What will he do to Father?"

Rather than react to Audrey's agitation, Sally studied the door where the colonel disappeared. "He didn't act upset by my comments if he heard them."

"Oh, he heard you," Audrey said, marching across the kitchen and thrusting the rack at Phebe who flinched as if she expected Audrey to hit her with it.

Audrey glared at Sally. "We have candles to make. Just because Mother's not here doesn't mean the work stops."

Sally scowled. "Pray, who left you in charge?"

Not sure she understood what upset Audrey, Sally's bewildered gaze focused on Liss, who offered her a conspiratorial grin before adjusting a rack of cooling candles.

Still not understanding, Sally got back into the rhythm of her work and tried to put the handsome colonel from her mind but found that impossible. He now lived with her.

"So, Colonel Simcoe," Father said, standing behind his chair at the dinner table. "Tell us about yourself. Where did you grow up? What does your father do?"

Distrust burned John's features. He lifted his chin. "Why do you ask?"

All eyes turned to him. He lowered his hands to his sides, and it felt suddenly hot and stuffy in the kitchen.

The fire crackled and popped on the hearth. Outside, the storm continued, whistling past the house, and down the chimney, blowing ashes onto the brick apron. He watched as Miss Sally grabbed a broom and swept the embers behind the andirons, but when his gaze returned to Mr. Townsend's he cringed at the man's hard stare. John expected a rebuke, but instead, he bowed his head to say the blessing. John prudently bowed his head and closed his eyes.

After saying Grace, Miss Sally placed the stew at her father's elbow before sitting down on his left. Her choice of seat pleased John. She settled across from him so anytime he wanted he might glance up and admire her beauty.

Mr. Townsend scooped food onto his plate and passed the bowl to her. She fumbled a little, then served herself before passing it to her sister.

John understood the insult just offered him however, he chose not to respond. He did overreact.

After Mr. Townsend spooned out applesauce, he again handed it off to his left. This time, Sally was ready.

John sat back as Mr. Townsend leaned close and stared into his eyes. "Forgive me for sounding intrusive, Colonel. I simply wish to learn about the stranger whom I must feed, host, and entertain for the indefinite future."

The first bowl arrived at John's elbow. He scraped out the remnants of gravy and bits of meat and potato before the next appeared. He dredged the remains of applesauce, then laced his fingers together.

"Forgive me, Mr. Townsend. I spoke harshly. I'm uneasy around strangers. I always have been. It's a fault of mine but I'm sure that will change as we all become better acquainted. However, please understand, I'm not here to make friends. I have a job to do." He let his gaze roam to each person. He couldn't undermine his authority by befriending the locals.

But when his eye fell on Sally, his resolve flew out the window. His features softened and he couldn't keep his admiration from showing.

She colored and not wanting to frighten her off, he shifted his regard to Mr. Townsend.

"However, I take your point. If I'm to live here, we should become better acquainted." He picked up his fork.

"I grew up in Exeter," he said including everyone. "I went to school at Exeter, Eton, and Oxford. I entered the military as an ensign in the 35th Regiment of Foot in 1771 and received a promotion to Captain of the 40th Foot in the same year. He chose not to admit he bought his captaincy, recalling how General Howe frowned upon the practice. What if Mr. Townsend held the same opinion? After the Battle of Brandywine, I advanced to major and then named commander of the Queen's Rangers, founded by the celebrated Robert Rogers in the Seven Year's War."

Distaste curled Mr. Townsend's lip. "I'm aware of Mr. Rogers and his regiment. An unsavory character. I hope, Colonel, if you're in charge now, you'll raise the level of their conduct to gentleman."

"Such is my intention, sir," John said, placing his fork on his plate and bracing his hands on either side of the dish. "And I intend to make the Queen's Rangers the finest light infantry unit in the entire British Army."

"Why the Queen's Rangers?" David asked, breaking off a chunk of bread. "If you were successful with a regiment, why not stay and continue your promotions in regular service?"

"Promotions are d—uh quite, glacial in the army," John said, shrugging. "Besides, the Rangers is an elite light regiment and esteemed the best mode of instruction for those who aim at higher stations."

"Be careful of higher stations, young man." Mr. Townsend said, dipping his bread in his stew. "Don't reach too far above the will of God in what you do."

The words, sounding like something Grandfather would say, took the breath from John's lungs. His mind fumbled for something to say. "Yes, sir," he said sounding like a whipped schoolboy.

"Tell us what you did at Brandywine?" David's eyes shone.

At the foot of the table, Mrs. Townsend's sharp intake of breath warned John not to go into too much detail. He studied the young man. "You're a strapping lad. How old are you?"

David bobbed his head. "I'm twenty-one," he said, face flushing with the admission.

Mr. Townsend thumped a fist on the table. "Taking another man's life is against God's law, Colonel."

Though he directed his words at John, Mr. Townsend's steely-blue gaze was only for his son. "War or no. You would do well to remember, young man."

David ducked his head and paid attention to his meal.

Heat flowed up John's neck and into his cheeks. He should change the subject. "I hope, while here in winter quarters, my men and I may recuperate and refit for the next campaign season."

His gaze strayed to Sally again, but she kept her head down as she ate. "Your name is Sally, correct?"

Her head snapped up and she blinked before turning a questioning eye to her father, who gave her a slight nod.

Sally raised her chin. "My name is Miss Townsend."

She returned to her meal, but as she lifted her fork, John noted her hand shook.

"Of course. I only meant to gain a sense of who is whom."

Phebe straightened. "Oh," she said. "You're correct, Colonel."

She jerked a thumb at Sally. "She's Sally. I'm Phebe," she said, indicating Audrey across the table from her, pointing with her fork.

"And she's Audrey. David is sitting next to you. We have—well had—five brothers, but now only four. Solomon sails for His Majesty, Robert and William live in Manhattan, and Samuel...."

"Enough, Phebe," Mr. Townsend said.

"Died."

The word spilled from her as she shrank in her seat. She speared her food, bringing the fork to her lips like she expected to eat poison.

Except for the silverware clattering on dishes, the silence around the table stretched.

Uncomfortable with the silence, John shifted in his chair, directing his words to David. "When I first took command of the Rangers, they were a light infantry unit. My first change was to form an associated mounted company called, 'The Hussars,' but I call them my Huzzars."

He laughed, while David offered a polite chuckle.

Chagrined for the stupid joke, John continued. "I'm also teaching them more hit-and-run tactics so they can attack, advance, and deploy with stealth or speed, as the situation may require. Their uniforms were the bright red of the other troops, but I insisted we go to the green coat and black pants and black light infantry style hats for the Rangers and black bearskin for the Hussars. I designed the white metal crescent with the words the Queen's Rangers engraved across the front."

"Mmm," David said, raising an eyebrow.

"How did you convince the army to let you change colors?" Phebe shot a frightened glance at her father, but when he didn't reprimand her, she turned to John, interest brightening her blue eyes.

John offered her a smile, reassuring and friendly. "Well, it was a struggle, I must say. They wanted to remain in red, but I explained how green would be best. In the spring when the coats are new, they match the surrounding countryside and as the year wears on, the color fades with the seasons and by autumn my men are again indiscernible." He raised an amused face to them. "Besides, in the green we can sometimes blend in with our foes and surprise them."

To his surprise, Sally snapped her head up and stared at him as though he turned back flips across the table. What had he said?

"But Colonel," Phebe said forcing him to focus on her again. She took a sip of cider and set her cup down. "The fighting isn't here on Long Island. What will you do when the winter is over?"

"That remains to be seen, Miss Townsend. Depends on whatever orders I receive. For now, my men need rest and recuperation. My job is to prepare the area for defense against raiders from the Connecticut Colony and bring them to justice."

12

John opened his eyes to absolute darkness. With no hearth, the room was pitch-black, and bitter cold preventing deep sleep. He pitied the brother they said occupied this room and wondered how he didn't freeze to death. John had better nights sleeping in military tents in January.

The bitter cold penetrated the walls and wrapped icy tentacles around his legs and leaving his feet like two blocks of ice.

Sitting up, he pulled aside the curtain. The storm moved on. The stars brilliant against a backdrop of black. He dropped the curtain and huddled under the meager blankets, clutching the covers under his chin. He scrunched his body onto the mattress, drew his knees up tight, and breathed into the blankets, to warm his nest.

The wind whistled past the corner of the house and a shiver rocked him from head to toe. Closing his eyes again, he tried to sleep for another hour, but he was too uncomfortable.

Patting the small table next to his bed, John searched for the flint striker and when he found it, he wrapped the blanket around his shoulders before lighting the candle. The small flame, with its orange-yellow halo, extended inches into the darkness, enough to locate his clothing. He drew on his tunic and then held his hands over the candle flame to warm his fingers to button his coat, then carried the candle across the room, his body warming with his layers of clothing.

He considered requesting a warmer room. But all the other bedrooms were on the upper floor, and this one allowed his men access to him and enabled him to come and go freely. Today, he would bring Israel here. He needed his aide.

John drew a sheet of parchment close, as well as a small vial of ink. He held the vial above the candle flame careful not to burn his fingers as he thawed his ink. Making himself comfortable in the chair, he scratched out a message to General Erskine, informing him where he and his men were. Oyster Bay was perfect for his mission. He would make the town so formidable the raiders would hesitate to challenge him.

He folded the finished note, which he set aside. With a new sheet, he dipped his quill intending to create a map. When he finished, he uttered an amused scoff. Instead of a map of the town, he stared at a face with almond-shaped eyes, a short straight nose, heart-shaped lips, and a strong chin. With a smirk over his foolishness, he added a bun on her head and let two curls stream down either side of her face.

Elizabeth, his fiancée would never hold a candle to Sally's fiery loveliness. He dropped his quill and lifted the sheet of paper. Such daydreaming over a woman of questionable loyalty would never do, no matter how beautiful. He crumpled the page. Taking up another sheet, he concentrated on his map. As he worked, the sun broke the horizon.

John's stomach growled. He withdrew his father's timepiece and snapped open the lid. Noting the time, he hoped breakfast was ready. With a click, John slipped the piece into his inside pocket, patting the spot against his heart.

Picking up the wadded drawing of Sally, he straightened the page, and gazed at her face for a long time before exiting out the sitting room door. At the hearth, he laid his drawing on top of the glowing coals. The image blackened, then burst into flame and turned to ash.

The sound of voices from the kitchen drew him to the door and looked nothing like the candle-making factory from yesterday. The back door was now closed against the brutal cold, and a heavy black drape drawn across prevented errant drafts from finding their way inside. The lightening sky laid a foursquare pattern on the kitchen floor from the window beside the door.

Sally worked at the hearth lifting the lid off a Dutch oven and poking a finger within. "They still have a few moments, Mother," she said over her shoulder before straightening. She must have caught sight of him because her hand flew to her heart as she uttered a sharp intake of breath.

"Heavens, Colonel Simcoe, you startled me. Is this a habit of yours, skulking in the shadows?"

"Sally!" Mrs. Townsend said, stepping around the worktable. "Good morning, Colonel. Breakfast will be ready soon. Please make yourself comfortable."

She was polite and friendly, but her concern was evident over Sally's rudeness.

But he didn't consider her rude. More like a challenge.

He didn't acknowledge Mrs. Townsend, but locked eyes with Sally and refused to be the first to break eye contact. A smile curved his lips.

She did say she would hate him on principle. How long might she hold out? Her down-turned mouth and hard set jaw left no doubt he would need considerable effort to warm her heart. Fine. Winters were long, and he had all the time in the world.

The back door opened, and Sally turned as the men clumped across the kitchen with their heavy work boots.

Their servant, at the moment, he couldn't recall her name, grabbed a broom and shooed the men along. "Look at what you're doing to my clean floor," she said, slapping another servant, a man, in the back of the legs before pushing the clods of snow back outside.

"Careful woman!" He yelped as the bundled straw smacked him again making him hop out of the way of the flying broom.

"I declare, it's a never-ending task keeping this house clean with you clodhoppers stomping about," she said, but the smile she gave the man, clearly her husband, belied her complaint as she stamped the broom into the corner of the hearth.

Mr. Townsend laughed. "We are sorry, Patty. Don't berate poor Hiram. In the future, we will remember to remove our boots."

Patty grunted, hands on hips before she returned to her task of making breakfast.

John grinned, watching the domestic antics.

Mr. Townsend nodded acknowledgment of him, then bowed his head to bless the meal.

"So, Colonel Simcoe," Mr. Townsend said after finishing the blessing. He made himself comfortable. "Tell me more about your family. Is your father also an army man?"

John folded his hands together as Sally approached with a bowl of porridge.

"No, sir. My father was a navy man, but I can't abide water, so I joined the Army."

John dipped his spoon into his bowl and stirred. "He died on board his ship during the siege of Louisburg in fifty-nine. I was eight years old."

The cold note in his voice caught him off guard. At home, no one spoke of his father's death. The unexpected rush of anger pushing through him made him pause. He glanced at Mr. Townsend, who gazed at him with sympathy. John lifted a spoonful of porridge and blew on it before slipping the spoon into his mouth.

"I'm sorry for your loss, young man," he said.

The kindness offered made John study his host met his eye with solemnity and without mockery.

"Thank you, sir."

John shifted his gaze to his bowl. "After his death, my mother took my brother and me to Exeter where we lived with my grandfather on his estate."

Why was he telling this stranger his life story? Why did Mr. Townsend make him want to share personal details? The mention of Percy furrowed his brow, bringing the familiar pain...and guilt, which he pushed away with some effort.

"I see." Mr. Townsend ate. "And what is the occupation of your brother?"

John shifted and moved his spoon about in his bowl. What possessed him to mention Percy? "My brother died when I was twelve and he was ten years of age, Mr. Townsend. Drowned in my grandfather's pond."

They all eyed him with various degrees of sympathy, but he didn't want their pity. He concentrated on his bowl.

Mr. Townsend laid a gentle hand on John's forearm and

squeezed. "My deepest condolences, son," he said before removing his hand. John slipped an oatcake on the plate near his bowl. He jerked his lips into a strangled smile that disappeared almost immediately. "If you'll excuse me, I must eat and return to my men. We have much training to do today."

"Of course," Mr. Townsend inclined his head. "We wouldn't want to keep you from your duties."

"What will you do here?" Phebe asked.

John smiled at her. "Phebe, am I right?"

He continued at her nod. "Well, we will strengthen the fortifications against the rebel army," he said, spooning a few last hurried bites. "And search for places where we can set up outposts to warn of, and stop, any rebel raids from the Connecticut province. Now, if you'll excuse me," he said, rising and wiping his mouth before dropping his napkin into his bowl. He walked to the hallway door where he stopped to bow at Mrs. Townsend. "Thank you for breakfast, Madam."

"You're welcome," she said, sounding pleased and surprised he acknowledged her.

He glanced at Sally before going to his room for his cloak and hat. She was as frosty as the winter morning but perhaps, for him, spring would come.

When Sally finished her morning chores, she entered Robert's—no—Colonel Simcoe's room now. On the far wall, nestled in the corner, a single bed rested next to the west-facing window where a small table claimed the best light, flanked by an armoire.

He closed the door to the sitting room, and beside the door stood Robert's desk, the top clear of all but a neat stack of paper, a quill, and an inkpot on the gleaming top.

She drew back the curtains, letting in more daylight. The colonel made the bed and placed his clothes in the armoire. She had nothing to tidy up. Simcoe was a man who had a place for everything, so rifling through his things wouldn't be prudent. He'd be aware if she mislaid something.

She gazed around the room, hands on her hips as she assessed possible tasks. The pine floor could use sweeping.

Her gaze fell on the desk where a pot of ink powder stood next to the inkpot. Despite her resolve not to touch anything, she lifted the powder urn's lid to find the container filled to the brim.

What Father wouldn't do for some of this! He diluted his dwindling supply of ink with water so often, that the writing was almost illegible, and he feared he couldn't obtain more. Well, the colonel had plenty.

She replaced the top and strode out of the room to find Father at his desk inside the parlor door, writing in his ledgers.

"Father, Colonel Simcoe has a pot of ink powder on his desk. Perhaps he'll lend you some."

Father glanced up from his work. "Perhaps," he said, tipping the feather toward his ledger where the faint numbers showed in the columns. "Fresh powder would be a godsend."

Sally leaned over his shoulder and studied the page. "Shall I ask the colonel when he returns?"

"Ask me what?"

Sally jerked upright, her eyes round, and spun toward his voice.

The colonel's lips twisted. He bowed to her. "Forgive me for startling you, Miss Townsend. A bad habit," he said from the doorway.

The idea struck her he was made for standing in doorways, as though the model around whom they were constructed.

His black cloak covered his green coat and fell to his thighs, making him appear taller and slimmer in all black. He removed his high fur hat, which he tucked into the crook of his arm.

Sally gestured toward his room. "Oh," she said. "I was in your room too—"

"What were you doing in my room?"

He lunged forward so fast; she jerked back a step. In a trice, Father was in front of her, blocking her from the colonel, arm out in a protective manner.

"I'm certain Sally meant no harm." Father held a palm out to Simcoe. By the hard set of his jaw, though his words were calm and polite, he would defend her--physically, if necessary.

Sally grasped his arms. "Of course not!" she said, more secure behind his stout back. "Mother sent me in to straighten up. If you hadn't interrupted me, I would have said so."

The colonel's brow furrowed, cold blue eyes evaluating.

She directed her words to Father, knowing he would believe her, but kept her eye on the colonel.

Would he believe she told the truth? Why should she care? "I only meant to do as Mother asked."

Colonel Simcoe squared his shoulders and lifted his chin, giving her the impression, he peered down his nose at her. Unconsciously, she matched his movements. Squaring up and stiffening her spine, she lifted her chin and waited.

Colonel Simcoe sketched a jerky bow from the waist. "My apologies, Miss Townsend. I overreacted."

As his cloak resettled about him, he lifted a hand, which he let drop against his trouser leg. "However, Mr. Townsend, I must request, in my absence, you will instruct your family to respect my privacy and stay out of my room."

"Your room?" Sally asked, prepared to make him aware of who "his" room belonged to, but Father clamped his hand down on her wrist and squeezed hard.

"Of course, Colonel," he said with a nod. "Tonight, at dinner when we're all gathered, we will explain your position. Isn't that right, Poppet?"

Her jaw worked, but the flint in Father's eye had her clamp off her ire. "Of course."

"Thank you," Colonel Simcoe said and started to walk away, but Sally stopped him.

"Colonel, you have ink powder on your desk, and as you can see," she said, indicating Father's ledger with its indiscernible writing. "We're almost out. Getting more is quite impossible," she said, crossing her arms. "I wonder if you might lend us some?"

"No, Miss Townsend."

"But why not? You have plenty. Father will buy some from you if you require it."

"I'm sorry, Mr. Townsend," he said, waving a hand, "but I'm not inclined to give away military stores, nor am I a merchant. It's impossible."

"I quite understand, Colonel," Father said, pulling his chair close before sitting. "I wouldn't want to place you in a compromising situation."

"Why you—!"

Father interrupted. "Sally, enough! The colonel has his orders."

Sally fisted her hands, her breath coming in impotent bursts. "Maybe you understand, Father, but I do not. Excuse me."

She marched toward the colonel and pushed him aside before stomping upstairs and slamming her bedroom door.

13

John allowed her to shove him aside as she passed, regretting saying no and almost giving in to appease her. But no, they mustn't think they might work around him if they wanted something.

He and Mr. Townsend each took the measure of the other, as Miss Townsend pounded her way up the stairs. The muffled bang of her bedroom door broke their standoff.

Mr. Townsend dipped his quill into his inkpot and searched for where he left off, then made a mark in the book.

John peered over Mr. Townsend's shoulder. They were not speaking idly when they said the ink was well diluted.

"Mr. Townsend, please understand..."

Mr. Townsend kept his gaze on his work. "I do understand, Colonel. We all labor under orders and instructions."

He dipped his quill again. "Where would we be if we disobeyed orders over the ire of a pretty girl."

Mr. Townsend lifted his eyebrows with a sardonic twist of his head before going back to work.

"Yes, sir."

Conversation over, John went to his room and hung his cloak in the armoire before surveying his room. All was in its rightful place.

He lifted the top of his ink urn, satisfied she refrained from helping herself. Sitting down, he picked up his quill, dipped the tip into his inkpot and tapped the side to shake off the excess ink, and poised his hand over a sheet of parchment, to make notes.

Sally's angry eyes—they turned green with her rage—flared into his mind. The hard set to her jaw and her stiffened body posture shamed him. Was he being ungentlemanly? Was he wrong to give out a small amount of ink? Such a minor request, but if he gave into one, what next?

As he once again reached toward the inkpot, his hand froze. What would Grandfather do? The question flew through his mind so fast that he wondered where it came from. Ever since meeting Mr. Townsend, memories of his grandfather prodded him.

John threw down the quill, folded a sheet of paper into a container, and poured in a small pile of ink powder.

"Mr. Townsend?"

Mr. Townsend, still sitting at his desk, lifted his gaze.

John placed the container on the desk. "Between us, and please understand I will not be able to do this again."

Mr. Townsend peered at the powder, raising an eyebrow. "Can you afford this, son?"

John stifled a smile. Grandfather always called him son, and he liked when Mr. Townsend did too. Despite himself, his lips twisted. "Just this once."

"Thank you, Colonel. This is generous of you."

"Please, Mr. Townsend, call me John."

When Mr. Townsend smiled but didn't respond. John started for the door where he paused, one hand on the door jamb. "Mr. Townsend, about your daughter."

The man met his eye. "She speaks her mind as her mother, and I, taught her. If you take an issue..."

Was he so transparent? He jerked back waving both hands. "I managed to start out wrong with her. How do I fix the situation?"

Mr. Townsend uttered a derisive snort. "She's a young woman, my boy, and the ways of women are a mystery."

He poured a stingy amount of the powder into his pot and stirred. "Thank you again for the ink. We'll discuss your request for privacy at dinner."

John nodded. "Of course, sir. Thank you."

Back to his room with the door closed, John sat at his desk and picked up his quill. Smiling, he got back to work.

After supper, Sally and her sisters approached the colonel's closed bedroom door. Sally hugged a folded Jacob's Ladder patterned quilt to her chest.

Audrey also carried one with a Crazy Quilt pattern, two homespun linen sheets draped over her right arm, and she held a silver tankard in her hand. Behind them, Phebe held a warming pan filled with hot coals. Audrey knocked three times on the door.

The door swung open, and the colonel filled the opening, clad in his shirt and breeches. Turning, he walked to his chair and grabbed the coat draped over the back, slipping it on. "Ladies—" he nodded to the blankets and warming pan as his fingers buttoned the coat.

"Our mother—" Sally couldn't hide the edge of anger still tinging her voice—"wanted us to bring you these if you'll permit us to enter a room in our own house."

Audrey nudged her.

Sally scowled back.

Audrey showed him the linens. "I fear we're in for another chilly night, Colonel," she said. "We've brought two more sheets, an extra quilt, and a coverlet, and Phebe has a warming pan."

When Phebe half raised the long-handled pan, the colonel gestured to let them in.

Audrey placed the tankard on the bedside table and the linens on the chair. Sally set her quilt down and helped Audrey strip and remake the bed, adding the extra blankets. Before they tucked them all in, Phebe slid the pan inside. She made three slow passes along the feather mattress from pillow to foot, then left the pan at the foot of the mattress.

Pulling the handle, she detached the pan and propped the long stick against the wall, before helping her sisters tuck everything in. When they finished, Sally threw the Jacob's Ladder quilt on top as a coverlet, and Audrey and Phebe helped straighten the edges, so they fell evenly.

"Thank you, ladies. I shall sleep more comfortably tonight."

Audrey and Phebe bobbed their heads and murmured "you're welcome."

Sally remained silent, unwilling to let him off so easily.

"Miss Audrey, Miss Phebe, may I have permission to speak to your sister alone for one moment?"

Head tilted to one side, Audrey gaped at Sally, questioning, while Phebe fidgeted.

Sally hiked up her chin. "Leave the door open."

"You're certain?"

At Sally's nod, Audrey held out a hand to their sister and guided her from the room. "We shall be right outside, Colonel."

Sally squeezed her lips together at the warning in Audrey's voice.

"I understand." He offered a courtly bow. "Thank you."

The two left and Sally crossed her arms and shifted her feet, ready to run if needs be. She chewed her lower lip and waited. He wanted to talk, so talk.

He rubbed his hands together, pushing his left thumb into his right palm. He grew so boyish and unhappy she relented in her anger—a little.

From beneath his lashes, he searched her face. "It appears, Miss Townsend, I owe you a most humble apology."

He dropped his hands to his sides.

Her eyebrows shot up. Of all the—what was this most unexpected ploy? Was he playing some game for which she had no rules? She uncrossed her arms. "For what, Colonel?"

He held his hands in a gesture of supplication as though seeking her understanding. "I grew up in a family of boys and spent the past three years in the Army surrounded by men. I fear my mother's teachings became lost in those years. My manners toward the more delicate sex...well, they remain something to be desired."

He smiled and his gaze, full of hopeful expectation, coaxed a smile from her.

She puckered her lips, not wanting to concede but unable to sustain her bad humor. He did apologize. Father would insist she accept an apology offered without reservation. "No, I owe you one, Colonel." As she said the words, their truth filled her. "First, I never should have said I would hate you on principle. You heard me, don't deny it," she said, rushing on when he started to speak.

He closed his mouth.

"That was a terrible breach of God's law."

She studied him, hoping he understood she meant what she said. "Second, my display today over the ink was inexcusable and I am sorry for that as well."

Her gaze moved about the room. "Also, when my brother is home, this is his room. I was jealous of your moving in."

"I see." The colonel said. "I can understand your jealousy and now I find nothing to forgive."

Sally held out her right hand in a businesslike gesture. "Truce? Can we try to become friends?"

The colonel took her hand, pumped her arm once, and let go. "Truce." A summer-like warmth lit his blue eyes. "I should like to be your friend, Miss Townsend. I should like that a great deal."

Sally offered him a half smile. She gestured with her chin toward the sitting room door. "If you keep yon door open at night, you'll be a lot warmer in here."

14

November came to a close while the Townsends and the colonel got better acquainted. In the evenings he took to regaling the family with his exploits and Sally discovered not only a dedicated soldier, but innovative and creative.

"This morning, I instructed about fifteen of my men to move the stable on the corner of South Road and Main," he said. "I require a new outpost to guard against rebel raids. That building was dashed tricky to lift and roll on rails for three miles, but my men accomplished the task well."

Outside the wind whistled past the house and falling snow swirled in the windowpanes. Father closed his eyes and rubbed his forehead. Tension filled the room and Sally concentrated on the stocking she knitted. She cast a nervous glance at Audrey whose answering glance matched her thoughts. Audrey returned her attention to the wool she spun.

Father sighed heavily and rubbed his forehead.

"Is something amiss, Mr. Townsend?" Colonel Simcoe asked, turning a puzzled gaze on Father.

Father shook his head. "A headache, Colonel. Nothing more."

"Oh. I'm sorry," he said offering a sympathetic smile and

changing the subject. "So, Miss Sally. What did you do today?"
Sally lifted her knitting needles. "As you see, Colonel. I'm in charge of seeing the servants have new stockings this year."

Behind her, Mother's spinning wheel whirred, as did Audrey's, Phebe scratched out more wool on her cards, while David whittled more spindles for the spinning wheels.

Father dropped his quill into the inkpot and slapped his ledger closed. "I think I'll head up to bed now. I am unwell," he said, bowing to Colonel Simcoe who rose from his chair.

Mother stopped her work and followed Father. Phebe glanced around at Audrey, Sally, and the colonel, and putting her wool cards away, she scampered from the room and up the stairs.

Colonel Simcoe resumed his seat and studied Sally and Audrey his brow furrowed in confusion. "Have I said something amiss? I fear I've upset your father, but I don't know why."

"No, Colonel." Audrey set her mending aside. "I fear 'tis an old wound that festers."

His gaze traveled between the two. "I don't understand."

Sally laid down her needles. "Last year, Major Hewlett turned our church, the New Light Baptist Church into the stables you moved. You're not to blame," she held out a hand to assure him. "I'm sure to you the building was only a stable, but the loss of our church—founded in our great-great grandfather's day—,"

"By our great-great-grandfathers." David put in.

"'Tis still a deep anger and hurt for him," Audrey added.

"Why would Major Hewlett desecrate a church? That doesn't sound like him."

"Major Hewlett is Anglican," David said, having a hard time keeping an edge from his voice. "The only church he didn't sully was the Anglican Church. He burned down the Quaker meeting house."

Brows furrowed, the colonel nodded, and his eyes took on a faraway cast making Sally wonder if he recalled such an action he caused. He pulled at his lower lip and stared into the fire, then turned a solemn face to Sally and dropped his hand to the arm of the chair.

"Thank you for telling me. Now, if you'll excuse me, it's been a long day and I have another tomorrow."

Sally and Audrey exchanged confused glances, but they both

bid him a pleasant night. Sally waited at the sitting room door holding a candle as Audrey banked the fire in the hearth, before, they too retreated upstairs.

Sally awoke with a start. Downstairs, the hall clock bonged out two times. Slipping back the covers, she rose, and in the dark of the night, lit only by the moonlight shining through her bedroom window, she sat at her desk and worked in silence, scratching onto her parchment everything she remembered about their conversation.

Phebe made a sound, and Sally jerked her hand from the page. She waited, holding her breath, but her sister rolled over and sighed. Turning her head, the other way, she inspected Audrey's bed, but Audrey's light snoring reassured her of deep sleep.

Taking a long breath, she finished her notes and dropped the quill into her inkpot before hiding her pages in her hope chest. After their luncheon on the day of Father's trial, Robert took her aside and suggested she might gain much from listening and asking what sounded like innocent questions. Sally found herself capable of both. Someday, her notes might prove useful. Until then, she collected and hid them at the bottom of her chest. She eased the top closed and climbed back into bed.

The Townsend's prepared for their annual holiday tea held on Christmas Eve, an event kicking off twelve days of festivities. This year, their tea was in the colonel's honor.

Sunshine pooled but still, Sally shivered and pulled the hood of her brown camlet cloak tighter about her curls when she stepped outside. As she neared Simcoe's training ground at the top of Norwich Hill, she hugged the packet of invitations for her friends and neighbors and stopped to stare.

The men engaged in some strange comical antics. As the mounted Hussars raced along at full gallop down the field, the infantry had hold of the horse's manes and were pulled along. Two or three men lost hold of their mounted companions and landed on their faces in the snow. She cringed at the cold and pain they must suffer, but each man rose, dusted themselves off, and some laughing, ran to catch up to their mounted partner.

Her curiosity was piqued, as another group of soldiers prepared for their dragging down the field. She stiffened. Why would the colonel allow an African in his unit?

Searching the grounds, she found John standing on the other side of the training ground, staring in her direction. He was too far away to determine if he was unhappy with her presence.

Her gaze traveled back to the lone dark man. His men accepted him as their equal, which gave her pause. Would Patty, Liss, Hiram, or Isaac want to join the British? Do they want their freedom? Liberty and Freedom. Two words pounded like stakes into the ground. If the war ended in favor of the Americans, would liberty and freedom be afforded them?

Colonel Simcoe shouted something, and the men stopped. Sally turned his way as the Hussars dismounted and tended to their mounts while the infantry gathered in clusters laughing and talking.

The colonel was making his way toward her.

Heart pounding, she gathered her skirts and headed down the hill, allowing the momentum of the slope to set her into a run. He was angry with her. She had no right to view this activity and now he was going to tell her to leave.

"Miss Townsend."

Sally ignored his call and headed for the Wooden's. She had invitations to deliver and work to do at home. She would apologize and explain tonight.

She returned from delivering her invitations and went upstairs to change into a fresh, dry dress. Once dressed, she stared at her hope chest. Should she sit down now and record their activities? But what if Phebe or Audrey walked in on her? How would she explain?

She lifted her head and listened. Faint sounds from downstairs, the voices of her family as they prepared the house for the party.

Where was Liss? Sally went to the door and peeked out into the empty hallway. Across the hall, her parent's room was empty. Easing the door closed, Sally tiptoed to her desk and grabbed a sheet of parchment. Writing fast for fear someone might walk in, her uneven letters reflected her shaking hand. With quick pen strokes, she drew a sketch, not sure anyone would believe her words. She didn't try to explain because she didn't understand everything and hoped a drawing would be convincing.

As she worked, an idea came to her, and grabbing another sheet of parchment, began a newsy letter to Robert, telling him about the family, and the holiday party, declaring she expected him to come.

She reread her letter before setting aside the pages. But before opening her hope chest, she listened and eyed the door. After a moment, she lifted the lid and dug out her notes, then returned to her desk.

Taking another sheet, she folded her wad and, on the front, wrote out, Robert Townsend, Oakman and Townsend Mercantile, Pier Street, Manhattan. Dropping her quill, she tied the packet with twine and brought it downstairs.

"Father," she stood in the doorway hugging the packet to her chest. "I have a letter for Robert. Can you deliver this for me?"

Father grabbed a linen rag and wiped ink stains from his fingers, his lace cuff swinging with his movements. He removed his coat and worked in his shirtsleeves, cravat, and waistcoat. He rubbed the back of his neck, leaving a black streak near his ear. Cocking an eyebrow, he jutted his chin at the packet. "That's some letter, Poppet"

Her jaw worked and she self-consciously squeezed the packet tight as her head bobbed on its own. "Well, I included an invitation to the party and a long letter. I haven't written in months." Did she sound guilty? She bit her lower lip. *Please don't ask me anymore!*

With his quill, he pointed toward his desk. "Leave it here, and I'll have a courier come soon."

"Thank you."

She hesitated, and at his questioning gaze, she wadded handfuls of her skirt in her grip. "Um...May I ask your advice on something?"

He gestured toward a chair, so she hefted one from the dining table and set it down next to him. She settled and adjusted her skirts, unsure how to proceed.

"What's on your mind, Poppet?"

She squirmed. "This morning, I was delivering invitations and the colonel's men did some unusual training exercises, and... well..." Her gaze roamed the room and stopped at Mother's prized corner cupboard where she kept her fine China. Through the upper glass doors, Sally studied the bone China teapot and cups painted with dahlias and lilies, which Mother only used for important company. In the bottom cupboard, they kept the more utilitarian bowls and dishes for the family. She forced herself to return her attention to Father. "I was curious, so I stopped. But do you think he

103

might consider that spying?"

Father picked up a quill, which he twirled, lips pursed. "I doubt it, my love. But if you're nervous about what he might think, I'm sure you can explain—should he ask. I wouldn't broach the subject though."

Fingers toying with a pleat of her skirt, she prayed he didn't ask since she spent the past quarter hour writing everything down for Robert. Sally peeped at Father through lowered lashes, but he didn't appear concerned and took her at her word. Should she confess her activities? Should she tell Father she stopped not out of curiosity, but hoping to discover something to pass on to Robert? She drew in a breath and pursed her lips.

She rose and slipped her arms around his neck. "All right. Thank you."

When he patted her back, she pulled away. "I'll let you return to work now."

"Sally."

At the parlor door, she stilled and peered over her shoulder.

His blue eyes dimmed beneath a furrowed brow. Did she sense fear?

She raised her brow. "Sir?"

"You did just stop because you were curious, right? Nothing more?"

Sally cocked her head, and she uttered a false laugh. "What more could it be?"

Her heart pounded. Her gleaming white packet on the corner of his desk mocked her. Her gaze bounced up to meet his eyes and returned to the desk. Her cheeks hurt from the too-wide grin on her face. "Why do you ask?"

As Father studied her, she worked hard to meet his eye. A slow exhale deflated his chest and curved his shoulders inward. "Nothing," he said with a sad smile. "Nothing. Go on about your chores."

A confession surged, but somehow, she kept the words behind her lips and teeth. "Thank you, Father."

Sally stood behind her seat at the kitchen table waiting for Father to finish washing up as everyone gathered around their places.

Colonel Simcoe entered the kitchen, and rather than go to his usual seat, he stopped at the bench beside her, forcing her to sidle down to make room. Startled, she offered Phebe an apologetic glance as she pushed her down, but appearing amused, Phebe shrugged.

Father first glanced at the Colonel, then at Sally, who lowered her lashes and refused to meet his gaze. He cleared his throat and bowed his head.

Sally bowed her head and laced her hands together in front of her. She closed her eyes, blinking back tears of humiliation, as Father intoned the evening blessing. When he finished, she slid into her seat.

Colonel Simcoe sat down and accepted a plate of food from Father. He took what he wanted before passing the platter to Sally who tried to take the dish without touching him. She passed the dish to Phebe, who sent it on to Mother and then Audrey, and finally, David now sitting on Father's right. They began to eat, but Sally sensed their humorous glances cast her way and her face burned.

She crossed and uncrossed her ankles, laid her napkin across her lap, and let her gaze fall anywhere but, on the man, sitting to her right. Why was he sitting there?

Patty placed a platter of chicken on the table with a teasing glance at Sally, who clenched her fork so hard, the metal cut into the backs of her fingers. She wanted to cry. Why was he embarrassing her like this?

Beside her, he picked up his fork and began to chat, as though nothing was unusual.

Sally shifted closer to Phebe to gain some distance from his arm that kept bumping hers as he ate.

Colonel Simcoe laid his hand so close to hers on the table Sally trembled. "I saw you at the training ground today, Miss Townsend. I called out to you, but you didn't stop."

Sally moved her hand to her lap using her napkin to hide the gesture. *Please don't berate me in front of my family!* Looking past him, she sought out Father. He met her eye but kept his face inscrutable.

"I'm sorry," she said in a whisper.

"Sorry?" It was his turn to jerk his hand away. "Why?"

Shoulders hunching in, she dared lift her head.

His full lips curved upward in a slight smile. His eyebrows raised in question.

She straightened her back and squared her shoulders. "I heard you," she said. "But I assumed you were going to tell me to leave and recalling the fate of Mr. Hale I didn't want to be accused of nefarious activity, so I left. I had no wish to embarrass either of us."

The colonel bobbed his head. "I understand. First, you could never be of such a low character as Mr. Hale. Second, let me state right here if any of you ladies, or you, David, wish to partake in my training tactics, you have only to come to the training ground. If you wish, I'm happy to instruct and educate."

Sally locked shocked gazes with her brother. If he was foolish enough, her mind hollered, she should take full advantage, but her conscience gave her pause. To use him in such an unfair way was unchristian. Glancing down the table she found Father's censorious gaze on her as the colonel once again regaled the family with his war experiences. Was Father aware of what she was thinking? Was he trying to communicate to her what her pricked conscience was telling her? Sally focused her attention on her food and barely listened.

15

John took his seat at the breakfast table and smiled as Sally brought him a bowl of porridge and a platter of bread and sausage, returning for a teacup and the pot of steaming tea.

"Mr. Townsend, might you spare Miss Sally and perhaps Miss Phebe this morning?"

Mr. Townsend's hand froze as he brought his tea to his mouth. He took a slow sip and returned the cup to its saucer. "Why?"

John's face grew hot, and his heart thudded in his chest. He squirmed. "Well, I—I have to go to Lloyd's Neck and inspect the work being done, and I thought the ladies might accompany me. I would enjoy their company." John held his breath.

"How long will you be gone? They have work to do."

"I understand, sir. We should be gone only for the morning and return by early afternoon if all goes well."

Trying not to squirm under the man's scrutiny, he rushed on. "If you're worried the girls cannot ride so far in the cold, please be assured, I ordered a carriage. They'll ride in comfort."

Mr. Townsend sat back in his chair and dropped his hands on the table. "You ordered a carriage."

"Yes, sir. I did." John's pleased smile slid off his face at the hard line of the older man's jaw. His mouth went dry, and he licked his lips.

"You assumed my consent and went ahead and ordered a carriage? What, may I ask, would you have done if I refused permission?"

"Well, I thought—that is," John's gaze sought out first Sally, then Phebe, but they refused to meet his eye. His hand splayed across his chest. "Not at all, sir. I just thought...if you did say yes...I didn't want to waste time trying to procure a conveyance. I assure you I did not assume your consent."

He cast a quick glance at Sally's face. Tread with care her expression communicated. But how was he to do that? He returned a steady gaze toward Mr. Townsend, hoping by sheer will, to convince the man of his innocent intention.

"I see," Mr. Townsend said slowly, breaking off a chunk of bread, which he placed on his plate, before spooning up some porridge. "I assume your desire to take Phebe with you is not about giving the girls an outing, but because you wish Sally to accompany you, which she may not do without a chaperone. Am I correct?"

Heat flushed John's face, which he tried to hide by holding his napkin to his mouth to regain his composure. If he wanted to spend time with Sally, the truth would be best. He respected Mr. Townsend and imagined his father might have been much the same type of man.

"You are correct, sir," he said, sensing Sally's eyes on him, but John kept his gaze fixed on her father.

"I thank you for your honesty, son." Mr. Townsend buttered another chunk of bread. "Be sure they're back by mid-afternoon. Mrs. Townsend still has a deal of spinning yet to be done."

"Yes, sir. Of course." John ate his meal with gusto. He would spend the morning with Sally. It was his fervent hope she would be impressed with his work and, by extension, with himself.

Dirty snow drifts lay along the side of the road. But away from the road, the drifts sparkled in the sunshine. The cold, bracing air touched Sally's cheeks with a slight tingle as the carriage bumped along frozen dirt roads. A small warming pan on the floor kept their feet warm, and she was cozy bundled in her camlet cloak and a lap robe over her and Phebe's laps.

Colonel Simcoe's piercing blue eyes studied her, and Sally grew uncomfortable with his intense scrutiny. Not knowing where to rest her gaze or what to say, she stared out the window. But every so often she peeked at him from her lashes, only to find him regarding her. Phebe didn't help. She was as tongue-tied as Sally.

"Oh, Colonel, stop the carriage!" Sally popped her head out the window, hoping to distract him, but when the colonel leaned close to peer out, she regretted drawing him so close. The scent of sandalwood soap and mint carried to her. Where had he gotten mint?

Sally retreated so fast, her back slammed against the carriage cushion. Phebe gawked at her.

On the parade ground—the village common until the Queen's Rangers appeared—his men, with bayonets fixed, ran at straw dummies tied to stakes.

What attracted Sally was the noise. As they ran toward the straw dummies, the men screamed, then rammed their bayonet points into the hearts of the "enemy."

He rapped the roof, and the carriage came to a stop. The colonel exited the carriage first, then helped her, and Phebe down. As they took in the activity, Colonel Simcoe kept up a running commentary.

He pointed as he talked. "The charge is never to be less than three hundred yards," he said. "They will gradually increase in distance, taking care the grand division keeps its ranks close, and their pace adapted to the shortest man."

"How terribly barbaric," Phebe said, cringing. "I don't understand how you men can enjoy exercising such brutality on each other."

He turned to Phebe, amusement, and sympathy in his blue eyes. "Well, no one enjoys brutality, Miss Phebe, but sometimes it is necessary."

Sally, watching in silence, now regarded him. He didn't act like a brutal man, but he was hard to get to know.

When Colonel Simcoe caught and held her gaze, she turned away, unsettled.

The colonel cleared his throat. "The soldier," he said, "is taught to keep his head erect. Graceful on all occasions, but absolutely necessary if the enemy dares stand a charge."

Sally challenged him. "Why?"

The colonel pointed with his chin. "Behold."

Such pride and satisfaction boosted his voice!

The men reformed and prepared to make another charge. He timed his words to their movements. "When the British soldier fixes his eye on his opponent, and, at the same instant pushes with his bayonet without looking at its tip, —" at this point, the men stabbed the dummies—" he is certain of conquest."

Brow furrowed, she leveled a questioning eye on him, but he kept his gaze focused on his men, evaluating their performance without the least bit of irony.

"You may call them your opponent, but they are our countrymen." Phebe broke the moment. Crossing her arms, she shifted her stance. "We better continue our journey, Colonel, if we're to arrive at Lloyd's Neck and return on time."

When Phebe turned to climb back into the carriage, he held out his hand to her. "Quite right, Miss Phebe."

He helped Sally in next but turned to examine his men for a bit longer. He climbed in after the girls and made himself comfortable in his former seat across from them and Sally sighed.

He rapped on the carriage roof and the conveyance jerked into motion.

"So, Colonel..." Needing something to do with her hands, Sally pulled her skirts out from under Phebe's leg before readjusting the robe across their laps. Perhaps if she got him talking, he would stop staring at her in such a forward fashion. "What are we going to find in Lloyd's Neck?"

"Outposts, lookout posts, strong points, fortifications. That sort of thing." His eye lit with shy pride, surprising her. "We must defend against possible rebel raids across the Devil's Belt. We're only separated from Connecticut by twenty miles of water."

Sally pressed her lips together, amused at his self-important declaration. She tried not to roll her eyes. "We're aware, Colonel."

A deep chuckle rumbled in his chest. "My apologies, Miss Townsend."

Drawing in a deep breath through her nose, she exhaled and returned to her study of the passing countryside.

"We're going to visit Fort Franklin."

110

Phebe sat up. "Named for William Franklin, the estranged son of Benjamin Franklin. He was Royal Governor of New Jersey, I believe."

"So he was," the colonel said. "Good for you."

Sally snorted. "We may be girls, Colonel, but we are not uneducated ones." Beneath the robe, Phebe pinched the back of her hand. Sally ignored her.

Colonel Simcoe bowed his head accepting her rebuke. Speaking with more humility, he said, "the fort guards the approach to Oyster Bay Harbor, which I believe is strategic in defending this section of Long Island against waterborne raiders from Connecticut."

They spent more than two hours at Fort Franklin, listening to Simcoe's descriptions and explanations and even met many of the men working there. By the time they left, Sally's head fairly spun on her neck and as the carriage rattled home, Phebe dozed, her head on Sally's shoulder.

When they arrived home, Sally woke Phebe and thanked the colonel for the visit.

Phebe hopped down from the carriage and thanked him before running to the kitchen.

Colonel Simcoe helped Sally down but didn't relinquish her hand. His solemn blue eyes plumbed the depths of her soul as her heart pounded in her chest.

Sally was using the colonel's obvious attraction to her advantage, but one question gnawed at her. Could she be his friend and betray him at the same time? Would the Lord forgive her duplicity? The colonel was charming in an awkward yet sweet way. Deciding he held her hand long enough, she gave a gentle tug.

Colonel Simcoe broke eye contact and released her hand. He contemplated his boots before returning his gaze back to her face. "I hope you enjoyed our outing, Miss Townsend."

If he only knew! She tucked her thoughts behind a slow smile she couldn't conceal. "I did, Colonel, very much. I hope we can do this again soon."

He bobbed his head. "I'm glad."

His grin broadened. "I'll try to come up with another inspection site soon."

"Wonderful," she said and gestured toward the house. "But

now, I must go inside and back to work."

He stepped back. "Of course. I'm sorry. I didn't mean to keep you from your duties. I have work, as well. I'll see you at supper tonight."

She bestowed her warmest smile on him. "Goodbye, Colonel, and thank you again."

"Well dear, did you enjoy yourself?" Mother asked when she entered the house. She was on her knees, cleaning the hearth of ashes.

"I did. Where's Phebe?"

"I put her right to work carding wool. I'll need you to spin this afternoon."

"Do you mind if I change my clothes first? I wish to freshen up."

"Of course. Go change your dress and hurry down."

Sally went upstairs, keen to write everything down while still fresh in her mind.

16

Two days before the holiday party on Christmas Eve the door knocker rattled. Sally, who was making her way to the parlor with clean soup tureens and platters, dropped her cargo on the table and answered the door.

A portly man with gold epaulets on his shoulders stood on the door step. He removed his cap to reveal bushy gray hair and bangs which made his pudgy face pudgier.

"Yes," she said. "May I help you, sir?"

He offered her a slight bow. "My name is General Erskine, and I am in search of Colonel Simcoe. I'm told he resides here."

"That is correct, sir but the colonel is not here at the moment. It's cold outside, please come in," Sally said and pulled the door wide for him.

General Erskine entered as David approached and took his cloak and hat. Sally led him into the sitting room and offered him a chair by the fire.

"I'll send someone to fetch the colonel, General," David said and left.

Sally went in search of her parents. Mother told her to bring tea and some cakes to entertain the general.

When Sally returned, she tried to lower the tray without rattling the pot or cups, but her hand shook, and she could barely breath. What did General Erskine want with John?

"Good afternoon, General," John said, saluting. "This is a wonderful surprise. What brings you here?"

The general unfolded his long frame from the chair before returning John's salute, his gold epaulets draped across his broad shoulders, bounced with his movements.

"I'll come straight to the point, Colonel." As the general spoke, his gray hair, sitting like an inverted bowl on his head and curling at the tips, bounced, earning him the nickname "Wooly". Bangs fell over a high forehead. A long, straight nose accentuated pudgy cheeks and eyes and contrasted with thin lips and a receding chin.

Sally pitied John who looked like a schoolboy about to receive a whipping but had no idea why.

"Do we need to speak in private?" John held out a hand indicating his room.

When Mother and Father rose, General Erskine waved them back down. "No. We can speak here."

Phebe entered with a tray of party cakes then sat down. David stood by the door leaning against the jamb.

This reminds, me, General," Mother said, reaching for a cup, which she handed to General Erskine as Phebe offered the tray of cakes. "We're hosting our annual holiday tea the day after tomorrow in honor of the Queen's Rangers and Colonel Simcoe. We would be pleased and honored to have you as our guest."

General Erskine took the cup. "Thank you, Mrs. Townsend, but I'm afraid my duties in Jericho will not permit such a pleasure."

"I'm sorry to hear." Mother handed John a cup.

The general offered her a perfunctory smile before turning to John. "Which brings me to the point of my visit, Colonel."

John sipped his tea. "Sir?"

"I want you to relocate your troops to Jericho."

John choked on his tea.

Sally gasped, then covered her lips with her fingers. Did the sound escape? *No. No. No!*

"Sir..." John eased his cup back onto its saucer. His cautious gaze met Sally's briefly before returning to the general. "May I ask why?"

"Your troops would be better served if you were in Jericho."

"I disagree, General, and if you will stay until tomorrow, I'll take you on a tour. You can assess the work we've done to strengthen our positions and appreciate how close we are to the Sound. It was your desire, was it not, to be able to patrol the Sound for raiders from Connecticut?" John held his breath, not willing to do anything to provoke a negative response. He clutched the arm of his chair so hard, his knuckles whitened.

A reluctant nod dipped the general's head, and his receding chin became a double chin. He waved a reluctant hand. "I can stay through this afternoon. I do want to view your accomplishments in your month here."

Soon after the tea, John and General Erskine left.

The two men rode to the top of Norwich Hill bisecting the town and John's mind was in a whirl.

Why Jericho? His men would be too far away from the coast. All their work building fortifications and reinforcements would be for naught. General Erskine couldn't be entertaining the idea of moving his men twenty miles away.

"As you can see, General..." John swept a hand to show him the spectacular view of the town and waterfront. His men were building fascines and gabions and digging earthworks around the perimeter of the conical hill.

"Colonel DeLancey designated this hill as a strong point for the defense of Oyster Bay, but for some reason, he didn't proceed much beyond clearing brush and cutting a few trees," John said, waving an expansive hand at his men. "My men are hard at work. When complete, it will be adapted for arms, and the outer circuit of the hill fortified by sunken fleches."

He grasped the general's elbow and guided him to the spots he described. "A square redoubt, capable of holding seventy men, will cover the summit. Platforms erected in each angle will be ready for field pieces and the guardhouse they're building in the center will provide cover for the entire earthworks with no more than twenty men."

General Erskine locked his hands behind his back and took in the work, turning and studying the activity until he made a three-hundred-sixty-degree rotation. He jutted his chin.

115

"Impressive, Colonel. I must admit. Impressive."

Thank you, thank you, thank you! John turned his back and stared out over the bay until he reined in his joy. He cleared his throat and offered the general a curt nod.

John loved to build and create, and General Erskine's praise rained on him like manna from Heaven. "Thank you, sir."

Grasping a log making up part of the redoubt, General Erskine peered out over Long Island Sound, toward Connecticut. The pleased smile dropped from his face. He pointed. "Colonel, what are those men doing?"

Below them, a team of twenty oxen hauled a cabin on log rollers toward the beach, moving with care to keep the building intact. John was pleased with this brainstorm. "They're moving the cabin to the beach. I learned Major Hewlett desecrated a church, which he turned into a stable. I moved the stable to the beach, not knowing its original use. I don't feel right using it, so I'm moving the cabin as a replacement," John said with a deprecatory shrug at the general's scrutiny. "I plan to house the Highland Grenadiers there so they can spot and respond to any waterborne attack at a moment's warning."

The general rubbed his receding chin, his eyes widening. "I approve, Colonel. Most heartily. I must say I had no idea how well-suited this village is."

"Thank you, General."

John held his breath, while he clenched and unclenched his fists. He didn't want to go to Jericho. He wanted to complete his work here. He wanted to stay in the Townsend home.

General Erskine shivered and clutched his cloak tight about his neck. "I'm satisfied, Colonel. It's chilly out here. Can we return to the house now?"

"Of course," John said, leading him back down the hill to their horses and casting sidelong glances at the general. Would he learn his fate or not?

They rode back to the house in silence, where John dismounted. He expected the general to join him inside, but he remained in his saddle. He gestured toward the front door. "Aren't you going to come in, General?"

"No. I need to return to Jericho," he said, gathering his reins in his hands. "Keep up the excellent work, Colonel."

John saluted. "Yes, sir!"

General Erskine chuckled as he returned his salute. "I wish I had entire companies of men such as you, but as it is..."

He broke off, nudging his horse into motion. "Good day, Colonel Simcoe."

A young corporal approached to take Salem. Handing over the reins, he grabbed the boy's arm. "Give him an extra measure of oats."

Brows raised and mouth open at the unexpected gesture from John, he clicked to Salem and walked him back to the barn.

Vindication of his achievements filled him with pride and happiness. The only thing that would make him happier was if Sally waited for his return.

Sally sat in the Louis XVI chair by the fire working her sampler, uninterested in the needlework—the single most tedious task anyone ever concocted—but the task gave her an excuse to await his return.

When he stopped inside the sitting room door, filling the frame as only he did, she dropped her work in her lap. "Well, what did the general say? Can you stay?"

He sauntered forward, seeming to fill the room as he filled the door, and gazed down at her. "Would that please you?"

The watered-silk quality of his voice flowed over her, and she stood. "Of course, I want you to stay," she said glancing at him through her lashes, a coy smile tugging her lips. "Besides, I'm quite used to you skulking in the shadows."

A rush of laughter surged up his throat. "I can stay."

Catching her lower lip with her teeth, Sally picked up her needlework and sat back down. "Wonderful!" She pulled the thread and with a mischievous glance she added, "I don't want to lose our guest of honor for the tea."

He claimed a chair across from her. "I'm looking forward to this tea, as are my men. They're pleased you're honoring them in such a way. Though the villagers are polite and welcoming, it's hard to live in a place without family or friends."

"I'm glad."

The threads bled into a blur. What a stupid task. Still, she forced herself to focus until the colors revealed themselves.

They sat in silence. Once when Sally glanced up, she found the Colonel watching her, and when she met his eye, he held her gaze with his own.

Heat flowed up her cheeks, and the needle pricked her thumb. She snapped her hand away and shook it out, before sucking on the bleeding finger.

"Did you hurt yourself?" Colonel Simcoe asked jumping from his chair, but she waved him back down.

"I'm all right. I do that all the time." Laughing, she kept her head down, trying to poke her needle into her sampler. But her hands shook, and the tip kept coming up in the wrong place.

As he reclaimed his seat, his shadow fell on her sampler until she raised her gaze.

A nervous smile twisted her lips. "Did you want something, Colonel? Your hovering is unsettling." She cast him a mischievous glance to soften her criticism.

Sally had to stifle a grin at his diffident smile.

"Are you glad, Miss Townsend? Because if you are, I shall live on the knowledge of your happiness."

Sally studied him. Did he mean that or was he playing a jest. "Yes, Colonel. I am glad you can stay. It makes me very happy." She dropped her gaze to her sampler. *It makes me immensely happy.*

Sally baked the Christmas cake while Mother, Patty, and Liss cleaned the house.

Audrey and Phebe made pine boughs into wreaths and garlands, and strung them across the mantelpiece, interspersing them with bayberry candles and sprigs of holly.

David was out collecting mistletoe which Phebe planned to make into small nosegays for Father to hang from doorways.

Between the cinnamon and nutmeg from her baking, evergreen boughs, and holly, the scents of Christmas permeated the house, reminding her of the solemnity and the promise of hope in the season.

This year, her Christmas prayer was for peace. She prayed for the American soldiers, encamped at Morristown, New Jersey. With God's grace, this winter would not be as critical as their last in Valley Forge, a place, until this past year, she had never heard of.

118

Once she mixed the cake and poured it into the pan, Sally placed the batter in the oven. Her next task was to cook the oly koeks, small balls of dough filled with currants and chopped apples.

Using a slotted spoon, she eased the balls into the hot oil two at a time, watching them sizzle in the kettle, enjoying the bubbles erupting around the uncooked dough. Then she set the platter down to prepare a cloth-covered dish to accept the fried dough.

She worked without conscious thought. Oly koeks was a treat she made often and only needed to keep half her mind on her task.

Sally scowled as a new problem crowded her packed mind. For some time, Colonel Simcoe had been sending her signals which Audrey assured her indicated an infatuation. She didn't know what to do or how to react.

He was handsome, daring, and smart, and in her heart, she believed she might have found her soul mate, which dismayed her. He was a British Officer. She wanted the Americans to win. How could she reconcile the two?

The back door opened, and Audrey and Phebe entered, laughing at some joke.

Sally dropped two more donuts into the kettle. "Aren't you two all rosy-cheeked and laughing."

"Sally, can you put water on for tea?" Phebe asked, hanging her cloak. "All these wreaths and pine boughs, my hands are becoming sticky and chapped."

Sally wiped her hands on her apron, then reached for the kettle. "Wash your hands. I'll boil water."

"Mm, what delicious aromas in here," Audrey said, sniffing the cinnamon on the donuts. She moved to the shelf and took down the tea container, measured out a quantity, and placed the tea in the pot.

Sally smiled. "Well, I hope so. I baked my fingers to the bone this morning." She set the kettle on the trivet to heat over the fire before dropping two more dough balls into her hot grease.

Phebe sat at the table and brought a piece of marchpane to her lips. "I wonder if your beau likes marchpane," she said with a giggle as her teeth touched the confection.

Sally pointed to the treat in Phebe's mouth. "Put that down!" She huffed. "If you want treats for the party don't eat another one," she said, hands on her hips squeezing the woolen material. "And he's not my beau."

Turning her back on them she tried to hide the blush flowing up her neck, warming her ears and cheeks.

"You might want to explain that to the Colonel," Audrey said. "Phebe and I went in search of more pine boughs as we were short what we needed to make one more wreath. We stopped on our way back to watch his men and all he asked was where you were and why you didn't come with us."

Phebe jumped into the story. "When we said you were home preparing food for the party, he said he was looking forward to eating what you made but disappointed he must wait to see you."

Sally scoffed as she fished out the oly koeks and dropped in two more, using her task to end the conversation. She hoped.

Audrey picked up the steaming kettle and poured the water into the teapot before returning the lid. Then she got three cups and brought them to the table. Raising her brow in question, at Sally's shrug, she took three oly koeks off the platter and brought them to the table. "Sit with us. Enjoy some tea."

After fishing out the last two, Sally placed them on the platter, before joining her sisters.

Audrey placed a teacup in front of her. "In all seriousness," she said, also placing a cup in front of Phebe, "Colonel Simcoe is infatuated with you. You must be aware."

Sally nodded, keeping her gaze on the table.

"You're not pleased," Audrey said with gentle persistence. "You know it strikes me, encouraging his infatuation, might make things easier, especially if people thought there was a relationship between you and the Colonel. And if Father condoned it, well, perhaps they would relax their belief he's a Whig and he could regain his business."

Audrey presented a new side of the argument to Sally. She was so caught up in her own roiling confusion she'd never considered how she could benefit Father.

Sally turned to Phebe, including her in the conversation. "What do you think?"

Phebe chewed her oly koek, then swallowed. "I think Audrey's right. I also think he's a handsome man who is smart, comes from a well-connected family, and no matter the politics, he's a man who esteems you. I think you should encourage him."

Her sisters laughed. Phebe eyed them in confusion. "What?"

Sally shook her head as she picked up her teacup. "Of course, you would offer a practical response," she said, bringing her cup to her lips. Could she be so practical? For Father's sake, she should find out.

17

Though Erskine had visited John the day before, late last night, orders arrived stating the general desired an audience with him in Jericho before day-long meetings. Uncertain of what his commanding officer wanted, John polished and spit-shined anything going on his person. Erskine claimed he was pleased with his progress, so what changed since yesterday?

They still had much work to do, to be sure, but despite the deep snow and freezing temperatures, his men made wonderful progress and he couldn't help a certain measure of pride.

Exiting his room, he carried his boots in one hand and tiptoed to the kitchen. Stopping in the doorway, he found Patty and Liss readying the morning meal.

Israel sat at the table with the other Townsend slaves. John scowled. He respected Mr. Townsend, but the one personality flaw he couldn't ignore was the man's penchant for owning other human beings. Otherwise, he would esteem Mr. Townsend as he did the memory of his own father.

"G'mornin' Colonel," Patty said, placing the round of bread dough on the wooden peel which she carried to the brick oven. She laid the peel inside and with one deft movement yanked the long-handled paddle out before closing the door and setting the peel down. "Breakfast isn't ready yet."

She gestured, and Liss retrieved a teacup but, eying the table filled with colored men, questioned where to put it.

The men began to rise, but John waved them back to their seats. "Put the cup on the table, Liss. I can sit with these men."

Liss cast a questioning glance at Patty but did as he instructed. She backed away from the table and returned to her work of serving the men.

John took his seat and studied his aide, who never took his eyes off Liss, as she moved about.

Every so often her glance found Israel, and a small, pleased smile tugged the corners of her mouth.

If a romance was burgeoning, he would need to nip it in the bud.

"Israel," John said, his tone sharper than he intended.

Israel jerked his gaze away from the woman.

"When you finish eating, prepare the horses. We ride to Jericho today. General Erskine demands an audience."

Israel spooned the last of his porridge before popping an oatcake into his mouth. "Yes, sir," he said around his food, rising and dusting his hands of crumbs, while still chewing, he left out the back door.

John approached Israel holding Salem's reins. 0 0 "You understand romances are impossible, yes?"

Israel's eyes darkened, but he didn't answer.

"When I was commander of the 40th Foot, I had a standing order. I did not allow my men any romantic relationship with any woman on Staten Island. My order still stands. You may not engage in a relationship with Liss."

"I don't engage in a relationship with her, suh, but I want one."

Appreciating the honesty, John mounted Salem and took the reins from the man's hand. Israel started out as a personal attendant and did well at his duties, but John saw a deeper, more interesting, and intelligent man than just a servant, so Israel entered his ranks.

Steering south, John discussed with Israel what the general might want with him. "Did I make a mistake in calculation or miss something important in my placement of fortifications?"

He glanced at Israel who shrugged.

123

"Do you suppose General Erskine changed his mind about removing my men to Jericho?"

"I can't say, Suh," Israel said, and his expression showed his regret over his inability to answer John's questions. "But I often find I do my best frettin' after I find out what I need to fret about."

John chuckled. "Sage advice, my friend."

As they passed through Norwich, the sun broke the horizon. Their breath plumed in the cold.

"Liss says we will be able to celebrate in the kitchen," Israel told John as they discussed tonight's holiday party. "Except to serve the officers and such, we remain in the kitchen."

"You cannot continue any dalliance with her. You'll land her in trouble. She's not free."

Israel glanced at him but said nothing and in his eyes was a fury so dark, John didn't pursue the subject. Besides, what might he say?

In the distance, a lone tree poked bare branches into the bright blue of the sky. Small piles of snow lay in the crooks of its branches like small blankets. In a sudden burst, John kicked his horse into a ground-eating canter. How wonderful to be outside on this Christmas Eve morning, the sun shining on his shoulders and the icy air biting his cheeks! With the increased speed, the wind bit his cheeks a little harder. Behind him, Israel's horse pounded.

The spires of Jericho soon came into view. He slowed Salem and the two men walked their horses the last mile or two into town. Once he located the general's quarters, John dismounted in front of a stone mansion and clacked the brass door knocker shaped like a lion's head with the half-circle of the knocker held in the animal's teeth.

When the butler let him in, John removed his high fur cap. In the long hallway shining oak floors made a gleaming path to the back of the house. On his right, an ornate spiral stairway rose to the second floor. He indicated a room to John's left and indicated he should wait there.

Giving the butler his cloak and hat, John walked to the fire crackling in the hearth and held out his frozen hands. His gaze took in the portrait of a lovely young woman above the mantle and recognized the work of the renowned artist, John Singleton Copley. He was expensive, but worth every shilling, as this portrait showed.

The glint of humor in her clear brown eyes, and the pink in her cheeks, reminded him of Sally. Though she did not possess the same intensity in her gaze as Sally, whose hazel eyes took in everything and missed nothing. And rather than red curls piled on top of her head with ringlets falling to her shoulders, this girl was flaxen haired.

Footsteps in the hall broke his reverie so he presented his backside to the flames to greet General Erskine who entered with an aide. "Greetings, Colonel. Thank you for coming early and on a short summons."

"My pleasure, General."

John slipped his hands behind his back and took an "at-rest" posture, staying close to the fire, enjoying the heat on his hands and backside.

General Erskine moved to a table below a south-facing window and studied the contents of a sheet of paper. John's brow creased, but he remained silent until the general made his request known.

He handed the sheet to his aid, picked up a quill, and scratched his signature on another before handing that off. "Take these to the courier."

The aide saluted. "Yes sir."

Erskine said nothing until the door closed behind him. He shifted his feet, and lowered his chin, causing the appendage to double. His somber brown eyes studied John.

"Colonel, some disturbing reports are coming my way, and before I pass judgment, I wish to hear your side."

Disturbing reports—his side? John tensed. Behind his back, he grasped his left wrist and squeezed it tight. "Sir?"

General Erskine shifted his gaze to the window, before turning to John. "I'm not sure how to proceed with this. The claim sounds so outrageous as to appear silly, but I must ask. I hope you understand."

John didn't dare breathe.

"I'm receiving reports of an infatuation with one of the young girls in the house where you're staying."

When John started to speak, Erskine held up a hand, stopping him. "I can quite understand the attraction, Colonel," he said, "but residents of Oyster Bay bring me stories. They say your feelings for the girl, while understandable, are causing more strain on their

125

households than your hosts. Don't be unwise, Colonel Simcoe. Don't play favorites in this mess. Is it true you take the young lady and her sister for drives? Allow them to examine the training of your men?"

Sweat trickled between John's shoulder blades. He resisted the urge to squirm as he locked his gaze on the wall over General Erskine's left shoulder.

"I invited the entire family to go out on drives with me, General," he said, hoping to minimize the situation. "So far, these two ladies are the only ones to accept the offer."

"And you don't think showing them what you're doing, your training tactics, you're not taking a dangerous risk? How can you be sure they don't pass on their knowledge to," he said, waving a hand— "shall we say—interested parties?"

John's throat constricted. The fire overheated him and stepped away. He considered the possibility, but enjoyed Sally's company so much, he justified his actions by reminding himself she was a woman.

"General, they don't understand what they're looking at. I don't explain beyond the bare minimum, and there isn't anyone to pass their knowledge on to. The only other people they might tell are in their own house or their friends who are all loyalists. All the young men are in Captain Youngs' militia."

"Reports are Mr. Townsend is not a friend to us, Colonel."

"Mr. Townsend is a man who takes his faith, and his oaths seriously. I found a loyalty oath he signed three years ago. Countersigned by Judge Hicks." John bit his tongue, wanting to take back his words at the sudden angry set of the general's face.

Erskine straightened. "Is that supposed to placate me? The allegations against him must have been dire indeed if he went before Hicks."

John deflated. A demotion was coming next. He could almost envision the Queen's Rangers slipping through his fingers. How would he look Sally in the eye?

"Sir," he said but stopped when Erskine's jaw tightened, and his brown eyes pierced him with a warning.

General Erskine laid a hand on his shoulder. "Had I not been with you yesterday and received the pleasure of meeting Mr. and Mrs. Townsend, and had I not seen the fine work you are doing, I would reprimand you and transfer you to another regiment."

He sighed. "However, my comment still stands. If I had regiments of men like you, there is no accounting for what we could accomplish."

He clapped his hand down on John's shoulder. "Stop the rides and demonstrations. Be more discreet in your dealings with the family, and for heaven's sake, end the relationship," General Erskine said wandering back to the table as though, having said his peace, the meeting concluded.

John was willing to do all but the last thing. He tried one more tack.

"General, you don't think—."

He stopped at the angry flush of the general's face, fearing he stepped over a line from which he might not recover.

"It isn't what I think that matters."

Erskine waved a negligent hand, as though this entire conversation bordered on the ridiculous. "I understand you didn't allow your men to enter into relationships with the young ladies when you were with the 40th Foot."

That was true. He'd told his men to either end their relationships or marry the girls, but to stop messing around. But with so many accusations of rape, he believed it the best course of action to protect his men.

He studied the general, who kept his gaze firm on John, as though waiting him out. Retreat being the better part of valor, John brought his fist to his mouth and uttered a small cough. "Was there anything else, General?"

All day, Sally occupied herself with work. After cleaning away the morning meal, she went through the house, replacing candle nubs with new, slim tapers for the party. A small bucket hung off her arm, and she dropped the old candles into the bucket for next year's candle-making.

Sally entered the sitting room. Horse's hooves rang on the cobbled street outside. A soldier rode by, but not Colonel Simcoe. The clock chimed out eleven times and Sally shook her head. What was she thinking? She had a long stretch of the day ahead of her before he returned. Shifting her focus to her task, she plucked candles from sconces and replaced them. She would die of shame if a candle burned out in the middle of the dancing or dinner.

She touched the knob on the sitting room door leading to Simcoe's bedroom. Locked. Brows furrowed, she tried again, but the doorknob remained unyielding. Determined now to get inside, she strode to the hallway to try the other door.

Fingers inches from the doorknob, she pulled her hand back. He had made clear they were not to enter in his absence, but she reasoned he must need candles. Biting her lower lip, she turned the doorknob. To her astonishment, the door opened. Heart pounding and breath clogging in her throat, she stepped inside.

His presence was strong in here, and she feared to touch anything. The desktop was clear of all but the inkpot, the powder urn, and a quill. Not a single piece of paper marred its gleaming surface or a wrinkle on the bed, so Sally feared somehow, she'd leave a clue of her presence in here. A candlestick was in the center of the nightstand next to the bed, a nub of candle poking out of the top. This was the purpose of her being here, so she plucked the candle bit out, and dropped it into her bucket, then replaced it with a long, slim taper. On impulse she lay another taper beside the candlestick.

Task completed, she strode toward the bedroom door, but the empty desk intrigued her, its smooth, clean top a siren call to investigate. She padded to the bedroom door and listened, but discerned nothing beyond the usual house noises, the clock ticking, the creaks, and pops of the house.

Back at the desk, she drew open a lower drawer. Supplies. Paper, and dispatch pouches.

She pushed the drawer shut and reached for another. A door closed in the back of the house, sounding like a pistol shot next to her head. She jerked upright, staring hard at the bedroom door, half-expecting to find a scowling Colonel framed in the doorway. Drawing a relieved breath, she swiped her sweaty palms down the front of her apron. She went to the table, and after yanking out the candle, she replaced the nub, grabbed the extra taper, and beat a hasty retreat.

18

Sally and Audrey worked at their spinning wheels. Mother insisted the girls do some spinning before guests arrived. They still had two hours before they needed to dress for the party.

Audrey spun flax while Sally worsted wool for knitting. Nearby, a strong fire snapped and popped, in the hearth, keeping them warm. Beside the window, Phebe knitted stockings. Every so often, Sally glanced out the window before returning to her work.

Phebe giggled. "Don't worry, Sally. I'll tell you the minute he appears. That's why I sat here."

As Audrey's laughter rang out, Sally scowled. "I'm sure I don't know what you mean."

She shoved the wheel harder than she intended, allowing her ire to direct the speed. The wheel whirred snapping the yarn. Slamming her hand down, she pulled the line back and fed in more wool as she willed herself to slow down.

"Relax, Sally," Audrey said, stopping her own wheel, and scowling with exasperation. "There's nothing to be ashamed of."

She restarted her flax wheel, creating linen thread. "Colonel Simcoe is a handsome man. He's ambitious and, I suspect, wealthy," Audrey said wetting her fingers. "If he were infatuated with me, I'd jump at the chance."

Sally said nothing, instead, watching the twist before shrugging. "If you want him, you're welcome to him."

Audrey stopped her wheel again and dropped her hands into her lap. "What bothers you so much about him?"

Sally made a show of moving the thread to the next hook as she searched for the right words. "He's handsome and smart. I'm certain he will rise to importance in the world after the war ends, and I would do well to marry him."

"But?" Arching a sandy brow, Phebe purled a stitch.

"But, well. He's British."

Phebe scoffed. "We're all British."

"No, we're not," Sally said, fighting a rush of frustrated anger. "At least, I'm not. I'm American. I'm not sure I can work past that."

Oh, how their confused, skeptical expressions irked! "I don't want my heart broken." Unexpected tears suffused her eyes. She blinked and shook her head as if to say she didn't want to discuss it, which she didn't. "And please you two, stop teasing me."

Audrey squeezed her shoulder. "I'm sorry. We will stop teasing, won't we, Phebe?"

"I'm sorry too, Sally," Phebe said in a whisper. "I wasn't aware you felt this way. I'll be more sensitive."

Sally sniffed and squeezed Audrey's hand. "Thank you. Now, Mother will be displeased if we don't finish."

The tedious ride back to Oyster Bay gave John too much time to think. Israel's silence respecting John's desire to be alone with his thoughts.

Where had he allowed things to go beyond the appropriate?

From the first, she left him smitten and John admitted that even when in his room with the door closed, knowing Sally was present, made him giddy with longing. He promised General Erskine he would end his courting of Sally, but his resolve lasted only to the Jericho town line.

Long horizontal rays of the late afternoon sun gleamed across the snow-scape, setting the world in shades of blue and white. Bare limbed trees rose in stark relief against the backdrop, and his fortifications gleamed in the late afternoon winter light when he entered Oyster Bay. His men moved about, and he stopped to assess their progress.

Lieutenant Wright saw him and rushed over.

John sighed as he turned to Israel. "No doubt he has something he needs me to attend to. Ride on ahead and ask Patty to prepare a bath for me and lay out my dress uniform for this evening."

Israel saluted. "Very good, suh."

He booted his mount and headed toward the house.

Wright stopped in front of Salem and saluted. "Afternoon, Colonel. We didn't expect you back so soon."

John dismounted before returning the salute. "We have a party to attend tonight, remember?"

Wright chuckled. "Yes, how could we forget?"

He sobered and gestured toward Norwich Hill. "Sir, can you spare a moment? I wish a word with you."

"What's the problem, Lieutenant?"

"Well sir, the men can't find enough timber to support a section of the fort nearest the edge of the hill."

They walked over to the section indicated and he showed John a gap in the fortifications.

"Sir, we need more wood for the walls and redoubts and there is none left, except for yon fruit orchard."

He pointed. "I want to send some men to cut down the trees."

John hesitated. Wright referred to Mr. Townsend's extensive fruit orchard. He surveyed the area for more trees hiding somewhere, but his men clear-cut much of the surrounding forest to construct their encampment, for firewood and fort construction. New trees wouldn't pop, full-grown, out of the ground. He turned back to Lieutenant Wright. "Can't you scavenge more wood from the townsfolk?"

Wright's irritated glare caught him up short. "Colonel, we've scoured and scavenged from here to Setauket. There is no wood available in the quantities we need. We must chop down the orchard. There are over one hundred trees, sir."

Mr. Townsend would be furious. The entire family would turn on him. No. There had to be another way.

Wright scowled. "She's a woman, sir. She'll get over it."

John's back stiffened. "I beg your pardon, Lieutenant."

Wright said nothing more. He put his hands behind his back

and stared off into space, lips pressed together, as though restraining his words.

He reminded John of his reaction when General Erskine dressed him down. John placed his own hands behind his back and rocked up on the balls of his feet. "Clearly you have something on your mind, Lieutenant. Speak plain. What is it?"

The younger man glanced at him, uncertain. He nodded once, and concern written all over his face began. "The men are talking, sir. To me. They're talking to me. About how she comes around here all the time, watching, asking questions, and about how you welcome her with so much warmth. We can understand why. She's beautiful and a glance from her would leave me jelly in her hands too, but sir—." Wright broke off, casting his gaze on the snow.

John crossed his arms and widened his stance. "Go on," he said, the back of his neck goose-pimpling and a hard knot of anger forming in his gut.

A pained expression crossed Wright's face. "Well, sir. It's common knowledge they're Whigs. You can say what you want, but that family is Whig," he said pointing toward the house to emphasize his words.

"I grew up in this area, and I know the affiliations of everyone, so believe me when I tell you. Which makes me wonder why she's here all the time. Why you show her what we're doing and why we're doing it. Sir, you're a fine officer, the best, but I think you're dangerously blind where she's concerned."

Wright stopped. "Thank you, Colonel for allowing me to speak."

He straightened up into the position of attention and falling silent, pursed his lips.

He could demote this man right here and now. Make him a private for what he said. John drew in a deep, calming breath.

"You say the men are talking," John said, glancing at his men, who, though they kept at their labors, every so often glanced their way, as if they knew this confrontation was underway and gave their support to Lieutenant Wright.

Anger surged. They should be supporting him. "Gather as many men as you need to cut down the orchard."

He spun on his heel and stormed back to his horse. A reprimand from General Erskine was one thing, but his men, something else entirely. By allowing the cutting of the orchard, they would change their opinions. Not that he cared what his men thought.

By the time he entered the yard, he had to work hard to rein in his fury. The Townsend slaves bustled about preparing for their guest's arrival. The sight of them enraged him. John hated the idea of slavery, and if it were in his power, he would free them all to spite the Townsend's. The slave, Isaac, walked toward him and John jerked the horse to a stop. Irritated by the sight of the boy, he threw the reins at him and dismounted.

John never approved of the idea one person should own another and it cast appalling hypocrisy on the entire liberty idea the Americans espoused. He had no idea how they would solve the dilemma, but he wanted to be around when, or if, they ever did.

He noted the hour. Three o'clock. He had time to change into a more appropriate attitude and dress uniform.

At the side of the barn, a flash of green caught his eye. Was Israel loitering? He walked over.

"What are you doing?"

Israel and the servant girl, in his shock he forgot her name, were wrapped in an embrace.

Israel stepped in front of her and stretched his arms out to his sides, but she dodged beneath his arm and ran to the house.

John crossed his arms, eyes narrowed. "How long?"

Israel fidgeted and shuffled his feet. "Almost since we got here, suh."

A million things entered his mind to berate Israel, but under the circumstances, what gave him the right?

Israel kept his gaze fixed on John's feet. "I love her."

John sighed.

"And she loves me," Israel said, raising defiant, brown eyes. His chin jutted as if daring John to deny them.

John uncrossed his arms, placing his hands on his hips. "You'll get her into trouble."

"We understand the consequences, suh. More than you realize. We both been slaves."

John opened his mouth to speak, but a long sigh left him instead. He waggled a finger in Israel's face. "Be careful. Don't get caught."

He turned on his heel and strode to the house.

In the kitchen, the two slave women worked with frantic speed, taking food and party platters back and forth to the parlor. At his entrance, the younger woman eyed John, terror in her eyes. He gestured to her, and she walked over to the door.

Taking her elbow, he pulled her to the yard and drew the door closed, holding onto the doorknob.

"You could be whipped," he said without preamble.

She raised her chin in defiance but refused to speak.

"Do you love him?"

"Yes."

John studied her and he found the truth shining in her eyes. He glanced away, not sure how to proceed. "If you're caught, I won't be able to help you. I hope you know that."

"If we're caught," she said, crossing her arms, "we don't expect help."

"What would you do? Run away?"

"If it comes to that, yes," Liss said. She glanced at the door. "If you'll excuse me, Colonel, I need to go back inside before I'm missed."

He let go of the doorknob and Liss disappeared. He cursed himself for not having the desire to discipline the two of them, but who would discipline him? He intended to ignore General Erskine. He loved Sally Townsend.

19

Outside, horses' hooves clattered to a stop outside the window. Sally went to see who might be arriving so early. "Robert's home!" She spun toward the door. "I'm going downstairs to say hello."

She pounded down the last stairs as Robert hung his cloak. She ran to him, wrapped her arms around his neck, and squeezed. "I must speak with you in private," she said, whispering in his ear.

He hugged her back and as he kissed her cheek, he said, "after the party."

Mother hustled them all into the sitting room, urging Robert to warm himself near the fire. She introduced him to Colonel Simcoe, just coming from his room. They shook hands.

Robert stretched his hands to the fire. "The wind is picking up. A snowstorm is on the way. Indeed, clouds are beginning to billow in the west."

"Oh, I hope that won't deter people from coming to the party," Phebe said and ran to the window to peer out as if searching for either guests or the snow. "We've done so much work to prepare."

Audrey greeted Robert with a kiss on his cheek. She waved a hand about the room indicating their decorations. "Don't worry. Mother's holiday tea is the talk of the town. Everyone waits all year for it. A little snow won't deter anyone."

When Robert glanced at Colonel Simcoe, her heart skipped a beat when he addressed the colonel.

He sat forward, a guarded smile on his lips. "Colonel, you may not remember me, but I remember you."

Sally's gaze darted first to Colonel Simcoe, then to Robert, and back to the colonel.

The colonel cocked his head. "Now you mention it, Mr. Townsend, you're familiar to me. Enlighten me. Where did we meet?" He held up a hand. "No! Wait! Let me guess. I pride myself on never forgetting a face."

Sally drew in a breath. He never forgot a face. Did he and Robert encounter each other in some way that might put her brother in danger? How had they met before now?

"Mm, the scent of pine and bayberry fills the room," she said to deflect the conversation away. She smiled at Phebe and Audrey. "You two did a wonderful job on the decorations."

A candelabra stood in the center of the mantelpiece surrounded by pine boughs and red ribbon. Four lit bayberry tapers with flames danced in the eddies of air. Candles burned from sconces all around the room.

In the parlor the servants brought food to the table, leaving little room for diners. Ham and a roast sat in the middle surrounded by custards, puddings, potato dishes, beans, Sally's Christmas cake, and her favorite, Syllabub.

A murmur of agreement traveled about the room and Sally congratulated herself on diverting the two, until Colonel Simcoe dashed her hopes.

He slapped the arm of his chair. "Ah ha! General Howe's holiday party last year at Mr. Duncan's mansion in Manhattan."

Robert chuckled. "Correct, sir. I too, never forget a face. I recognized you right away."

The colonel sat back his smile now guarded. "Did you?"

Robert inclined his head and cocked an eyebrow before turning away. "Tell me, Father, of the goings-on around here. How does business fare?"

Father shrugged and took a seat. He wore the same suit of brown Manchester velvet he wore on the day of his trial. "We've had better years, son, but we've had worse," he gestured toward

Colonel Simcoe. "The Colonel's presence has been a help. People have been more willing to come back and do business knowing an officer of his caliber is residing with us."

A scowl crossed the colonel's face, but he chased it with a smile and a deprecating wave. "Hardly, sir. Your integrity is what draws them back. I have little if anything to do with that."

Sally's brow furrowed. Had she seen the flash of irritation, or was that her imagination? She studied him and when he glanced at her, the admiration in his gaze made her lower her lashes and play with her hands in her lap. Still, she questioned. In the short time, since his arrival, he had never refused to take credit wherever due.

She glanced at Robert. His intense regard made her nervous and, she fought the urge to leave the room and compose herself. He needn't be surprised. She wrote to him countless times about the Colonel's growing infatuation and asked what he thought she should do. His responses had been vague and unhelpful, but now, seeing firsthand, he might appreciate her predicament.

Robert crossed his legs. "So, Colonel, how long will the Queen's Rangers be in Oyster Bay?"

"We'll be here all winter, Mr. Townsend until we receive further orders," John said folding his hands and placing them in his lap.

The two men regarded each other, sizing one another up. Sally's gaze darted between them. They met before. Did they dislike each other? Become enemies?

Upstairs, Sally changed into an apricot brocade gown with a moss green petticoat. The gown gave her complexion a peaches and cream appearance and complimented her red hair.

Audrey was at the dressing table, her face in a cone while Patty powdered her hair. A frown drooped the older woman's lips and her movements and mutterings made clear she was unhappy.

"Patty, the holiday party will start any minute. What makes you so grumpy?" Sally asked twirling to admire how her new skirts swirled and swished.

"Hmmph," was all Patty said.

Sally cocked her head, now staring at the woman. "Hmmph what?"

Audrey lifted her head.

Patty wiped the white powder off her dark hands. "I ain't one to speak out of turn, but that Liss. She's supposed to be up here helping you all girls while I help Miz Townsend downstairs, but where is she? Why is it I always gotta go looking for her whenever I need her?"

Audrey turned in her seat and studied Patty, her brow furrowed. "Do you think Liss is unhappy here?"

Patty huffed again. "I think Liss is in love." She took hold of Audrey's shoulders to turn her back around to finish powdering her hair, but Audrey refused to move.

She stared up at Patty's unhappy face. "With whom?"

Patty shook her head. "I shouldn't say nothing."

She moved to turn Audrey again, but again, Audrey dodged her.

Patty sighed. "Who do you think? Who else could she be in love with," she said with a snarl, "but that uppity aide of the Colonels. I seen them together more than once, though I ain't said nothing till now."

"Why not?" Phebe asked.

Patty played with the powder horn, her fingers twitching with nervous tension at her sudden disclosure. She shrugged a shoulder. "Because I remember when Hiram and me first fell in love," she said glancing at the girls. "I didn't want to get her into trouble. Your ma and pa were kind to us, but we lived here. He doesn't and I don't know what your folks'd do to them."

Patty cast a pleading gaze at the girls. "Please don't say nothing to your folks. This might be an infatuation. I suspect when the Rangers are gone that'll be the end of it."

"We can do that, can't we?" Sally said, gathering her sisters in on the secret. "Phebe, do you think you can keep quiet on this?"

Phebe nodded.

Audrey tsked. "I don't think we should keep secrets from Mother and Father."

"Oh, come on, Audrey," Phebe said, warming to the idea. "I think it's romantic. Besides, I'm sure Patty's right. When the Queen's Rangers are gone that will fix things."

Audrey still appeared skeptical, and Sally realized she was ready with another objection.

"How would it be," she said, gripping the bedpost, "if I speak to Liss and find out the situation? In the meantime, do you think you can refrain from saying anything to anyone?"

Audrey sighed. "Clearly, I'm outnumbered."

Phebe squealed with delight, jumping up and down and clapping her hands.

Audrey turned back around to let Patty finish her hair. "I will keep your secret if I must, but I want you all to understand, I don't care for the idea."

"Thank you, Audrey," Sally said, checking her dress and patting her hair, done in the style John liked the best, with a top knot on her crown and ringlets falling to her shoulders. Two strands of soft red curls framed her face.

Audrey sat at the dressing table, her gown on her bed, and her face in the cone while Patty powdered her hair.

"Sally, help me, please," Phebe, said dressed in her chemise, and stays, holding her skirt out to her. She refused to dress too early, fearing getting the fabric dirty. Now, minutes before guests were due to arrive, she recruited Sally to help her.

Downstairs amid the joyful sound of arriving guests offering holiday greetings, Sally grabbed the spruce green petticoat and draped it over Phebe's head. Grasping her sister by the shoulders, she spun her around and tied the skirt around her slim waist, all the while struggling against impatience to be among her neighbors and friends.

Next Phebe stepped into the garnet over-skirt, and Sally drew the bodice over Phebe's raised arms, settling the cloth on her slim waist. Sally smiled. With Phebe's hair more auburn than the bright red of her own, the red and green brocade were lovely on her.

Because she was nervous and excited about her own appearance, she commented on Phebe. "This red is a beautiful color on you," Sally laid her hands on her sister's shoulders and pressed her cheek to Phebe's. "You look like Christmas. You'll turn many a male head tonight." She was about to fasten the stomacher when Phebe stepped back, eyes round, lip quivering. She wiped her hands down her skirt as though thinking twice about wearing the garment. "I will? What should I do?"

Behind the cone, Audrey laughed. "Why you laugh and chat, silly. Use your fan to hide your face and stay aloof. Men can't stand when you remain aloof."

Patty tsked. "Be yourself, child. It's the best part about you."

Sally kissed her cheek. "Listen to Patty. She's right. And if you have trouble, find Audrey or me, and we'll help you." She drew Phebe close and finished buttoning her up. "Now, let's hurry up you two. It won't do to hide up here while the party goes on."

A sharp rap at the door elicited a squeal from Audrey. She grabbed for her robe, which she held to herself. "I'm not decent."

"Open the door! I must speak with you," David said, and though the wood muffled his voice, they heard his urgency.

Sally grabbed the handle and yanked the door open. She jerked back at the distress on her brother's face. She sucked in a breath and pushed out one question: "What's wrong?"

David stepped inside, pulled the door from her grasp, and held it, his knuckles growing white. "Father's so upset he's taken to his bed. Mother can't coax him downstairs, and guests are arriving."

Audrey spun from the dressing table.

Phebe strode to Sally's side. "Is Father ill?" Her voice shook.

David shook his head. "No! He's...he's I don't know."

He gestured with both hands and glared at Sally, freezing her with deep, cold blue eyes. "They cut down our orchard. The entire thing. Not one tree did they leave standing."

Sally rooted to the spot, unable to breathe. Or think. She gawked.

Phebe began to cry.

Audrey kept asking why.

Robert appeared. "Patty," he said, "can you please go downstairs and help with our guests?"

She slipped past him as he pushed David further into the room and closed the door.

Sally exploded from her shock. "We'll see about that!"

She tried to push past her brothers, but David grabbed her by the elbows, and Robert blocked her way. Sally stepped back, yanked free of David, and glared her rage. "Let me by! I'll give him a piece of my mind. How dare they do such a thing!"

Both boys shushed her. David pressed his hand over her mouth. "They'll hear you!" He hissed.

Sally slapped his hand away. Tears spilled down her cheeks. What were they to do? Father's prized orchard, more than one hundred fruit trees. That was their food. What were they to do? She tried again but couldn't find a way past her brothers.

"Ughhhh!" She said, holding her arms rigid at her side, hands curled into fists. She spun away from them and found herself in Phebe's arms. Sally buried her head in her sister's shoulder and tried to stop the tears.

Robert took hold of Sally's shoulders and guided her to the bed. He pushed her to the mattress. "Sit down, Sally."

She wiped her eyes as she perched on the edge. Robert sat beside her, and David knelt before her. Audrey and Phebe stood behind David.

"Listen." Robert laid a gentle hand on her arm. "You're angry. We're all angry, but you must keep your emotions hidden." He held out his hands now for the other girls, squeezing their hands as he included them in his advice. "We must all keep it hidden. Colonel Simcoe most likely ordered the cutting of the trees as a military necessity to build his fort."

Sally sat up straight ready to rail at him, but Robert pressed her back down.

His grip tightened on her shoulders. "Shhh! Let. Me. Finish."

She lowered her gaze to her lap. Her new dress blurred through her tears.

"Simcoe is astute enough to comprehend his infatuation with you is common knowledge, so perhaps wanting to appear impartial, he tore down the orchard."

Sally stared at him. Was his infatuation common knowledge? Then the whole town knew. Her stomach flipped and she feared getting sick. Heat suffused her body, and she covered her face with her hands. How would she face her friends? They would laugh at her. More rage followed on the heels. Forget herself. What of Father? The loss of the orchard would ruin him. "He might have found another way."

Crying beneath her hands, Sally sank down in abject fear for their future and drew in a ragged breath. "He didn't have to do that."

Robert curled an arm about her shoulders. "I think he did, Sis. I think he did. And I need you to wipe your eyes and pretend this didn't happen," he said opening his arms and gathering the other girls into a hug. "I need you all to pretend this didn't happen. Can you do that?"

Audrey and Phebe gawked at each other. Sally dropped her hands to her lap. She sniffed and wiped her nose. "I'll try." Stiffening her spine, she raised a tearful face. "It won't be easy, but I'll try."

"Do it for Mother and Father," he said with a smile.

Sally pushed from the bed and reached for her sister's hands. "For Mother and Father."

20

Sally made her way downstairs gathering her wits and reining in her tears. On the landing behind the chimney, she hid from view and surveyed the party underway.

People gathered in the sitting room or the front hallway in small groups laughing and chatting. Under the doorway to the sitting room, Mr. Cooper made a show of kissing Mrs. Cooper under the mistletoe amid much laughter and cheers.

She made her way down the remainder of the stairs and stopped inside the sitting room door. In the far corner, Robert chatted with Daniel Youngs, Absalom and Solomon Wooden, and John and Nathaniel Coles. He smiled and talked as if minus any care in the world. What did they talk about? Daniel was the head of the loyalist militia. Was he obtaining information from Robert about the patriot movement or did Robert attempt to glean the movements of the British? How did they maintain their friendship on opposite sides?

Sally's hands shook, and she clasped them tight, hiding them in a fold of her skirt. She wanted to go over and listen to their discussion, but the moment she did, they might stop talking or change the subject. Over Solomon's shoulder, Robert met her eye, gave a slow nod of acknowledgment, and returned to his conversation.

A hand fell on her arm. Her cousin, Hannah Townsend Green, her husband, Joseph, and Sarah Coles each kissed her cheek and wished her a merry Christmas.

"Well, Joseph," Sally said, trying out her new attitude. "How's life with Aunt Mercy?"

Hannah laughed at her husband's sigh. He kissed Sally's hand. "She's a delight."

His comment drew laughs from all of them. Since Uncle Jacob's death, Aunt Mercy made no bones of her decided Whig leanings and often lamented her son-in-law being a British soldier. Sally assumed, due to Aunt Mercy's age and widowhood, her caustic comments went unchallenged. Everyone else understood her daughter's marriage saved her from retaliation by the occupiers.

Sally glanced around the room. "Where is Aunt Mercy? I should say hello."

Hannah waved toward the stairs. "When we arrived, Phebe said Uncle Sam was ill, so Mother went upstairs to help Aunt Sarah."

They moved to chairs near the hearth. Joseph excused himself and moved off to a group of Queens Rangers across the room. Sally half-listened to Sarah and Hannah discussing fashion, and the inexhaustible topic of Lady Georgina Spencer, the Duchess of Devonshire.

Sally smiled at her cousin as she lifted her punch cup. Spotting a platter once filled with sweetmeats she set down her cup, excused herself, and grabbed the tray to refill. A pass around the room listening in on conversations might turn up an interesting verbal tidbit while she handed out real ones.

Tray in hand, she approached Colonel Simcoe, who spoke with two of his men.

"Gentlemen?" She held up the tray, wishing she had the gall to press the entire thing into all their faces. Instead, she gritted her teeth and pasted on a false smile while they made their selections. The colonel turned his warm blue eyes on her. She glared back, letting her expression say what her brothers forbade her to utter. The warmth in his gaze died. He took a candied apple from the tray and brought the treat to his lips.

The tray trembled in her shaking hands. "Enjoy," she said, her back stiffened. "Thanks to you, there will be no more fruit."

As the men exchanged chagrined glances and shifted their feet, she spun on her heel and stalked away. She couldn't help herself.

Sally carried the tray around offering refreshments, smiling, and chatting as if nothing changed in her world. She soon found herself talking with Solomon. Earlier in the summer, he joined Daniel's militia unit alongside his brother, Absalom.

"So how is military life treating you, Solomon? Is being a British soldier everything you wanted?"

He furrowed his brow at the men dressed in redcoats and white pants or the green of the Queen's Rangers, then turned his scowl on her. "I thought it would be," he said and sighed before turning his back to the room and speaking to the hearth.

Sally set her tray down on a nearby table and leaned close to catch his words.

"The British...the real British...have a hard time distinguishing loyalists from patriots. I joined Daniel's group to remove any possible suspicion and because Daniel's job is to remain here in Oyster Bay supporting the British Army."

"So, you won't be doing any fighting?"

He chewed a candied apple. "I can't say. Anything is possible. But I'm sorry I joined them," he said as his angry gaze cut to a group of Hussars, led by Lieutenant Wintzengerode, who burst into loud, raucous laughter.

"So, what will you do?"

He shrugged.

Audrey strode over and wagged a finger between them. "What are you two discussing so seriously?"

While Solomon sipped his punch, Sally offered a negligent wave of her hand. "Nothing in particular."

Audrey scowled when neither Sally nor Solomon said anything more. She flicked her fan at Sally. "Perhaps you should attend to our guests and pass more refreshments."

With half a mind to tell Audrey to pass around refreshments herself, Sally nodded to Solomon and moved off. Instead of passing refreshments, she walked over to Robert, speaking with Colonel Simcoe, curious about what they discussed.

The colonel sipped his punch from a silver coconut-shaped mug. "My father was commander of His Majesty's ship, The Pembroke," he said rocking up on the balls of his feet. "He carried

General Wolfe up the St. Lawrence River to his famous attack upon the Canadian capitol city." Simcoe's smile shifted to a frown as his brow furrowed and his blue eyes grew dark. "He died in the Royal Service against Quebec in 1759. I was eight years old."

"My sympathies, Colonel," Robert said, gesturing with his own cup of punch. "Your father died an honorable man who served his country well. You must be proud."

Sally moved away uninterested in their conversation and not wanting Simcoe to think she might give him the time of day.

Patty stopped inside the sitting room door. When she made eye contact with Audrey, she made an eating motion with her hands.

"Everyone, dinner is served," Audrey said.

The room quieted at her words. Robert walked to her and held out an arm. She dropped her hand on his forearm. "If you'll follow us."

The guests moved to the parlor/dining room and a table laden with ham, roast, pickles, relishes, and custards.

Sally entered the room on Solomon's arm. He held out a chair for her, settling himself on her right.

A young officer attached to the Queen's Rangers, Captain McGill, sat at her left. He and Solomon were deep in a discussion about the whaleboat raiders coming across the sound from Connecticut, and their discussion gave Sally something else to think about besides her father's orchard and her burning anger.

"I understand the True Blue captured a loaded schooner a week ago," Solomon spoke around Sally.

She ate her syllabub but offered up a question. "Wasn't that near Huntington?"

"A great loss and one a loyal maid should regret." Captain McGill bit into a custard tart.

Sally huffed having had enough of British officers for the evening. She lowered her spoon. "Of course, I do."

Did he doubt her loyalty? Had she done or said something to reveal her true feelings? She glared back.

Solomon nudged her, then peered at her with a glint in his blue eyes. Was he warning her to be careful? When he returned his concentration to his meal, she said the first thing to come to mind. "I fear attacks at sea." So feeble. But...she disguised her true feelings.

Captain McGill sought to reassure her. "You need not fear a raid from the mainland by the rebels. Not while we are here," he said, pointing his fork down the table at Colonel Simcoe as if to suggest he had everything well in hand.

Sally's gaze followed and she found Colonel Simcoe sitting next to Robert, his blue eyes on her. She sneered, gratified by the confused furrow of his brow and the angry set of his jaw.

She offered McGill a flirtatious smile, gratified again when the colonel stiffened.

McGill leaned close and spoke in her ear. "Alas, we cannot protect all of the inhabitants from treacherous attacks by whaleboat men and marauders unwilling to distinguish between loyalist and rebel."

McGill's words irritated her, which she displayed by jabbing her spoon into her syllabub. The clank of her silver spoon against the pewter cup warned her to tread carefully.

Allowing the sweet cream to fill her mouth, she held the concoction on her tongue to prevent a scorching reply to his arrogance. Her silence went unnoticed as Solomon and McGill resumed their conversation. They discussed lawless men who took plunder, and though she kept quiet, she identified more than a few redcoats who participated in the same activity. She tried to swallow her anger with her food.

When McGill placed a hand over hers, she jerked her gaze up disarmed by his smile.

"Do not be so somber, lass." He let go of her hand. "While we are camped here in winter quarters, all you need do is bestow a few lovely smiles on your protectors."

McGill nodded at Solomon. "Enough of talk of warfare, sir. We are beating the lady's ears most unkindly."

Solomon snorted. "I can tell you from personal experience, Captain, the lady in question is tougher than you think," he said and winked at her.

After dinner men moved the furniture against the walls as women called for dancing. Hiram entered with his fiddle. He stood inside the door of Simcoe's bedroom and played merry tunes. Soon after, Israel joined him, with two spoons, which he slapped against his thigh in counterpoint to Hiram's fiddle.

Sally and Phebe stood near the hearth as men and women paired up. Phebe nudged Sally's elbow and jerked her chin to Simcoe, who approached them. "Someone wants to dance with you."

Sally crossed her arms over her chest, her chin jerking up. "Not if I have anything to say on the matter."

Phebe chuckled. "We'll see about that." She sobered. "He's coming. You better dance with him. Remember what Robert said."

Colonel Simcoe stopped in front of them and held out a hand. "May I have this dance, Miss Townsend?"

Phebe giggled, and ignoring Sally's shut-up glare, she flounced away in a swirl of skirts, leaving Sally on her own.

Sally gave him her hand and let him lead her to the dance floor. As she settled into her place to begin Grimstock, Robert lined up with Phebe. Audrey paired with John Coles while Robert Stoddard and Sarah Coles stepped up to the end of the line.

Hiram started playing, and as Sally waited for their turn to dance, she glared at Simcoe. Should she speak? Simcoe bowed and she curtsied. Their turn came, and she moved to the music as her brain rehearsed the next dance steps. She didn't dance often, though she knew how, and feared she might forget the pattern or step on his toes. If she did, he would never let her live that down.

When the music ended, Sally murmured her thanks and started for a chair. She turned at his hand on her elbow.

"One more dance, Miss Townsend?" The colonel asked gazing down at her with such schoolboy hope in his eyes her ire softened.

"Of course, Colonel."

She moved back into position as Hiram began "Mr. Beveridge's Maggot", a complex dance making her heart skip a beat.

Sally and Simcoe circled each other, keeping eye contact, broke apart, and circled the couple to their right. When they regained their original position, Simcoe smiled. They approached again and touched palms before circling their partners again and moving down one position. When their turn to circle came again, they joined the other two in the center.

"Please, Miss Townsend, I'd like to understand why you're angry. You are angry, that much is obvious. What have I done?"

What had he done?! Who was he trying to fool? Heat flooded her face, and she gritted her teeth against a caustic comment. Luckily, they broke apart again and moved further down the line, standing across from each other as they waited for their turn to dance again.

Rather than meet his gaze, Sally concentrated on the other dancers to rein herself in. Undone, she started too early and bumped into Audrey who circled her. Sally waved an apologetic hand at Audrey's irritated glance. Face burning, she peeked at Simcoe. Had he seen her gaffe? If he did, he made no sign as he stretched out his hand for her. She touched her fingers to his palm.

"Do you not wish to tell me?"

"You know why I'm angry and you're pretending—," they broke apart again and moved down the line. She waited for them to come back together again. "Your pretending is only making me angrier," she said.

"How could you"—separate, return—"cut down our orchard?" Break, return. "What gave you the right? After the welcome my father gave you. You ungrateful..."

The music ended, and her voice rang clear throughout the room.

21

Sally's eyes narrowed, and her chin jutted forward. "You had no right to cut down Father's prized orchard without discussing it with him."

Robert and David edged their way through the crowd. Determined now to get in her say before they stopped her, Sally took one menacing step forward. "How dare you? After everything we've done for—,"

Colonel Simcoe cut her off, stepping forward so fast, she retreated. "And what have you done for me, Miss Townsend?"

Fighting the urge to step back once again she held her ground, aware her brothers were behind her, and prayed they wouldn't intervene.

Simcoe pressed. "Hmm? What have you done for me? You come to my training grounds and ask a myriad of questions. I take you places, and like a fool, I shared with you all my knowledge. So, again, what have you done for me?"

Sally's jaw worked but no words ushered forth. Oh, Lord, help her. Was she so transparent he saw right through her? Fingers brushed the back of her arm. She didn't turn but knew Robert's warning to be careful. She straightened to her full height, but still only came to the level of Colonel Simcoe's breast.

"You invited me." Raising her arm, her index finger indicated the kitchen. "You sat at our kitchen table and told all of us that any who wanted to come and learn were welcome to do so. I was curious, so I took you up on your offer. So, my dear Colonel, the fault is yours and not mine."

His face flushed and his eyes scanned the room. He started to speak, but she spun on her heel and marched from the room, ignoring the whispered remarks and comments.

Hiram tucked his fiddle under his chin and started another tune, which faded as she stomped upstairs to her bedroom.

Sally paced back and forth, fury and terror waging war within her. What had she done? Had she damaged their relationship so much? What if he never takes her places or tells her things? Did he comprehend what she was doing? Was he baiting her all this time?

She was halfway across the room on her third trip when a quiet knock broke her reverie. She didn't want to open the door. Another knock.

"Who is it?"

"It's me." Robert's voice floated toward her. "Please may I come in?"

Her shoulders sloped, every muscle sagging until she could scarcely stand. She didn't want a lecture now but pulled the door open and stepped back.

Robert faced her then eased the door out of her hand and closed it.

"Please don't lecture me. I stood his arrogance for as long as possible."

"You'll need to apologize."

She needed to what! "No!" She said crossing her arms over her chest, wrinkling her gown. "I'll do no such thing. I'm not in the wrong! He is. If anything, he should apologize to us!" her voice lowered to a whimper. "To Father."

Robert perched on her mattress. He grabbed hold of the bedpost and squeezed as if the motion helped organize his thoughts. "Let me tell you what's going on in Manhattan. Almost everyone, whether Whig or Loyalist is suffering abuse from the occupying force."

He cocked his head, sympathy twisting his hard set features. "Many of the soldiers treat the citizens with contempt. The homegrown loyalists are worse, demeaning people, and if someone objects, they're denounced as a 'damned rebel' and liable to be punished."

He let go of the bedpost and clasped his hands together in his lap. "The homegrown loyalists have a new name. People call them Tories. They go about the countryside telling the farmers when to harvest their fields and when and which animals to slaughter. Soon after, they return and take the produce and meat, telling the farmers they are required to sell to the British Army. Not just crops and livestock either, but seed grain, tools, furniture, and clothing. And neither the British nor the Tories pay for what they steal. The Tories also tear down barns and homes and use the wood to construct shelters or turn their horses loose in meadows and gardens to graze and trample crops. A way of settling scores, real and imagined. In truth, with every injustice, they make more patriots."

She opened her mouth to reveal what Solomon told her, thought twice, and closed her mouth.

Robert came to stand before her and laid gentle hands on her shoulders. "You must understand, dear Sally as difficult as this is and will continue to be, you must bear these indignities alongside the rest of the family. Otherwise, the British and Tories will become vindictive. You must think of Father's position. Despite signing the loyalty oath, he is still considered a loyal Whig."

"Is he still drafting portions of the New York Constitution?"

Robert drew back, shock and surprise registering in his eyes.

Sally cocked an eyebrow. "I told you," she said, crossing her arms and answering his unspoken question. "No one pays attention when a woman sits at a spinning wheel or works a sampler. You men talk, but we have ears to hear and functioning brains."

A soft smile lit his blue eyes. Then sobering, he squeezed her shoulders. "tell no one, but yes, he is. And if he's arrested because of some action on your part..."

He didn't finish the sentence. Her gesture of acquiescence said he didn't need to.

"I'll go downstairs and apologize to Colonel Simcoe. I must apologize to you, first. You told me to keep myself together, and I didn't. I'm sorry, Robert. I'll be better. Please don't lose faith in me."

He gathered her into his arms. "I have all the faith in the world in you, Sally. If anyone can pull this off, you can. I wouldn't trust Audrey or Phebe to do what you're doing. I don't tell them half as much as I share with you."

He drew back. Was he warning her to be careful even around her sisters?

She nodded. "Phebe asks wonderful questions on our trips, but she talks too much. Audrey...Audrey follows the rules."

Letting go of her shoulders, he tweaked her nose. "I'm impressed with the information you gave me. The details are so intricate as to be stunning. Later, after everyone goes to bed, we'll speak more. You'll be an invaluable asset."

She gave a florid bow. "I shall endeavor to do my best," she said waving him toward the door. "Now come on. I have a relationship to repair. Publicly."

Sally and Robert returned downstairs and stopped in the doorway of the sitting room. The dancing was still in full swing. Colonel Simcoe danced with Phebe.

Robert's gentle fingers on her back pushed her into the room. He signaled to Hiram who stopped playing, bringing everyone's attention around to them.

Sally's body and face flamed, but she took a deep breath, and with a quick glance at her brother, she grabbed her skirts and moved with determination to the colonel.

He stared down at her, his blue eyes guarded, his brow furrowed. She couldn't blame him. She attacked him in public, and he had a right to be on guard.

She didn't know how to start. She crossed her arms and glanced around her. All eyes were on them, and the room was silent.

Robert came to stand next to her and she offered him a pained smile of gratitude. She uncrossed her arms and kept her gaze focused on the buttons of Simcoe's uniform coat.

"Colonel Simcoe, please allow me to apologize to you. I had no right to say the things I did. I allowed my anger over the orchard to get away from me."

She stopped, feeling inadequate in her apology. "I'm so sorry. I hope you can find your way to forgive me for my inexcusable behavior."

When he didn't say anything, she raised her gaze to his face.

He continued to stare at her, but his expression was inscrutable. Then he nodded once.

"I forgive you, Miss Townsend. I understand how my actions shocked and frightened you. Please understand I had no choice in the matter."

She lowered her gaze again. Did she appear as a sufficient supplicant? "I do."

He reached for her hand, which he raised to his lips, placing a light kiss on her knuckles and as he dropped her hand, he leaned close and hissed in her ear. "Don't you ever embarrass me in front of my men again," he said, and though a smile played on his lips his blue eyes were in deadly earnest.

Sally's blood ran cold.

He turned to Hiram and signaled him to start playing again. The colonel held out his hand. "Care to dance with me, Miss Townsend?"

Sally stopped in front of John's room and peered at the crack under the door. It was dark. She drew her shawl close around her shoulders and tiptoed to the kitchen where she built up the coals into a fire. Taking down the kettle she poured water for tea. A creak on the stairs made her freeze. Barely breathing, she eyed the doorway. Robert appeared in stocking feet. She relaxed and returned to making tea as he sat at the table.

When the tea was steeping, she brought over two cups and the pot then took down pastry's leftover from the party.

Robert slid a filled cup close. "What's on your mind, Sis?"

Taking a pastry, she broke small pieces and ate them. She kept her eyes on her dish and scratched the side of her nose. She told him about Colonel Simcoe's growing infatuation with her and how Audrey and Phebe teased her.

"Do you dislike his attention?"

A half-shrug lifted one shoulder. "Nooo. But I'm not certain I like it either." Should she tell him what the colonel whispered to her? No, she would deal with that herself. She pinched her lips tight together, then blurted, "He's handsome. He's interesting. Ambitious. He'll be important someday, but he's British."

"I see."

154

But did he? She twisted the teacup in her hand, pressing the heat into the hollow of her palm, wishing he would say something to ease the hollow in her heart. But sitting here was doing that. Robert had always been her safe harbor.

He sipped his tea. "Would you be averse to encouraging his affections?"

She jerked her head up. "Whatever for?"

His whole face softened as he smiled at her response. "Sweet Sally..." He cocked his head and one eyebrow lifted as if asking her to fill in the answer herself. When she didn't, he touched her hand. "You could possibly learn a lot, which would help us."

"Us?"

"Us. I don't want to say more. It's safer for you. But I believe you found a way to gain helpful information."

When she didn't respond, he continued. "Remember when you sent me the invitation? You included a drawing of those men being dragged down the lane by the horses."

Sally nodded, so he continued. "I understood what I was looking at, even if you didn't. I passed your information on to those who will most benefit." He sipped his tea. "And I thought you are in a unique position to help us."

Why was she so surprised? Was this not her precise idea? The memory of luncheon on the day of Father's trial filled her mind. His words inspired her. She focused on his face.

"Wait here." Rising, Sally padded upstairs to her bedroom, eased open the door, and tiptoed to her hope chest.

Shuffling aside the contents, she swept her hand around for the papers and laid them on the floor beside her. When she decided she found them all, she restored the contents and silently closed the lid.

Phebe sighed in her sleep and rolled over. Audrey snored. Sally froze, then gathered up her sheets.

Laying the pages down in front of Robert, she poured them both more tea. "I told you I needed to speak with you privately. I kept these hidden, waiting for you to come home."

They talked by firelight, but now, Robert lit a candle to study her sheets. Alarm and admiration crossed his features and widened his eyes as he studied her layout of Fort Franklin, troop numbers, where Simcoe planned to put his outposts, and where he anticipated landing places for rebel raids.

She included written notes of what Colonel Simcoe told her during his various training exercises. Her information was extensive. She left nothing out she thought might be useful. Robert plucked at his lower lip as he flipped page after page. "How long have you been keeping notes?" He didn't look up but turned a page, which he laid aside.

"I started about a week after he arrived. I was delivering invitations for the tea and saw them doing the exercises you mentioned and stopped, fascinated. Colonel Simcoe started toward me, and I assumed he was going to tell me to leave, so I did." She lifted several pages and pointed to her notes.

"When he returned home, he told us all we were more than welcome to come to visit the training field, so I started to accompany him. Then he asked Father's permission to take Phebe and me out into the country to inspect his outposts. He likes to explain things. So, I listen and ask questions, which encourages him to talk more. Everything I learn I write down and hide my notes at the bottom of my hope chest. I was hoping you would come home sooner because I don't understand how to send this information to you any other way. I don't trust the posts."

"Nor should you," Robert said, sitting back and tapping the pages. "This is incredibly detailed. Not to mention dangerous." He eyed her with wary concern. "If he were to catch you or to find these...." The look in his eye communicated his worry.

She stiffened. Of course, she understood the risks. Did he think her a half-wit? She laid a hand on the table and splayed her fingers. "I realize, but if he were going to willingly tell me and show me these things, the least I could do was record what I learned. My question is, how do I pass this to you faster? I keep thinking something he tells me might be terribly important."

Now Robert told her to wait. He gathered up the sheets and took them upstairs, returning with a slim book.

He sat back down. "Say nothing to anyone about what you see or hear. Tell no one about this book. Offer no opinions. If someone asks for your opinion, dissemble. Even if you think they may be on our side. You can't be certain who is who in this struggle. Play the silly female. The redcoats don't consider women capable of much more than gossip and making tea. They don't understand gossip is our currency. Clearly, neither does the colonel and that, my dear sister, is his fatal flaw."

"I understand." Meeting his gaze, she didn't as much as blink. "So, how do I get what I learn to you?"

He pushed the book across the table. "Use this."

In his small, cramped handwriting, he listed columns of words, numbers, letters, and headings. To use the letter A, substitute E, B:F, C:G, D:H, E:I, F:J, G:A, H:B, I:C, J:D, K:O, L:M, M:N, N:P, O:Q, P:R, Q:K, R:L, S:U, T:V, U:W, W:Y, X:Z, Y:S, and Z:T. Numbers denoted people: 711-General Washington; 712-General Clinton, 713-Governor Tryon—and what's this—726-Rivington!.

Sally jerked her head up and stared at him. It was too much to comprehend, but his soft smile reassured her. Returning to the pages her eye fell on two unfamiliar names. 722 Culper, Sr. and 723 Culper, Jr.

Other names she knew like Mr. Austin Roe who owned a tavern in Setauket and Caleb Brewster whose family also lived outside Setauket. Numbers also denoted place names such as 727 for New York and 728 for Long Island.

Certain letters also stood for numbers: e 1, f 2, g 3, i 4, k 5, m 6, n 7, o 8, q 9, u 0. Her brow furrowed at the gibberish. Holding the book open, she turned the pages toward him. "Did you come up with this?"

"No."

Sally nodded, still studying the columns. "Who are these people? Who is John Bolton or Culper? Who is Culper, Jr?"

Robert's steady, blank stare told her she just made a huge mistake.

"Sorry." She returned to studying the book. "How do I use this?"

Robert charred a small stick in the candle flame. On the plank of the table, he wrote BIELV. "This alphabet is to express some words not listed above. Look at the list of letters and find the letter B. You'll find the corresponding letter H. I is for E, E is for A, L is for R, and V for T. Spelling the real word, heart. Instead of writing New York or Long Island, use the corresponding number. The same for numbers of things, use the corresponding letter. So, for instance, 2,456 would look like f.i.k.m. N.q.u is 790. Do you understand?"

Sally barely breathed. "My b-i-e-l-v is pounding. Is this safe in the house?"

Using his sleeve, he rubbed away the charred writing. "Keep the book well hidden. This is a matter of life or death. I'll give you a quire of paper. When you need to send me notes, use the quire. Place the notes about fifteen pages in, but always make sure the quire has twenty-five pages. Write me a newsy letter to place on top. Give the package to Father and ask him to send it to me."

"Father?" Sally gasped.

"Shhh!" Robert laid a finger against his lips. "Yes, Father, and I assure you, he won't ask questions."

"Father is involved in what you're doing?"

He leveled a warning stare at her with Father's same steely-blue eyes. "Did I say that?"

"No. I'm assuming."

"Assume nothing. Father won't ask questions because we correspond back and forth for business all the time. Last thing. If something comes up and you cannot wait for Father, go to Daniel."

Shock hit her like a snowball in the face and she drew in a sudden breath. "But he heads the loyalist militia!"

"That's right." Robert leaned across the table and laced his hands together. He stared hard into her eyes. "Which means he can get notes and letters into the city faster than anyone else. Trust me, Sally. If you're not willing to trust me, I can't let you do this."

When he reached to take the book from her, she jerked it away. "I trust you. And if you trust Daniel, I will as well."

"Good. Remember, though. Only in the case of an extreme emergency."

A floorboard creaked on the stairs. Robert laid a finger on his lips and rose.

Sally scooped the book off the table and into her lap, leaned forward, and folded her arms.

He tiptoed to the kitchen door and spoke softly. Phebe answered. He returned and sat back down. "Phebe got cold. I told her you'll return soon."

"Do you think she overheard us?" Sally kept an eye on the door, half-expecting Colonel Simcoe to walk in on them.

"No. She's half asleep. I doubt she'll remember coming down."

Phebe's arrival broke the moment. Sally rose and gathered up their dishes. "I should go to bed now anyway. It's late." She cleaned the dishes and banked the fire again.

He also stood and blew out the candle. "One other thing. It's dangerous just talking late into the night like this. Avoid any situation that might appear suspicious."

Sally slipped the book into a fold of her robe. "I'll hide this upstairs, and I promise not to tell anyone." Her fingers squeezed the binding, and her heart did a flip in her chest.

"Good." He kissed her cheek. "Goodnight, Sis."

Sally padded up the stairs behind her brother. In the case of an extreme emergency, he wanted her to go to Daniel. If he insisted, she would comply, but she prayed the day never came that she would have to trust Daniel that much.

22

As John dressed the morning after the party, he recalled an incident shortly after arriving at Grandfather's. They were on a walk together and he asked why his mother cried so much. Laying a loving hand on John's shoulder, Grandfather explained that women crave security first above all other things. Otherwise, they become frightened and when women are frightened, sometimes they cry, and sometimes they become angry, but underneath is fear.

He frightened Sally, which he regretted. After dressing he sat at his desk. Drawing a sheet of parchment, he tapped his quill and began a letter to Grandfather, wishing him and his mother a wonderful holiday season. After inquiring about news from home he tapped the feather against his cheek.

He dipped his quill and started a new paragraph.

Can you please send me one hundred of the finest apple tree seedlings you can find? If you send them now, they should arrive in time for spring planting.

He reread his letter, decided he approved of his impetuous decision, and taking his sand shaker, sprinkled the letter before folding and addressing it.

He left his bedroom for breakfast. The family was standing at their places, waiting for him so they could say the morning blessing. He stopped short, surprised to see Mr. Townsend at his seat.

"I apologize. I didn't realize you waited for me. I trust you're better, Mr. Townsend?"

"Thank you, Colonel." Father held out a hand to him, inviting him to take his place. "Come and join us for breakfast."

After the blessing, John sat and placed his napkin on his lap. He glanced at Sally, who focused on her dish of ham and eggs. *Security and fear.* He kept an eye on Mr. Townsend, expecting an assault for his actions and John's nerves grew taut. He leaned toward the man sitting at the head of the table. "Mr. Townsend, I hope you can understand why."

Mr. Townsend held up a hand, cutting him off. His jaw hardened and he pressed his lips together. "Let's not discuss the matter now, Colonel. You did what you must, but not in front of the women." His tone shut down any further words.

Security and fear.

"Yes, sir," he said picking up his fork. He tried to eat, but the food was like dust in his mouth. He shifted in his seat. "I understand an Anglican Church is located in Huntington." He said to have something to say. "The Christmas holiday reminds me I have shirked my religious duties since my arrival."

Mr. Townsend wiped his mouth. "You best be on your way. You have a twenty-mile ride ahead of you. You don't want to be late."

"Oh, yes. Thank you," John said scooping up the rest of his breakfast and slurping down the last of his tea. He rose. "Do you not exchange gifts?"

Mr. Townsend regarded him. "We do."

John couldn't help flicking his gaze to Sally before bowing to Mr. Townsend. "Thank you, sir."

The front door closed. When Father regarded her, Sally's face grew warm. She wanted to be anywhere else right now. Her appetite disappeared and she pushed her food around.

Father laid a gentle hand on hers. On his pinkie finger, he wore a simple gold ring with a plain square face. "Well, daughter. You weathered your first storm."

Somehow, she lifted her gaze from his ring. He patted her hand. "Finish your breakfast and come to the parlor to talk."

She lifted her fork to her mouth and took a listless bite.

Audrey picked up her own dish to carry to the washbasin. "Well, I don't see what she's being so squeamish about. If a man like Colonel Simcoe admired me the way he does her, I would have my wedding dress sewn and ready to wear."

Phebe jutted her chin at her oldest sister while her fists found her hips. "You're older. Everyone expects you should marry first. Besides, this is Sally's first beau. I'm sure I would be confused as well."

On impulse, Sally kissed her cheek. "Thank you," she said standing and glaring at Audrey. "I can't help if you're jealous, but please! Leave me be about Colonel Simcoe. I'm trying to work things out."

As she returned her gaze to her food, she found Robert's sympathetic blue eyes on her. Lifting his teacup, he saluted her and took a sip. She took comfort from his sympathy.

Sally closed the parlor door and sat in a chair where Father waited for her. She said nothing, prepared for whatever he would meet out.

He reached out with both hands and cradled hers. Her hand, chilly from trepidation, warmed under his gentle touch.

"Robert told me of your notes and drawings."

The hair on the back of her neck stood up. She drew in a breath through her nose and tried to withdraw her hand, but Father tightened his grip. "I want to warn you of the dangers if you proceed."

"I understand the dangers, particularly to you. Robert told me," she said, brow furrowed. "But I wish he'd kept silent."

"He was concerned for you *and*," he said, stressing the word, "I need to protect you if necessary."

She relaxed her fingers and slid them through his. "You're part of this?"

His gaze went past her, to the portrait of Solomon, and spoke as if to the image of his eldest. "To some degree. The last time I went to Manhattan, Robert and I talked about how we could keep each other informed about business but soon transformed. When the Colonel started showing an interest in you, well, I must confess I had misgivings. But Robert suggested your activity might bring an advantage to us."

He shifted his hand and the gold ring picked up the sun and twinkled its reflected light. "While I'm leery of 'signs from God,' I am aware that Simcoe's warm feelings for you can be turned to our advantage. That's why I don't object, though I don't care for the situation. I am watching closely. "

"I have a question."

"Of course."

Sally shifted in her seat and crossed and uncrossed her ankles. "Well... what happens if I encourage his affections and find myself..."

How could she say what was in her heart? "I sometimes have well, affection for him." There. The words escaped. She couldn't recall them now. "He can be charming in his own awkward, self-conscious way that touches my heart." She sighed. "But then the other night at the party, when I apologized to him, he accepted but..."

"But what?"

Sally exhaled, relieved to speak the words. "He leaned close and whispered in my ear never to embarrass him in front of his men ever again," she said peeking at Father through her lashes. "I confess, by the tone he used, a shiver ran down my spine. Sometimes he makes me nervous, and I wonder, do I like him or don't I, and I become so confused."

Father pulled at his lip.

"And what if he asks me to marry him? He will return to England. I don't want to live in England. I'm an American."

A chuckle rumbled in his chest. "Let's cross that bridge if we arrive at one. You have my permission to pursue this relationship for whatever reason you choose but beware of the dangers. Guard your heart zealously. You would be considered a spy and recall what happened to Mr. Hale."

Shivers coursed through her. Two years before, British officials hung the twenty-three-year-old as a spy in New York City after being duped by Robert Rogers into admitting his mission. Could she keep from such an end? Believing herself smart enough, she drew her shoulders back and allowed a satisfied smirk to twist her lips. "Thank you, Father."

She crossed her arms and braced them on the table. "I have one other question."

"Yes?"

She squirmed. "I'm troubled. He loves me. He hasn't said so, but in his own awkward way, he shows me he does. But, Father, I simply cannot summon the same emotion and I'm sorry for that. I feel as though I'm twisting a bayonet into his heart," she said reaching for his hand. "If I pursue this course of action, aren't I being duplicitous?"

Father braced his elbows on the table and laced his fingers, leaning his forehead against them, not seeming to pray, but to think. "In a normal time of peace, I'd say yes."

The response sounded dragged from deep within him. "But this is not a normal time of peace. The British government disturbed our peace and committed acts of atrocities against our fellow human beings. While I do not advocate picking up arms against them, I will do whatever my conscience bids me, and I suggest you do the same."

Father patted the back of her hand. "He picked up arms against his fellow human beings. As a British soldier, he represents a government that broke the peace and committed atrocities. He has also killed. And it doesn't seem his conscience is bothered by these facts."

As a soft gasp whistled past her lips. Sally jerked her elbows off the table and cradled her arms. "What makes you think he's killed?"

Father squeezed her arm. "He's a soldier, my dear. He's told us of his battles. You do not survive battles without killing. Trust me."

Father had been a soldier in the French and Indian War. She cocked her head to one side, trying to picture the young man who, before embracing his faith, left home to fight for his country. "Did you kill?"

The words escaped and couldn't be drawn back.

Father gave her a sharp, stern stare but didn't answer. His elbows slid from the table and his hands fisted as the corners of his mouth pulled down and she understood the truth.

He pushed his chair back and crossed his legs. "If the idea worries you, don't continue your activities. But if you choose to allow him to pursue you, I'm here to protect you and Robert is in

Manhattan ready to do the same."

The gleaming tabletop reflected the bright window. She chewed her bottom lip. "I believe I can handle whatever happens."

Father clamped a hand on her shoulder. "One more thing and I cannot stress this enough. He must never find out what you're doing. If he discovers your activities, your relationship—your life—will be over."

John returned home late. Inside the door, he doffed his snowy boots, then hung his damp cloak. He sneezed twice as he moved toward the sitting room door.

"God bless you."

He jerked to a stop and peered inside the sitting room, seeing nothing in the shifting shadows of the firelight. A movement caught his eye. Sally! She sat on a sofa Father and David had moved closer to the hearth. "Thank you," he said, entering.

She came toward him. "You must be chilled through to the core. Come sit by the fire."

John didn't argue. He grabbed his saddlebag and settled on one end of the sofa. Sally perched on the other. As they faced each other, he couldn't think of anything to say, entranced by the way she chewed her lower lip and stared at the dancing flames.

When he shifted, she glanced his way. "You're up late, Miss Townsend."

A smile softened her lips and her intelligent eyes glowed. "I waited up for you."

She tucked her lip over her bottom teeth and turned again toward the fire. Such an endearing habit from an endearing soul. The light of the fire caressed her rosy cheeks and revealed the shyness in her hazel eyes that charmed him to his soul.

He would die for her, yes, he would. The idea of Elizabeth Gwillum twinged his conscience less and less these days. He didn't have time to become well acquainted with Elizabeth, his grandfather's ward. She came to live with them before John left for the colonies. Time and distance being what they were...well, Sally was here, and Elizabeth was not. He wanted Sally as his wife. Now, all he had to do was figure out how to bring her around.

He cleared his throat capturing her full attention. Keeping his gaze on her, he picked up his saddlebag, which he dropped into his lap to withdraw a small blue box wrapped with a gauzy white ribbon. "I meant to buy you a gift for Christmas but feared it might be inappropriate. I hope you don't mind."

He placed the gift in the palm of his hand. The ribbon wrapped much the way she wrapped her heart around his. He extended his hand. "Merry Christmas a little late."

A myriad of expressions crossed her features and her hands twisted in her lap. What was she thinking? He withdrew the box. "I was right. This was inappropriate. Please accept my apology, Miss Townsend."

He flipped the top of his saddlebag to replace the box, but his hands shook, and he fumbled with the latch.

She laid a gentle hand on his arm. "I'm sorry, Colonel. I didn't mean to appear unkind, but...well, you brought me chocolate in the past, which I shared with the family, making it less like a personal gift. But a gift for me...I don't understand how to accept...what it means to accept...such a gift." Offering an apologetic half smile, she said, "besides, I'm embarrassed. I didn't get you a gift."

He chuckled. "The fact you waited up for me is gift enough, Miss. Townsend," he said, his heart melting at the uncertainty he saw in her hazel eyes, now shaded more to brown. He sat forward and gripped the back of the couch. "Miss Townsend, no doubt by now you are aware I'm not very good at...well..."

He broke off and focused on the crackling fire, before returning his gaze to her face. "I'm not well versed at these things. I never have been."

Unsure of what he wanted to say, John wished he had the easy grace of Andre, but he was dumb and clumsy.

He laid the box on the cushion between them. "I want your affection, Miss Townsend." The boyish hope in his voice embarrassed him and he cleared his throat. "You would honor me by accepting my gift as a token of my affection for you."

He studied her face, forehead wrinkled, one brow lowered. She touched one corner of the box, then raised troubled eyes. "Colonel, I like you a great deal, which scares me. So much could go wrong."

John flinched as though slapped across the face. "Like what?"

She rubbed her arms as if chasing away an inner chill. "What happens after the war? You'll want to go back to Britain?"

166

"Of course."

She pursed her lips and inclined her head. "And I'll want to stay here," she said, whispering. "What would I do without my family? My life is here, Colonel."

"I understand," he said and tried to swallow his disappointment. John fiddled with the ribbon. There had to be a way to change her mind. He licked his lips. "I care for you, Miss Sally Townsend. I care for you deeply, and I wish to declare to you right now, my abiding affection."

With the tip of his finger, he nudged the box closer to her. "Please accept this as my pledge to you, my declaration. I wish to be your suitor," he said watching her face for a sign he should retreat.

Her jaw jutted and her brows knit. Ever so slowly, she closed her fingers around the box. Her teeth grabbed her lower lip again as she plucked the ribbon, untied the satin, and set it aside. She opened the box and freed a delicate crystal bottle. Closing her eyes, she unstopped and held it to her nose.

"Mmm, rosewater."

Sally tipped the bottle to her fingers and touched them to a spot under her ear, near her jawline. She dipped again and touched her fingers to her wrists, then slid the stopper back on and nestled the bottle back in the box. "Thank you. You are so kind."

Again, John's heart melted, and he dared not breathe. "Don't give me an answer until you're ready," he said, hoping his elation didn't come through in his words. "But when you are, allow me to ask your father's permission to court you," he said, lifting a finger. "But only if you wish me to."

When she opened her mouth, he placed his finger against her lips. "I said don't answer me right now. Tell me when you're ready."

She didn't pull away, which made John's heart leap. He withdrew his finger lest she discovered how his hand shook. She offered him a small but encouraging smile and rose. "Good night, Colonel."

"Good night, Miss Sally," he said, walking her to the stairs, enjoying how her skirts swished. She stopped at the foot and turned to him. Lifting the box, she smiled. "Thank you for the perfume." Then taking hold of her skirts she disappeared. John listened to her trot upstairs, his heart matching the rhythm of her shoes.

Sally clutched her bottle of rosewater as she ascended the stairs to bed. Her heart pounded with excitement. She passed her first test. She entered her bedroom and placed the candle and the bottle on the nightstand next to her side of the bed. The blankets rustled.

"Sally?" Phebe's sleepy voice questioned.

"Yes."

"Is the colonel home now?" Phebe rose on an elbow, wiping at a corner of one eye.

Sally unhooked her bodice and prepared for bed. "He is."

"What's that?" Phebe asked pointing toward the bottle gleaming in the candle glow. "Did he give you a Christmas gift?"

"He did." Sitting on the edge of the mattress, Sally plucked up the bottle to hand to her sister. "Rosewater."

Phebe sat up straight, pulled the stopper off, and sniffed. Her eyes widened. "Mmm, roses—in the middle of winter! How lovely," she said and handed the bottle back. "May I try it sometime?"

"You may try some tomorrow if you like."

"What were you and Robert doing up so late the other night?" Phebe asked while Sally finished undressing.

Sally's fingers froze on the ties of her stays. She shrugged and prayed the light of the candle didn't show her blush. "We were catching up. He's been gone so long."

Phebe yawned. "He's special to you, isn't he?"

Sally smiled. "Don't tell the other boys, but Robert is my favorite brother. I'm not sure why, but he is."

"You two are a lot alike." She lay back down. "Now come to bed. The hour is late, and I'm cold without you here."

Sally tucked the bottle back, climbed into bed beside Phebe, and snuggled close. "If you're cold, I can go downstairs for a warming pan."

"No. I'm fine. Your feet are cold."

"Sorry," Sally said, yawning. "All right. Sweet dreams."

She awoke to Phebe shaking her. "Hmm, what?"

"I changed my mind," Phebe said in a whisper. "I'm cold, but I'll go down for the pan."

Sally patted her arm. "Stay put and snuggle down. I'll go." She threw back the covers, grabbed her wrap and slippers, and headed for the door. The hallway clock bonged twice.

At the bottom step, she stared at John's bedroom door where a deeper shadow caught her attention. She widened her eyes to let in more ambient light.

The lack of eyesight improved her hearing, and something rustled down the hall. Seeing nothing but the white panels of the front door in the dark, she headed toward it. Pulling her wraps tight about her shoulders, Sally padded down the hall. She stopped in the sitting room doorway, but the glow of the banked embers revealed an empty room.

"Sally."

The sharp whisper pierced her breast like a bayonet.

Drawing in a sharp breath and spinning on her heels, she threw her hands over her heart. "Colonel Simcoe! You startled me. What are you doing?"

He was behind her. "Were you in the parlor?" Father kept his important papers on the desk inside the parlor door.

"Why aren't you in bed?" His hands on her elbows, he steered her toward the stairs.

"I came down for a warming pan. Phebe and I were cold. There was a noise."

John nodded. "I came out to investigate. We've had reports of raiders attacking in the night."

He changed course with her to the kitchen. "Come, let's fill a warming pan so you can go back to bed. All is well. Probably a night creature roaming outside."

After he helped her fill a pan with hot coals and carried it to the stairs for her, she took it from him. "Thank you for the help and thank you again for the rosewater. I love it."

The colonel's teeth gleamed in the darkness. "You're welcome."

Sally could think of nothing more to say. She waited a moment, but he didn't speak either and she sensed he wanted her to go upstairs. "Sleep well."

"Good night, Miss Townsend. Sleep well."

She stopped on the landing. The colonel stood inside his bedroom door, watching her. She raised a hand and waggled her fingers at him before disappearing up the stairs

23

Simcoe strode through Hanover Square, named for the family occupying the throne. As he approached Bowling Green Park he scowled and turned away from the empty base where the King's statue once stood.

At the beginning of the war, hotheaded rebels pulled down the statue of King George III to melt down for bullets. Now the stone block on which the once magnificent statue stood appeared forlorn, but not forgotten as graffiti smeared all over made clear.

The desecration matched the mood he gained in his campaign meeting. Though mid-January deep winter was not too early to plan for the spring campaign season. But instead of planning a campaign, he once again found himself defending his uniform color choice.

A vague shout reached him, but he ignored the sound, still grinding with disdain for his upper command.

"John! John Simcoe!"

His head snapped up and he peered over his left shoulder. A grin stretched his lips, and he raised a hand to wave at John Andre riding toward him.

"John Simcoe, what are you doing here in Manhattan?"

After Andre dismounted, he approached, hand outstretched.

"I knew if I came to Manhattan, you might show up," he said teasing Andre as they shook hands with vigor. John gripped his friend's elbow.

"Like a bad penny, as my late lamented father would say," Andre said, slapping him on the back and John's breath caught from the impact. "I always turn up."

They started walking. John glanced at his friend. "I haven't seen you in almost a year. What have you been up to?"

"Can you spare some time? I found a wonderful coffee shop around the corner."

"I can," John said.

Andre handed his horse to an aide who remained in the saddle and dismissed him for the rest of the day. When the aide nodded and moved off, John and Andre fell into step. "I understand you were in a planning meeting for the coming season."

John's upper lip curled, and he snorted. "Spare me from generals and members of Parliament who prefer to execute the war from afar."

He clapped his friend on the back. "So, tell me, did they throw you out of Philadelphia or did you leave of your own volition?"

Andre laughed. "I left on my own, although, I did leave a sweet little dish behind. Miss Peggy Shippen, the most beautiful angel in Philadelphia. Her father, a wealthy Tory, has been instrumental in keeping the Army in Pennsylvania well supplied. Her charms are beyond compare." Andre held open a door. "Here we are."

The sign above the door hanging from a bracket above, showed a printing press with pages flying in all directions, and a tilted coffee cup amid the swirl of paper announcing the establishment as Rivington's Coffee Shop. He arched a brow. "James Rivington of the Royal Gazette?"

Andre swept a hand indicating John should precede him. "The very same. He runs this coffee shop, which I assure you, is the most popular in town."

The room was noisy with red-coated men in buoyant moods who behaved more like boys at break from school than soldiers and two men served coffee. Was that—yes, Robert Townsend served coffee and greeted soldiers as though he greeted old friends.

John pointed and leaned toward Andre. "I recognize yonder man. I live in his father's home."

Robert, speaking to a soldier, straightened as he and John made eye contact. Townsend glanced down at the man, said something, and strode toward John and Andre.

"Colonel Simcoe," Robert said, extending his hand, which John shook. "Welcome to Rivington's Coffee Shop."

"Thank you, Mr. Townsend. May I present my friend, Major John Andre?"

After shaking Andre's hand, Robert surveyed the room. "There's a table available out of the way for you. Quiet."

"Sounds wonderful," John said, rubbing his cold hands together. "Thank you."

Robert led them to a corner, away from the crowd where they could talk in private. "I never thought to find you in an establishment like this, Mr. Townsend."

Something gnawed at him—but why?

Robert chuckled. "Mr. Rivington is a friend of mine and asked me to work with him."

"This work doesn't interfere with your business duties for your father?"

"My brother, William, finished his apprenticeship with our uncle, Thomas Buchanan, and is now doing daily duties at the store, which frees me to work here, giving me a chance to pursue a lifelong dream."

John took a seat. "What is that?"

Robert offered a self-deprecating shrug. "I like to write, and Mr. Rivington gave me an outlet here. I pen articles for soldiers. Personal articles they can send home to their families. It's becoming quite popular. In fact," he indicated the table of men he spoke to when Simcoe and Andre entered, "I was accepting a request when you came in."

Andre settled himself in his chair, adjusting his uniform to smooth out any creases. "I'm interested in reading your articles, Mr. Townsend." He glanced up at Robert. "Perhaps I might avail myself of your services if I like what I read."

"Perhaps, Major. I just completed an article, and I'm waiting for the young man to come in and retrieve it. Would you like to read the piece?"

Andre raised his eyebrows. "Indeed, I would. Thank you."

Robert straightened. "Certainly. But, for now, may I take an order?"

The two men ordered coffee and Chelsea buns.

Robert returned with their order and placed their coffee cups in front of them along with a plate of buns in the middle of the table. He left and returned with an oversized sheet of parchment which he handed to Andre his blue eyes guarded as the major took the page.

When he finished scanning the sheet, he handed the page to John. "There's some detailed information here, Mr. Townsend," Andre said, as John finished and handed the sheet back to Robert.

"I agree," Simcoe said. "Why?"

Robert shrugged. "The men like to inform their families what they're doing, what units they're with, who their friends are. I write these and give them to the men to send home."

He and John held eye contact. Neither blinked nor shifted their gaze.

Andre rapped a knuckle on the table. "Well, Mr. Townsend, I'm convinced. I should like you to write my article."

Robert gave a short bow, quirking up a crisp grin. "Excellent, Major. Come back soon and we'll sit down to discuss the particulars."

Andre idly gazed at Robert as he went back to work. He turned to Simcoe. "We'll see how much of my false information appears in Mr. Rivington's Gazette."

John smiled. "That would be most fascinating," he said, folding his arms on the table and leaning close in the noisy tavern so they didn't have to shout to be heard.

"So, Andre. Tell me what's been going on with you."

Andre curled his fingers around his cup, which he hoisted in a salute. "I will, old friend, but first, how fares the Queen's Rangers?"

"We fare well. All is quiet in Oyster Bay."

Andre downed much of his coffee and thumped the cup onto the table. A sly grin split his face as his bushy brows bobbed up and down. "How would you like to stir things up?"

John ordered his men on a foraging expedition. Captain Youngs' militia oversaw finding the forage, but too often returned empty-handed. Youngs reported that, though reliable reports put livestock and foodstuffs in the area, as soon as his foragers arrived, the supplies melted away, so John decided to go along to see for himself what was happening and to see to it the loyal citizens gave their fair share.

Once at the encampment, he met Captain Saunders, who thank heaven had replaced Lieutenant Wright. In Saunders, John found an officer who reminded him of Captain Bamford, who now led the 40th to distinction. He should write him a note.

John dismounted at Saunders's tent. He stamped his cold feet and shook the snow off his shoulders while clearing his mind for the coming day.

Saunders saluted. "Good morning, Colonel."

John saluted back as he entered Saunders's tent and approached the small table where a map awaited him. Fabulous how the man was all business. No blustering about collecting the tools John expected on hand.

Refocusing his attention, he gazed at the town of Setauket, circled on the map. The town lay on the island's eastern side, about fifty miles east from Oyster Bay.

Saunders now tapped the circles. "Yesterday, I sent out Captain Youngs' militia to scout farms with livestock. I warned him to be discreet, not to explain their mission, just to scout and report. They found several excellent locations. Youngs also reported most of the rebels in this area are gone to join Mr. Washington's group of rag tags, so we don't anticipate any trouble with the locals. I received independent reports of whaleboat men from Connecticut using the cove here," he tapped a thick finger on Setauket, "to resupply the rebels, and a goodly supply of forage materials and foodstuffs delivered two days ago. This morning, I ordered Captain Youngs' men to deny the rebels those supplies."

John studied the map. "He's gone already?"

"Early this morning, sir, so he can thus join us for the rest of the forage expedition."

John nodded. "Excellent, Captain. Do you mind having company? I'm in the mood for an excursion today."

"Not at all, sir. It'd be my pleasure."

By midday, the Rangers approached Setauket. The cove discussed extended out toward Connecticut on John's left, and a village emerged from low hills on his right. He studied the water. They had no boats and no supplies. With any luck, Youngs was successful in retrieving the supplies bound for the rebels. He had little time to ponder the question as cattle lowed nearby, hidden behind an elevation in the land.

John whistled. "If I could but fortify this place, what wouldn't I do?"

He liked what he saw, as much as he liked Oyster Bay. But Sally lived in Oyster Bay, and Setauket was noted for its decided Whiggish leanings. In fact, the town politics aligned more with its New England neighbor, the Connecticut province, than with New York.

"Where are Captain Youngs and his men?" He asked, scanning the landscape looking for the cattle lowing out of sight, and for his missing militia captain.

"I'm ignorant, Colonel," Saunders said sounding uncomfortable "Perhaps he found it necessary to bring the supplies from the cove back to Oyster Bay. I did tell him to use his discretion."

John could deal with Youngs later. He had more important things to worry about now. "Our job today is to retrieve the cattle calling us, and the forage to go with them and return to base. The troops on Manhattan need us to be successful."

Saunders urged his horse to a faster pace. "Yes, sir."

The men splashed across a stream flowing to the Long Island Sound. John held up a hand for the men to stop. Atop a rise in the land to their west, a group of horsemen marked their approach. A harbor dominated the north, the ground around them flat, rising several hundred yards into the hills from which the enemy waited. Staying in the lowlands would not do. He had to find high ground to reconnoiter his surroundings.

As they approached, their observers fled into the woods. The man in front raised a sword, which he waved over his head, a clear signal to others to retreat. He was close enough for John to call out. "You are a brave fellow, but you must go away."

The officer stopped waving his sword to glare at John, before resuming with a defiant swing of his arm.

John swung around in his saddle. "Captain McGill!"

The young captain rode up and saluted. "Yes, sir."

"Fire on that man. Persuade him thus to leave."

McGill dismounted. "My pleasure, Colonel," he said, going

down on one knee and taking aim.

The defiant enemy soldier stood his ground as McGill raised his weapon and drew aim. After he fired, the unharmed soldier turned his horse and disappeared into the woods. A few other straggling shots chased him away before John sent a contingent of light infantry, supported by his Highlanders to clear the front.

When they reached the top and occupied the territory vacated by the enemy John gained a commanding view of the surrounding area. He stiffened in the saddle. The lowing cattle were being driven east and disappeared behind a ridge. He knotted his hand around the reins, aching to go after them, but not knowing the strength of the enemy gave him pause.

How in Heaven's name did they find out he was coming? Who had been listening? Who gave him away? Determined to find out, John would make sure the good citizens of Setauket did their part and supplied the British Army. Even if he had to burn down every home in town.

The front door latch rattled, and the door opened and closed with a quiet click.

"Welcome home," Sally said in a soft tone. "Did you have a successful mission?"

The colonel raised an eyebrow at her. "I did." His gaze swept over her, and a smile quirked one side of his mouth. "Did you wait up for me?"

Sally clasped her hands. "I did," she said returning his smile. "Are you too tired to sit up for a while?"

John contemplated his bedroom door before entering, the sitting room. "I am tired, but I'm happy to sit up."

He stirred the fire in the hearth until the flames crackled and danced. He sat in the chair next to the sofa. If anyone were to enter, there would be no question of compromising her.

"Was your raid successful?" Sally bit her lip. Did she ask a safe question? Would he consider his actions a raid?

"Yes, thank you," he said stretching his hands toward the fire, letting its warmth soothe his aching fingers. He crossed his legs, settling in. "Thank you for asking. We rounded up some cattle, though not as much as we needed. We got the forage, food, and many other supplies. All in all, quite successful."

"And burning the barn. Another military necessity?" *Go carefully.*

John's grin disappeared. "How did you hear about that?"

For a split second, she regretted the words, but she stiffened her back. "What does that matter?"

He regarded her with a pained expression, then shrugged. "It doesn't, I suppose," he said, turning glacial blue eyes on her. "So, to answer your question, yes," he said, cold steel hardened the word.

"Why?" She poured all her despair into the word.

He drew in a deep breath through his nose and exhaled. "We came across some resistance and became necessary to establish who was in charge. Had I to do this again, I'd do no different."

He gripped the armrest. "If you're planning to argue about my tactics, I'm going to bed. As you said, it was a long day, and I'm tired."

When he started to rise, she touched his arm. "I'm not going to argue, John. I see no point in doing so. I don't understand why you felt your actions were necessary. My mother always says you attract more flies with honey than with vinegar. Aren't you creating more enemies when you do such heartless things as burning down someone's barn?"

"The more heartless thing would have been to burn down the house, don't you think? Especially in January?"

She didn't think of that. "I suppose," she said, as the logic of her argument slipped away once again.

A heavy breath slipped from his lungs, and he rubbed his eyes. They remained closed once he pulled his hand away, braced his elbows on his knees, and rested his chin on his hands. "I would never cause anyone to be homeless in the winter. That, to me, would be the epitome of heartlessness, would you agree?"

When he opened his eyes, she turned away.

"But these people," he said, "the ones who identify as members of the opposition need to understand this war will end someday and they better get right with their King."

But what if the King loses? Sally bit back the question lest the words escape. Instead, she stared down at the floor, as though finding her next words carved into the pine boards. Soot and ash gathered around the edges of the hearth reminding her the house needed a thorough cleaning.

"I understand. You did what you felt necessary. I won't question or judge you, but I will say your actions speak of gratuitous violence. Gratuitous and unnecessary. You'll have to understand I will never accept or understand the need for violence."

A half smile twisted the corner of his mouth. John took her hand. His face softened in the shifting shadows of the firelight. "War is frightening for women and I'm sorry you have to experience such things. If I could shield you, I would."

He gave her fingers a light squeeze. "I don't enjoy when I have to do these things, but they are military necessities," he said, his tone pleading for her to understand.

She bit her lower lip, and as she met his eye, her shoulders drooped.

He cleared his throat and drew his hand away. "We will not speak of these things again. I cannot justify myself to you. Since now I understand you will never understand or accept any actions, I may deem necessary, we will consider this one of those things we will allow to lie like a sleeping dog, and as long as we leave it alone, it should not rear up and bite us."

He rose. "Please understand, I have a job to do. I must act to the best of my ability, and if at times you're unhappy, well, I'm sorry, but in the end, I answer to King George."

24

True to his suggestion, Sally and John ceased discussing his tactics and actions and focused more on learning about each other. Sally never considered the reality that John answered to superiors and reconsidered her criticisms. If his actions were the necessary result of orders given, then it didn't necessarily mean he liked what he had to do.

But he confused her. He still took Sally, Phebe, and sometimes Audrey out on rides. He was considerate of their needs and even joked with them. And though he didn't have the gift of easy humor, the fact he tried warmed her heart.

Whenever he had to go to Manhattan or Jericho, he never failed to return with a small token for her. He declared himself to her in all the correct ways and she found herself more and more confused about her own heart.

January moved, as slow as a glacier in that frozen winter of seventy-nine, into February. Winter storms increased in frequency as the cold battled for dominance over the warm weather which would soon prevail. By mid-February, the southern winds and more temperate ocean climate melted the snow and brought the mud season. On the thirteenth day, the Townsends hosted a tea in honor of the changing seasons and for some social engagement with neighbors' unseen since the twelfth-night festivities. As usual, the invitation included John's men.

Unlike the Christmas party, this was an informal affair, so no dancing, but people gathered in small groups, chatting, and laughing.

Solomon and Absalom arrived dressed in their red and white uniforms. The boys were grand. Solomon clubbed his brown hair with a blue ribbon. Had anyone besides Sally recognized his subtle declaration by adopting the fledgling colors of the new country?

When their eyes met, she smiled her praise at his bravery. He stood alone in front of the hearth, staring with envy at his brother who laughed and talked with Daniel and their militia group, Sally decided to keep him company.

Pouring two cups of tea, she carried them to him. "Solomon, I'm glad you came. I feared Daniel might keep you busy elsewhere," she said arching a teasing brow and handing him a cup. "As penance for your last foray into mischief."

Shocked by the red flow up his neck and brightening his ears and face, Sally expected him to understand she teased. Her fingers flew to her lips. "I learned a little of what happened. Do you want to tell me the rest?"

Solomon shifted his stance and turned his face away. He was a kind boy but always full of antics without a hint of meanness. His doings often frustrated and angered his brother, Absalom, who harbored a strong responsibility for him, since their mother's passing after Christmas.

"Remember the time you gave me a birthday gift? A small box with a beautifully tied bow, I think for my thirteenth birthday. You said, to mark my years marching toward womanhood. Do you remember?" She asked, hoping to distract him from his embarrassment.

She tried to read his face but couldn't because he now stood in profile to her. He flicked his brown-eyed gaze in her direction before regarding his shoe tops. She squeezed his arm. "When I opened the box, a salamander ran up my arm."

Having coaxed a rueful smile from him, Sally released his arm and sipped her cool tea.

Solomon chuckled. "You screamed something awful."

181

"He scared the daylights out of me. I didn't expect a lizard. I was expecting, oh, I don't know, a pretty bauble of some sort. A hair ribbon. But, in the end, no harm done."

Sadness drooped his facial muscles, turning down the edges of his mouth when he glanced at her. "You were angry at me though."

She ducked her head and shrugged. "Momentary anger. Once I got over my shock, I thought the whole thing quite funny." She was lying but decided no harm would come from saying otherwise.

Sally gestured to his teacup. "Would you like a fresh cup of tea?"

Together they strolled to the parlor. As they circled the table, choosing tidbits she leaned close and offered a mischievous smile while speaking in a low tone. "I like your hair ribbon. Interesting choice of color."

His brown eyes studied her. She raised her brow making him smile.

"Thanks," he said, touching his hair. "I hoped you might appreciate the gesture."

She refreshed her cup and poured one for him before handing it to him. "Do you want to talk about what happened the other day?"

He balanced the dainty cup and saucer in his massive hands and peered across the hall where his brother talked with Robert and David.

Solomon met her eye and swigged a gulp of tea. "I was on patrol duty one night and set snares to catch a rabbit," he said, his gaze swerving to John speaking with a couple of his officers. His expression darkened.

Reaching for her arm Solomon guided her back into the sitting room. "They don't feed us provincials well. The redcoats. They keep all the food to themselves and give us the crumbs, like dogs at their table," he said close to her ear.

He drained his cup and clattered the saucer on the mantle.

"If not for Daniel. He..." Solomon cast a wary glance at his militia captain and then at Sally.

"He looks after you," Sally said, supplying the narrative.

Nodding, Solomon continued his story. "One of my snares snapped, so I investigated and found a giant vole hanging in the tree. Well, since I don't much care for their meat, I let the thing go and was resetting my snare when something rustled in the

182

undergrowth. I grabbed my gun and jumped up and called 'Who's there,' but ducked when I heard gunfire. I didn't get hit, but Daniel, Absalom, and the Coles boys surrounded me." His gaze searched the room once again as he picked up his cup.

This was a different version and she realized there were two sides to every story.

"They were furious with me. Daniel most of all because I left my post and they fired, thinking I was the enemy. When I tried to tell him why I was there, he wouldn't listen. Absalom boxed my ears."

He rubbed an ear, as though the very mention, brought remembered pain. "Now they don't talk to me. They don't come anywhere near me, and I think Daniel wants me out of the corps," he said. His eyes sheened over, and he blinked fast.

"No, Solomon. I don't think that's true. Despite what he says, Daniel likes you and will keep you."

How weak she sounded! But what else might she say to reassure him?

He shrugged. "I don't want to talk about this anymore." He drew in a deep breath. "Thanks for your concern, Sally, but I think someone wants your attention now."

Sally followed his gaze and found John's angry glare fixed on them. Her spine stiffened.

John excused himself from his friends and approached her. Solomon stepped away, squeezing in between his brother and Daniel, who continued to talk with her brothers. Daniel shifted to let him in and laid a gentle hand on the back of Solomon's shoulder. Gratified, Sally turned her full attention to John.

She raised a teasing brow, ready to diffuse him if necessary. "Good evening, Colonel."

"Good evening, Miss Townsend."

He offered a half bow and swept a hand toward a sofa. When she perched on the edge and laid her teacup and saucer in her lap, keeping one hand on the edge, he sat at the other end of the sofa. "This is a splendid party. Did you and your sisters throw this one in our honor like the Christmas tea?"

"I'm sorry, but we didn't." Sally spread a hand in a deprecatory manner as if to apologize. "We decided a midwinter party was in order to help push out the winter blues and encourage spring," she said before taking another sip and laying her cup on the saucer. "I don't know what winters are like in England, but here they can be isolating if you don't have a social gathering once or twice. It's not unusual for someone in town to throw an end-of-winter tea or host a frolic, to socialize and remind themselves they're not alone. Some people can become melancholy at this time of year, and a frolic helps revive one's spirits."

John surveyed the room, his expression revealed he wondered who among their guests might suffer such hardship.

Pretending to be unaware, Sally put the cup and saucer on the table next to her side of the sofa.

John returned his attention to her. "Is your tea cold? May I freshen your cup or bring you a sweetmeat?" He rose and held out a hand for her cup, which she gave him.

"Thank you."

"Don't go anywhere."

As he wended through the room to the refreshments laid out on the parlor table someone tapped her shoulder. Sally shifted in her seat. Captains Saunders and McGill stood behind her. "Gentlemen. Colonel Simcoe is getting refreshments."

"Miss Townsend, perhaps you don't remember me." Captain McGill said, placing his right hand over his breast.

"Of course, I do, Captain McGill. You came to our holiday party, and I acted like a boor. I do hope you can forgive me."

Captain McGill straightened. "Why, Miss Townsend, I do not recall any such behavior. I found you quite charming and a wonderful table companion. I also assure you we've done as I promised and kept the hated rebel raiders at bay. You're quite safe in our company."

Her lips twisted in a sardonic smile, and her eyes squinted from humor. "Well, I'm quite relieved at the news, Captain."

They laughed as Captain McGill glanced into the parlor. John stood deep in conversation with Uncle Thomas, a good-natured man, married to Father's Whig sister, Almy, he remained loyal to the Crown.

"Who is that gentleman?" Captain Saunders asked.

"He's my uncle, Thomas Buchanan," Sally said, shifting for a better view. "And don't worry. A more loyal subject you're not likely to find on Long Island. He came here from Scotland as a young man with not a penny to his name. Just the clothes on his back, as he likes to tell the story."

She stood and smoothed the skirt of her blue satin gown. "We've all heard the story a thousand times. He made his fortune in shipping, along with Father, and he credits the Crown for his success rather than his own hard work."

She bit her tongue, not wanting to sound disloyal. "Among my many uncles, he is my favorite. You have no cause to be suspicious of him, I assure you."

"I'm sorry, Miss Townsend. I didn't mean to sound suspicious. I'm new here," he said by way of explanation.

"Would you like an introduction?"

He glanced at McGill, who nodded encouragement. "No thank you, not necessary," Saunders said, arching a hopeful brow. "What I would like is an introduction to your brother, Mr. Robert Townsend. I understand he writes articles for the men."

"He does," she said managing to sound perky. "Would you like one written?"

A sheepish smile twisted his lips. "Yes, I would. Very much."

John strode toward them. "Captain Saunders, there's someone I want you to meet."

Saunders excused himself and followed Simcoe into the parlor where Uncle Thomas waited.

She laced her slim fingers together and leaned toward McGill, her red curls bouncing against her shoulders. "Well, he's getting an introduction all the same."

She regarded McGill. "Would you like an article written as well?"

McGill jutted his chin as he admitted his desire. "Perhaps. May I show you a trick?" He reached into his pocket and drew out a diamond ring.

Suspicions rising, she furrowed her brows. the diamond had to be worth at least two years' salary for him. "Where did you get that Captain?"

"Would you like to see my trick?" He asked, not answering the question.

She nodded, letting her curiosity go for now. There were other ways of finding out.

He drew her to the side window and pulled back the damask

curtain. Using the diamond, he scratched out the words: *'The Adorable Miss Sally Townsend--J. McGill.'* As he used the diamond to write on the windowpane, he drew a crowd. When he finished, Sally gasped, clapping her hands. "How did you do that?"

She plucked the ring from his fingers to examine but she didn't recognize it as belonging to anyone familiar to her. Sally tried to make a scratch in the window but didn't make a mark. She handed the ring back.

"You have to use considerable force to make a scratch."

McGill glanced around and his eye fell on Audrey. Moving to the next squared-off pane, he wrote: *'Miss A.T. The most accomp'l. young lady in Oyster Bay.'*

He grinned at Audrey, who mock pouted. "I see how it is, Captain. I'm Miss A.T. while my sister is Miss Sally Townsend."

Her grin belied her complaint, and Sally took up the gauntlet of teasing the young man.

"As to that, Captain McGill, I hardly think we know each other well enough you can get away with calling me, Sally. My formal name is Sarah. I demand a correction."

"Please allow me to make amends," he said as laughter surrounded them. "Forgive me."

Using the ring, Captain McGill scratched out the name Sally and above wrote Sarah.

She dipped a curtsy. "I accept."

"Who else would like to be immortalized?" McGill said, waving the ring above his head making the gold setting twinkle in the winter sunshine streaming through the window.

When several ladies' hands shot into the air, he used the ring to point out Sarah Coles. Once she supplied her name, McGill, with a mischievous glance at Sally, scratched 'Sally Coles into the glass of the third pane.

"McGill!"

The room went silent, freezing McGill. Red-faced he turned to his superior. John stood beyond the knot of young ladies; his arms crossed. "When did you receive orders to vandalize our host's windows? Is this how you repay their hospitality, Captain?" John's emphasis suggested he might not be a captain long, especially when his gaze flicked to Sally and, scowl deepening, returned to McGill, who slipped the ring into his pocket.

He bowed to John. "My ap-apologies, Colonel," McGill said. "Merely a game. I meant no disrespect."

He sought out Father and bowed to him as well. "I offer my most humble apologies, Mr. Townsend, and if you desire, I shall pay you for the cost of a new windowpane."

Father waved away the apology. "Not necessary, son. I perceive the entire thing was in a spirit of fun and humor."

"Thank you, sir," McGill said, excusing himself and moving away.

Sally hugged her arms around herself. The fun disappeared from the room. Why did John have to embarrass the poor lad unnecessarily? She touched the windowpane. How did a diamond do such a thing?

Poor Sarah. Now the entire world would think she was not comely enough to merit much more than her name. Sensing a presence at her side, she slipped an arm around Sarah who studied the windowpane bearing her name. She squeezed the other girl's waist. "I'm sure he would have said something lovely about you."

Sarah didn't answer as Cousin Robert appeared, and taking his fiancée by the arm, drew her away.

Sally touched her name etched in the cool glass. Why did John have to go and ruin their fun?

John paced his room, closeted behind the protective walls of his bed chamber. The party ended hours ago, but he did not enjoy himself. Sally attracted too much male attention. Not on purpose, but it rankled. He had no intention of demoting Captain McGill— the lad was too good an officer—, but he felt compelled to warn him away from Sally.

Every time Sally spoke with another man, a desire to throttle him and drag her away assailed him. He struggled to appear unconcerned, but when McGill scratched her name in the window, he snapped.

He lit a candle and sat at his desk before reaching for his quill, ink, and some paper. Burying himself with work might take his mind off his torture. He inked his quill and began to doodle. Of its own accord, the quill drew out two hearts, one behind the other. Next, an arrow-pierced both hearts, pinning them together. On the back heart, he wrote the initials *ST*, and on the front heart *JGS*.

187

He laid the page aside. There was no hope. He must declare himself or go mad. Sitting forward, he reinked his quill and, gathering his thoughts, wrote.

From Lieutenant Colonel J.G. Simcoe to Miss Sarah Townsend:

Written and delivered at Oyster Bay, L.I. St. Valentine's Day, 1779.

That sounded formal, but he could go back and change it later.

Fairest maid where all are fair,
Beauty's pride and Nature's care.
To you my heart I must resign.
O choose me for your Valentine!
Love, Mighty God! Thou know'st full well,
where all thy Mother's graces dwell,
where they inhabit and combine
To fix thy power with spells divine.
Though know'st what powerful magic lies
within the round of Sarah's eyes.

John read the words. Would she like his efforts? He dipped his quill and wrote.

My happier days no more to range o'er hill, o'er dale,
in sweet Employ, of singing Delia, Nature's joy.
Thou bad'st me change the pastoral scene forget my crook.
with haughty mien to raise the iron spear of war,
Victim of Grief and deep Despair; Say must I all my joys
forgo and still maintain this outward show?
Say, shall this breast that's pained to feel be ever clad in horrid steel?
Nor swell with other joys than those of conquest o'er unworthy foes?

He considered this new stanza, thought to cross them out, but then chose to let her see his heart. He ended with a flourish he hoped, prayed, she would like.

Shall no fair maid with equal fire awake the flames
with soft desire. My bosom born, for transport, burn and
raise my thoughts from Delia's urn?
"Fond Youth," the God of Love replies, "your answer, take from Sarah's eyes."

His quill jiggled in his hand as he reread his poem. He would never come up to Andre's abilities, but still, not half bad. He laid the quill down and topped his poem with the hearts. He folded the pages in threes and pushed them to the edge of his desk. Satisfied with his efforts, he blew out the candle and went to bed. As soon as John's head hit the pillow, he was sound asleep.

Sally sat down to breakfast with the women. All the men, including John, ate, then left to do their chores.

As she reached for her fork, her fingers connected with something sharp under her plate. Lifting the porcelain, she found a folded sheet of paper with her name written in John's handwriting.

With a furtive glance around the room, she slipped the sheet from the table and tucked it into her pocket beneath her skirt.

Grasping her fork with shaking fingers Sally ate, resisting the urge to touch the sheets hidden in her lap, and doing her best to chat with her mother and sisters with complete nonchalance.

"Sally," Mother said as she sat down with a cup of tea. Audrey brought her a bowl of porridge. "This morning I want you to clean the hearth in the sitting room. I almost died of shame when I saw how sooty and dirty it is."

Sally wanted to laugh for joy. This was the excuse she hoped for. "Of course, Mother, but may I go upstairs and change into a different dress first?"

Mother studied her and Sally anticipated her denial, but she sighed and shrugged. She spooned some porridge. "Put on your linsey-woolsey and come straight back down. We have a lot to do today."

Sally finished her breakfast and after bringing her dishes to Patty to wash, she ran upstairs. After closing her bedroom door, she sat on her mattress where she unfolded the sheets. "Oh..."

A soft gasp whispered past her lips, and her heart swelled at the two arrow-pierced hearts. Her heart mimicked the physical pang of the tip. She laid it beside her hip and began to read, whispering the precious words. "Fairest maid where all are fair. Love, Mighty God! Though know'st full well, where all thy Mother's graces dwell, where they inhabit and combine to fix thy power with spells divine. Though know'st what powerful magic lies within the round of Sarah's eyes."

When she finished the poem, she read it again and laid back, pressing the page to her heart. He cared for her and in his awkward way demonstrated how much. This poem plumbed the depths of his heart, and her conscience mocked her. She should reconsider her own mind and heart and give him a chance. Daydreaming about becoming Mrs. John Graves Simcoe, Sally lived happily ever after, but she only pictured them doing so in this home.

Like the arrows piercing the two hearts together, a pain shot through her heart, so intense, for a moment she couldn't breathe.

Tracing her fingers across the pages, her heart warmed with pride that a man such as John Simcoe would choose her. She needed to hide this from her sisters. This note was private. Only for her eyes. She jumped from the bed to kneel in front of her hope chest.

Pushing aside quilt pieces and clothing, Sally slipped the sheets inside the side pocket, then lifted out the contents to reorganize and hide the pocket against potential prying eyes. Refolding bolts of cloth intended to become sheets and pillowcases Sally laid them back inside. One bolt of woolen cloth crinkled with an unnatural sound. She unfolded it and extracted her notes for Robert. She studied them, unsure now of what to do. The pages shook in her hands. What if... what if she burned them and devoted herself to John?

She raised up on her knees, eyes on the door, listening for movement in the hallway. Quickly, she laid the pages out on the floor and studied them. Information about his raid on Setauket. Comments his men made when they visited the house.

Now, she felt duty-bound to destroy them.

"Sally!" Mother's voice rang from the stairway, and she almost jumped out of her skin. With frantic haste, she refolded the pages and tucked them inside her chest. She bounded from the floor and slammed the top of the chest before rushing to the bedroom door.

"Sally!" Mother said, sounding impatient.

Sally drew open the door. "I'll be down in a moment. I'm changing and I need a fresh apron."

"Well, hurry up, child. We have a much cleaning to do."

Back at her hope chest, she reached into the side pocket for the poem, making sure it was well hidden. Her fingers hit something hard, and she drew out her small codebook.

After a glance at the door, she flipped the pages. Her eye caught a particular number, and, in her mind, she went back to the night Robert gave her the book. Number 355. "The designation for lady," he said. "Like you."

"Three-five-five," she said, breathing out the words. She snapped the book closed and tucked it into the side pocket next to her poem, determined to give it back to Robert the next time he was home. She closed the top again before crossing to her armoire, changing into her linsey-woolsey gown, and grabbing an apron. She left the room while tying the strings behind her back.

Downstairs, Mother, Audrey, and Phebe were hard at work.

"It's about time," Audrey said with a growl.

"None of that, girls," Mother cut her off. "We have a lot to do, and I don't want any bickering while we do it."

She nodded to Sally. "Clean the hearth and sweep around the edges. It's become quite filthy."

"Yes, ma'am," Sally said, retrieving a broom, scrub brush, and a bucket of water and set about her task. While she worked, a small smile played on her lips, as the lines from the poem drifted in and out of her thoughts. "O choose me for your Valentine!" She did choose him for her Valentine. "The answer take from Sarah's eyes."

"What are you grinning about?" Phebe asked, sweeping the floor.

Sally peeked up from the hearth. "I was thinking of last night. It was a fun party."

A sigh deflated Phebe's shoulder. "It was fun and now everyone will remember you and Audrey for all time." She gestured toward the window. "Do you think John was angry about the glass?"

Sally shrugged "I don't know. I don't understand why he should be."

"Mother!" Robert's voice rang in the hallway "I'm ready to go now."

When the women stopped their chores, Robert waited by the stairs for Sally, his saddlebag slung over his right shoulder. Once the others left, he glanced at her. "Do you have anything for me?"

She almost said no, but something stopped her. "Upstairs in my hope chest."

He handed her the bag. "Quick."

Sally ran upstairs, unfolded the bolt of cloth, praying John would forgive her, and tucked the pages into the bag, all the while promising herself this would be the last time. Dropping the top of the hope chest, she hurried back downstairs.

25

The landscape around Oyster Bay changed from mud brown to the light green of new leaves on trees and green grassy fields not yet turned to summer gold. Birds chirped and swooped, attracting mates, and building nests. Foxes and other hibernators left their dens often with young in tow. The ocean breezes brushed Sally's cheek like a warm, soft blanket, lifting strands of red hair.

Carriage rides began again, and John promised a picnic with her and her sisters for the next day. The girls planned a feast for the occasion and Sally prayed the weather remained warm and sunny.

But for now, chores needed doing and the bright though chilly early April morning drew her. She took the butter churn outdoors to the front yard, and as she worked the handle, she let the stirring of a new spring fill her soul with a sense of contentment new since John's November arrival.

As neighbors passed the house, Sally called hello to friends unseen since the February tea. A sign people, as well as animals, were coming out of hibernation. The liquid in the churn thickened. A little more before it turned to butter. Using both hands, she put more vigor into the work, now wanting the chore done.

The clip-clop of a horse's hooves stopped at the end of the

walk, and a lanky British Officer prepared to dismount. She slowed her motions and straightened, shaking her head to remove a wayward strand of hair.

He stamped both feet and adjusted the bottom of his uniform, before tying his horse to the hitching post. He said something to the animal as he swept a hand down the horse's muzzle and patted his neck. When the horse bobbed his head as if in response and snorted, the officer chuckled and patted him again before turning Sally's way.

Bushy eyebrows shot up onto his high forehead, and blue eyes lit in obvious appreciation of her appearance as they traveled from her face to her shoes and back again.

Sally resisted the urge to make certain her clothing covered her. Who was he, and what did he want?

A friendly smile curved his full lips and shone from his blue eyes.

Sally's shoulders drew back, and she straightened her spine, prepared to run inside if necessary.

"Good morning," she said, offering a friendly, yet guarded, greeting.

The soldier doffed his hat and offered her a gallant bow, one foot extended forward, and with a swirl of his hat, tucked his arm in at his waist as he bent over it. When he straightened, he dropped the hat onto his brown hair. "Ah, the gods are smiling upon me this morning, if this is the house I seek."

Sally scowled in response to his grin. "I have no idea what you're talking about, sir. In this household, we recognize the one true God, and we do not hold with any other such silliness." Why did she take such a sharp tone? Perhaps because he was disarmingly handsome, and she recognized his charm in an instant. A charm that might prove hard to resist.

He approached her but stopped short at her sharp tone. His mouth formed an O and his blue eyes widened. He tilted his head, acknowledging her stand. "My apologies, miss. I merely wished to compliment you on your rather stunning beauty, but if I overstepped, permit me to make amends."

Unsure what to do or say, she shrugged, still struggling with suspicion. "What can I do for you...?"

He approached again. "Major Andre," he said supplying his

name. "Major John Andre, and I believe Lieutenant Colonel Simcoe resides in this house. Am I correct?"

"You are," she said, smiling for the first time. "I'm sorry, but the colonel isn't here right now. He left about an hour ago for the training grounds."

Major Andre pursed his lips. "How unfortunate."

"I can send someone to fetch him if necessary." Why did she make such an offer? She could simply direct him to the training ground, but this man discomfited her with the merest glance. She concentrated on the butter churn to hide her confusion, lifting the top and checking inside. The butter was ready.

Andre peered in as well. "Normally, I wouldn't want anyone to go to such trouble, but urgency demands I see him. I come from General Clinton's headquarters."

When he said General Clinton's headquarters, concern pierced her. Sally slammed the lid back onto the churn and dashed into the house calling for Isaac. She should have expected this. Spring arrived with the resumption of the war. This man was here to take John away.

When she returned to the yard, the lump of butter sat in the wooden bowl beside the churn, and Andre poured the buttermilk into a pewter pitcher, also set beside the churn.

"Thank you," she said, gesturing to the pitcher. "Usually, one of my brothers does the pouring."

Andre chuckled. "The least I could do for a fair maid."

Sally's heart pounded, and heat tingled up her neck and face. "I sent Isaac to fetch the colonel."

John wouldn't like this man flirting with her, but how was she to stop him? His broad smile and kind blue eyes were...she cast about for the word but couldn't find one. This officer made her feel delicate, and feminine in a way John didn't. John loved her. His poem, which she still found time to read daily, told her so. But he didn't gaze at her the way Major Andre did now. He didn't make her experience the softer things as she did at this moment, which puzzled her.

Andre pushed the wooden bowl into her hands, breaking her reverie. He took up the pitcher. "Where shall we take these things?"

"Follow me," she said, heading into the house, and the charming British Officer's boots clumped on the wooden floor behind her.

John rushed into the house, slamming the front door. "Andre!" He found him in the kitchen with Mrs. Townsend and the girls, a happy grin on his face. John notched his shoulder against the doorjamb. "I should've realized you would hold court with all these beauties."

Andre sat at the kitchen table, a teacup in front of him and some pastry on a plate, the girls sitting around him, with Sally at his right hand. His heart thudded hard in his chest, and he fought to keep a scowl from his features. The last thing he wanted to do was act like a boor and ruin the joy of his friend's visit.

Andre rose, hands spread. "What was I to do? They were all so kind and gracious." He waved a hand at all of them, stopping too long at Sally, "and lovely. I must say, quite lovely."

John faked a grin as he sucked in a sudden breath.

Andre's eyebrows went up, his head tipping from John to Sally. A deep blush stained her cheeks as she focused on her satin slippers peeking from beneath her skirts.

Full of bright humor and understanding, Andre eyed him with a mischievous grin.

"So, Andre, what brings you to Oyster Bay?"

"A most treacherous complaint, my friend, brought on by my Sisyphean labors at headquarters."

"How long has the general given you leave for? You must stay here."

Rubbing his hands together, Andre laughed. "As long as I need, provided I'm back within a fortnight."

"Mrs. Townsend," John slid his shoulder off the door jamb and ambled into the room. "Major Andre will stay in my room."

The woman's eyebrows closed in on each other, and a frown crinkled her lips before, she foisted off a false smile. "Of course, Major. You're welcome to stay as long as you like."

"Thank you, Mrs. Townsend, but as I said, I can only spare two weeks," he said with a flourished bow. "I promise to be a stellar house guest. You'll never think I'm here."

John clapped his hands and the sound cracked across the room. "Settled! Come with me, and I'll show you your new quarters."

They left the women in the kitchen, and once in his bedroom, John waved a hand around and closed the door. "Well, it isn't much. But the bed is expansive enough for the both of us, and we can work and talk in relative privacy."

Andre dropped his hat on the desk. "As I said, Clinton gave me a two-week leave due to illness. He believes, from our herculean task of managing this war. He wanted me to go into the country to rest, and I thought, what better place than with my dear friend, John Simcoe," Andre said clapping him on the back. "We can plan a strategy while I'm here."

He leaned close and spoke quietly in John's ear. "There is much work to do, Simcoe. I'm here, not only to recuperate—which is necessary—but also to serve the general who wants us to begin in earnest to ferret out a new menace, a possible spying operation."

John cocked an eyebrow. Sitting at his desk, he indicated Andre should sit on the bed. He said nothing as Andre settled himself but leaned forward to listen to what his friend had to say.

Andre leaned his right arm back while draping his left across his crossed knee. "Well, as I said, the general is under the impression clandestine activities are going on here on Long Island."

He gestured toward Simcoe. "Your foraging expedition for example. How did the rebels remove the livestock? Who told them you were coming? These are the things he wants to get to the bottom of." Andre stared hard at Simcoe and changed the subject. "Mrs. Townsend didn't appear pleased to offer me shelter."

It took a minute for John to comprehend Andre's implication but when he did, he scoffed. "I'm sure she's thinking of the extra work involved in having a houseguest."

Straightening his cuffs, Andre thought about that. "You're certain we don't need to start searching for spies right here in this house?"

John shook his head. "Positive."

The late afternoon sunlight streamed in the window sliding up the stones of the hearth and reaching for the ceiling. Major Andre sat in a chair near the hearth, legs crossed, a small book balanced on his knee. A quill in his right hand moved over the page while he and Father discussed shipping.

John had been called away for tasks not including the major, so he remained home, getting better acquainted with the family. In only a day or two, not only Sally but the rest of the Townsends were enamored of the charming Major John Andre. He spoke with Father on any number of subjects with authority, including business.

Sally sat on the sofa near the hearth working a sampler, tilting her work away so the major wouldn't see her uneven stitches. The sun warmed her face. She followed his conversation with Father by glancing up and smiling occasionally.

"You are quite knowledgeable on the subject, Major. Is your family in the shipping trade?" Father asked.

"My father," Andre shifted in his chair, "a Huguenot, left France as a boy and settled in Switzerland. He became quite a successful businessman, and that business took him to England where he got involved in the shipping business. There, he met and married my mother."

"I see." Father sat across from Andre. He sipped tea before setting the cup on the small table between them. He smoothed the ruffles of his cravat with one hand, and the gold ring on his pinkie finger flashed in the fading sunlight.

"What's the name of your father's business? Perhaps we've traded with each other unknowing."

"Oh, I doubt it, sir." Andre swung his foot as he waved away Father's suggestion, sounding almost jovial. "My father died when I was quite young, and the business went defunct soon after."

Father offered a grave smile. "My condolences, son."

Andre tipped his head back, his mouth opening and closing, as warmth lit his blue eyes. "Thank you, sir."

"Do you speak French, Major?" Phebe asked as she spun a distaff, having graduated from wool carding over the winter.

"I do, Miss Phebe, as well as German and English," he said, straightening in his chair and tugging at his white cuffs which peeked from his red tunic gleaming with gold braiding. He leaned forward. "Gelb steht dir, deine frisur gefallt mir, fraulein."

Phebe's ogling eyes and open mouth elicited a laugh from everyone. "Whatever did you say?" She asked stopping the distaff but forgetting to wind the wool.

Blue eyes narrowed with humor as he bowed his head toward her. "I said, yellow suits you well."

He gestured first to her gold satin gown, then her hair. "And I love your hairstyle miss."

He indicated the simple knot on her head, one strand left to fall over her forehead an imitation of how Sally often wore her hair.

Under his full attention, Phebe blushed and ducked her head, focusing on her task, of winding the wool.

Her sister's cheek pinked, and Sally's heart warmed. Andre's charms were indeed hard to resist.

"And I do wish you would call me Andre. Everyone does."

"How did you come to speak German, Major—uh, Andre?" Sally asked pulling a stitch. She didn't glance up, fearing she might fall victim to his charm again too.

"I spent my childhood in Switzerland, Miss Sally, the English not being too fond of those with French last names." He made a self-deprecating shrug. "In Switzerland, they speak both German and French."

Sally poked her needle through the linen before grabbing it. "And yet, you serve the British Army? Why?"

"Sally," Father said, a note of warning tightening his voice.

"Oh, not to worry, Mr. Townsend," Andre said, waving away his concern. "I've been asked that question many times." Bracing a small book in his lap, with swift sure motions, he drew lines across the page.

"My grandfather, whom I lived with after my father's passing, died when I was a lad of seventeen. I returned to England with my mother, and as I had no vocation or direction in my life, she suggested a military life might give me an anchor."

He tilted his head at the lines on the page, considering. "Of course," he drew a few more lines, "she frowned upon my desire to be a playwright or artist. She didn't want me starving in the streets of London."

He turned the book to reveal his sketch of Sally, hand poised gracefully in the act of pulling a stitch.

Andre turned back one page and showed Sally a sketch of Audrey sitting at her spinning wheel. Raising her eyebrows, Sally glanced at her sister as she laughed and clapped her hands.

"Oh! You're quite a gifted artist. You captured Audrey most admirably."

Andre turned the book to show Audrey, who glanced at the sketch, sipped tea, and smoothed her flowered linen frock. She didn't smile, but she failed to hide her pleasure at her likeness.

He tilted his drawing back and studied his work. "Hmm, you're right. Not bad if I may say so."

Grinning, he snapped the book shut. "I shall keep this one to remind me there is more beauty in Oyster Bay than meets the eye." He cast a grin at Audrey, who smiled but turned away.

The front door opened and closed.

Andre called out. "Is that you, Simcoe?"

John appeared. "It is I, and much as I hate to pull you away from this gentle company, Andre, we must get to work."

Andre rose. "Then let us be away to our task."

"If you'll excuse us," John said.

"Of course," Father said.

The two men disappeared into John's bedroom.

26

Soon after John moved into the house, her parents moved their
stores and supplies to the bedroom of their two eldest sons,
Solomon, and Samuel. Above the room shared by Simcoe and
Andre.

Mother asked Sally to fetch a bolt of cloth from this room.
Unable to locate the cloth, Sally yanked open cabinets and armoires,
slamming them closed when they didn't reveal the garnet silk. A
frustrated huff of breath escaped as her hands jammed onto her hips
and her gaze swept the room.

The room puzzled her. Someone stacked items in a haphazard
manner, making her search more difficult. How unlike Mother to
allow such a mess, even in an unused room and she should restore
order, but not today. Another day when she was in the mood for
such a herculean task—as Andre would say. Why had Mother
allowed the room to stay this way?

Aha! She spied an unchecked cabinet and bustled over, tripping
over a shin-high chest hidden among the clutter.

"Ouch!"

She rubbed the spot as the pain intensified and migrated up her
leg. Well, since she tripped over the thing, she might as well search

inside. Kneeling, she opened the lid and lifted out the items. Red flashed at the bottom. The silk! Thank heaven, with her other chores awaiting, she wasted too much time on this task already.

Below, John's bedroom door thumped closed, and his and Andre's voices drifted up as if they spoke right beside her. Sally froze as she tried to discover why their voices carried so well.

The chest she sat in front of sat on the floor above an open grate, designed to allow warm air to rise and heat the room.

"So, Simcoe... Those beacons are genius. But Norwich is some distance away. Why are the signals there? Why not erect them here?"

"Well," John said his voice rising clear as a bell, "I had them built a distance away in case of a surprise raid here in Oyster Bay. It's possible they can be destroyed but will take effort to reach Norwich from here. We can see them well enough from here. We've tested them to be sure."

"General Clinton will want to be made aware of this. He'll also want to discover how they will operate."

"Simple."

A chair creaked as someone sat in it. "Depends on where our unworthy foes land. We've numbered each harbor. So, if they land in force from the east of Norwich, we'll use the beacons. Depending on the harbor, the number of beacons. Lloyd's Neck is one beacon, Huntington Bay is two beacons, and so on. Fire by night and smoke by day. Telling us in an instant where to go based on the number of beacons lit."

Something rustled, did Andre sit on the bed? "What if they land to the west of Norwich?"

"That's Colonel Tarleton's problem," John said. "My territory is Oyster Bay and points east."

Andre laughed, then came a sound as though he clapped his hands together. She imagined his boyish grin lighting his face. The image made her smile despite their somber words. She'd sat on her knees, and her feet began to tingle from the lack of blood flow. She wanted to shift her weight and relieve her legs but didn't dare move, lest they catch the sound.

The tingling grew more insistent, so she laid a palm on the floor, lifted herself off her legs, and stretched out on her side next to the grate laying her head on her arms.

There was nothing for some time, and Sally began doze off, when Andre's voice again drifted up, again with an almost lazy tone. "Have you heard of a man named Culper?"

Sally jerked her head up. She waited for John's answer, but he gave none, so likely not. Andre went on to explain, verifying John's ignorance.

"General Clinton believes the espionage ring here in Long Island is headed by someone named Culper."

Sally almost laughed. The name was a nom de guerre.

"Well, when we find them," Sally held her breath for his next words "we'll destroy them utterly."

A chair scraped on wood. "Come, Andre, let's go for a walk. I sometimes think these walls have ears."

Something rustled, footsteps vibrated, and the door opened and closed. The voices went silent, but she didn't dare move as she processed all she learned. With a start, two of John's words penetrated her concentration—unworthy foes. He called her compatriots unworthy foes. The lines in his poem, lines she long since memorized and oft repeated during the day stung her now. 'Say, shall this breast that's pained to feel, be ever clad in horrid steel? Nor swell with other joys than those of conquest o'er unworthy foes?'

After a few minutes, she sat up and, with care, eased the lid closed. Fury ran her blood cold. She grabbed the cloth and, as she turned to leave, sighted Father's desk, which he always kept in the parlor downstairs. The desk disappeared sometime after the night John helped her get a warming pan. There must be paper in a drawer to use to inform Robert and show John how unworthy his foes were!

Setting the cloth on top of the chest, Sally wove through the clutter. The boxes and storage chests were like a kind of maze, and when she reached the desk, she smiled at the careful design, giving the impression of not being worth the effort to work one's way through.

She lifted the lid and rummaged through for a sheet of paper. She found Father's book in which he often wrote letters. She intended to tear out a page but again, her breath stopped in her throat. A letter, dated three days ago to the Continental Correspondence Committee outlined British activity in Oyster

203

Bay--. Troop numbers, training tactics, command structure, and much more.

Her heart pounded. Was Father the mysterious Culper? How to be sure?

It was best not to know. She closed the book and opened a drawer, found a quire of paper, took a sheet, and, after closing the desktop, wound her way through the clutter. Her cheek itched and she brushed her fingers on the spot. They came away wet with tears.

Sally worked in the kitchen making oly koeks for the afternoon's tea. So many friends and neighbors stopped by the house on supposed errands during the week for a peek at the famed Major Andre, Mother suggested hosting a tea party in his honor so their friends may all meet him at once.

Sally plucked out the last of the small donut balls from the hot lard, rolled them in sugar and placed them on a tray, which she covered with a damp cloth and left on the table to finish cooling.

"You are a vision of loveliness."

Sally gasped, spinning toward the kitchen door. Major Andre leaned negligently against the jamb. Behind him, the stump of a once towering oak tree framed his slim body and back lit him as the sun shone through the kitchen door. Warm spring air flowed in around him, like God's breath on the vibrant man. He raised a hand, thumb up, as though assessing her for a portrait.

She relaxed and returned to her task. "What are you doing?"

"I'm seeing you in a portrait. I cut silhouettes." He drew his body off the door jamb in a lazy motion and approached, staring down at her in mock seriousness. "I do. And I'm quite accomplished, I'm told."

"Oh, I believe you," she said, brushing a hand down the front of her apron. As always, she had the feeling she should check to make sure her clothing was in place when Andre was close by. "I've just never seen a silhouette done before."

He stopped close in front of her. "Then, I shall make a cut of you this evening."

Although he towered over her, Sally felt no sense of danger. Indeed, she believed he would defend her life with his own, if necessary, but an aura of maleness flowed off him like the waves of the ocean, overwhelming her until she felt vulnerable in ways never experienced, not even with John.

Stepping back, she smiled up at his magnetic blue eyes. "I'd like that," she said. "If you'll excuse me, I must change for the party now."

He swept a hand to the tray of donuts and lifted the cloth. "Did you make these?"

"I did. They need to cool, but I'll put them out later."

Leaning close he drew in a deep inhale. "Mmm," he said. "Cinnamon." He dropped the cloth. "I shall look forward to tasting one. I'm sure I'll find them delicious."

Her heart thudded. Did she remember all the ingredients? She would die of shame if she left out something crucial, or cooked them too long. Clutching her skirts, she backed toward the stairs. "I hope so."

He waved a hand at her. "Go, change your clothes. Put on your prettiest dress."

Inside, their bedroom Audrey sat at the dressing table, still in her shift and stays, preparing her hair. Sally leaned back against the wood her hands pressed to the panels. Her pulse raced and her chest lightened. "Audrey, what are you planning to wear?"

"That," Audrey said pointing to a peach-colored linen dress spread across her bed. "Your green linen would be lovely in comparison. And appropriate too. The color of spring."

Sally drew out the dress from her armoire, which she laid next to Audrey's. A perfect complement. "Have you ever had a silhouette cut of you?"

Audrey paused in twisting a curl. "No. Neither have you."

"Is it a bad thing to do? Do you think Father would object?"

Seating a pin in her hair, Audrey eyed her from the looking glass. "No."

She gestured with another pin. "Why are you asking about silhouettes?"

"No reason." Sally's head tilted as though silhouettes were of no consequence. "Major Andre said he might cut one for me at the party today if I want one."

"Oh."

She sauntered over and tugged at one of Audrey's perfectly sprung curls, and sing-songed, "I'm sure he'll make one of you, as well. I think he likes you."

From the looking glass, Audrey shot her an oh-please glare.

Wagging the captured curl, Sally cocked her head and furrowed her brows. "Don't you like Andre?"

Audrey seated the pin and twisted another curl. "I like Andre a great deal," she said, extricating the curl from Sally's hand.

Sally dropped her hand and went back to sit on the bed. "I detect a but, in your statement."

"But" Audrey spun around in her chair, careful to keep her head from moving too much and ruining her hard work. "I'm a one-man woman, and I do not believe for a moment Major Andre is a one-woman man. So, I like him. But not that much."

"I see, and I don't blame you." As her sister went back to her preparations, Sally removed her sweat-stained day dress and threw it into the wash pile along with her shift. She fumbled with a clean shift and mob cap. "I always want," cloth muffled her words as she waded through the shift, "to make sure I'm dressed every time he looks at me."

She settled the garment on her body. "And I get the disconcerting sense he knows what's beneath my chemise."

Turning on her seat, Audrey placed her hands on her knees. "Has he been discourteous to you?" She asked her blue eyes narrowed with concern. "Because if he has..."

Sally held out her hands to stop Audrey. "No, he's been ever the gentleman. I just think beneath the gentlemanly exterior lies the heart of a lecher."

Chuckling, Audrey patted her coiffure. "Hence my earlier statement." She spun back around and continued pinning her hair. "I like him, but I don't like him that much."

She came to stand behind Audrey, while her sister slid another pin into a curl. Sally shook out her own curls, brushed them, and pinned them in a knot atop her head. She allowed red tresses at her temples to fall to her shoulders and frame her oval face. She tapped Audrey on the shoulder. "Don't take too long. Our guests will be here soon."

She snugged the cap on her head and released the two front curls to fall in loose ringlets.

"I'll be down in a few minutes."

Sally made some last few adjustments to her dress, making sure the garment fell in a smooth flow to her ankles.

Sally glided down the stairs. Mother was in the sitting room. Mrs. Coles and Mrs. Underhill gathered by her. Sarah Coles Stoddard, having married Sally's cousin, Robert Stoddard, in March, stood by the window chatting with her new husband.

Stepping into the room, Sally waved a hand. "Hello, everyone."

"Why, Sally, how pretty." Mrs. Underhill shifted in her seat for a better look, her hands in her lap, one over the other. "Are you wearing the colonel's favorite color?"

An embarrassed chuckle escaped her, but she took the ribbing in stride. "I didn't inquire." She held her skirts open and did a slow turn. "It reminded me of spring."

"And so, it does," Mrs. Coles said. "I must say, green is a lovely color on you."

"Thank you, Mrs. Coles," Sally said with a pleased smile. "If you will excuse me, I must go get the food ready."

Pleased by Mrs. Coles' comment, Sally flounced her skirt.

In the kitchen, she froze, horror ripping a hole in her heart. Her donuts! She left the platter on the table for her guests. The cloth covering them lay crumpled on the table, but no platter. Perhaps someone moved them to use the space. Sally opened the cupboards and peered under the table.

"What?" Her breath left her in a whoosh. "Where are they?" She went through the cupboards again and considered looking in the oven but dismissed the idea. No one would put them in a hot oven where they would be ruined. Did someone bring them to the parlor? Going down the hallway, she began to imagine all kinds of scenarios. Were they thrown out? Mistaken for a snack by the boys?

Standing inside the parlor door, she examined the table laden with food, teapots, cups, plates, and silverware. No platter of donuts.

Now her heart pounded hard. What would she do and all her hard work? Where did they go?

Sally entered the sitting room. "Mother? Excuse me, ladies. Mother, did you do something with the donuts? I left them on the kitchen table, but now they're gone."

Wincing at the sound of her own screech, she nevertheless continued. "I spent all morning making them. Where did they go?"

Mother rose to her feet. "Keep calm, dear. Perhaps someone moved them. I'll help you find them."

Phebe came downstairs, making the last adjustments to her blue Lutestring gown, which was Sally's last year.

"Phebe, what did you do with my oly koeks?"

Her sister gawked; her brows furrowed. "What are you talking about?"

Sally's stomach broiled. Someone was playing a trick on her, and she didn't find it funny. "The oly koeks I made for the party this morning. Did you take them out to the field for the workers? Did you hide them? Where are they?" At her strident tone, Mother laid a calming hand on her shoulder.

Major Andre opened John's bedroom door. His brows crowded the top of his nose. "Is something amiss?"

She clenched and unclenched her fists. "The donuts I made this morning. They disappeared. Now I won't be able to serve them at the tea."

"Well, it wasn't me," Phebe said, pushing past her to the sitting room.

"I see," Andre said rubbing his chin as if thinking the matter over. "This sounds like a military expedition."

He pursed his lips and waved Mother back into the sitting room. "Mrs. Townsend, go back to your guests. I'll help Sally find them."

Mother's smile told Sally she thought this a small matter. "Thank you, Major."

Andre held out a hand to Sally and winked. "Come, my dear. Let's go find your wayward treats."

With a huff, she crossed her arms over her chest. "You can all laugh at me, but this isn't funny. I spent the entire morning making them. If we don't find them, or someone ate them already, it will be time and energy wasted, and that makes me angry."

The humor leaving Andre's eyes, he straightened his shoulders. "Well, we must find them," he said, grasping her arm. "Let's start in the kitchen, shall we?"

I did so already! Sally bit her lip, keeping the remark behind clenched teeth, and followed him. She stood in the doorway as he walked to the table and made a show of lifting the towel and cursing the donut thief. Her hands fisted as she held back laughter. But why would someone eat them, knowing they were for the party?

"I shall find the thief and hang him by the neck until dead!"

John entered the kitchen, and Andre spun toward him, finger pointed. "Ha! Have we caught our thief? You, sir, did you steal this poor young lady's food?"

John froze. His features crinkled and he stared at Andre as if he were a rabbit caught in a trap. When he switched his gaze to Sally, she rolled her eyes.

He removed his cap. "What foolishness is this? Of course not. I was gone all morning and only returned to change for the tea."

"Hmm," Andre said rubbing his chin again.

Suspicion brewed, but losing patience, Sally stamped a foot. "Andre, please, I must find them or discover what happened."

"Andre." John tsked. "If you have some idea what happened, then please put the poor girl out of her misery."

He walked to Sally and stood so close; his sleeve brushed her arm. His index finger found her pinkie and brushed against her knuckle.

Her breath left her body as she gazed into blue eyes filled with yearning.

Andre clapped his hands, and the sound cracked in the room, making Sally start and jerk her hand away. John's eyes clouded over as Andre raised an eyebrow at him.

"If you'll excuse me," John's breath brushed her cheek. "I must change." He squeezed past her.

"Come, Sally," Andre said, bracing his hands on her shoulders, and turning her around. "Let's check the parlor again, shall we?"

She allowed him to lead her back to the front room. He took her arm and walked her to the far side of the parlor table. "Now..." He gave her a gentle shove toward Mother's corner cabinet. "Let's begin looking, shall we?"

"Andre, I searched the table over."

The side window framed Daniel and Susannah walking up the road. "And now more guests are beginning to arrive."

A smile crinkled up his eyes. "We must concentrate," he said. "You're quite warm, though."

She was warm? Had he lost his senses? What did he mean? Sally took a tentative step toward the fireplace.

With a mock frown, he shook his head. "Oh, now you're cold."

Sally moved back toward the cupboard. His encouraging smile made her study the glass-covered shelves hosting Mother's China soup tureen, pewter bowls and pitchers, and other valuable items. Wouldn't he just tell her where they were? It was clear he was the culprit.

His gaze dropped to the cupboard beneath the shelves and back to her face as he cast her a significant glance. Her shoulders dropped, and she reached for the cupboard door handles. There were her donuts. She relaxed, and exhaled pent-up breath, grateful her back was to Andre as she pushed down her irritation. It was a harmless joke. He was famous for harmless jokes.

Sally reclaimed the platter with a silent and giant sigh of relief and placed it on the table.

Once their guests were enjoying tea and refreshments—and her oly koeks—, Major Andre pulled Sally to her feet. "Miss Sally, shall we regale our friends here of your near disaster?"

"Must we?"

She crinkled her forehead, half joking, not wanting to appear silly in front of her close friends.

"What say you all?" Spreading out his hands, Andre waved to encompass the room. "Do you wish to learn how Miss Sally almost came to a refreshment disaster before I swooped in to save the day?"

People gathered close, cheering and clapping.

At the chorus of encouragement, Andre extended his hands to calm the clamor "If you insist!" He called to a chorus of laughter. "I call this poem, 'An Ode to the Lost Donut.'"

Covering her face with her hands, Sally couldn't help laughing.

"Before I begin," Andre, said tugging at each cuff, "I must beg forgiveness as I compose this ditty in my head without the proper time to create a true masterpiece."

Daniel called out. "Tell us."

Andre bowed.

"Very well, 'An ode to the Lost Donut.'" He took hold of Sally's hand and faced her.

"Oh, fairest maid where all are fair...,"

Lightning tingles singed her as her mouth slid open and her gaze slipped to a scowling John. Since Andre's grin suggested the line came off the top of his head, she smiled and played along.

"Doth labor long and hard,

"To provide a treat of uncommon fare

"To friends—," his hand swept the room and came to rest on his chest-- "and this humble bard."

A wave of mirth rolled through the room forcing Andre to raise his voice.

He pointed to the back of the house. "The repast on plank in yonder room."

"Dark villain—," he said, again slapping his chest to alert all who that dark villain was—, "to gain fair maid's attention..."

His eyes twinkled at her.

Sally shook her head, as their guests' laughter murmured through the room.

"Said treat did vanish, an attempt to escape their doom. Cast down in veils of gloom, he must win fair maid's affection."

Andre affected a clownish frown with his fingertips pulling at the corners of his lips.

"Determined maid entreated villain,

"The donuts he must rescue, there was no question,

"He searched lowly cupboard and highest mountain,

"And now he pleads for mercy, this poem you do not mention."

Sally held her free hand over her mouth as gales left her sides aching. Andre found a way to make her laugh at the joke he played on her, and she loved him as laughter filled the room and their guests clapped and praised him.

Sally shook a finger at her tormentor. "You said whoever took them should be hung by the neck. I warn you, if such a disaster should happen again, I shall be judge, jury, and executioner."

27

The time arrived for Andre to return to Manhattan and John accompanied him to speak to General Clinton.

Sally waited on the front walk as the men adjusted their saddles and packed whatever items necessary to take with them. John glanced over his shoulder at her, dressed in the light green linen gown he found so beautiful on her.

He walked around the other side of his horse and checked the cinches. Again, he glanced over the back of his horse to find Sally blinking back tears, which made him wonder. Every time he thought he won her over, she withdrew, pulling back, making him start over. Well, he was undaunted. He would win her love if he had to plan as though a military action. He intended to marry Sally Townsend. Nothing else would do.

"Are you almost ready, Simcoe?" From atop his mount, Andre broke into his thoughts.

John patted Salem's rump. "One moment, Andre."

Andre nodded. "Say goodbye to your lady. I'll wait." He rode a few paces away from the front walk and stopped, so his back was to the house.

John approached Sally and extended his hands, and she placed her warm hands in his. Keeping his eyes on her trimmed nails, he closed his fingers around hers and brushed his thumb over her soft skin. How slim and small her fingers were in his generous palms. He feared to gaze into her eyes, she might make him change his mind about leaving.

She drew in a breath, drawing in also his attention. She was smiling at him, but her eyes shone. He squeezed her hands, and she responded in kind.

"I shall return in a day or so. What would you like me to bring back from Manhattan?"

"Yourself."

John chuckled at her singsong response and raised an eyebrow at her. "Understood. Anything else?"

She smiled, and his heart melted. "Surprise me."

He squeezed her hands again. "I love a girl with an adventurous spirit," he said, glancing over his shoulder at Andre. "I must go, but I'll be back in a couple of days."

"I'll be waiting and watching for your return." She drew her hands back, and with strong reluctance, he let them go.

"Goodbye, Sally...dear."

Before she could respond, he walked fast to his horse and mounted, then glanced back at her one more time, before stopping next to Andre. "Are you ready?"

Turning in his saddle, Andre removed his hat in a flourishing salute to Sally.

Her tinkling laugh reached them while she curtsied back.

"Now I'm ready," he said, laughing at the exasperated expression twisting John's features.

"I swear, Andre, women will be the death of you, someday."

His friend's laughter rolled with their horses' gentle stride. "Then it shall be a pleasant death, my friend."

John waited outside General Clinton's office while inside they finished up a staff meeting. He checked his timepiece, noting a quarter of an hour had passed. Stifling impatience, he put the timepiece back in his inside pocket and tapped his fingers against his knee and waited. When he pulled the timepiece out again, only five minutes had gone by. *Patience, Simcoe. General Clinton is a busy man.*

The door opened and John rose as a stream of officers left the room. General Clinton gestured to him to enter.

"My apologies, Colonel, for keeping you waiting, but some of my junior officers like to complicate things that are quite simple, and it becomes almost impossible to convince them otherwise."

"I understand, sir."

Andre stood next to a table, a map laid out and waiting. "Andre has been showing me your fortifications and redoubts on Long Island, Colonel. I must say I am most impressed."

"Thank you, General."

He nodded his thanks to Andre. "My goal is to prevent the rebel raiders from any landing zone on the island's north side. In my professional opinion, we've achieved that goal. Throughout the winter, they attempted a half dozen raids. All of them failed."

"Andre also informs me he filled you in on our need to locate and destroy a possible espionage ring on Long Island."

Clinton handed him a folded sheet of paper. "This list details all suspected Whigs living on Long Island."

John's heart almost stopped at the name atop the list. He lowered the sheet. "General Clinton, I live in Samuel Townsend's home. This man is not so much a Whig as he is a businessman who is careful to remain neutral."

"I would agree with his assessment, General," Andre said, sauntering over. "Having spent two weeks with the family myself, I found them nothing but kind and generous with their food, time, and affection."

Clinton eyed them both, head tilted, eyes slit as though assessing the truth of their words. "My sources tell me Mr. Townsend involved himself with the Correspondence Committee for the so-called Continental Congress."

John locked his hands behind his back and widened his stance, trying for an impartial but certain posture. "I searched his private papers, General, and found no such evidence. Perhaps he was, in the beginning, but I believe Mr. Townsend accepted the situation and withdrew his loyalty to the rebels."

Again, the narrow-eyed stare. Moments passed before Clinton gave one emphatic nod. "Fine. Find out about the rest of the names. I want that ring destroyed. They are reducing our supplies daily and making resupplying our army more difficult. How they always anticipate where we are and what we are doing must be stopped."

He flicked a hand and bent back over his map. "Converse with Captain Youngs. Give him orders from me he is to discover the method with which the rebels are staying one step ahead of our foraging parties. I want those raids stopped." Another emphatic nod of his head. "You have your orders, Colonel."

John folded the sheet and slipped it into a pouch at his side. He saluted. "Thank you for placing your trust in me, General Clinton. You won't be disappointed."

Andre walked him to the door. "Too bad I'm not attached to your Rangers, now, John. This sounds exciting."

"Same here. You have a way of engaging people in conversation that fills me with envy. However, I'll find these men and make them pay for their disloyalty to the king."

Before riding back to Oyster Bay, he stopped at a shop and purchased a small box of chocolate-covered almonds recalling Sally's delight the last time he brought her some of these treats. He wanted to experience that pleasure on her face again.

As John rode, he slid the list out of the pouch. He dismissed Samuel Townsend straightaway. John would know if the man was disloyal. David was young, but not impetuous. John suspected he wanted to be involved in the war and only needed to say the word and John would register him with the Queen's Rangers.

What of Robert? He was much like his father. Quiet, polite, unscrupulously neutral. Besides, he worked in James Rivington's coffee shop and wrote glowing articles about the men in the Rivington Gazette. True to his word, no information regarding military matters ever found its way into the published articles. That, most of all, declared Robert's allegiance to the king, didn't it?

Convinced the list was incorrect, John crumpled the sheet and shoved it back into his pouch. Taking up the reins, he jogged Salem into a canter. The sooner he got home and began work on finding out who these men were, the better.

When John rounded the corner the Townsend home came into view. Smoke rose from the center chimney, a comforting sign of welcome. He was home. Funny, how the place felt like home, eliciting a feeling of belonging he hadn't known since leaving England. He dismounted at the end of the walk where Isaac waited to take the reins.

The front door opened, and Sally waved a hand, beaming as she waited for him to open the gate and walk through.

When he reached her, he took her hands and gently squeezed. "You are a vision of loveliness," he said, releasing her hands and reaching into his pouch. "I brought you a gift." He withdrew the small box and extended his hand. "I remembered how much you enjoyed these the last time I brought them."

He laid the box in the middle of her palm and watched with delight as Sally lifted the lid and uttered a cry of joy. She bounced on her toes. "Are these the almond ones?"

"They are," he said. "I missed you so."

She gave him an impish grin. "You were only gone one day, Colonel."

He smiled. "Where you are concerned one day is the equivalent of one year to me, Miss Townsend."

Sally clutched the box to her chest, the sparkle in her eyes made his heart soar and a soft chuckle escaped him.

Mr. Townsend appeared at the front door. "Welcome back, Colonel."

John released her hand and stepped back. "Thank you, sir."

An awkward pause ensued as John reconsidered the names on his list. But no, it couldn't be so. He had too much respect for Mr. Townsend to consider such a thing seriously.

Mr. Townsend tucked Sally's arm in his and pulled her back inside, John followed, his tired legs complaining of his one-hundred-mile round-trip ride, and a deep sigh escaped him.

"Oh, John, you must be exhausted, and here we are chatting your ears off."

She linked her other arm through John's. "Perhaps Liss can prepare water for a bath? Then you can relax and get to work. Are you hungry? I can bring a tray to your room."

At her father's nod, she lifted her skirts an inch or so and headed for the kitchen, while Mr. Townsend clapped John on the back.

"I think you have your marching orders, son. I wouldn't advise objecting."

His knees wanted to buckle as the last reserve of energy drained from his body. John slumped his shoulders. A bath and a rest sounded wonderful. Nevertheless, he chuckled and tried to join in with the older man's bantering, but the best he could come up with was, "yes, sir."

When she disappeared, John and Mr. Townsend eyed each other. Should John tell him about the list? A wedge now formed in his heart that would alter his dealings with the man. A wedge he regretted, as he found no cause for concern, but caution shot through him like a red-hot poker.

"If you'll excuse me, Mr. Townsend, I think I'll prepare for my bath."

Mr. Townsend half bowed. "Welcome home, son," he said with a nod, before going outside.

John made his way to his room. After a moment, Sally knocked on the open door before she and Patty wrestled the cast-iron tub into his room. They plunked the heavy thing in the center. Both women huffed with their efforts.

"I got water on to boil for you, Colonel," Patty said clutching her abdomen while she caught her breath. "I'll bring it as soon as it's ready."

"Thank you, Patty," he said, turning to Sally. "I thought you were going to ask Liss to help."

She shot an anxious glance at the older woman and then squared up to John. "I have something I would discuss with you and has to do with Liss and one of your men."

John drew in a breath through his nose and held it a moment before releasing the exhale. "I see," he said, as he placed his hands behind his back. He should have realized. "And what would you like to discuss?"

Patty stepped forward. "Colonel, sir, one of your boys been sparkin' our Liss and must stop. She doesn't do her work. She runs to your camp and spends her time with Israel."

She glanced at Sally and, gripping her skirts, Patty dug in. "Now I ain't one to deny love but she disappears too often, she's gone too long, and Mr. and Mrs. Townsend are taking note, sir. It has to stop."

"So, you want me to do what, exactly? Speak to Israel? Liss? And say what?"

"Tell them to stop," Sally said, her furrowed brow communicating her growing annoyance.

John had been gone all day and the last thing he wanted on return was an argument. He held out a hand to her and nodded. "Please forgive me, Sally. I'm trying to be sure I understand the situation."

"Colonel, sir," Patty broke in between them. "Please tell him or her or both, they cannot continue. She is very near the verge of bad trouble. I don't want that."

Sincere concern and compassion in her deep brown eyes convinced John of her intent. He nodded once. "Very well, Patty. I shall sit Israel down this evening. When I commanded the 40th Foot, I had a standing order among my men of no dalliances. I shall impose my restriction once again."

He glanced between them. "Will that suffice?"

Patty and Sally appeared grateful. "Yes, thank you," they said together.

Patty laid her hands on Sally's shoulders and guided her from the room. "Thank you, Colonel," the older woman said as they walked to the hallway door.

He closed the door behind them, undressed, sank into the hot water, and relaxed. He emptied his mind of everything, except confronting Israel. He knew this day was coming, warned them both at one point, and now he had to deal with the consequences. He closed his eyes and sighed, releasing that complication with his exhale, and letting the water soak his tired bones.

Needing to be outside in the warming spring air, Sally walked to the parade ground to witness the men training. The scent of wet loamy earth and dung filled the air as did the sound of birds singing for their mates.

With the Rangers, something was in the air, she could feel it, and this was the best way to find out. She straightened her shoulders and waved as John trotted toward her.

"Good morning," she said to him. "You don't mind if I'm here, do you?"

"Of course not."

He reached for her hand before remembering himself and slipping his hands behind his back. "Why would I mind?"

She shrugged. "I just want to be certain my presence doesn't cause you problems," she said, turning toward the training field and waving a hand. "So, what are they doing?"

The men rode six horses across, bayonets fixed, charging, and shouting at straw-filled sacks tied to poles. When they reached the sacks, the men shoved their bayonets into them and twisted, then with one sharp tug, yanked them out and made way for the next group of six.

A gasp slipped from her. She remembered seeing the men charging on foot, but now, men on horseback, using the horse as extra leverage against foot soldiers dealt more cruelty. This was a new training tactic and it dismayed her to think those straw figures represented her friends and countrymen.

"Oh, John..." Sally said, and dizzy, she grabbed hold of his sleeve.

Hands up, he made a placating gesture. "The new campaign season will open in June, and I need them battle-ready."

A pleading note quivered in his words. She accepted his declaration as John placed light fingers on her elbow and led her closer to the training. Further away additional Hussars trained by horseback.

Her brows furrowed. "Do you have more Hussars than you did last year?"

"You didn't think I was idle all winter, did you?" He asked smiling. "I spent my time recruiting, not just Hussars but also foot soldiers." His gaze went to the men, still charging the straw sacks.

Sally's gaze swept the men milling about after having made their charge and those still waiting. Why he must have three thousand soldiers and more than five hundred horsemen! Trying to keep her face neutral, she nodded at the horsemen. "Whatever are they doing?"

The Hussars wheeled and charged each other, clashing swords and shouting.

"They're going to kill each other before they engage in battle!" Did she sound silly enough?

He lowered his head to hide a chuckle. "They're training for combat without dismounting. I find they can cause more confusion and fear when they charge into a platoon of men. Colonel Tarleton taught me."

Colonel Tarleton? An alarm bell rang in her head. 'That's

Tarleton's problem,' he told Andre. She cleared her throat. "Who is he?"

"He's serving in the south right now. I met him in Manhattan. A brilliant strategist, he taught me this strategy of charging a troop of foot soldiers. They become confused and, better still, terrified."

He rubbed his hands together, like a proud father boasting of his children. "The rebels won't have any idea what hit them once my Hussars have a go at them."

Smiling took effort. More like clenching her teeth so hard she feared cracking one. She walked away a few paces to gain distance from his glee and her dismay.

John walked up behind her, and she braced herself against cringing.

"I have to go out and inspect some fortifications this afternoon. I wondered if you might like to go with me?"

She raised her eyebrows at his request, rearranged her face to a more neutral position, then faced him. "Well, if my presence isn't an intrusion."

She raised a hand to forestall a scowl wrinkling his forehead.

"I'm not trying to start a squabble," she said in an even tone. "But at Christmas, you made clear you did not want me at the training ground anymore."

She ducked her head. "And here, I'm disobeying by showing up today. I'm sorry. I'll go home. It was such a beautiful day, I decided to go for a walk, and I found myself here," she said, peeking at him through her lashes. "I wanted to see you."

She started to leave, but he blocked her path.

His face reddened, and genuine contrition shone in his blue eyes. "I wish to apologize, Sally. I was wrong to say those things," he said, grasping her elbow and drawing her away from the men.

His gaze went over her head, as though he tried to organize his thoughts. "A lieutenant in my corps said some things and made allegations I have since found untrue. But they stung, and—I reacted. I'm ashamed to say for a brief time, I believed him, but more out of embarrassment and indignation than anything else. I was wrong."

He looked her full in the face and his features softened. "I must also confess when you dressed me down in front of your guests about the orchard, I reacted from a defensive posture. I want it on record how much I esteem your opinion, but if I may request, if you must dress me down again, I would prefer a more private setting."

Now was Sally's turn to squirm. "I was wrong, and I don't believe I apologized to you properly. When I apologized, I was still angry. Please allow me to express my regret for my bad behavior and I further promise I will not 'dress you down,' as you say, and I will not contradict you in public again."

She pressed her lips tight, then forced them to open into a smile. "Give me time to go home and change my clothes."

John leaned close. "I'll be along in an hour or so."

Sally squeezed his hand before running home. In her room, she sketched the training exercises and wrote a newsy letter to Robert, full of family and town gossip. In the margins, with the invisible ink, she listed troop numbers, noting they were going out this afternoon to inspect fortifications.

Placing her letter on top of a quire of twenty-five sheets of paper, she tucked her drawing fifteen pages down. She brought the package to her parent's room to lay on their bed where Father would find and deliver it.

28

The hour drew close marking the change from April to May and the four young people played a new card game that John taught them.

Phebe drew a card, which she slipped into her hand. She sighed with disappointment, but her cheeks were rosy from laughter. "I wonder when Major Andre will return. I suspect he'd like this game."

John chuckled. "I know for a fact Andre would like this game since he taught me. Though Andre has much to do in Manhattan, I do hope he's able to return soon as well. I miss him."

His comment made Sally study him. Such a declaration was unusual. She laid a hand on his arm. "Dear friends are a treasure to behold."

The play of cards went to Audrey. "Pass."

Sally tsked. "Audrey, must you? I had an excellent hand, but if my partner passes, I must concede the game." She'd fanned her cards in her right hand and now snapped the fan closed and threw them face-down.

Phebe and John, partners in this round due to how they bid before the round started, played their cards now to reach Ombre, or solo winner.

John beat Phebe with almost obscene delight but softened the blow as a disappointed frown drew her brows together.

"You're learning the game well, Miss Phebe. I never would play the queen first, and you made me stop and think. I suggest a few more rounds of the game, and you'll become Ombre in no time."

A sigh passed across the table as they all threw their cards in. Sally's turn came to deal, making her the "queen". When she dealt each their ten cards, she arranged hers by suit.

She started to ask John his bid, but his gaze was fixed out the dark window. Rain slashed against the pane and an errant draft of wind blew ashes from the hearth. Something was going on. *Leave it alone. Everyone is enjoying themselves. Don't start anything.* "Your bid, John."

John had offered to teach them this game, but clearly his heart wasn't in it—except when he won the final round. Resentment spiking, her heart pounded, and her breathing quickened into short shallow breaths. She rubbed her thumb across the hated stamp embossed into the deck of cards.

"Quite right," he said reaching for the deck. Outside a horse and rider clip-clopped on the lane. John's hand froze. When the rider passed, he plucked a card off the top and drummed his fingers on the tabletop.

Audrey leaned forward. "What do you call, John, pass or play?"

"Hmm? Oh, I am sorry, Miss Audrey. I forgot where I was for the moment."

He made a show of studying his cards, moving, and adjusting them. "Um, I call...play...and I vote spadille." He lay down a king of diamonds.

"Ombre," Phebe said, bouncing in her chair and casting down as many cards as she needed to form a run from the two of diamonds to the queen and with John as her partner, the king completed the play. Amid much laughter, she gathered up the small pieces of wood used for chips and placed them at her side.

John sat back laughing. He threw his hand face-down into the center of the table. "Here I thought Sally would be my most formidable opponent, and I find Miss Phebe challenges me."

Phebe giggled as she sorted the cards and made a clumsy

attempt to shuffle. She handed the pack to John, who shuffled with an expert hand.

Phebe passed ten cards, and as Sally gathered hers, she eyed John. "I didn't realize I'm a challenge to you. How should I correct the condition, or should we discuss this later?"

She crossed her left arm over her abdomen and tucked her fist under her right elbow she made a show of studying her cards basking in the irritation flowing from him. She couldn't help herself. He divided his attention. Something was happening, and he was listening for it. But what? She slapped down a combination of cards. "Manille."

His only response was a sharp glare before he took extra time choosing his cards. Then he laid out an ace of spade, two, and three, calling out "Spadille."

When Phebe, still his partner and sitting across from him, gave a sharp inhale, John reddened and offered her an apologetic smile. She shrugged but Sally experienced her sister's ire in the form of a venomous glare.

Sally's partner, Audrey drew, but Sally didn't pay any attention to the cards, not when John was playing another game. Before the evening was over, she determined to find out what.

The game ended after the hall clock bonged out a dozen times. Phebe won most of the rounds, and they all cheered her.

"Well, ladies, I had a most enjoyable evening, but the hour grows late. I must be up early tomorrow."

He gathered up the cards and put them away, while Phebe and Audrey threw the wood chips into the kindling basket. Sally returned the candlesticks to the mantle above the hearth and blew them out.

Audrey and Phebe said goodnight and went upstairs, leaving Sally and John a private moment. He walked with her to the hall stairs.

He wanted to reach out and take her hand but having sensed her negativity all evening realized he failed to deceive her. He had been too distracted.

For weeks, he and McGill planned a raid into Connecticut, and tonight the raid took place. For the first time, John sent subordinates to do a job and he worried. Would they carry out his orders to the letter? He sent them to Fairfield, Connecticut to capture two rebel generals, Gold Selleck Silliman, and Samuel Parsons. He'd faced them in battle twice. First at the Battle of Brooklyn and again at the Battle of White Plains.

John still didn't like to think about that day in Brooklyn when he feared he lost his friend, Andrew Bamford.

A sudden shake of his head drew Sally's sharp eyed attention. He offered a smile as he refocused his attention on the job at hand.

Parsons was the mastermind behind the Long Island raids, the last in Setauket in seventy-eight before John arrived.

John brushed his knuckles against hers, but Sally drew away. He scowled. Life was full of disappointments. High time she learned.

"Well, thank you for letting me teach you the card game. I hope you enjoyed yourselves." He made no attempt to hide the formal edge his anger gave to his words.

She blinked as though his comment required a moment for her brain to process, then she pulled her lips into a smile. "I did. It was fun. I had no idea Phebe would be so adept."

John chuckled. "She has talent. Some people can remember every card played and those still in the pack. I believe Phebe might have the skill. It comes naturally to some people."

Why this inane prattle? He wanted to say so much more, to tell Sally what was in his heart, but he couldn't. Not yet. Besides, her obvious suspicion created a chasm between them, which he needed to repair. "I'm sorry about this evening. You're quite right to think I was of two minds tonight."

Her eyebrows rose, but she didn't speak.

"You see, I entrusted Captain McGill with some tasks. He asked for the responsibility and," a self-deprecating shrug of one shoulder, "well, you know how I can be about letting others do things I believe I can do better myself."

Though he didn't intend it, Sally sputtered with a small laugh. "Yes, John," she said, relaxing her stiff posture. "I do."

The tension broke, he took her hand, and she squeezed back. "You won't be angry with me anymore?"

She laid her free hand atop their clasped ones. "I am sorry. I was jealous of your divided attention. I thought perhaps you were dreaming of another woman?"

She arched a brow.

Heat swept his face. Elizabeth, whom he had not thought of since the day he walked into the Townsend home sprang to his mind.

"I only think of you, Sally." Not a lie, though not a full truth either. He edged closer, and her breath touched his cheek. The heat intensified as he stared down at her. Her warm hand trembled under his palm, her eyes, now limpid pools of hazel, gleamed, and her cheeks glowed. He foresaw an uncomfortable night ahead but didn't care. He wanted to kiss her. He lowered his head toward hers but stopped at her sudden intake of breath.

John straightened as Sally retreated, pulling her hand loose. He let go, fascinated to see she didn't know what to do with it once set at liberty. She touched her hair, brushed her face, then slid her fingers down her bodice, coming to rest at her side, squeezing the fabric of her skirt.

"I need to go upstairs now," she said in a whisper.

"I know," he said, whispering back. Neither moved.

He drew close to her again. "Sally," John said, just to say her name.

"Sally!" Phebe called from the top of the stairs.

As he shot upright, Sally jerked away from him. "What!"

He stifled a smile at her sharp tone.

"Hurry up. Audrey wants to blow out the candles and go to sleep."

"I'm coming."

Without saying a word, he took her hand again and placed a lingering kiss on her knuckles to convey his longing. He gazed deep into her face, letting his eyes say what his tongue would not. His heart burst with joy. He released her hand before she detected his tremble from the tidal wave of emotion coursing through his veins. A red stain mottled on her cheeks, and the same longing shone in her eyes.

"Good night, Sally...dear."

He entered his bedroom and closed the door, leaning on the planks to catch his breath and stop his body from quivering. In this battle for hearts, Sally won, and John was happy.

John worked in his room, but with the door open, alert to McGill's arrival. As the morning wore on, however, he shifted in his seat and paced with worry over what might be keeping McGill. John paced. Had something happened to him? Was the raid unsuccessful?

Their plan was meticulous. What detail did he overlook? Yes, with every undertaking—and with the best-laid plans—things still go wrong. But they covered every contingency, so why wasn't McGill back yet? He took to pacing the hallway and occasionally opened the front door to peer down the street.

Before lunchtime, someone knocked at the front door. Sally moved into the hallway to answer, but John shoved her aside to yank the door open.

"You're late!"

Captain McGill whipped his hat off his head and saluted with sharp movements, snapping his heels together and straightening to his full height. "Yes, sir, I apologize, sir," McGill said.

Four of his men appeared, guarding two others who were barely dressed, disheveled, and bloody with their hands tied before them. "We had some problems with them on the way back, Colonel, which is why we're so behind schedule. Again, sir, the fault is mine, of course."

John drew the door open. "Bring them inside."

As they passed, Captain McGill nodded to Sally, who stared dumbfounded. "Good morning, Miss Townsend."

As the two captured men passed into the hallway, their faces darkened. John's men shoved the two from behind, and they stumbled into the sitting room.

John dismissed her. "Sally, don't you have chores to do? This is not your concern."

He stopped in front of the two men. Their swollen faces and blackened eyes spoke of strong resistance. Dried blood left a streak from the left side of the older man's broken nose.

This older man tilted his head back and studied John with the same arrogance John offered him. As if in response to John's silent challenge, he squared his shoulders and widened his stance.

"Well, well, well," John said, slipping his hands behind his back and rocking up on the balls of his feet. "How many men received injuries?"

"None, sir. We all returned unharmed."

John waved a hand at their prisoners. "Who are they?"

McGill pointed to the older gentleman. "This man is General Gold Selleck Silliman, sir, and the younger his son."

The young man inhaled and made to spit at John, but the older man knocked his shoulder into his son's arm. When they made eye contact, General Silliman shook his head, inclining his chin at John, or so John thought until the younger man's gaze went past his shoulder and he swallowed.

Sally stood inside the door, watching. John glowered. "I thought I told you this is none of your business?"

As the men had done, Sally straightened and lifted her chin. "This is my father's house and what happens in it is his business. Since he is not available to be a witness, I shall be one for him."

She marched over to a chair and sat.

John flipped a hand toward her and, with a shake of his head, dismissed her. If she wanted to be a witness, well, fine. That was to his advantage.

"Where is Mr. Parsons?"

McGill shifted his feet. "Well, sir, once we beached our boats, we decided not to risk a raid on Mr. Parsons, as we knew we could capture Mr. Silliman. One of our men used to work as a carpenter for Silliman and was familiar with his house and grounds. We thought it a better use of our resources." McGill's voice faltered as though fearing he had done wrong.

"Yes, and it is sure that man and his family will pay for his treachery," Silliman growled.

John would have berated him, but Sally's presence changed his mind. Besides, half a loaf was better than none. He bowed to McGill. "Well done, Captain."

McGill exhaled. "Thank you, sir."

Hands behind his back, John sauntered over to Silliman, as if to suggest he was unarmed and challenging the man to fight. "How do you feel, Mr. Silliman, to be captured by the finest men in the King's Army? One Queen's Ranger is worth ten of your men. My men would never be captured so ignominiously. In their beds. Asleep."

"John," Sally said in a soft voice behind him, her tone disapproving.

"Be quiet!" He spun around. "You wanted to be a witness, be

a silent witness."

She shrank in her chair, and her face stiffened as she glowered her distaste for this business. Why didn't he force her from the room?

He turned his back on her and her sanctimonious disapproval. "Who has been giving you information on Long Island's defenses?"

Neither man answered.

John moved so close to Silliman, that he could feel the man's warm breath on his cheek. "Who helped you in your raids? I want names."

Again, the two men remained silent. Sally's presence forced John to curb his urge to violence. Instead, he relaxed and stepped away as though he gave up on getting information from them. He sneered. "Take this" he waved a negligent hand toward his captives "so-called general and his son to Manhattan and deliver him to Provost Marshall William Cunningham and no one else. Let them become acquainted with Wallabout Bay."

"John! No!"

Sally jumped from her chair and tried to grab his sleeve, but he jerked away.

"I told you, this is men's business, Sally. You should listen to me." Changing his tone to one of speaking to a small child or to an adult with a limited capacity to understand, he sneered. "Why don't you find something to do? I'm sure your mother needs help in the kitchen."

Sally clenched her fists at her side, and her jaw worked as though she wanted to speak but couldn't force the words out. She studied the men, hands bound, but still standing tall and proud. Her face softened.

"Sally," he said, hoping to warn her off.

She rubbed her arms, then hugged them around herself. "You will answer to God for your actions, John. I hope it's worth it."

John recoiled as though struck. He didn't expect her words and decided female squeamishness, not sympathy motivated her. He relaxed; confident her anger would fade soon enough.

29

"Sally," Mother said, stirring the coals before adding more fuel to the small flames. "Where have you been?"

She couldn't answer. Hot blood thrummed in her body and pulsed in her ears.

At the worktable, Patty skewered a chicken on the roasting spit. "There's work aplenty in here if you're of a mind," she said fitting the spit into the roasting pan before reaching back to wind up the key.

Captain McGill arrived with two men he took captive in a raid last night," Sally said, helping to lift the spit and carry it to the open hearth.

Patty released the key, and the mechanism whirred as the belt spun the chicken.

"He is sending them to Wallabout Bay," she said, unable to hide her distress. "I tried to intervene, but John grew angry and exiled me."

Mother opened the oven to check her pies. "Of course, he did. I don't blame him."

Sally whipped around, astonished. "Mother!"

Patty jammed her hands on her bony hips. "She's right."

Sally's mouth dropped open. "I don't understand either of you. How could you say such a thing? Do you have any idea what those prison ships are like?"

Mother snapped. "Of course, we do. Do you think I forgot your father was almost imprisoned in one of those death traps?" Rubbing her temples, she closed her eyes and shuddered.

"I simply meant you must never contradict a man in public and absolutely never in front of his inferiors. Nothing will anger him more than injuring his pride. Speak to him in private later when you can get your complete say and try to make him understand your point of view."

Mother was right. The few times she discussed an issue with him in private, he listened with respect and once or twice, took her advice. While every time she took him to task in public, he lashed out and got back at her. She eyed the door as if expecting John to walk in. "But if I wait for an opportune moment, General Silliman and his son will be on a prison ship."

"Some things can't be helped, but you can advocate for them later and perhaps encourage him to release them."

Mother crossed the room and rested her hands on Sally's waist, lowering her voice. "If you are sympathetic to the cause, don't give yourself away."

Tears heating her eyes, Sally braced her forehead against her mother's.

"When John decides on a course of action, it's as well as completed," she said.

"Then General Silliman and his son's fate are in God's hands, as they always were." Mother gave Sally's waist a squeeze, then moved to the plank table to start cutting carrots. "Now, come and help us fix dinner."

While Sally mended, her conversation with Mother and Patty filled her mind and she had to concede they were right. The first time she tried to publicly express her point of view John made clear she was not to question his military decisions. But each time they discussed her concerns in private he listened with respect. She'd handled the situation with Mr. Silliman and his son badly. When she found a private moment, she would apologize and then, perhaps, he would listen to her concerns.

As she worked on a basket of mending, Father bent over his ledgers at a table near the front windows. His task required less and less of his time these days. He had nothing to sell. John confiscated most of Father's supplies for the Army.

Nowadays, Father's ships sailed no further than the wharf in Manhattan right in front of his store where Robert took the supplies off and sold them. Each week he returned home with a pouch full of money, keeping the family alive.

She and her father worked in companionable silence because John was in his room, with the door ajar. When she finished mending one of Phebe's petticoats, she dropped the garment into the completed basket with a heavy sigh.

"What troubles you, Poppet?"

"Nothing. I wish Phebe would do her own mending on occasion."

Father chuckled. "She's in the kitchen learning new cooking skills. I recall you did the same at her age."

"True."

A fist pounded on the front door. She and Father exchanged surprised glances before he went to answer.

"I need to see Colonel Simcoe!"

"Who are you?" Father's concerned voice drifted back.

Sally stood up when John opened his door and walked through the sitting room to the hallway.

"I'm Colonel Simcoe," John said, gesturing toward the sitting room. "Please come in, sir."

The man's hair stuck up every which way in keeping with his most unkempt appearance, while beneath his dark blue peacoat and dark breeches, his dirty white hose needed mending.

"Your name?" John's commanding tone settled the man.

"John Wolsey, sir," The man said, knuckling his forehead. "At your service. I was, until a few days ago, a sailor on a merchant vessel. We got captured by the Limeys...I mean the British Navy, sir."

"And they released you?"

"No, sir. I'm still a captive, but I have information and was told to come to you. An officer with General Clinton sent me."

John grinned. "And what was this officer's name?"

Wolsey shrugged. "I don't recall, sir. Andrews, Anderson,

something like that."

"Andre?" Sally asked.

Wolsey pointed at Simcoe. "That's the one. Andre."

John's gaze flicked to Sally and held a warning.

Squaring her shoulders, she moved around Mr. Wolsey to stand with her father.

He put his arm around her shoulder and, leaning down, said in a whisper, "say nothing. Show no emotion. Whatever you hear do not react."

"Well, Mr. Wolsey." John crossed his arms and widened his stance, imperious, "I'm waiting."

"Yes, sir. Well, sir, we was taken captive off Cape Hatteras where I was interrogated for a long time. We was brung back to Long Island." His eyes lit. "I'm from Setauket, ya see. I got to visit my family when I returned."

He sobered at John's annoyed scowl. "Anyway, me cousin told me, his friend's brother told him that Abraham Woodhull of Setauket is the mastermind of a spy ring here in Long Island."

Sally bit her lip to avoid the sudden intake of breath. She tipped her head enough to see Father standing stone-faced. She worked to arrange her face into a neutral position, and knowing her eyes often betrayed her thoughts, she cast her gaze to the floor.

They were acquainted with the Woodhull's. Genuine terror for young Mr. Woodhull clenched her stomach, wrenched, and twisted at it. Should they warn him?

"How sure are you this information is correct?" Father's question brought her out of her panicked reverie.

Wolsey squinted at him. "I beg yer pardon?"

"You said you heard this information fourth-hand at best and it doesn't sound as if from reputable people, so how positive are you that what you heard is correct? To accuse someone of espionage is a dangerous accusation, Mr. Wolsey. You may end a man's life, so is your information correct?"

Wolsey spread his hands. "Me cousin told me. He heard from—reputable people."

"Thank you, Mr. Wolsey," John said, clapping his hands, then reached for the man's elbow to guide him from the house. "I appreciate your coming here today."

"Well, do I get my freedom or not?" Wolsey's whiny tone

grated.

"We shall see what your information brings," John said, walking him to the door. "Good day, to you, sir."

"Father," Sally said with a hiss.

"Say nothing. Do nothing," Father said, clamping his lips tight together when John slammed the front door.

He strode back to his room, muttering to himself.

Father stopped him. "Colonel Simcoe."

Hands behind his back, which Sally learned from experience meant nothing Father said would make a difference, John cocked his head. "Yes, sir."

Sally, glided to her chair. Weak-kneed, she sank into the cushion.

"I meant what I said," he said, placing a paternal hand on John's shoulder. "This kind of accusation could kill a man. Please, I implore you to be sure your facts are correct before you proceed."

John appeared to consider what Father said. He bowed his head in acquiescence. "Thank you for your concern, Mr. Townsend. I shall take your suggestion under advisement."

He smiled at Sally. "Now if you'll both excuse me, I have work to do."

Father removed his hand. "Of course, you do," he said, returning to his table and ledger book. "We shall not disturb you."

Sally's head swiveled back and forth between them. A small squeak issued from her. She scooped up her mending and ran upstairs.

Robert was a friend of Abraham Woodhull and now lived in his sister's boarding house in Manhattan. He needed to know about Mr. Wolsey's accusations.

Before daylight, Saturday morning, John and his men prepared to leave for Setauket. Only the Hussars were going and were mounting up when Sally rushed outside to find out what was going on.

John saw her and met her halfway down the walk hoping to intercept her.

"What's happening, John? Are you called to the war?"

She was a vision. It was clear the noise awakened her since she still looked sleepy with a warm quilt around her shoulders, hiding her nightclothes. Her red hair fell in disheveled wisps from her nightcap, and he had to squelch a shot of desire.

"Nothing to worry your lovely head about, Sally dear. Go back inside before you catch your death," he said, trying to edge her toward the front door, but she wouldn't budge and gazed past his arm.

"You're going somewhere," she said, tightening the quilt about her shoulders. "How long will you be gone?"

"Just for the day. I'm taking my men on a training exercise."

"The men are ready when you are, Colonel," a young lieutenant said, stopping his horse at the gate.

The soldier's timing was unfortunate, and he prayed Sally would let the moment pass without adding to his troubles. John didn't dare take his eyes off her and she held his gaze with equal intensity.

"Thank you, Lieutenant," he said over his shoulder.

She disengaged first. "Where are you going, Lieutenant?"

"Setauket, Madam."

John could have cheerfully shot him.

Her whispered plea twisted his gut. "John, no!"

He clenched his jaw and grasped her quilt-shrouded shoulders. "Sally, go in the house this instant, and don't make a scene in front of my men. Go inside. We will not discuss this now. I must leave."

"But the Woodhull's are upstanding people, loyal to the King. Don't do this! Did you verify your information as Father asked?"

His hands squeezed her shoulders tighter, and a quick flash of pain darkened her pupils. He jerked her once making her teeth click. She might stop trying to make a fool of him in front of his men. "Do. Not. Argue. With me."

He turned her around and pushed her toward the house. "Go inside and dress. You're making a spectacle of yourself, prancing around out here half dressed in front of my men. For shame on you, Sally."

He shoved her into the house and slammed the front door before she might whirl and shout anything derogatory. He stomped down the walk and mounted his horse.

The front door creaked open again, but he refused to peek. "Queens Rangers," he said, as he mounted Salem. Raising his left arm, he held it straight out in front of him. "Tally ho!"

They rode the fifty miles east to Setauket, on the northern side of Long Island, facing Fairfield, Connecticut. The sun had long since risen when the Queen's Rangers arrived, and after an inquiry or two, John led his men to Judge Richard Woodhull's yard.

A middle-aged servant woman answered his knocking at the door. "Yes?" Somehow, she dragged the word out so slowly that she sounded almost bored.

John straightened to his full height and looked down his nose at her. "My name is Lieutenant Colonel John Graves Simcoe of His Majesty's Queens Rangers, and I'm here to arrest Abraham Woodhull on the charge of espionage. Now, kindly step aside so I may be about my duties."

When John took a step forward, the woman didn't move. He halted.

"My name is Abigail, and Mr. Abraham ain't here," she said and started to close the door, but he put up a hand and stopped the door from swinging closed. The flare of surprise in her dark eyes suggested she was lying. He pushed the door open and forced his way into the house, his men following.

Abigail shouted. "Just a minute! You can't come barging in here."

"I can and I will. I'm on the King's business."

"Abigail!"

Dressed all in black, except for a white shirt and white hose, an older man stormed into the foyer. "What's the meaning of this, sir?"

John, one hand on the hilt of his ceremonial sword, demanded. "Who are you?"

"Judge, these men are looking for Mr. Abraham. They say they're here to arrest him for some such, I don't know," she said, waving a disgusted hand, her lip curling.

The judge turned toward his servant. "Thank you, Abi, I'll handle this."

She bowed her head and took herself to the back of the house.

"You have your orders," John said. "Search the house!"

"Hold up!" Woodhull tried to grab a soldier or two as they passed by, but they shook him off. One soldier pushed the Judge aside and the man wobbled before righting himself, bracing a hand on the wall while he regained his feet. John smirked. This was what disloyalty to the king brought.

"My son isn't here," the judge said, turning this way and

that, hands out as if he could stop the soldiers from entering the rooms. "He had errands in New York City and left yesterday. He's not here."

John fisted his hands. "Your son is a spy. Spies are hanged, which is fitting for the scum of the earth that they are."

Judge Woodhull stood agog. Then he burst out laughing, a harsh wheezy sound. "My son? Have...you met...my son?" Woodhull asked, composing himself.

He coughed once. "My dear, Colonel. My son is a bright young man, but espionage takes bravery. And—trust me—he lacks bravery. He's the last man alive who would ever involve himself in anything dangerous. He doesn't even carry a rifle with him when he's out working the fields. He doesn't like to shoot things."

Woodhull's derision for his son must be a ruse, covering for him, as any father would, to protect a loved one from such an ignominious fate.

Deeper into the house, Abigail screamed, and something crashed. In the library off the hallway, books began to splat and thump onto the floor. Pottery and dishes smashed.

Judge Woodhull didn't move. "Do you think my grown son is hidden in a vase or a book?"

"Where is he?" He asked, grabbing the older man by the upper arms, much as he had Sally, and shook him. "Where is your son?" He kept his patience on a short leash today.

"I told you," Woodhull said, raising his arms between them, and with an outward motion, pushed John's hands off his shoulders. "And I refuse to say anymore."

John didn't expect such strength from an old man and without thinking, he punched him in the nose.

When the judge fell to the floor with a cry of pain, John grabbed him by the shirtfront, and hauled him to his feet, pulling the man's hands away from his face. They came away from his crooked nose bloody. He shoved the old man to a subordinate. "Interrogate him. Thoroughly."

"Yes, sir," the officer said, grinning. He waved over another man, and they dragged Woodhull into a room and closed the door.

Grunts and cries of pain emanated from the other side before John searched the house for himself. After entering yet another empty room, he fisted a hand and punched the gold-flocked wallpaper. He refused to come up empty-handed, but after a thorough two-hour search, they returned to Oyster Bay without Abraham Woodhull.

30

From the kitchen window, Sally spied John stalk across the yard from the barn. Over his shoulder, he barked something at his man, Israel, whose face darkened, but he did as bid. Her heart thudded. He didn't appear happy, which could only mean his mission was unsuccessful.

Wiping her hands on her apron she went to the kitchen door. At his approach, she opened the door.

He stalked past without acknowledgment or thanks.

She pushed the door closed. "What happened?"

"Mr. Woodhull was not at home. We missed him by one day."

"Oh," Sally said, returning to the table and picking up a knife, began slicing vegetables before putting it back down. She bit back a caustic suggestion that he might have saved himself a great deal of trouble if he'd verified his information first.

"Would you like me to make you some tea?" She asked.

John stopped at the hall door. He eyed her before nodding once, and though he didn't smile, his face relaxed some. "Thank you. That would be wonderful. Would you care to join me?"

"Of course. I'll meet you in the sitting room."

As Sally laid out the tea, John entered dressed in a less formal uniform. He settled himself in a chair near the west window and she handed him his cup of Bohea with light milk and sugar. Closing his eyes, he savored the smoky wood aroma.

Sally picked up her cup of Earl Grey and seated herself across from him. "I'm sorry your mission didn't go well."

He opened his eyes and studied her, but she was certain she kept any form of judgment from her voice.

"Thank you," he said before sipping his tea. He set his cup on the table next to his chair, folded his hands in his lap, and faced her. "What do you know of the Woodhull's?"

Sally's heart thumped hard in her chest. She lifted her cup to her lips and sipped, giving herself time to form her thoughts.

"Well, I'm acquainted with Judge Woodhull a bit. Father used to be the town clerk here in Oyster Bay and if any dispute arose, he relied on the judge to help him settle matters, but he hasn't been town clerk since the beginning of the war." She didn't add Father's Whig leanings were the cause of his dismissal.

"I remember the judge was very formal, but always kind to me and my sisters."

As they talked, the door knocker rattled. Liss answered and led a courier into the sitting room. He handed over a packet to John, saluted, and left the house.

Taking out the missives, he sorted through them. His face lit as he lifted one small note. "It's from Andre. Do you mind if I open this one right now?"

"Not at all," Sally set her cup down. "Will he come to visit again soon?"

His eyes skimmed across the lines. His brow quirked once then his eyebrows went up.

Fascinated, Sally wondered at the panoply crossing his features. He refolded the note and put it back in the case, frowning.

"Sadly, no."

"He's unable to visit?" she asked in a genuinely disappointed tone. It wasn't hard. She enjoyed Andre's company.

John shook his head. "Not for some time. What about Benjamin Floyd?"

The sudden shift caught her off guard. "Benjamin Floyd? I know of the family. Why?"

A negligent shrug of one shoulder. "Andre writes to say a

Colonel Benjamin Floyd appeared before him yesterday and vouched for Abraham Woodhull. I find it curious Colonel Floyd, a loyalist, would find out so fast Mr. Woodhull needed to be vouched for. Where is the information coming from?"

Sally sipped her now tepid tea. "I don't."

At John's questioning gaze she set her cup down. "Consider," she said, folding her hands in her lap. "The Floyds, Mr. Wolsey, and the Woodhull's all hail from Setauket. Like Oyster Bay, everyone knows everyone, so word gets around. In fact," she said, lifting a finger as a new thought came to her. "Benjamin's cousin, Ruth Floyd, married Abraham's cousin, Nathaniel Woodhull."

She stopped there, choosing not to share that Ruth Woodhull, widowed by the Battle of Brooklyn, was as fervent a Whig as her cousin Benjamin and his family were militant loyalists.

But why had Ben Floyd chosen to defend the so-called traitorous side of the family? Perhaps because, despite their differences, they were a tight-knit clan.

Sally picked up her teacup and sipped. Whoever supplied him information, John acted on it swiftly, which led her to wonder. Did any of her information find its way to General Washington?

Spinning the last of the previous year's flax into linen thread, Sally's mind wandered, and for the fourth time, the line snapped, jolting her from her reverie.

"Ugh!" She stopped the wheel, snatched the hook, and jammed it into the feeding line, attempting to pull the thread back. She needed several tries and was about to throw the hook across the room when she managed to catch the line and draw it back. Muttering under her breath, she tied off the ends.

"Patience, Sally. If you snap the line too many times, we will have to dispose of the entire roll, and you'll have to spin more. If you cannot manage the work, I'll have Audrey do the spinning and you may return to skeining."

Mother walked her giant spinning wheel, making more yarn from the last of the previous winter's wool. There was urgency to their tasks. Next week was sheep shearing. This year's flax seed was already in the ground.

Sally dropped her hands into her lap and lowered her head.

Eyes burning with unshed tears, she covered them with her palm.

Mother's wheel stopped whirring and a soft hand dropped on her shoulder. Sally raised her face and sniffed, wiping her eyes. "I'm sorry."

"What troubles you?"

So many things. Where did she start? She shook her head and released another sob. Mother knelt beside her and gathered her into her arms. Sally collapsed against her and wept. After a while, Mother's lavender-scented dress calmed her, and Sally sat up wiping her face.

Mother smiled and brushed back strands of Sally's hair slipping from her mobcap. "Now would you care to tell me what that was about?"

Sniffing back her sobs, she probed her mother's concerned faced. "How did you decide Father was the man for you?"

"Oh." Mother's gaze went to the floor. "Well, let me see." She took Sally by the hand and led her to the sofa. They sat down facing each other. Mother clasped her hand and called for a servant.

A moment later, Liss appeared in the doorway. "Would you be kind enough to make us some tea?"

"Yes, ma'am," Liss said, and with a bob, disappeared.

"Your father courted me gently. He came every day to visit my brother," as Mother spoke, a soft smile tipped her lips. "I needed several months to realize he was coming to visit me. When he did make his intentions clear he courted me as any young gentleman would and followed all the correct customs, always treating me with the utmost respect and kindness."

Liss returned. Mother sat back as their servant set the tray on the table without one rattle of a dish. "Thank you, my dear," Mother said, dismissing her.

Liss nodded once and disappeared again as Mother poured them each a cup of tea.

Sally took hers and sipped. The hot liquid comforted. "John is not gentle. I think he likes me. I'm sure he does, but he's not gentle. I try to overlook those things, but after what he did to Judge Woodhull, I..." she broke off and stared over Mother's shoulder.

"He is rather inelegant," Mother said, "but I agree with your assessment. He cares for you very much."

Sally set her cup on the table lest the trembling cause her to spill and faced her mother with the agony of an answer she feared making her heart pound hard. "Do I have to accept him?" Sally asked, her voice sounding small and scared.

Mother's head snapped back brows furrowed. "Of course not." She took Sally's hand in both of her own. "The man makes his affections clear. He brings small gifts and trinkets. That's expected. He may pay court to the lady, but in the end, it is always the lady's choice," Mother said, squeezing her hand. "Always." An emphatic nod pressed her point.

Sally chewed her lip as she studied the small flowers in her skirt. After a moment, she raised her gaze to her mother. "I like him. At least, I like the attention he's given me. He's a man who can be kind when he wants to be, but then he'll do something and I think, perhaps not. I don't know how to express myself, but I believe he is of two personalities, and I cannot figure out which is the correct one."

Mother sipped her tea. "And what have you decided?"

Sally retrieved her cup but didn't drink. Instead, she gazed at the small fissures in the porcelain zigzagging through the cup. When she raised her eyes to her mother, she realized the resignation washing through her showed in her countenance. "I believe the kind man is who he wants me to see, but the real John is ruthless and vindictive."

Mother's shoulders relaxed and for the first time, a smile tugged at her lips. She raised her cup, and a sigh escaped her. "I'm glad to hear that. I feared you might accept him."

Surprise forced a small laugh from Sally. "You don't like him?"

Mother hedged. "He's a fine soldier, but I am glad he won't be my son-in-law." Mother set her cup down and folded her hands in her lap. "Are you going to be honest with him?"

Should she tell Mother her reasons for cultivating her friendship in the first place? What would she say? Father was aware of her activities and didn't prevent her, but would Mother take the same attitude? "I don't think I should."

Mother arched a brow. "Why not?"

"I fear if I disabuse him of any hope in a deeper relationship, he might do something to retaliate against Father. I would never forgive myself if harm came to him at my hands."

"Your father can take care of himself."

"I know, but still..." She broke off not daring to tell the truth.

Mother adjusted her skirts around her legs. "Fine." She set her saucer on the table with a clack. "I hope you realize what you're doing."

So do I. Sally grasped her mother's hand. "I think I can work with more patience."

She rose and returned to the flax wheel while Mother picked up the tray and took it back to the kitchen.

John and his men were all in a lighthearted mood. The warm sun, the scent of fresh earth, and the prospect of a new campaign season propelled them forward. He shared their excitement about being back in the field again, but he had to admit he would miss Sally. As he worked his men, he kept one eye on the road, waiting for her to return from her mission.

When she rounded the corner from Cove Road, he strode to the edge of the parade ground to await her approach. Standing with his hands on his hips as the horse plodded along, his heart swelled when she waved and urged her horse forward.

She stopped in front of him. "Good morning, Colonel Simcoe. A fine day, yes?"

John laughed at her playful tone and reached up to help her from the saddle. "Must you return right away, or can you stop and visit?"

She dropped her hands on his shoulders as he lifted her down.

"I can stay but not for long. Mother is doing spring cleaning today and I must return."

His strong hands encircled her tiny waist. "I shan't keep you long." He set her on her feet, and they stopped at the edge of the field.

Sally pointed to a half dozen empty wagons lined up, ready for the harness. "Are you preparing to go?"

"Yes," John said, shading his eyes and looking in the same direction. "I appropriated those yesterday. I don't have orders to leave yet, but summer is coming."

Out of the corner of his eye, he saw her glance in his direction. *Ask her!* A surge of urgency flowed through his veins, and he shifted his feet. "Will you be sad when we leave, Sally?"

"Of course."

She sounded surprised by the question, and he studied her more closely.

"What I mean is, will you be sorry when I leave?"

Turning toward her when she didn't answer right away, he found her staring at his men, her lips twitching. For a crazy second, he had the impression she was counting. Then, her bottom lip tucked itself into her teeth, an endearing habit of hers, and she smiled her beautiful smile.

"I'm unsure how to answer, John, without perhaps giving the wrong impression." She laid a hand on his warm woolen sleeve. "Of course, I'll miss you, but how do I interpret the question? As a friend? Or as something more?"

John took her hands in his. "I hope as something more."

His stomach clenched and his heart pounded hard. He couldn't meet her eyes. What if she rejected him? What would he do?

"Sally," he said, forcing himself to meet her eye. "When I return to the house tonight, may I ask your father's permission to receive your hand in marriage?"

As soon as the words were out of his mouth, he felt a small tug on his palm. He almost released her hands but didn't. If he refused to let go, she might say yes.

Her hazel eyes swam with tears. He released her. "My dear, why the tears? Might I assume them to be tears of joy?"

She shook her head and his heart plummeted to the ground as he visualized her trampling it into the mud.

"I'm sorry, John. I must say no."

He had to lean close to catch her words.

She sniffed. "I admit, I suspected for a while this question was coming. Don't misunderstand, I recognize the honor of being Mrs. John Simcoe, but I cannot. Not while the war rages. I do not wish to become a war widow."

He started to defend himself, but she held up a hand and he stopped.

"I understand you may survive, but you may not, and what would happen to me if you did not? When the war is over, and if you still live, I give you delirious permission to ask Father, but not yet."

Though crushed, John took heart. Not an emphatic no, she forced him to respect her position. She understood what happens to a young widow. His mother, widowed with two small boys, having to live off the charity of her father-in-law, softened the blow and he gained admiration for her courage to refuse.

He nodded once. "I understand, my dear," he said, smiling to show he did not harbor ill will. "And I respect your answer. I must work harder to end the war, mustn't I?"

She chuckled. "You must at that. Now, if you'll excuse me, I have to go back home before Mother scolds me."

He walked her back to Farmer Girl and helped her into the saddle. "Thank you, Sally, for being frank with me."

"Thank you, John, for flattering me enough to consider me worthy of a man such as you."

Don't turn around, he'll be watching. Sally rode home, holding Farmer Girl to a steady walk, but her heart wanted her to prod the mare into a ground-eating gallop. She hoped he wouldn't propose. She felt—not better—but more confident after her talk with Mother. Knowing she didn't have to accept him gave her strength.

For months, she tried to tell herself she loved John, but the truth was hard to accept. She didn't love him. He angered her too often, did things she didn't like, and didn't care for the way he justified his actions. She only told him he could ask Father if he came back so he would come back, and she could continue to press him for information.

The house came into view and now she did urge Farmer Girl into a quicker pace. Mother would be annoyed if she stayed away too long. Spring cleaning arrived, and she needed every hand.

As Sally rode into the yard, she spied Liss leaning against the side of the barn, laughing and talking with someone, but when she spied Sally, her smile disappeared, she pushed off the building, and headed back to the house.

Sally's brow creased. Isaac came out to help her out of the saddle. His eyes darted to Liss, now disappearing inside. He made a tsking sound as he reached for Sally.

"What was she doing?" Sally asked bracing her hands on

Isaac's shoulders as he lifted her down.

"Not my place to say, miss," Isaac said managing to sound pompous and annoyed at the same time.

"Make it your place," Sally said. She grabbed Farmer Girl's bridle so he couldn't lead the horse away.

Isaac studied the tops of his worn leather shoes. "Well, miss, the colonel's man has been sparking her."

He raised his gaze to her for a brief second before tugging the horse's bridle from her hand. "Now if you'll excuse me, miss, I got to bring the horse in the stable."

When Isaac led her horse away, Sally walked to the corner to discover where he went. After traversing the length of the barn, she didn't find him. Throwing up her hands in defeat, she headed to the house. Tonight, when things were quiet, she would confront Liss.

While Sally helped clean up from dinner, John and Israel disappeared behind his bedroom door. She brought dishes to the washtub where Liss scrubbed. Sally picked up a towel and began to dry. She said nothing while Phebe swept the floor, but when she finished and left, Sally laid a dish aside and picked up another.

"What were you doing this afternoon, Liss?" Sally asked slowing her movements as the girl's face darkened and her hands stopped moving in the tub.

"Do I got to answer?"

Sally set the dish down and picked up another. "I can't compel you to answer."

At the girl's questioning glance, she relaxed some. "No," she said. "You don't have to answer, but I desire one."

Liss returned to washing dishes, dropping a cup into a barrel of clean water, and setting it down for Sally to dry. "You gonna tell your ma if'n I do answer?"

"I suppose that would depend on what you tell me."

Liss considered her response for so long, Sally thought she might refuse.

"He loves me. And I love him."

"Oh," Sally said. She picked up the cup to dry with absent motions. "How do you know?"

"What?"

"How sure are you that you love him? And how sure are you

247

that he loves you?"

Liss's mouth worked, and a shoulder jerked up and down. "I just...I just do."

Sally inhaled through her nose. Not the answer she expected. "No, I won't tell Mother, but you must promise me not to let your romance interfere with your work or Mother will find out on her own."

"The colonel caught us together once," Liss said swiping the cutlery and dipping it into clean water. She handed them to Sally.

Sally gawked. He never told her. "How long has he had this knowledge?"

Liss shrugged again. "A few months. He said the same thing. "'Don't get caught.'"

"Excellent advice."

Fighting a surge of annoyance, Sally put the cutlery away. One more sign of his dishonesty with her. Should she confront him? To what point? She refused his suit so what John Simcoe did or said no longer concerned her. Besides, Israel would be leaving with him soon and perhaps the whole thing would end.

31

The Queen's Rangers left in the middle of May. To immense fanfare, they rode out of town and Sally and her family stood in the front yard, waving goodbye, and wishing the men well.

Now would be a perfect opportunity for the Americans to raid the island while the army was elsewhere.

Before John turned the corner onto Jericho Road, he turned back one more time.

Sally waved her hand over her head. "Hurry back!"

John waved back before he disappeared behind Cooper's home. She kept her gaze on them until the last man disappeared, and as she returned to the house, emptiness and loneliness pulled at her, like chains around her ankles, making her steps drag. She would miss John and the prospect of a long and uneventful summer filled her with dread.

Upstairs in her room, she sat at her desk, grabbed a quill and a sheet of parchment, and began a letter.

Dearest, brother—

Our house guests left town today, and I fear our other friends missed a chance to visit. I would be sad indeed if they could not come, for I believe a more propitious time may not be found. We do wish to see our dear friends again, soon.

She tapped the feather against her cheek, mindful of structuring her sentences to be as inane as possible, restraining the urge to ask when and if the Americans were going to seize upon her information and why they did not retaliate against the raid of Judge Woodhull.

John's attack on the old man so infuriated her, she wanted justice done. Dipping her quill, she poised her hand over the page.

Send us some signal alerting us if our friends can come to visit. We sent every means of invitation, but so far, they failed to respond. I fear we may have offended in some way. Love to you, dear brother, and to our friends.
Your loving sister,
Sally.

When she finished, she sanded the sheet, folded her letter in threes, and sealed it with wax. She tapped the packet into the palm of her hand. What would John's unworthy foes make of that?

The summer passed in slow motion for Sally and one thing became certain in her mind. Though she had no wish to become Mrs. John Graves Simcoe, she missed John's presence. The rooms felt bigger, emptier, and her days lonelier without him to wait for and to speak with in the evenings.

She no longer corresponded with Robert as there was nothing to tell him. When the Rangers left in May, Sally made daily rides to Daniel's. He told her the Queen's Rangers were in Westchester. But as May moved to June he had no more information and she stopped visiting. Still every day she cast her gaze toward the signal beacons, looking for some evidence the Americans took advantage of the Rangers' absence, but alas they remained untouched.

In the second week of July, Sally made a delivery for Susannah.

"Look what the cat brought home." Susannah teased as Sally

entered the house, arms loaded with her supplies. "Daniel isn't home so I fear he can't tell you anything of Colonel Simcoe's whereabouts."

Sally smiled as heat having nothing to do with the summer air warmed her cheeks. "That's all right," she said handing Susannah her packages. "I brought the supplies Father said you needed."

After dropping the items in the kitchen, Susannah extended her arm toward a chair in the front room. "Have a cool drink. Can you visit?"

"Where is Daniel?" She asked, taking a small bite of her biscuit.

Susannah regarded her as she poured herself cider. "He's on patrol."

Sally wanted to ask why the rebels failed to attack with the Rangers out of the area, but how to approach the topic? "Is that all he does?"

Susannah's steady gaze made Sally nervous. She shifted in her seat and gave a deprecatory shrug. "I only mean, I'm curious about what he does in the militia."

"They patrol the island and gather supplies for the army," Susannah said, her voice going a bit cold.

Sally studied her. "Are you alright?"

Susannah sipped her cider. "Fine." Her cup clocked on the table.

Sally laid a soft hand on her friend's arm. "I meant nothing untoward by my question," she said, rushing to assure her friend.

"Sally, may I speak freely?"

"Of course."

Susannah nodded, but several long seconds passed before she said anything. Taking a deep breath, she plunged in. "The reason Daniel doesn't tell you much is..." she scratched the side of her nose. "Well because we're not sure what we say doesn't end up in the enemy's hands."

Sally gasped. "You think I'm a spy?"

"No!" Susannah placed a hand on her arm for emphasis. "And neither does Daniel. But what if he tells you something that results in an action that could only have come from you? A slip of the tongue or an "'I-know-something-you-don't' type of situation.'"

Sally's hand shook as she gripped her cup. Never in her life did she suspect Susannah and Daniel distrusted her. She kept her gaze locked on the far wall, while she raised her cup to sip for something to do with her hands. Slowly, she lowered her cup. "I understand. We're Whigs and you and Daniel are Tories, and you think I would betray you, our friendship. For what? Extras supplies? Extra consideration? Is that who you think I am, Susannah? Do you really think me that shallow?" The sense of betrayal broke her heart, and she strove to hold back her tears of shame and hurt.

"I must go." Sally jumped to her feet and handed Susannah her cup. "Thank you for the cider."

"Sally, please don't go. That's not what I meant." Susannah jumped to her feet and tried to stop Sally from leaving.

She rounded on her, tears in her eyes. "You have no idea, Susannah, the difficulty of living in a house with a man you consider your enemy, having to be polite and kind and pretend feelings you don't feel until all of a sudden you do and then you're so confused you can't remember if you're supposed to like or dislike him. Guarding your tongue until you're mute because you you don't know what you can or cannot say. And when you're convinced, he's not so bad, he does something to one of your friends or countrymen and it's as if he's slapped you in the face."

Susannah stepped forward arms outstretched, but Sally raised her arms, stopping her. "You can't know what it's like, so don't tell me you can't trust me."

Turning, she stormed from the Youngs' home maybe for the last time.

Sally wanted to finish the harder chores before the building heat made such work difficult. As she dipped her scrub brush into the bucket, she let the water splash across the floor of John's room, using the puddles to soften the deeper grime. August dragged and she didn't know when John would return, but she wanted the room as clean as possible for when he did. Why, when she had no intention of becoming his wife, did she want to display her domestic skills?

Weeks had passed since her outburst at Susannah, and she thought about the incident with shame for her behavior but didn't know how to make amends. A straightforward apology was best, but Sally had been so hurt when Susannah revealed they didn't trust her, she couldn't find a way to an apology.

Was she not as circumspect as Robert would wish? Did she give herself away so easily? So many questions, but how was she to evaluate herself to discover the truth?

A breeze riffled the curtains at the open windows and the draft blew soft on Sally's cheek as she scrubbed.

Outside, Phebe shouted, but Sally paid no attention. Her mind filled with other worries.

Phebe shouted again and this time, Sally rose on her knees as she heard Phebe call hello, and... did she say...John?

A rush of excitement made her heart hammer. Throwing her brush into the bucket, Sally jumped to her feet. Lifting her skirts, she ran through the sitting room and out the front door, emerging in time to see John lead his men down the road toward the house.

Dust rose off the road to the height of the fetlocks and his uniform was dirty, his face dirt-streaked, but her heart soared at the sight of him. She jumped up and down giving in to the wave of happiness surging through her body, as she hailed him with frantic abandon.

He waved back and urged his mount to the gate. Isaac waited to retrieve Salem.

Gathering her linsey-woolsey work skirts in her hands, Sally bounced on her toes as he dismounted, stretched his back, and shook out his legs, one at a time, before walking through the gate Hiram held open for him.

"Welcome back, John," Phebe said, waving as she ran to greet him.

He took her hands in his. "Thank you, Miss Phebe. I am most happy to be back," he said as his gaze went over the top of Phebe's head and came to rest on Sally. After some perfunctory inanities, and questions about how she spent her summer, he moved around Phebe.

Sally's breath caught in her throat when he approached. His teeth gleamed white against his brown-stained face. He stopped before her, and her hands disappeared into his generous paws. His blue eyes roamed her face, as though he couldn't get enough of looking at her until a red stain arose beneath his tanned visage.

"Sally," he said, squeezing her hands and running a thumb

253

across the backs of her knuckles.

A sweet pang hit the pit of her belly, surprising her and causing heat to explode from her core and fly up to the roots of her hair.

"Welcome home, John," she said, squeezing the words from her emotion-clogged throat. She tugged her hands and half turning, indicated the front door. "You must be exhausted. Come indoors."

John dismissed his men and Israel darted around the corner of the house. Sally's heart sank when Liss darted after him. John assured her he spoke to his man. Oh well. Time enough to bring up the issue should another problem arise.

As they entered the house, Audrey, David, and her parents rushed to greet the returning warrior.

Mother laid a welcoming hand on John's sleeve. "I gave Liss and Patty instructions to lay out a bath for you, Colonel," Mother said. She'd never adopted the habit of calling him John.

Sally gasped. "A bath!"

She flapped her hands in an uncharacteristic show of confusion. "I was scrubbing the floor in your room. I'm not finished!"

Skirts flashing, she whirled and raced back to his room to gather up her things. The floor was half-washed, but now he was home, casual access to this room was once again forbidden.

She turned to leave and found him framed in the hallway door. Without thinking she bobbed a quick curtsy. "I can return tomorrow if you wish and finish the floor."

"Fine," he said smiling. He glanced around the room. "My but it gleams in here."

"Well, I calculated you must return sometime if you were to come back to Oyster Bay, and I wanted your room to be in immaculate condition when you did."

He chuckled as he once again surveyed the room. His steely-blue gaze came to rest upon her once again. "All shipshape and Bristol fashion."

Unsure of what he meant; Sally didn't respond. The bucket cut her fingers, and due to his absence, she was awkward in his presence.

"Well, if you'll excuse me, I'll go put these things away."

She started toward him, and he stepped out of her way.

As she passed, he leaned close and she thought he was going to speak to her, so she slowed, but he allowed her to pass so she kept moving, the only indication of her confusion was a small hitch in her step. Then, she left

32

John dressed and went to the kitchen for his breakfast and greeted the family as he seated himself.

Israel appeared at his elbow. "Suh, they's a captain at the door saying he got to speak with you. He's from Lloyd's Neck, suh, saying something about a raid there last night."

The room went silent, and John stared at Israel as though the man had grown two heads.

"A raid."

"Yessuh."

"At Lloyd's Neck."

"Yessuh," Israel said picking at the cuticles of his left index finger. "Fort Franklin, suh."

John was vaguely aware of the murmurs from the family, and he saw, as though detached, Sally and her father exchange a glance.

His mind was numb, embarrassment thrummed through him. What must these people think of him? A raid at Fort Franklin? The place was impregnable. Not possible.

With effort, he pulled himself together with a long deep breath. He would get none of the answers staring at his aide-de-camp.

John rose and went to the sitting room where Captain Diemar paced the room.

"What happened, Captain Diemar?" John said without greeting or fanfare.

Diemar rose and jerked a quick salute. "Well, sir. Last night Major Tallmadge and fifty dismounted dragoons, almost thirty infantrymen, and some fifty whaleboats left Shippan's Point in Connecticut. They crossed the Devil's Belt and landed on Lloyd's Neck where they fell on Fort Franklin, sir. They surprised the five hundred Tories there and destroyed the garrison. Some of the loyalists managed to run off into the woods, but they were captured and brought to Connecticut. Before they left, sir, they burned all of our watercraft so we couldn't launch a rescue."

"How many men did they lose, Captain?"

The captain cleared his throat and his expression said he prayed the floor would open and swallow him. "None sir."

John raised a brow. "None."

"None," Diemar confirmed then shifted his feet and glanced at John before sliding his gaze away, uncomfortable at what he had to say next.

"Major Tallmadge said he had a personal message for you, sir."

At this point, the poor captain began to squirm, and his expression said, "'keep in mind I'm only the messenger.'"

John crossed his arms and widened his stance. "What was the major's message?" John said, returning his gaze to the hapless messenger.

"He said to tell you that was retaliation for General Silliman and Judge Woodhull."

Standing in the hallway, out of sight but not out of hearing, Sally pressed her hands to her mouth, dumbfounded. A raid. The Americans conducted a raid at last. Her emotions warred between the thrill at the daring raid, and remorse for John.

From where she stood, she saw his face redden and he looked like a boy who had been publicly humiliated. Then his expression changed again to implacable anger.

He turned to Israel. "Go to the campground and retrieve Captains Saunders and McGill posthaste."

Israel nodded and bolted out the front door.

She entered the room." John, I'm so sorry. Are you alright?"

His face reddened and his shame and embarrassment flowed at her like a torrent. "Not now, Sally!"

His expression changed to implacable anger as he spun and strode to his room and Sally followed.

He snatched his chair back and slammed the legs onto the pine floor before dropping his heavy frame into the seat.

"John?"

Slamming his fist on the desk, he growled at her over his shoulder. "I said not now!"

She retreated as Israel returned with McGill and Saunders. They greeted Sally with somber nods, and she made herself busy setting up her spinning wheel close to the bedroom door to listen without being seen.

"Captain McGill, you will dictate this message to General Erskine for me," John said without greeting his men.

"To General Erskine. Sir."

Sally's heart went out to him. The mortification in his voice, as he related the details made her heart sick. At the end of the note, to her surprise, he took full responsibility for the failure and promised to do better in the future.

As her wheel spun a small smile crossed her lips. So, the Americans conducted a successful raid on Fort Franklin right under his nose. Unworthy foes indeed. She was dying to ask and never could: did her notes and drawings help?

33

To John's relief, the repercussions from the rebel raid on Fort Franklin were minimal, he believed, from his swift response. A few days after informing General Erskine of the incident, the general wrote back with words of regret, support, and sympathy.

General Erskine stated his opinion, that these things happened, and he would still love battalions of men like John.

Returning to the house early, he found Sally cleaning the hearth in the sitting room. A bucket of filthy water by her elbow, her hands in canvas work gloves, she wore her linsey-woolsey work dress as she scrubbed the stone hearth. As she greeted him, she used the back of her hand to push an errant stand of hair out of her face, leaving a streak of soot across her cheek.

"John," she said, with a smile as he entered, his cloak draped over his arm. "You're home early."

"I have work to do here, my dear," he said, enjoying the sound of the domestic chit-chat and wishing to make it a permanent fixture between them.

He waved a piece of parchment. "I received word from General Erskine to prepare the men for some action in the not-too-distant future."

"Oh? You're leaving us? But winter is coming."

Sally gestured toward the hearth she cleaned in preparation for winter use. "Where are you going? How long will you be gone?"

John chuckled. "Wonderful questions, dear Sally, but none for which I can give you answers. All I can say is Monsieur D'Estaing is due to arrive from the West Indies and we must prepare."

"Monsieur D'Estaing? Who is he pray tell?"

"The leader of the French fleet. We have word they are on their way to poke their noses into this terrible business and must be stopped."

Her raised eyebrow made him wonder if he'd said too much. John had been getting the feeling more and more that Sally understood far more than she let on, but then, he kept coming back to the same conclusion. She is a woman. What would or could she do about the things he told her?

He smiled at her as he moved to his bedroom, stopping at the door. "Pray may I have some tea sent to my room while I work?"

"Of course."

She stood and picked up the bucket before leaving the sitting room. "I'll go find Patty or Liss."

John made himself comfortable at his desk as he made lists of what he thought he might need. Israel appeared at his elbow, an ever-present, though silent, companion.

Once again, the sound of Sally's scrub brush scratching against the hearth made a reassuring backdrop for his work. The plunk of the brush in the bucket, the splash of water as she scrubbed again.

Liss entered with a tray of tea and biscuits which she set on the desk at John's elbow. When she made to pour, John flicked an absent-minded hand her way and she retreated.

He picked up a folded piece of parchment and held it out to Israel. "Send this to Captain McGill. Tell him we will need all the wagons and conveyances he can beg, borrow or steal."

"Yes, suh," Israel said, pocketing the note.

John poured himself some tea and sipped.

From the sitting room, Captain Saunders spoke to Sally.

"He's in his room," she said, and Saunders knocked lightly.

"Come," John said, sitting back.

"A message, Colonel. From Lord General Cornwallis, sir." Saunders held out the note.

John read the message aloud. "We are to rendezvous with Lt. Colonel Tarleton in Jamaica then proceed to Yellow Hook, thence to Staten Island."

John made a disgusted sound as he dropped the note on the desk. "I so dislike Staten Island."

Neither man responded and the only sound was the slow swish of Sally's brush on the hearthstones.

"Anyway, once there we are to join the earl's command along with the seventh, twenty-third, twenty-second, thirty-third, and fifty-seventh regiments."

"Excellent, sir," Saunders said. "When should we prepare to leave?"

John considered. "When we receive word to move out, Captain, and not a moment before."

On October nineteenth, the Queen's Rangers arrived on Staten Island. Though he despised the island, John was gratified by the cooler climate. Still, sickness prevailed and when he and his men arrived in Richmond to relieve a garrison struck with illness, he ordered their huts burned. Then had his men build new huts.

John waited for the meeting between Generals Clinton and Lord Cornwallis to begin. He had a plan he wanted to put into action, and he prayed they approved, but at this moment, his thoughts went to his old friend and aide-de-camp, Andrew Bamford. What became of the young, gifted officer? Was he still head of the Fortieth Foot? He should draft a note to Andrew asking about his health.

"Colonel Simcoe," Lord Cornwallis broke into his thoughts. "Do you wish to contribute to the discussion?"

John shot to attention. "Yes, sir, if I may approach."

General Cornwallis signaled and John stepped up to the table.

"Various reliable sources tell me Mr. Washington plans to attack Manhattan City with approximately fifty flat boats conveyed along the Delaware Road. Each boat can hold seventy men. I understand they assembled at Van Vactor's Bridge on the

261

Raritan River. I propose to burn the boats, thereby preventing an attack on the city."

General Clinton crossed his arms and squinted at John. "What is the estimation of the enemy in the region?"

John shook his head. "Not at all, sir. I understand Mr. Lee left that part of the country, taking his force further inland to protect Philadelphia. I don't expect to run into much more than foraging parties and some local militia."

Clinton and Cornwallis stared at each other, and John held his breath.

"Tell us your plan," Cornwallis said, and John relaxed.

Simcoe set off on a cold and blustery day in late October with eighty members of his Hussars, riding toward Middlebrook, New Jersey.

At dawn, the rebel militia stirred at their approach on the road, but to his incredulous disbelief, most believed his men to be a faction of General "Light horse" Harry Lee's men.

Simcoe arrived at Middlebrook, disappointed to find only eighteen boats, not the fifty reported, on the Raritan River.

"They have mistaken us for rebel cavalry," he said. "We shall keep up the deception, if possible, but we shall need a guide from here on out because we cannot risk moving through what is now an alerted countryside. McGill," he turned to the captain.

"Yes, sir."

"Go find us someone who is loyal and familiar with the countryside to lead us to Hillsborough."

McGill saluted and rode off.

"In the meantime," he turned to the rest of his men. "We will destroy these eighteen boats. We won't leave them for the enemy to use."

The men set about pulling the boats ashore and chopping massive holes in the bottoms.

Satisfied at first, John began to think over the situation and realized the rebels could repair them.

"Take the chopped wood from each boat," he ordered, "place it within and set them afire."

While the boats burned, McGill returned with a young man who claimed to know his way to Hillsborough.

They set off before noon stopping at a rebel forage depot to feed the horses, still pretending to be some of Lee's men. Once they reached Hillsborough they came across the courthouse. Three British soldiers were held prisoner, all chained to the floor and looking starved. Furious, he ordered the men released and then burned the courthouse. Once engulfed in flames, he turned east back to Perth Amboy.

He intended to bypass the enemy post located at Brunswick and meet up with the infantrymen he sent to South River Bridge earlier, but the guide McGill commandeered, led them into an ambush by a force of militia rebels. Seeking to protect his men, John rode, spurring Salem, who galloped forward as he attempted to break through the rebel lines, but Salem stumbled and went down.

Careening through the air, he landed on his back and his breath whooshed from his lungs as the back of his head contacted the frozen ground. As he drew in a gasping breath, a young, red-headed boy appeared, holding a bayonet pointed at John's throat. He peered at the youth through watering eyes. What was Sally doing here dressed in boy's garb? Why did she threaten his life? John attempted to swat the bayonet away, but the sharp tip pressed into his throat.

"Don't move," the boy said, and John was only too happy to comply. Shaking his head to relieve the dizziness, his captor grabbed his shoulders to drag him off the road. Another appeared above him, bayonet ready to plunge into his heart.

"Leave off!" The young rascal dragging him shouted. "He is dead enough already!"

Then the world went dark.

34

Sitting at a table inside a noisy tavern, John's body ached, his head pounded, and he wished those clamoring for his blood would clamor more quietly.

The last thing he recalled he was charging an ambush before the world went dark. Now, as far as his addled wits could follow, he was a rebel prisoner. These men insisted on an eye for an eye, or in his case, his life for that of Captain Voorhees, whoever he was. The clouts didn't even have the decency to provide him ale and his throat burned.

Glancing around the room, he assessed his level of danger. They'd seated him in the back of the room, away from the warmth of the fire burning in the hearth, as well as the door. To escape, John would have to work his way through a crowded room of angry men. To his right, a stocky man with arms the size of tree stumps moved about serving ale and beer. Every so often he sent John a malicious glare, which informed him who his guard was.

A patron shouted, waving a flintlock in the air. "Bring him to the captain's grave and skew him."

As the patron shouted, two men entered the tavern. One of them waved a piece of parchment but didn't speak. Gradually the room quieted, as he gained their attention.

"Gentlemen," he said, greeting the room of men dressed mostly as farmers.

The tavern keep stood behind the bar, his arms outstretched, hands braced on the edge, as he too eyed the man with suspicion.

"My name is Clarkson, and I'm here," he said, again waving the parchment, "on orders from Governor Livingston to remove the prisoner before any harm befalls him."

John tilted his head and studied the man, ignoring the pain searing his brain with every movement of his head. Was this a ploy? Had Captain Sandford sent men disguised as agents of the governor to secure his release?

When Clarkson approached, John rose, his back and lower extremities protesting his movements.

Clarkson held out a hand, indicating the door. "Colonel Simcoe, if you wish to join me,"

John said nothing but held up his hands. Clarkson nodded and produced a knife which he used to remove the bindings. As he sheathed the blade, Clarkson's stern blue eyes met his.

"I released your bindings, Colonel. I trust as an officer and a gentleman you will not attempt to escape me."

Slowly John inclined his head. "You have my word, sir."

Clarkson extended an arm. "Let us proceed."

Two days later, John found himself at yet another tavern in Bordentown, New Jersey owned by a man named Colonel Hoogland of the New Jersey militia. Unlike those in Brunswick, he received treatment befitting officers of His Majesty's Army.

Having been granted an interview regarding his possible exchange, John sat at a table across from the American Lieutenant Colonel Harry Lee. His men referred to him as "Light Horse Harry" and John liked him the minute they met. Colonel Lee was resplendent in a blue coat with gold lace on the collar and breast, gold epaulets on his shoulders, and thick white lace stock cascading down the front. His open friendly face, with full cheeks and warm blue eyes, met John's with the respect due a fellow officer.

Lee leaned forward. "So, Colonel Simcoe. Tell me how you come to be in my company as a prisoner of war, sir?"

"I can hardly describe the circumstances, Colonel," he said, sipping from a tankard of ale. It was tasty. Why couldn't the tavern keeps in Staten Island make ale as delicious as this?

"While foraging with my men, we became aware of the local militia in our rear as evidenced by one person in particular firing off a weapon every so often to pinpoint our location."

Lee nodded and sipped his ale, but his eyes never wavered from John's face.

"Well, sir, fearing an ambush, as you might imagine, I approached a home where several women worked on their laundry."

He waved a hand as if to suggest Lee would have done the same as him. "I told the women to warn whoever came after us that if gunshots continued to mark our location, I would burn down every home I came to."

Lee's eyebrows shot up and consternation shone in his eyes.

Again, John made a deprecating gesture and Lee sat back.

"Colonel," John said, leaning close. "I believe, as officers, we understand each other, and would not run amiss with you if you allowed my release. I can return to my unit, taking with me my full regard for you and your obvious skills as an officer. I understand your men call you Light Horse Harry due to your skills in the saddle. I too am a capable officer and without my guidance, my men will not know what to do next."

Lee said nothing but studied John for several long minutes. He lifted his tankard to hide a smile, sipped, and carefully set the tankard down, fitting it on a stain on the table.

"My dear Colonel Simcoe," he said and slid the tankard back and forth across the wood planks. "Were your request within my power, I would secure your release immediately. However, I have orders and those orders do not include securing your release." He let go of his tankard and sitting back he reached into his coat and removed a leather pouch, which he dropped on the table between them and chinked with coins inside.

"Allow me to offer some expense money to see you through your captivity. It is the least I can do for you," he said as John was about to protest.

"Please, it is my wish you take the money," Lee said. "But

unfortunately, my orders are to see you to Burlington where you will be held in the common jail for the duration of the war, or parole for your release can be secured. I am sorry, Simcoe. I like you, truly I do, but this is the most I can offer."

John studied him and from the set of the man's shoulders and the regret in his blue eyes he spoke the truth. Reaching over, he plucked up the pouch and slipped it into his coat next to his father's timepiece.

"Thank you, Colonel. I shall not forget your kindness."

35

As October closed and the new month began, John readied himself for his march to Burlington, New Jersey to begin his confinement as a prisoner of war. Each day he prepared and each day he went to bed inside the tavern. He rarely ventured away from the premises as rumors of his cruelties to the populace gained unfair traction. Yes, he threatened to burn down each house he came to but that was merely a threat to stop the person behind his men from warning them of their location. He didn't actually do any damage.

Someone warned the rebels he was coming. Certainly, the buffoon who guided him to Hillsborough lied when he claimed he knew the way. Instead, the man led John and his Rangers into an ambush and if not for John's quick thinking, the entire Ranger corps would be imprisoned.

John drew in a deep breath and let it out, releasing some of his vexation. He should be in Oyster Bay, with Sally now, celebrating a one-year anniversary with her. How quickly the year passed.

As he sat drinking in the tavern, the poem he composed for her danced through his head. Fairest maid where all are fair. Hmm, that could stand improvement. Fairest maid of all the land? How about just fair maid? Oh, why didn't he possess Andre's skill?

His reverie broke when the front door opened.

"McGill!" John's utter surprise made him call out in an uncharacteristic fashion.

McGill, flanked by two men, started toward John, only to find his way blocked by his two companions.

"That man, kind sirs, is my commanding officer," McGill said. "Now stand aside."

The command in McGill's tone had the desired effect and both men did as bid.

John returned McGill's salute when he approached, then grabbed him by the upper arms. "My God in heaven, man, it does me well to see you, but what are you doing here?"

To his shock, McGill's face burned red as he shrugged. "Several of us couldn't accept the idea of your death, Colonel so we searched for you and were ourselves captured. We scattered and everyone managed to escape, except me and Colonel Billops."

John glanced around the tavern. "Where is Billops?"

McGill waved his hand toward the door. "He is a loyalist, sir, so they are keeping him outside. They are treating him most unjustly Colonel, but there is a deep anger among the continentals for their brethren who remain loyal to the King."

McGill lurched forward as his captor shoved him from behind. "Enough a yer palavering you two. Next thing, you'll be plotting yer escape. Well, it ain't gonna happen."

The man shoved McGill again, this time to the side. "Siddown and shut up."

Scowling, both men did as told.

The following day, John and McGill readied for their trip to the prison camp in Burlington. They stood quietly while their captors bound their hands with a thick rope and tied the other end to their saddle horns. John prayed he might survive the trip. "Brace yourself, McGill," he said under his breath.

"Stop this at once!" Colonel Hoogland shouted, storming toward them.

"Perhaps we've been paroled," he said in a soft voice. "He told me yesterday he's been negotiating for our release."

Hoogland stopped a few paces from John and gestured behind

269

him where an empty wagon approached.

Hoogland glared past John's shoulder. "Untie these men immediately. They are to ride in the wagon, not dragged behind like chattel."

Cowed by Hoogland's rage, the men untied Simcoe, and McGill, and allowed Colonel Billops to climb into the wagon.

Once settled, Hoogland dropped his hand on John's knee. "I am sorry, Colonel. I was not able to secure your release. You will go to Burlington until such time as you either serve out your term or a prisoner exchange may be had for you."

He removed his hand from John's knee. "I did my best."

"I appreciate your efforts, sir," John said while swallowing the lump of disappointment sitting like a boulder in his throat. There was nothing for him to do but make himself as comfortable as possible for the ride to Burlington.

The wagon bumped along the rutted dirt road, jostling the three prisoners as they rode southwest into captivity. A northwest wind goose pimpled John's body beneath his green woolen coat and black cloak. He raised his face to the warmth of the sun shining in a deep azure November sky, but the frigid North wind gusting across his body, left no doubt of the approaching season.

They followed the Delaware River south, ice already forming on the edges and John calculated it wouldn't be too much longer before the river caught over completely. Winters were damnably cold in the new world. Why anyone would want to endure such weather in this God-forsaken land was beyond his comprehension.

Across from him, McGill curled in a tight ball, his knees pulled to his chest and his arms tucked between, to conserve his body heat, though he still shivered. He stared over John's shoulder with a blank expression.

"How did you come to be here, McGill?"

McGill's slow blink alarmed him, and he suspected the man might succumb to the cold, so he sought to keep him conscious with conversation.

With effort, the captain shifted his gaze and studied his superior officer. "Forgive my bold, rash behavior, Colonel, but the rebels captured me whilst looking for you."

John already knew this but nodded to keep him talking.

McGill lowered his legs but pulled them close again as a

strong, frigid blast of wind hit him in the chest.

"Aye, Colonel," McGill said with a gesture toward Christopher Billops sitting to John's left, shivering uncontrollably.

Over his and McGill's objection, their captors removed Billops's coat and hat, leaving him in his shirt and breeches. They refused him anything with which to keep warm. If they didn't reach their destination soon, Billops would freeze to death. He gestured to him, and Billops sidled close to John. At least they could share body heat.

McGill continued his story. "Billops and I came looking for you. We discovered Salem, lying dead on the road when rebels ambushed us. They hid in yonder cornfield." He shook his head. "I am deeply ashamed, Colonel as you must be, over my lack of adherence to your training, but we rejoiced your body was not with Salem and contemplated what happened to you when the dastardly enemy quite literally popped up out of nowhere."

Billops joined the story. "We tried to pass ourselves off as Americans, but they wouldn't have it."

He huffed a discouraged breath. "Said we tried that one too many times to fall for it, despite my New York accent. They called me a Tory bastard and threatened to shoot me on the spot, but Captain McGill promised to see them all hanged if they did, so here we are."

"Here we are." John mused.

They reached Burlington by mid-afternoon and arrived at the courthouse in the center of a small town.

The three men climbed down and milled about, stretching their legs, and stamping their feet to get the blood flowing again.

A man exited the courthouse and trotted down the steps toward them, a rolled piece of parchment dangled in his hand. When he reached the bottom step, he stopped and eyed the three prisoners.

"Which of you is the Tory who claims to be Colonel Billops?" He didn't ask so much as he demanded.

"I am."

The man descended the last two steps and approached Billops, holding the parchment under his nose as if he wanted to scrape the appendage off Billops's face. "This here is a mittimus for you, Colonel," he said, sneering at the title. "It is dated the sixth of November, three days ago, and comes from none other than our

271

Commissioner of Prisoners for New Jersey, Mr. Elisha Boudinet."

None of the men reacted. They didn't know who Elisha Boudinet, was but something told John they would become well acquainted with him by reputation if not by person before too much time elapsed.

"You, sir, will be clapped in irons, both hands, and feet, and will be chained to the floor in a closed room in the jail. You will receive only bread and water from now on."

"Barbaric!" John said, stepping in front of Billops as though to protect him from a violent attack, but Billops merely straightened his shoulders and remained silent.

"I protest this vile treatment. Billops is an officer and a gentleman, not some common criminal."

Billops placed a gentle hand on John's arm. "Thank you for your defense, Colonel, but I can take care of myself."

He offered his hands. "I will go without protest."

"This is barbaric!"

John protested again as real fear for his person seized his heart. What would they do to him and McGill if they could heap such abuse on Billops?

"He is a Tory!"

The prisoner official shouted back grabbing Billops by the arm and yanking him away.

The man shoved John and McGill into a tiny, dark and dank room with weeping stone walls and a dirt floor. They were in the bowels of the courthouse and here they would remain until such time as—in the words of the supercilious prison guard— "'until his own side saw fit to release him, but if Simcoe remained a prisoner for the duration, the fault would lie with the British.'"

After the door slammed and locked behind them, they stood in the semi-darkness of the poorly lit cell.

"Rats," McGill said, making it sound like an expletive.

"What?" John asked peering at him in the gloom. His heart pounded and he struggled to regulate his breathing. The room was too small for two people, and he was uncomfortably close to McGill. He stepped to the side to gain distance, but his shoulder bumped into the stone wall and came away wet.

McGill gestured. "Rats," he said again. "Listen to them scurry."

Bloody fantastic, John glanced around the floor and sure enough, one the size of a guinea pig scampered for the darker corner. He shuddered. *Please, God*, he cast the plea into the ether. *Rescue me and return me to Sally.*

The door to the cell clanked open again and a threadbare blanket flew at each of them, and a bucket dropped inside the opening. Then the door clanged shut again leaving them in almost total darkness, one small window far above their heads in the eastern wall, their only source of light.

John recoiled at the odor emanating from the blanket, an odoriferous combination of sweat, urine and, might it be, vomit? He suppressed a gag. Reluctantly, he wrapped the blanket around his shoulders.

After a few days, John had the schedule down. The jailer arrived every morning, at dawn. A repulsive little man who dropped an empty bucket beside the door and brought them a half loaf of bread and some gruel in a wooden bowl.

John avoided the gruel and ate the bread after prying the weevils out. The sight of them made his stomach turn, but he intended to keep his strength up for the day he might be exchanged. He encouraged McGill to eat and drink the water, though he was sure it was the cause of their dysentery.

"Billops is in the cell next to us," McGill said. He took up position beside the door and discovered he could detect the conversations of their jailers clearly. "Chained to the floor by his wrists and ankles. Colonel, is there nothing we can do for him?"

"The jailer should arrive soon. When he comes," John said, rising from his reclining position, "I shall ask again for quill and parchment. We are officers. Perhaps I can prevail upon him to give poor Billops some quarter."

The key rattled in the lock and John wrapped his blanket tighter about his shoulders and coughed. His lungs felt tight with illness.

"Ya dyin?" A gruff voice said as soon as the door swung open. "Well hurry yourself up. I got enough to do wi'out coddlin' the likes a ye."

His brows drawn John shot a surprised glance at McGill. Their jailer didn't usually speak to them and for the first time, the long and stringy man entered. His lean muscles showed wiry strength.

Greasy hair hung in strands to his shoulders and cold blue eyes bore into John's, who straightened his back and shoulders to increase his height. John stood six feet tall, and he had to raise his eyes to meet this man's steely gaze.

"I demand a quill and parchment. I wish to write a letter and as an officer and a gentleman you cannot refuse such a request." *Gentlemen indeed. More like the scum of the earth.*

"I canna, can I?"

John paused to figure out what he said. He sucked in a breath. "No, you cannot."

McGill sidled around to John's side, ready to defend, if necessary, but John held the man's gaze, determined to let him know who the superior man was. For a full three seconds, they locked eyes, and finally, the jailer nodded. I'll bring ye your writin's with yer supper tonight and not a moment before. He kicked over the bucket and slammed the door shut. The keys rattled in the lock, giving John and McGill time to discuss what they wanted to write in the letter.

Lieutenant John Simcoe and Captain John McGill entered Manhattan City on the last day of seventeen seventy-nine. They had been prisoners for thirty of the worst days, John ever experienced.

Now, they rode to General Clinton's winter quarters where John Andre waited for them.

After a bath, shave, and a change of uniform, the three men sat in front of a warm fire, sipping whiskey while Simcoe and McGill related their experiences to General Clinton and Andre.

"Well, I must say," Andre said, shifting in his chair. "We prepared to send forty...shall we say...friends of government, all armed and ready with a rescue plan if the damned rebels didn't release you."

"It was a capital idea you had, Simcoe, to write to Governor Livingston and Mr. Washington regarding your situation," Clinton said. "It astonished me to learn they held you as criminals."

He sipped whiskey. "Indeed," he went on. "What a sad state the world is coming to if an officer's rights can be swept aside so easily. I wrote a letter to Mr. Washington straight away. Major Andre was most industrious in his efforts for your release."

Andre waved away the compliment. "I was at your disposal as always," Andre said downing the last of his whiskey. He got up and went to the sideboard where he grabbed the decanter.

"Still, we're most grateful to you, Andre," John said holding out his glass for more. Again, Andre waved away his comments as nothing more than what one did for one's friends.

John turned to General Clinton. "General, there is one favor I would ask of you, if you're of a mind to grant me one."

"Speak out, Colonel. What can I do for you?"

Rather than answer the question, John turned to Captain McGill. "I'm grateful to you for your services in the prison, McGill. You kept my sanity in many ways."

McGill said nothing but the red flush flowing up his neck and into his cheeks was all that needed saying. He let Andre refill his glass.

John turned to Clinton again. "I would request Captain McGill either receive an annuity for his services or be promoted to Quartermaster of Cavalry."

Clinton bobbed his head. "Which would you prefer Captain?"

Taken aback, McGill rose to his feet. "Colonel, you honor me." He held out his glass in salute to John who smiled warmly.

"You earned it, McGill. You fought for better food, for better treatment for poor Billops, and you had a knack for finding other prisoners with specific skills designed to keep us all alive. Were it not for you..."

His voice faded. He understood in his heart that if not for McGill, John would have died in prison. He did not possess the temperament to be locked up, but McGill adapted quickly and easily to the situation and made it work for them.

"You earned it," he said again and downed the last of his whiskey to hide an unexpected rush of emotion.

McGill turned to General Clinton. "If given a choice, sir, I'm not ready to leave the military. I should like the post of Quartermaster of the Cavalry."

Andre, ever the efficient assistant, already had parchment, quill, and ink ready for Clinton to write the necessary orders. When finished, Clinton signed the document with a flourish and John added his signature beneath the general's before giving it to Captain McGill, newly named Quartermaster of Cavalry.

After McGill and Clinton retired for the night, Simcoe and Andre sat by the fire drinking. Andre signaled to John they had things to discuss and though exhausted, John remained seated, the combination of fire and whiskey making him pleasantly warm and drunk.

"I am corresponding with Mr. Arnold."

Andre poured more whiskey for himself. He held out the decanter to John, who shook his head. If he had any more, he might have trouble keeping up his end of the conversation. He raised his brows in question.

Andre nodded. "He is disenchanted with the rebel cause, in no thanks to his charming wife, the former Miss Peggy Shippen." At the mention of her name, a shadow crossed Andre's face so fast, John almost missed it.

"Is Mrs. Arnold an acquaintance of yours?" John asked.

Andre waggled his head from shoulder to shoulder and offered John a lecherous grin. "Let's just say, Miss Shippen and I got to know each other...quite...well."

Andre sipped his drink while staring into the flames in the hearth. "Word from the other side is Arnold is disliked thoroughly by all, including Mr. Washington, who puts up with him because he must. He is the only general who can win a battle."

"I understand his unceasing complaints about lack of recognition for his bravery—and he is brave— are driving the nails in his coffin," Andre said. "From what my sources tell me, Arnold became enraged when Washington promoted a more junior general above him. His consolation prize, command of the garrison at West Point. He's to arrive there sometime in September."

"West Point?" John sat upright. "Why if we capture that garrison imagine what we could do to the rebels."

Andre smiled and nodded. He saluted John with his glass. "Imagine," he said.

276

36

John lay abed. A racking cough shook his shoulders and made him wish to curl up and die. He was staying in the headquarters of General Clinton, too sick to join his men, which besides seeing Sally again, was the only thing he wanted.

He'd survived a voyage to South Carolina and took part in the capture of Charleston before he and the Queen's Rangers boarded another ship for a grueling voyage back to New York.

They'd arrived a month ago, but his health had not returned as rapidly as he thought it should and that worried him so much, he threw back the covers and ignored another racking cough. If lying in bed didn't help his recuperation, then perhaps pushing through his illness and getting back to work would.

Once dressed, he moved carefully down the spiral staircase of the mansion General Clinton called headquarters. John moved slowly in order not to bring on another spasm of coughing and ruin his chances.

"Simcoe," Andre's friendly voice boomed from the bottom of the stairs. "Just the man I wanted to see this day. Since the day is more than half gone, I feared I would have to come to you." He held out his hand in welcome and his friendly grin belied his words.

"Andre."

John squeezed out his name before unsuccessfully suppressing another cough. He turned away pressing a handkerchief to his mouth.

"Gracious Simcoe, perhaps you're not up to activity as yet," Andre said and placed a hand on John's shoulder. "You look like death's head upon a mop stick."

There was genuine concern in his friend's blue eyes, which John waved away.

A knock at the front door forestalled their discussion as Andre moved to answer the door.

John recognized the young boy standing at the entrance.

"Private Wooden," he said before pressing the cloth to his lips again. "Absalom, am I correct? What are you doing here?"

"Absalom is my brother, sir," Solomon said, correcting him as he stepped inside, a dispatch bag held in both hands which he offered to either man. Andre took it.

"A message from Captain Youngs, sir. He says I'm to await your response."

"Excellent, Private. You may have a seat there," Andre said, indicating a chair in the hallway next to a room, which in days of peace served as a ballroom, but now, was General Clinton's war room.

Solomon sat as Andre and John disappeared behind the closed door.

"So," John said as he read the dispatches. "Washington is gathering forces across the Hudson."

"Yes." Andre handed him another. "But where did he get eight thousand more men? I would have thought this war was a lost cause by now."

Andre waved one sheet of parchment in confusion. "Eight thousand troops. The same number General Clinton has sent to Rhode Island. It sounds a bit strange to me, but I can't put my finger on why."

John laid one sheet aside and picked up another, studying it carefully. "Whatever you may think, these plans are fairly well detailed. I understand Mr. Washington to be a meticulous man. Short on luck but long on detail."

John could appreciate such a man, being one himself. "I think you should take this seriously, Andre. You must get word to General Clinton one way or another to return to Manhattan before Washington attacks."

After more discussion, Andre wrote out an order and as they reemerged from the war room, Solomon rose and saluted.

Andre handed back the dispatch bag. "Return to Captain Youngs and tell him to prepare his troops for possible action on Long Island."

"Wonderful, sir," Solomon said, and with another quick salute, he was out the door and mounting his horse.

Andre closed the front door. "Well, John, how long has it been since you've seen your wonderful lady or Long Island?"

"Too long," John said as a smile pulled the corners of his lips. "Far too long."

The late August days still held the warmth of summer, but the cooling nights and dew-covered grass forewarned of the coming cold. Weaving must begin in a month or two. After the wool, came the flax line to weave into linen cloth. Mother always said spinning was a never-ending task and Sally now understood what she meant. The warmth of the day beckoned so she brought her spinning wheel to the front yard to work.

More than a month had passed since the lighting of the beacons at Norwich Hill. From what Sally read in the Rivington Gazette, the British thought a raid on Manhattan by combined French and American forces was imminent, as indicated by the lit beacons, so they recalled their forces to meet an attack that never materialized, giving the French fleet time to unload troops on Rhode Island where they remained even now, training and preparing.

Solomon told her he saw John in Manhattan at General Clinton's headquarters and told her John was ill. Had something drastic happened to him over the winter?

Well, she would only find out if he returned. Clearly, he didn't think it necessary to write and put her mind at ease. She tried not to let it hurt, though it did. The dichotomy was that with his absence, she often put him out of her mind, sometimes for days.

Sally stopped the wheel to adjust the yarn on the hooks before restarting. A motion by the front door caught her eye and she raised her gaze to find Audrey standing in the doorway staring hard down Main Road.

With a sudden movement, Audrey raised her arm and shouted. Curious and concerned, Sally rose and trotted to the walk. A cloud of dust appeared on the road.

She grasped Audrey's elbow. "Who is it?"

"The Rangers," Audrey said, grasping Sally's hand and squeezing. "Look through the dust cloud. I'm sure John's coming."

Sally sucked in a breath. They clung to each other's hands and waited for the dust to clear. When it did, John indeed rode at the front of the line. The girls jumped up and down and Sally waved with frantic abandon as her heart pounded. An unexpected wave of joy crashed over her so hard tears threatened to overflow.

John raised a hand briefly but let it fall to his thigh. Sally's smile froze on her face. "What's wrong with him?"

Audrey tsked. "Oh, don't be such a worry wart. I'm sure he's fine. He's probably exhausted."

Sally eyed him critically. "No. Something's wrong. I can tell. He's having trouble sitting in the saddle. And he's not riding Salem. Something's happened, Audrey."

Her fears were grounded deeper when John made no effort to gallop forward as he had last year. Now tense, the girls waited for John to stop at the front walk. When he did, he remained in the saddle until a lieutenant dismounted and helped him from his horse.

Audrey turned and ran back up the walk calling for Patty and Liss. Sally remained rooted to the spot her hands tight over her mouth.

"John! Are you alright?"

"He's ill, miss." The lieutenant told her as he drew John's arm over his head to rest across his shoulders. Another soldier stepped up and put John's other arm over his shoulders and together they helped John walk to the house. Once inside, Sally directed them straight to his room where they lay him in the bed.

As he passed Sally at the front door, he smiled softly. "Hello, Sally, dear. I'm home."

37

John couldn't have it any better. He stayed in bed for a week, kept there by Sally's strict orders, and he happily obliged. Sally, Audrey, and Phebe plied him with warm and comforting food, Bohea tea, and forced rest. They kept guard over who could see him and who could wait. Though he felt much better, he allowed the women to coddle him a bit longer than necessary, because he enjoyed the attention, but this morning he awoke full of energy. Throwing back the covers, he bounded off the mattress and dressed quickly hoping to join the family at breakfast.

Entering the hallway, he was reminded of his first day at the Townsend's, and when he recalled how he treated them with suspicion, his face grew hot. Stopping at the kitchen door, he spied their activity with affection.

Sally bent to check the oat cakes and this time, not wanting to startle her by "lurking" as she accused him once, he stepped into the room. "Greetings, ladies."

The women stopped their work. "Good morning, Colonel," Mrs. Townsend said, still refusing to call him by his Christian name, but John no longer took offense. If Mrs. Townsend needed the formality, he would give it to her.

Months in a dank dungeon of a prison cell did much to humble him.

He took a seat as Sally brought him a cup of steaming tea. "I'm afraid it's not Bohea this morning, John but simple Earl Grey."

"Fine, Sally," he said and smiled at her. He felt so good, he didn't care if he drank hot water and lemon.

She gazed at him with a critical eye. "You have color in your cheeks today."

"Thanks to yours and your sister's careful nursing, I'm quite well today," he said and smiled his appreciation. He would have said more, but the men entered the kitchen and hailed John with morning greetings. Mr. Townsend shook his hand and welcomed him back to the land of the living.

"Though with Sally as your nurse, she would allow no other outcome."

Her father's words heartened him. Her nursing and gentle care of him hadn't gone unnoticed. Perhaps she found a way to love him enough to marry him. If so, he would ask her again today.

John ate his porridge with enthusiasm, genuinely hungry this morning and the food tasted delicious, even with the weak Earl Grey to wash it down.

"I'm afraid I must disappoint Nurse Sally today," John said, elaborating when Mr. Townsend raised his brows in question.

"I must get back to my men. I'm in full health and no longer have the excuse of illness to delay my work."

"Well," Sally said while bringing her brother, David, a bowl of porridge. "I shall be disappointed, but I am pleased my care brought you back to health."

After breakfast, John left the house. His horse, Hercules, waited, saddled at the front walk. The horse was well-trained and heeled to John's commands, but he still missed Salem, his fine stallion. There was something about a fine black horse to lend the animal a fearsome air that Hercules, despite his name, did not possess.

John thanked Isaac for holding the reins as he mounted the horse. Riding toward the parade ground John contemplated his men. How many bad habits would he have to undo, gained in his absence? Would they still follow his lead? Well, he wouldn't leave them a choice in the matter. When he arrived, he was pleasantly surprised to see a dear friend among his officers.

"McGill," John said. "What are you doing here? I thought General Clinton attached you to his command from now on to my everlasting disappointment."

McGill laughed as he shook John's hand. From their days in the cell together, their friendship grew, and John dropped the strict formality he maintained with other junior officers. On more than one occasion, McGill preserved John's life with his ability to scrounge and cajole for food and other necessary supplies. McGill flattered their heartless guard into supplies like writing paper and ink and even got him to agree to send the letters to Mr. Washington and Governor Livingston that resulted in their being paroled, exchanged for two majors and a lieutenant.

"Well, Colonel," McGill said, his blue eyes shining with delight. "I convinced General Clinton as your Quartermaster General, my services to the British Army would be best served. He agreed and here I am."

McGill leaned close and lowered his voice. "My understanding from the General is a major action of some sort is in the offing, and you will need me to procure supplies."

John clapped him on the back. "You are correct there, my friend. On both counts."

McGill straightened and putting his hands behind his back he turned to the field. "Well then," he said, "in that vein, I have not only brought supplies but men. Two more troops of Dragoons joined your regiment, courtesy of General Clinton."

Grinning, John clapped his hands together. The sound cracked across the parade ground. "Let's get busy."

Captain McGill became a frequent guest of the Townsend's as he came and went to visit John. Immediately, Sally detected the change in their relationship. Where once McGill was deferential and slightly in awe of John he now laughed and talked with him as an equal, as tonight, sitting companionably chatting in low tones while she knitted winter stockings.

Her gaze strayed to the window where Captain McGill once used a diamond ring to etch her name on a pane of glass. The entire thing was done in jest, but John reacted with anger, subtly threatening the poor Captain's rank for the action and his anxious deference.

Her spindle was full, and Sally stopped the wheel to exchange it for an empty one. From the corner of her eye, she spied them glancing at her. Pretending ignorance, she tossed the full spindle toward the basket of other spindles waiting for Phebe to skein with the niddy-noddy. The spindle bounced off the side of the basket and landed on the floor near the door. With a tsk of disgust, she rose to retrieve the spindle before the yarn got dirty.

"I procured about thirty carts and wagons," McGill stated. "I admit I commandeered almost all of them, but they are ours."

"Wonderful," John said. "What do you mean you commandeered most of them?"

McGill scratched his nose. "Well, sir," he said, "the local folks are less disposed to helping out these days. One farmer even went so far to say this was the third cart we'd commandeered from him without returning the last two so he supposed he wouldn't get this one back either. He then went on to have the audacity to present me with a bill of sale for three carts."

Sally resumed her position at the wheel and struggled to keep her face neutral. She'd heard about that. Mr. Coles was the one who presented the British with a bill of sale. The bravery of such an act went through town like a wildfire.

"Mm," John said. "We must remind them when the King restores order, their lack of loyalty will not go unpunished."

"It's not a lack of loyalty." Sally surprised herself by having the nerve to speak up.

"I beg your pardon, Miss Townsend?" McGill turned a smile on her. John scowled but she went on, speaking to McGill.

"It's not disloyal to ask to be paid for something about to be taken, especially when you know it won't be returned. It seems to me if you're taking something from someone and you know you have no intention of returning it, then it seems right you should pay the person for it. Either that or be upfront that you're stealing it and there is nothing they can do about it."

Sally's comment was met with silent stares.

"Sally, my dear," John said, pasting a sickly sweet smile on his face and rising. McGill followed suit. "Please excuse us." Without waiting for her consent, he led McGill into his bedroom and shut the door firmly behind them.

"Of course," she said to an empty room. During his convalescence, he acted so grateful she began to change her mind about her feelings for him, but now those fledgling feelings curdled like spoiled milk. When would she ever learn?

38

Sally stood at the front door gazing toward their former fruit orchard, a smile tugging her lips at the sight of them fluttering in the summer breeze. They arrived in late April along with a note from William Simcoe, stating he received a letter from his grandson asking for the trees to be delivered in time for the planting season. One hundred trees had been requested. Seventy-five now fluttered gaily in the summer breeze. Things like this confused her. John claimed he cut down the trees as a military necessity, but then ordered their replacement. What was she to think of such actions.

Father had wasted no time writing to Mr. Simcoe expressing his thanks and appreciation for the replacements, and he openly admitted, his regard for the stoic colonel raised significantly.

Sally moved to close the front door when a red-coated soldier rode into town from the Lloyd's Neck area. He rode pell-mell past the house, the third in the past hour. What was going on? Wrinkling her lips, she came to a decision and closed the door.

She found Father in the field harvesting this year's flax crop. "Father, do you mind if I take Farmer Girl and go visit Susannah?"

"Does your mother need you somewhere?"

"She says no," Sally said, though in truth she never asked.

Father studied her for a moment before nodding. "Be no more than an hour, Poppet. I'm sure Mother has spinning or knitting or some such she will need from you."

"Yes sir," Sally said, turning away before her smile of triumph gave her away. She had so much wool yet to spin but excess energy forbade her sit still at the wheel.

After saddling Farmer Girl, she rode down Cove Road. As she rode, she passed the training grounds in the center of the village, now empty with the Rangers on a campaign. When would they return? Sally couldn't possibly hope to expect them back before October if she were lucky and for the millionth time, she tamped down her impatience for John's return.

As she rounded the curve to Cove Road, the pounding of horses' hooves caught her attention. She pulled Farmer Girl onto the grass to keep from being run down as another red-coated rider flew past her.

Something was happening. She needed to find out what. Another rider closed the distance with her, and she hailed him to stop.

"Sir!"

The soldier reined in his horse, though impatience showed on his face.

"Yes, miss."

"What's happening? You're the third rider I encountered today riding like Beelzebub himself is on your heels. Are we to be attacked?" For extra measure, Sally glanced around her, as though seeing danger everywhere.

"No, miss, at least not imminently."

The soldier patted his horse's neck before gathering his reins. "However, I suggest you return to your home or seek safety where you may. Word is the rebels are on their way and events might become dangerous," he said, as he tipped his cap. "Now if you'll excuse me, miss, I must be on my way."

Sally thanked him and when he left, she booted Farmer Girl and rode with all haste to Daniel's.

Sally sat at Susannah's kitchen table sipping cool cider. "He was the third hard rider I encountered today. By the urgency in his voice and the tension on his face, something is amiss, and it frightens me.

What if we're to be attacked? What shall we do?"

Susannah sat back and rather than answer the question, she cast a long somber glance at Daniel sitting across from her. They locked eyes and the pair communicated something to each other, much the way her parents often did.

Daniel leaned forward. "Sally, calm yourself. No one is attacking anyone. Not at the moment anyway."

He sipped his cider and exchanged another glance with Susannah. They didn't trust her. That broke her heart. Aside from gathering information for Robert, and despite her outburst to Susannah earlier, they were dear friends and to lose their trust hurt deeply.

With a sigh, he set his cup down deliberately on the oak dining table. "Sally, if I tell you something, can I trust you to remain silent as the grave? Your life, mine and Susannah's will depend upon your silence."

A shiver ran down her spine and fear spiked her heart. She pushed it down and nodded once. "Of course."

She croaked, cleared her throat, and said again, pushing aside her nerves, "Of course, Daniel."

"I wouldn't say this, it's too dangerous, but Robert assures me you can be trusted above anyone else save your father."

He'd consulted with Robert. About her trustworthiness?

Daniel's words made her sit up straight and proud and scared the daylights out of her. What was so dangerous she must swear to take the information to the grave?

"There is no American attack imminent anywhere on the island or in Manhattan. That is what we want the British to believe so they keep their fleet in New York Harbor. What has happened," he said, breaking off to stare at his cup as though reassessing whether he should tell her. With the tip of his fingers, he pushed his cup of cider to the side, clasped his hands together, and placed them on the table. He stared hard into Sally's eyes.

"What is happening," he said again, "is the French fleet arrived a day ago and is anchored in Newport, Rhode Island with six thousand fresh French troops for General Washington, along with a good deal of money."

He stared hard at Sally his gaze asking if he made a mistake in telling her.

It was Sally's turn to contemplate the tabletop. Was Daniel in league with Robert? Was he using his position to pass information to General Washington?

Robert told her the night she became involved, if she needed to get information to him fast, Daniel would help her. Sally raised her gaze to Susannah. Her tense face and worried face suggested she too feared Daniel erred in being open with her. Sitting up, she pulled her shoulders back and came to a decision of her own.

Tilting her head, she studied him. "I think I understand now. As head of the loyalist militia, you learn things in the British command, and you're well placed to forward the information to Robert so he can pass it on to General Washington. You set up the raid last fall against John's fortifications. Did you tell them the best places to attack?"

Daniel sat back and his astonished glance at Susannah told Sally she got it right.

"You're not wrong," Daniel said, confirming her suspicions as a smile ghosted his lips. "We did inform the so-called rebel militia when to attack but not where. Someone else provided excellent and well-detailed information about the fortifications and the best places to land and such. I didn't have to do much, other than set the time and location based on the information sent to me."

Now Daniel smiled. "I received hand-drawn sketches and notes with which to plan my attack." He narrowed his eyes at her. "I had no idea you were so observant, my dear."

Sally gasped. "How did you discover it was me?"

He chuckled. "How many receipts did you write out for me when your father still had his store? I recognized the handwriting."

That made her stop and think. Fear tingled her scalp and made her hitch her breath. If he recognized her handwriting, John might too. Robert warned her this was dangerous work. "So, no attack is coming?"

"No. But the British don't know that. I recently sent Solomon on a mission with a dispatch pouch full of false information for General Clinton. Now, we're waiting to see if our dangling fruit will be plucked." He raised a brow at her.

"What they do know is that the French fleet is anchored off Newport, Rhode Island and General Clinton wants to attack them before they become organized. We want to stop an attack from happening, so an American attack on Manhattan was the best General Washington could come up with at the last moment."

Sally nodded at everything Daniel told her and her heart lifted. All these years, she wondered about his loyalty only to learn he chose to head the British militia to serve the American cause.

It explained why the rebel raids never reached his home, though the Youngs' lived so close to the Sound. It also explained why so many foraging expeditions were unsuccessful.

The grandfather clock further inside the house bonged out twice, startling her. She was late getting home.

"I must go," she said. "I promised Father I wouldn't be more than an hour and here I've gone and abused the privilege."

"One more thing, Sally," he said leading her to the front door. "Be on the alert for the lighting of the signal beacons. As soon as you see that, you'll know our plan has been put into action."

Daniel opened the door and smiled down at her.

On impulse, she rose onto her tiptoes and kissed his cheek.

"Thank you, Daniel," she said, and grasping Susannah's hand in a quick goodbye, she left.

Sally's sisters snored in their beds while she stood at the open window staring toward Norwich Hill. Two weeks had passed since Daniel told her about the signal beacons. Together with what she'd written to Robert about what John had disclosed about the French fleet, she surmised they had formed a plan. Now, she was anxious for them to carry it out.

So each night, Sally posted herself at the window, watching. Each day, while she did her chores, she cast frequent glances toward Norwich Hill and the tall beacons Robert assured her could be seen from Connecticut.

The steady crick of tree frogs punctuated by the cheeping of crickets in the fields were her only companions as she kept vigil. The night was so eerily silent she could hear the grandfather clock ticking below stairs.

A rustle of blankets made her turn. Phebe lifted her head. "Sally?"

Sally whispered back. "I'm here."

"What are you doing? Come back to bed."

"I couldn't sleep. I wanted some air."

Phebe lay back down and when her breathing returned to a slow deep rhythm, Sally turned back to the window. Still dark. She sighed with impatience, but then a bright flare of fire lit the night sky followed quickly by another and another.

Sally sucked in a breath. Cringing, she turned to see if her small gasp woke either Phebe or Audrey but each slumbered on, oblivious to the danger and intrigue surrounding them. Sally wouldn't miss it for the world. She turned back to the window in time to see another beacon set ablaze.

Her heart pounded. She didn't know what danger it portended for the British, but she prayed for success for the Americans. Lifting her fingers to her lips, she kissed the pads and sent a prayer to the Lord that whatever happened, it would work toward the defeat of the British. As she climbed into bed and drifted to sleep, it never occurred to her that defeat for the British also meant defeat for John, and for Daniel and Susannah.

39

As Sally bounded down the stairs, the door knocker clacked. Launching herself off the bottom stair, she answered the door.

"Andre!" Sally clapped her hands together. "What a surprise. Why didn't you tell us you were arriving?"

"My darling goddess Sally," he said, reminding her of their first meeting. He took her hand in his and kissed her knuckles, sending the familiar shiver down her spine.

"I wanted to surprise you. Is Simcoe in the house or is he off abusing his men?"

Sally laughed. "He's off *training* his men."

Andre pretended that was what he meant to say. "Oh, yes. Training. My most sincere apologies."

She laughed with him. "Please come in if you can spare the time. Mother and Phebe are in the kitchen. Audrey will be sorry she missed you. She's at Sally Coles' helping her sew her wedding dress."

"Miss Coles is to marry?"

"In a few weeks. To my cousin, Robert Stoddard."

"I've met Mr. Stoddard, have I not?" Andre asked as he followed Sally to the kitchen.

"I believe so, at the ill-fated Valentine's Day party."

She giggled recalling the silly poem he made up on the spot to make her laugh for taking her donuts and hiding them on her. The undue consternation when she discovered her treats went missing embarrassed her now, realizing it was a harmless prank.

"Oh, that." Andre waved his hand and laughed with her. They stood at the door of the kitchen and before Sally could announce him Andre spread his arms and said, "Hello ladies."

"Andre!" Phebe squealed and ran to him, throwing herself into his arms with a joyful squeeze.

Andre hugged her as he would a younger sister he had not seen in many months. When he pushed her away, he gazed down into her sparkling blue eyes. "My dear, Miss Phebe, I declare you grow more beautiful every day."

He pushed her away further and eyed her up and down. "And how you have grown. I declare if I leave you alone for any longer, you'll be taller than me."

Always susceptible to Andre's charms, Phebe covered her mouth with her hand and giggled. Red-faced, she returned to the hearth and the stew cooking within the pot.

"Good morning, Andre," Mother said as she left the worktable and, wiping her hands on her apron, she extended them to Andre, who took her hands in his own and kissed her cheek. "Dear, Mrs. Townsend, it is always a joy to see you."

The note of sincerity in his words made Sally glance twice at him. Did he carry an infatuation for her mother?

"And how is your dear mother? When was the last time you wrote to her?" Mother asked, extending a hand to the table in an invitation to sit down.

Andre moved to the table and sat.

Patty heated water for tea.

Sally sat down next to Andre.

"I received a letter from her Tuesday last," he said, inclining his head in a gracious nod to Mother. "I told her all about my surrogate mother here in the colonies. She is pleased and hopes one day the two of you may meet."

"What a lovely idea," Mother said with a gleam of pleasure in her eye, as her expression acknowledged the truth of how remote the possibility would ever be.

"So, Andre," Sally said as Patty brought tea and cakes for them, though it was still early in the afternoon and there was much work to be done. "What brings you to Oyster Bay?"

"Well, my dear, I'm on a mission to find Simcoe. General Clinton gave us an important assignment and I'd hoped to speak with him so we may coordinate our efforts for the best effect."

Sally pouted. "Do you mean to take him away from us?" Consternation mixed with a touch of protective anger laced her words.

Andre's quizzical gaze and pause in his answer prompted Mother to speak up.

"Now, Sally, I understand the Colonel has been ill, but you may not coddle him any more than he wishes. The man has a job to do."

Sally's cheeks grew warm, and she turned away in humble chastisement. "Yes, Mother, you're right."

She turned a bright smile on Andre. "I do apologize, dear Andre. But John has finally recuperated from a terrible illness, and I hate the thought of you whisking him away again and having him fall ill once more."

Andre placed a warm hand over one of hers and gave her fingers a gentle squeeze. "Dear Sally, I do pray one day to find a wife as caring and concerned for my health as you."

John entered the kitchen with Luke on his heels. Patty had sent the lad to find him when Andre arrived. Andre rose and extended a hand.

"How are you, Andre?"

"I'm well," Andre said. "But Miss Sally tells me you've been in ill health."

John waved it away. "The same illness you saw me in. Eight months a prisoner of war, a voyage to the southern colonies, and another voyage back to the northern..." he broke off with a negligent wave of a hand. "Is it any wonder?"

He extended his hand to Sally, who took it with a gracious smile.

"If not for some of the best care in the colony, I probably wouldn't be here now."

He smiled at her, gratified when her face reddened with

pleasure and a shy smile tugged her lips.

He was positive now, after the weeks of dedicated care she gave him, her heart softened towards him, and he could once again propose to her. He needed the right moment, and he hoped beyond hope Andre brought such a moment.

With an abrupt gesture, he returned his attention to his friend. "So, what brings you here, my friend?"

Andre smiled and cocked a brow. "Are you ready to get to work on the plans for General Clinton?"

John sat back. From the corner of his eye, he was aware of Sally carefully following their conversation, but he didn't acknowledge her. Finally, he nodded and as one, John and Andre rose and went to his room.

Once John closed the door he turned to Andre, now all business. "So, what are the developments thus far?"

Andre lifted his hands in a surrender gesture. "The General and I meant to engage Admiral Arbuthnot in a discussion about the French Navy. He did not show so on our way back, I requested permission to stop here."

John sat at his desk twiddling a quill as Andre told his story. "Our friend will soon be capable of that 'one grand stroke' we discussed late last year," Andre said, glancing at John. As he spoke, Andre paced the room. "I received a letter in May and our friend, Mr. Gustavus, assures me he will soon be in a position to turn over that one prize we'd hoped for."

40

Andre stayed with the Townsend's for almost three weeks, during which he and John were uncharacteristically tight lipped and mysterious. Where they normally engaged Sally in their most banal conversations, now they didn't even discuss banalities in her presence and Sally was certain mischief was in the making.

All was quiet in the house and telling Mother she needed to find a certain color thread for the quilt piece she was working on, she went upstairs to her brother's bedroom.

Sally eased the door closed and tiptoed to the chest sitting partially atop the grate in the floor above Simcoe's room. He and Andre had been closeted in there for the past two hours and enough was enough. She had to discover what they talked about.

Holding her skirts so they wouldn't rustle, she carefully lowered herself to the floor. Andre was speaking in quiet tones, and she had to lay close to the grate.

"A lady friend of mine in Philadelphia has been in contact with me. She believes our fruit is ripe and ready for picking."

"What if Mr. Gustavus gets cold feet or decides he wants a better bargain?"

"The deal has been struck," Andre said with finality suggesting this Mr. Gustavus was out of luck.

Sally's foot began to tingle so she shifted and accidentally bumped the chest. She froze at the loud thump and held her breath. Her heart nearly stopped beating when Andre's voice floated up. "What was that?"

John's voice followed. "I'm not sure, but it sounded like it came from above our heads."

Silently she rose and opened the chest. She had better find her thread or else.

Two tense days passed with no recriminations from John and Sally soon relaxed. They hadn't suspected her of eavesdropping, but what Sally learned upstairs made clear something was afoot.

Once again, after supper, John and Andre locked themselves behind closed doors and Sally had had enough. She knocked firmly on the door. "John, 'tis I."

"One moment," John said, and his impatience came through the portal.

She leaned close to the door. "No! You open this door this minute."

The portal flew inward, and Andre stared at her aghast. "Miss Sally, what troubles you so?"

He took her hand and led her into the room.

Now that she was in, she couldn't think of a plausible excuse, so she stuck her nose in the air and feigned hurt feelings. She cocked her head and glanced at each man. John was annoyed by her interruption, so she turned to Andre who still stared at her with bewildered concern.

She feigned anger. "It's only that...well the two of you closed yourselves off in this room for almost two weeks now, or you've gone off on long walks together, and... well..." she broke off, not sure where to take this line, but to her delight, she didn't need to worry.

"My dear girl!"

Andre recaptured her hand and kissed the back of it. "We have been two boorish men, leaving you and your lovely sisters to your own devices. What churls we are. How can we ever make it up to you?"

He turned to John not waiting for a response from Sally.

"An entertainment. What do you say, Simcoe? Should we give the ladies an entertainment they shall never forget?"

John glared at Andre.

"Come, Simcoe," Andre said, unfazed by John's annoyance. "It will be like Philadelphia in seventy-seven."

Overflowing with enthusiasm, Andre turned to Sally. "In Philadelphia, Simcoe and I participated in the most sublime entertainments. We painted scenery and acted in plays. Hmmm."

Andre's eyes drew closed with the memory. "Those were the days. Such fun."

Now certain Sally had Andre in her pocket, she only need work on John, which she could do later, but for the moment, she feared he would refuse, and she'd lose Andre's attention.

"I know!" She said, clasping Andre's hand. His eyes popped open. "A tea! We'll host a tea, in your honor, Andre you and John can organize our entertainment."

"What a lovely idea."

"Sally," John cut in. "Andre has to return to Manhattan tomorrow."

Sally's face fell. "Oh." She didn't have to feign disappointment and her mind whirred with what to do next. She cast a wily eye at John through her lashes. "I suppose I shall have to get used to being ignored by you."

She affected a huff. "Fine."

Sally snatched her hand back from Andre and whirled toward the door, skirts flouncing.

She was in the hallway before John caught up with her. Grasping her arm, he turned her around.

"Sally, dear, I do apologize most profusely for your hurt feelings. 'Tis only Andre asked my opinion on some military matters and, well, I'm flattered the adjutant to General Clinton would want my opinion."

He glanced at Andre and returned his gaze to her, a smile lighting his blue eyes. "I didn't want to burden your sweet ears with mundane military matters. I assure you when we've completed our task we will join you, Audrey, and Phebe."

Sally studied the guarded hope in his eyes. Hope she accepted his tale. No. Something was afoot. He didn't fool her, but now, she must fool him.

"All right," she said with a gracious nod of her head. "I shall wait with strained patience for you two to complete your tasks."

She started to walk away, but John held her arm. "Sally one more thing," he said when she glanced up.

He glanced at Andre who leaned against the door jamb watching their interactions. "When we've completed our mission here," he said with a gesture toward his room. "Would you allow me to discuss our matter with your father?"

Sally's brows rose higher, and John rushed to explain.

"We anticipate wonderful success and if we achieve this success, I'm certain the war will end victorious, so may I speak to your father?"

Sally licked her lips and pulled her bottom lip over her teeth. What were they discussing? With effort, she curbed her impatient curiosity. "Well, John, you know what they say about counting your chickens, yes?"

He nodded.

"Let's await the outcome, and after you may speak to Father."

With as sweet a smile as she could muster, Sally withdrew her hand and left.

41

"Miss Sally, how about next Saturday, the second of September?"

Sally was in the sitting room, knitting more stockings when John and Andre emerged from John's room.

Andre's question came from nowhere and Sally's uncomprehending stare made him chuckle.

"The tea, silly girl. The tea you wanted to host in my honor. I requested leave to remain here through the next week, so if you host your tea next Saturday, I can leave on Monday with an exuberant heart."

"I think Saturday is a wonderful day to host a tea."

"Capital," Andre cried and squeezed her hands. "Then Simcoe and I will have time to prepare an entertainment as well," he said, narrowing his eyes in a conspiratorial manner. "You and your sisters will have the main parts, but I warn you, we are preparing Macbeth."

She gave him a mock ferocious glare. "Are you calling me a witch, Major Andre?"

Playing along, Andre splayed a hand over his ruffled heart. "Hardly, my dear! You three will be the prettiest hags ever made!"

"Why you..." She cried, resuming her knitting. "I shall have much to do preparing pastries and cakes for the tea."

"And I shall enjoy them. I must say, your cakes and pastries are a delight and I anticipate them every time I visit."

Turning to John who remained quiet during their discussion, Andre clapped his hands. "Well, Simcoe, we must get busy. The scenery doesn't make itself after all."

He grasped John's arm and turned him back to his bedroom. The door closed leaving Sally alone with her thoughts.

"Andre, what did that solve? You've just added to our tasks, and we have much to do to prepare for West Point."

Andre grasped John's elbows and stared him in the eye. "Patience, my friend. We must also appear as if all is normal and with all the skulking we've been doing, I fear we've aroused the curiosity of our hosts. One fine, perceptive young lady in particular."

John grunted. Andre was correct. Sometimes he suspected Sally understood more than she let on about his activities. Many times, he wondered if someone in this house found a way to alert the rebels as to his activities, but Sally was a woman. Curious and perceptive she may be, but certainly, not capable of acting upon her suspicions.

"Well, so now what?" John asked as he took a seat at his desk.

Andre sat on the bed. "I received correspondence from the wife of Mr. Gustavus, who has now changed his nom de guerre to Monck."

"You mean," John said, "George Monck the First Duke of Albemarle who assisted Oliver Cromwell in his overthrow of the throne only to turn on Cromwell and assist Charles II to restore the crown?"

Andre nodded. "The same. Monck received a reward from the King. Mr. Gustavus is hoping for the same and the name change is a coded way of expressing the hope of immense compensation."

Andre sneered. "I detest this man, but we must work with what we have, eh?"

John rose and moved close to talk without being overheard. "What does he say?"

"Well," Andre said, "my friend, Miss Peggy Shippen, now Mrs. Benedict Arnold, writes me."

John was watching Andre's face and didn't miss the shadow of sadness passing through Andre's bright blue eyes.

He recalled Miss Shippen, a beautiful blond-haired woman as spirited and fearless as Andre. He and the lady, a woman from a wealthy and loyal family, spent much time together and John suspected a broken heart at the mention of her marriage along with Andre's comment about how he detested her husband.

Andre continued. "She says General Arnold will be taking over the command of West Point in September. After that, he is prepared to turn the fort over to us...for a price...twenty thousand pounds."

John exploded. "Twenty thousand!"

Andre made a lower-your-voice gesture shushing him.

John threw a hand over his mouth then lowered it. "Is such an amount even possible?"

"Oh, yes, it's possible but probable?" Andre shrugged. "General Clinton hopes if such an officer as Arnold should defect, perhaps more will follow, and Mr. Washington will be bereft of his commanders. Not to mention, it would open the Hudson River and the navy would have a clear path all the way to Canada."

After dinner, Sally went upstairs to collect pieces from her Hope chest for a quilt she began a week prior. It was time, to begin building her trousseau. Tradition held she must have thirteen quilts completed before she married. The thirteenth being for her marriage bed. The thought made her blush to the roots of her hair.

John was growing persistent, and she couldn't—wouldn't—tell him no, so she put him off with evasive promises of the future.

Audrey had twelve of her quilts completed and was dutifully working on her "marriage quilt" so Sally decided to work on her first with the help of her sister.

As she descended the stair, she sorted the quilt blocks and tried to find a pleasing pattern for them. Meandering around the corner of the landing she held up two pieces and fitted them together, admiring the effect when Andre's voice, coming from John's room, floated to her as though he stood beside her. "West Point will fall like a stone."

Sally raised her gaze from the blocks and landed it on John's partially open door.

West Point! Why did they discuss West Point? Sally recalled reading that General Arnold was named the commander, due to take over in September. An officer of the caliber of Mr. Arnold meant the fort was in capable and strong hands. Was this the mischief she suspected?

Carefully, she lowered her foot down to the next step and stopped. John's door was ajar. Most unusual for him. Did he wish to invite someone to listen? She was aware he suspected someone was providing information to the rebels, but he often told her he suspected one of the men in town. Mr. Cooper, the newspaper man was his most promising suspicion. Or did he just tell her that?

"A long-fulfilled desire, then. Contact General Arnold. Tell him we agree."

Holding her breath, she leaned close, understanding if they caught her, they might accuse her of spying.

A chair scraped across the floor. They were rising. What if they caught her?

Breath stuck in her throat, she lifted her skirts, pivoted and rushed back up to the landing, praying they didn't see her. As they exited John's room, she came around the corner as though she hadn't a care in the world.

John smiled up at her, and she smiled back, moved past him without a word, and entered the sitting room where she sat beside Audrey.

Her hands shook so hard, she dropped her quilt blocks on the floor. After two tries, she retrieved them and placed them in her lap. "What do you think?" she asked, voice tight.

Audrey barely glanced at them. "Lovely," she said and continued to sew.

Sally held the pieces together, but her shaking hands couldn't manipulate the needle through the cloth.

From the corner of her eye, she saw Audrey lower her hands to her lap. "Are you well, Sally? You appear disturbed."

Sally tried to smile but feared it appeared as a grimace. "Fine," she said, refitting the pieces and trying to push the needle through the fabric, but when John appeared, the needle went straight into her index finger eliciting a gasp of pain. She shook her hand out, reminded of the time, she'd stabbed her thumb while working a sampler. Back when John first arrived at their home. Back when she was naive enough to think she could have him and American independence too. The needle stab to her finger might as well be a bayonet to her heart.

The two men, apparently oblivious to the fact she overheard them, left out the front door.

Lifting a hand to her forehead, she almost cried with relief. "Now that you said something, Audrey, I fear I have a monstrous headache. I'm going upstairs to lie down."

Audrey laid a sympathetic hand on Sally's arm. "Should I call Mother or Patty?"

This time Sally did smile, grateful for her sister's concern. "No, thank you. I'll be fine."

Audrey put aside her sewing. "I'll take you up some tea. How would you like that?"

Sally kissed her cheek. "Thank you."

42

Dressed in her shift, she did her best to appear as if she readied for bed when Audrey entered, teacup and pot on a tray. She placed the tray on the corner of the desk and faced Sally, who climbed into bed and pulled up the covers.

"I told Mother you're unwell. She said she'll be up in a thrice if you need anything."

Mother appeared in the doorway. "And a thrice it is," she said smiling as she entered the room.

Mother perched on the edge of the mattress and lay a cool palm on Sally's brow.

"I'm fine, Mother," Sally said in response to her mother's worried face. "No need to worry. I simply have a headache. I think I've been doing too much this week what with planning for Andre's tea and the part he wants us to play in his entertainment and the sewing and spinning and knitting. I may have bitten off a bit more than I can chew."

Mother nodded with understanding. "Over time, you'll learn your limits, but for now, lie down, rest and rejoin the family in the morning."

Audrey poured her some tea, which she placed on the table in front of the bottle of rose water. Sally thanked them both and resisted the urge to shoo them from the room.

Once gone, she sipped her tea, forcing herself to stay in bed in case someone returned. Leaning over, she placed her empty cup back on the table, picked up the crystal bottle of rose water, and slipped off the cork.

Holding the scent to her nose, she sniffed deep. Placing a finger over the top, she tipped and then drew her finger along her wrist, dabbing at the base of her throat before corking and returning the bottle to its place. She held her wrist to her nose and savored the scent.

West Point. What did they plan to do at West Point? Did they plan an attack? Was there to be a battle around the area? If the British captured West Point, how would it shorten the war? Clearly, John thought such a thing possible, but how? If the British win the war, he would press for marriage.

Sally dropped her wrist to her lap and stared at the door. No one was coming to visit her. Jumping from the bed, she went to her desk and grabbed her quill and inkpot.

Writing with frantic haste, she couldn't say what John and Andre were planning with regard to West Point, but her instinct told her Robert needed the facts as she understood them. She hadn't yet worked out how she would pass the note to him. She didn't want to wait for Father to send correspondence, but she may have no choice.

In her letter, she asked if he was coming on Saturday for the tea in Andre's honor. She wanted to speak to him and reinforce what she told him here in her invisible ink. Sally stopped writing as her gaze drifted toward the window.

Distracted by a constant indistinct rumble accompanied by the neighing of horses and whistles and cries of drovers with whips, she rose and went to the window. Carts rumbled down the road in a long line. What was the purpose of so many carts? The waning sun slanted into the west window. Darkness would soon be upon them, but still, a long line of carts and wagons moved past the house. She began counting and when the last empty cart rumbled past, she had counted thirty.

Returning to her desk, she wrote some more. *Our friends are gathering farm carts for which purpose I cannot comprehend, but I fear the reason must be nefarious.* She stopped to reread. Did she give too much away in her comment? Hard to tell. She made a mark and dipping her quill into the invisible ink, Sally wrote *I counted thirty but have no idea how many passed before I saw them.*

She continued with her newsy letter. *Please brother, tell me if you can come home three days hence for our tea. I miss you dearly and wish to catch up. So much has happened here, I can hardly relay it in a letter. — Your sister, Sally.*

Sally put away her writing implements and hid the note in her Hope chest. Tomorrow she would ask Father to deliver her letter and invitation to Robert for the tea.

Her head did hurt now from her efforts to try and discover what was afoot. She crawled into bed, lay down, and fell asleep.

Not wanting to appear too obvious in her quest to satisfy her curiosity, Sally busied herself with preparations for the tea, now two days away. Though John and Andre were out for the day on military business, couriers came and went with unusual regularity for a Thursday, so Sally buried her suspicions in her baking.

She made tea cakes as well as flummery and custard tarts before starting on the oly koeks.

As she mixed the dough, Sally recalled how Andre had hidden the donuts inside the bottom shelf of the cupboard in the parlor and she had panicked thinking her brothers or Phebe had eaten them.

More than fifty donuts? They would be sick for days but nonetheless, in her distress, she feared someone did exactly that, only to discover Andre, the scoundrel, tricked her.

As she fished the last of the donuts from the pot, she placed them on the table and covered them with a damp cloth. Most of the baking was done and Sally was hot, tired, and sweaty. After cleaning up, she changed into a linen frock and a fresh cap and was returning downstairs when she rounded the landing on the stairway and stopped short at the sight of a stranger striding into the parlor.

Sally grabbed the railing to keep from falling. Had he seen her? She didn't think so. She only caught a fleeting glimpse of him before he disappeared into the room, but what was he doing in there?

Gathering her skirts, she slipped down the remaining stairs.

Because couriers were to come and go today, John left his door open in his absence allowing them to leave their missives and be on their way, so Sally entered his room and rushed to the sitting room on tiptoes, hurrying toward the door. She slipped behind it and peered through the crack. She didn't see anything at first and feared she'd missed his leaving, but the man straightened and glanced about. She ducked back, fearing she'd given herself away.

He wore ill-fitting clothes with a dirty red stocking cap perched on his greasy head. Standing in front of the corner cupboard he peered around him as if fearing discovery.

What was he doing? After another furtive glance around, he bent down and the cupboard doors clicked open. Almost immediately, they closed with the distinctive snick of the lock engaging.

Straightening again, Sally held her breath as he tiptoed past and out the front door as silently as he entered.

She counted to fifteen, but he didn't return. Positive she was alone again; she slipped across the hall and opened the cupboard door. Inside, tucked behind chargers and other dishes a note leaned against the cupboard wall.

Sally snatched the envelope and read the name on the front. "James Anderson."

It was closed with a heavy wax seal, and she didn't dare open it, knowing she would have to break the seal, so she returned the missive to its place and went back to the kitchen. But a burning question filled her mind. Who was James Anderson?

43

Now feeling unsafe in the house alone, Sally moved out to the yard and sat down in the grass. What business did a stranger have hiding notes for a James Anderson in her house? Spreading her skirts, she raised her face to the breeze blowing across the yard. She was still over warm from her baking and the day had taken on an ominous cast. Couriers arrived and departed, but they were uniformed and identified themselves. They weren't dressed like ruffians sneaking into and out of her house hiding notes.

Andre's horse rounded the side of the house and she relaxed. She'd feel much safer with a man present to protect her.

"My dear, Sally, what are you about on this fine afternoon?"

She almost told him about the intruder, but a sudden impulse checked here. Instead, she forced a smile. "I'm sitting and cooling myself after a morning of baking. 'Tis hot in the kitchen and I desired some fresh air."

"Would you desire company?"

"I'd love some."

Andre pulled his belt and pouch over his shoulder. "Allow me to change into a fresh uniform and I shall return."

Sally nodded as he entered the kitchen. Was he James

Anderson? John? Father? Robert? Who? What? She sighed knowing she'd have no answers to her questions and that rankled.

Andre returned a short time later and sat down next to her stretching his long legs out before him and crossing his legs at the ankles. Planting his hands behind him, he leaned back, raising his face to the sunshine, and released a long sigh.

"Are you weary, Andre?"

He reclined with his eyes closed. "A bit. Such a warm day."

Sally studied him from the corner of her eye. He was a handsome man with a long, straight nose. His blue eyes always twinkled with humor, and his heart-shaped upper lip rested softly on his full bottom lip, giving him the false appearance of a pout. The corners of his lips were pulled upward, and she wondered what he thought about.

"Do you, perchance have a lady waiting for you in Britain?"

He turned and regarded her. "No."

He closed his eyes again and turned his profile to her. "I gave my heart to a lady once, but she refused me and wed another."

Miss Shippen, perhaps? I detest that man.

A surprising pang of hurt twisted her heart. Without stopping to think, she placed a sympathetic hand on his arm, the rough warm wool of his sleeve scratched her palm. Her touch was momentary, and she returned her hand to her lap.

Andre's lips drew into a full smile. "Thank you, my dear," he said before opening his eyes and straightening up.

Phebe entered the yard from the kitchen. "Oh, Sally, there you are, and Andre. Wonderful. Audrey and I completed our delivery of invitations. Everyone said they wouldn't miss a party if Andre will attend."

Andre stood and held out his arms to her. "Ah, Phebe. Vision light as air, flowerets should crown thy head, and never shall it e'er be said that I have added to thy cares. I have a task for you and Miss Audrey if you would permit me to impose upon you."

Giggling, she dropped into a curtsy. "Well, after such a verse, how could I refuse?"

"I would ask you and Audrey to copy out portions of Macbeth for our entertainment on Saturday."

He drew a copy of the play from his pocket and handed it to her. "I marked out the pages."

Phebe took the book. "Of course, we'd be delighted."

Sally started to rise, and Andre extended a hand.

"I'd best go inside and finish cleaning up from my baking before Mother returns and scolds me for leaving a mess."

The three went back inside. Sally stopped short. Her plate of donuts! Narrowing her eyes, she cast a warning glare at a laughing Andre.

"Cold," he said, playing the game he'd played with her the last time he'd hidden her donuts.

In mock fury, she slammed her hands on her hips. "Fool me once, Major," she said, though her chuckle belied her anger. "If you insist upon playing tricks on me, you'll discover how fast I can change from siren to wicked witch!"

With a determined stride, she marched from the kitchen to the parlor.

"I swear on my sainted father's grave, Miss Townsend, it was not I who played such a dastardly trick on you."

He followed her.

When he appeared in the doorway, she pointed to the cupboard. "Hot?"

His laughter was her answer and she bent, reaching for the cupboard door, heart pounding and hands shaking, she swung open the door.

Her laughter sounded forced to her ear as she retrieved the platter. The note was gone. So, Major John Andre was the mysterious James Anderson. What a shame.

Andre sipped tea while Sally finished cleaning the kitchen. She felt awkward around him now that she knew he posed as a man by the name of James Anderson. Did this have anything to do with West Point?

"Bravo, my dear girl, for being so smart as to catch onto my trick so fast," he said his eye alight as he sipped.

What are you doing, Andre? Sally smiled as she finished wiping flour from the worktable. "I recalled the last time you played the same trick on me."

She wagged her finger at him. "But you forgot what I said to you the last time you hid my treats."

He splayed his hand across his chest. "Ah, such a lovely judge, jury, and executioner. I simply could not refuse another jest on a maiden who would never take offense at my play."

What are you doing?! Why are you pretending? Who is James Anderson? "Of course, I wouldn't. I recognize beneath that rough and tumble exterior," she said, as her face smoothed out. "There lies the heart of one of the kindest men I've ever had the pleasure to meet."

His blue eyes softened, and a pleasing smile creased his lips. "You, my dear, are a true treasure," he said.

The back door flew open, and John strode in. "There you are, Andre," he said destroying the atmosphere. "Are you ready to start?"

Andre rose and handed his cup to Sally.

"Welcome home, John." Sally didn't try to hide a nip of irritation.

"Thank you, Sally," he said, completely missing her ire.

Andre peeked at her from under his lashes as a sardonic smile twisted his lips. He bowed.

"Excuse us, my dear. Duty calls."

"You're excused," she said and turned away as the two men left the kitchen.

Sally took down the tins of tea to do an inventory. She opened the Bohea and sucked in her breath. The tin was almost empty. John's favorite. What was she to do?

Returning the canister to the shelf, she ran upstairs to write a quick note to Robert asking for three pounds of tea.

Retrieving her coded book, Sally carefully recorded what she'd overheard between John and Andre, and about the man she'd seen leaving a note addressed to a James Anderson, earlier in the morning, and her certainty, Andre took the note. For what purpose she could not divine.

Getting up, she went to her Hope chest and removed other notes recording what she'd overheard about West Point and included them.

Sally ended her message by stating she feared the two incidents were connected but didn't understand how. The letter asking for the Bohea she placed on the top of a small packet and placed the coded information on the back page, praying no one flipped all the way through the pages.

In a burst of clarity, she understood what she must do and gathering her pages, she flew out the kitchen door calling for Isaac.

He appeared at the barn door. "Quick, saddle Farmer Girl for me. I must ride to Daniel Youngs'."

Isaac turned and disappeared inside the barn. Moments later he returned with the horse and helped Sally onto her mount.

Once out of sight of the house, she rode as if Beelzebub himself were on her heels and didn't stop until she reached Daniel's. He was outside speaking with some redcoats, but he broke off to help her from the saddle. In a harsh whisper, she told him she must speak with him urgently.

Taking her elbow, he led her past the officers and into the house.

"Sally," Susannah said when she spied her. "I haven't seen you in some time. How are things with you and your family? Has the Colonel proposed marriage yet?"

Susannah teased her knowing of his infatuation with Sally.

"Everyone is fine," she said, "and no, the Colonel has not proposed. I asked him to wait until after the war. Then he may approach my father, not until."

She wondered at the knowing glance the couple shared before Susannah hid it behind a friendly smile.

"Well, come sit down and have some cider and biscuits so we can catch up."

Sally whirled on Daniel. "I have to send an urgent message to Robert."

She sat down and handed him the packet. In her nervousness she blurted out, "Robert once told me if I needed, in an emergency, I could come to you, but you needn't look inside, I only have a letter and a shopping list."

Daniel's sharp gaze assessed her, and heat flowed up Sally's face and warmed her ears. Why did she say such a thing? She turned away as Daniel crossed his arms and lowered his brow. "Of course, my dear, but if only a shopping list and a letter, what is of such importance?"

Affecting a small laugh, Sally shrugged. "I'm sorry I spoke so sharply. But with the tea a few days away and in Andre's honor, I discovered this afternoon we're out of Bohea and since he is the adjutant general for General Clinton, I want everything to go exactly right."

Daniel smiled. "I see," he said as he untied the packet and scanned the letter, flipping the pages. When he got to the last page, he studied it carefully before raising his gaze to meet Sally's eyes.

"Of course, my dear," he said retying the packet. "I shall send a courier right now and tell him not to return unless he has the tea." He shot a quick glance at Susannah. "After all, Bohea happens to be our favorite as well."

Daniel left the room and returned almost immediately, a dispatch case in his hand. "Today is your lucky day, Sally as I also have correspondence that needs to be in New York post haste. I'll give this to my courier who is absolutely trustworthy and tell him not to return until he has the tea."

He stuffed the dispatch case full and took it outside waving away her profuse thanks.

She stayed for another ten minutes so as not to be impolite. "Thank you for the refreshments, Susannah, but I must return home in time to help Mother prepare supper and I still have baking to do for Saturday."

"We're looking forward to Saturday," Susannah said. "Wish your mother well for me."

"I will." Sally forced a chuckle. "I declare, with so much to be done, I don't know where the time goes."

Sally walked to Daniel and stopped beside him. He placed an arm around her shoulder and gave her a gentle squeeze. "Don't worry, my dear. You will have your tea by tomorrow."

He walked her to Farmer Girl and helped her into the saddle.

When she settled, he lay his hand on her knee. "Be careful, Sally," he said with firm determination. "Say nothing of what you gave me. I assure you no one will read your note but Robert. The dispatch rider I sent is my most trusted man."

Was he giving her a message or a warning? "Thank you, Daniel and I assure you I will be the soul of caution."

Daniel smiled and stepped back. "We're excited about your party Saturday, and I expect a cup of Bohea."

Sally laughed. "Well, if the colonel doesn't drink it all by himself you shall have some."

Tapping her heels, Farmer Girl broke into a trot and Sally rode home. She was fairly certain he was one of them, but how to be certain? There was only one way to find out. Either she would receive her tea or be arrested.

44

When Sally returned, Isaac helped her dismount.

"Hello, miss. The colonel's been looking for you."

The words no sooner escaped when the back door flew open and John stormed across the yard, Andre slowly brought up the rear.

"Sally! Where've you been?"

She stopped short, surprised, and caught off guard by his angry bark of impatience. "I...I... went for a ride," she said, stammering. Her gaze shot between the two men. "Is something amiss?"

"Not at all, my dear," Andre said, smoothing ruffled feathers. "Our illustrious friend here, went in search of you and discovered you were nowhere to be found. Fearing you'd abandoned him for some rake, well, he nearly fell into an apoplectic seizure."

Sally chuckled. "Well in that case," she said, with a gesture toward the road. "I was doing an inventory of our tea supply for Saturday and to my surprise discovered we do not have enough Bohea to serve one cup and as it is John's favorite, I realized I must act, so I wrote out a shopping list for my brother. As I further know Daniel Youngs can send messages quickly, I confess I imposed on his good humor and his friendship with Robert and prevailed upon him to be certain my request reaches Robert post haste. He has done so."

To her relief, John visibly relaxed, and a shy smile lifted his mouth. He stepped forward and claimed one of her hands. "You did all of that for me?"

"I did."

John raised her hand and kissed her knuckles. "How kind of you, Sally. Thank you."

Andre clapped him on the back. "You see, Simcoe, I told you there was nothing nefarious here. You're a lucky man to have such a comely lass go so far out of her way for you."

"I am," John said, smiling. "I am, indeed. Thank you again, Sally. Perhaps soon, I might have an opportunity to speak with your father."

Sally smiled. "Perhaps," she said, retrieving her hand.

John and Andre returned to the house. Glaring at John's back, Sally brought up the rear. *And your apology is accepted. This time.*

The next morning Sally, Audrey, and Phebe were up early preparing and practicing for their roles in the Macbeth production.

Amid teasing and laughter at each other's expense, Sally and Phebe created costumes and playfully emoted their roles. The party was tomorrow, and all the food was ready, but Sally worried about the tea.

Every time the sound of horses' hooves rang on the road, she expected either the dispatch rider or a group of soldiers, much like those who arrested her father years ago, dragging her away to Wallabout Bay.

With every fiber of her being, she pushed her fears to the back of her mind and played an entirely different role of the unconcerned maiden, practicing for a part she might never play.

After dinner, the family sat out on the lawn, catching a cool breeze. Father drew in a deep breath and released it.

"Is something amiss, Father," Audrey asked.

He shook his head. "No. I was only thinking today is September the first. The harvest season is at hand. We will have much work to do soon."

Sally's mind turned to the linen thread to weave, not to mention candle-making would begin again.

She studied John, recalling the day he arrived in the middle of candle-making, and he'd stared at her with undisguised interest, flattering and pleasing her. In the two years since he'd arrived, his interest in her had not waned and now he wanted to ask her father for her hand. The idea filled her with trepidation.

Shifting her gaze, she studied an ant making its way up a blade of grass. What he planned once at the top, she couldn't fathom, much like how she thought of being John's wife.

Two questions she struggled with. Did she love John Simcoe? What did love look like? Her mind whirred on these so often like a donkey at a gristmill. Round and round her mind went with no answers in sight. She missed him when he left and was euphoric when he returned, but those feelings never lasted long. She got used to his absence and his presence.

Her only other gauge for love were Hannah and Joseph Green. When Joseph had to leave for the campaign season, Hannah wept for days and nearly clung to him like a vine when he returned. Sally did none of those things, which confused her.

When Andre told her about the woman who spurned him, her heart ached. In the back of her mind was the suspicion that John would not endure such pain with the grace of Andre.

Deep in thought, Sally started at a touch on her hand.

"What are you thinking, dear Sally?"

John's concerned blue eyes probed her face.

She smiled and with her chin, she pointed to the ant now making his way down the blade of grass, not finding what he sought.

"I was watching yonder ant and wondering what he hoped to gain by climbing that blade of grass."

John chuckled. "Such an imagination you have for a lass."

Before she could ask what he meant, a dispatch rider arrived.

Together, John and Andre rose. "Do you have something for me or Major Andre?" he asked reaching out a hand.

The rider saluted. "No, sir," he said looking chagrined. "I have a package for a Miss Sarah Townsend of Oyster Bay." He made his sentence sound like a question. "Captain Youngs said I was to deliver this immediately."

With a silent sigh of relief, Sally rose. "I'm Sarah Townsend."

The dispatch rider offered her a quick smile, and with a bow, he handed her a packet with a folded note tied on top. "With Captain Youngs compliments, miss."

"Thank you," she said and gestured toward the back door. "Why don't you go into the kitchen and tell Patty I said to give you some refreshments."

The young man eyed the two officers warily. "No, thank you miss. I must return to Cove Road immediately."

Sally shook her head. "Nonsense. You've done me a great favor. The least I can do is offer you some cool cider and food."

Again, his gaze snapped to the two men who were reclaiming their seats. He turned back to Sally and smiled. "Thank you, miss. I rode straight here from Manhattan City. It was a hot and dusty ride. I could use something to drink."

When he walked away, Sally opened the note. "It's from Robert," she said, her eyes scanning the page.

Dearest Sally. Here is your Bohea three pounds. Tell Father to make note the cost is three shillings.

Disappointed, she turned to her father. "He's not coming."

She glanced at the note again and in the upper right corner of the page, in small letters he'd written, m.r. M.R? Sudden realization hit. M.R. Message Received.

45

The party was in full swing, but Sally found John and Andre in the yard, their heads close, speaking in low tones. Annoyed, she advanced on them. This party was in Andre's honor. They might show some appreciation for heaven's sake.

"What are you two speaking of so intensely?"

They broke apart as if caught discussing the assassination of King George.

"Oh," John gave a negligent wave of his hand. "Military matters. Nothing to worry your pretty head about."

Andre grinned but remained silent.

Pretty head indeed. She hated when he patronized her and suppressed a sudden urge to inform him exactly what her "pretty head" knew. Instead, she fell back on teasing humor.

"By the sly grin stretching Andre's lips, I'd say you two are up to no good." She lay a hand on John's arm. Beneath the cloth of his sleeve, his muscle flexed under her palm.

"I came to apologize to you for Aunt Mercy and to beg you show her some lenience. My uncle Jacob died some years ago and she's become something of a viper since, but she means no harm. Please, she's an old woman."

Andre's stern blue eyes belied a spark of humor. "Do you mean her caustic comments of lobster backs and villains?" He shook his head. "I shouldn't worry fair maid. I daresay every family has one such as her in their family tree."

He shifted to stand closer to John as if the two of them were together on his next point.

"We shall do our utmost to protect the Xantippe from Mr. Cunningham and his ilk."

Sally started to thank them before realizing Andre called Aunt Mercy a shrew. She should scold him, but the truth was the truth. Instead, she shot him an amused but irritated glance before thanking them both.

"Now, come inside. We're about to eat and this party is in your honor, Andre. You would mortify me to the ends of the world and back if you ignore my guests."

"Never, my love!"

He crooked his elbow for Sally to take his arm and John moved to her other side. With each hand firmly held, she allowed the two men to escort her inside.

As she ate her syllabub, she listened idly while Andre and Daniel chatted with Amos Cooper, the local reporter, about the pros and cons of Mr. Rivington's newspaper, which Mr. Cooper called a "rag."

His comments made Sally smile and when Andre looked affronted, she nudged his arm. "Worry not, Major. Mr. Cooper," she said, leveling her neighbor with a teasing grin so he wouldn't take offense—she hoped—"thinks any newspaper not his own is a rag."

Mr. Cooper's mouth dropped open in shocked surprise, then he laughed. "You want to keep your eye on this one, Major. She's a sharp-witted lass. Were she a man I would have her on my staff in a thrice."

Mr. Cooper chuckled and gave Sally a sideways glance before turning away to speak with Father.

"Well, as to that," Andre said to her. "Perhaps a better friend of Rivington than I has been several times pointed out to me, but dear me, I do not see him today. Such a disappointment."

"And who would that be, prithee?"

"Why, your brother."

Sally's silver spoon clattered in her pewter cup. "My brother?"

"Well, his articles are the talk of Manhattan. I read one once," Andre said, "and wished to commission an article for myself, but alas I've been far too busy to follow up."

What a coup that would be. "You must be truly disappointed," Sally said.

Thinking back to a tea last summer, she recalled Captain McGill, and Captain Saunders asking for an introduction to Robert. Sally smiled. Her brother was a genius. If Sally learned anything from playing the silly female, it was that men loved to talk about themselves. All she ever needed to do was ask one or two well-posed questions, sit back, and try to remember all they said.

"Andre!" Phebe sat across the table. "Do tell us the story of the Cow Chace. I'd read most of your poem in Mr. Rivington's paper but haven't learned the ending yet."

Sitting beside her was Captain Wintzengerode, who though thirty was smitten with the eighteen-year-old. Phebe, for her part, appeared unaware. Several people cheered Phebe's request, and Wintzengerode quietly called, "bravo!"

Andre sat back looking delighted with himself. He splayed a well-manicured hand across his chest, as he feebly waved all to silence.

"Well as you know," he said, rising to his feet. "I composed the ditty at Headquarters and Rivington published the second canto on August thirtieth."

Peering around the table, he stopped at Phebe and narrowed his eyes at her, teasing. "Perhaps I should let you wait for the final installment by Mr. Rivington!"

Many around the table begged him to recite the entire poem, but Susannah turned away to hide a displeased expression. Indeed, many women and some men squirmed with discomfort.

Solomon scowled and dug into his custard tart, eating great mouthfuls.

If Andre was aware of the differences in attitudes, he pretended otherwise. Instead, he laughed and flapped his hands as if in surrender. "All right, all right! I shall recite the entire poem if you so desire."

Amid a smattering of applause, he drew a deep breath and cleared his throat before taking a swallow of wine.

"To drive the kine one summer's morn," he said, reciting the

opening verse.

"The tanner took his way; The calf shall rue that is unborn,
The jumbling of that day.
And Wayne descending steers shall know,
And tauntingly deride, And call to mind in every low,
The tanning of his hide."

General laughter followed his insult of General Anthony Wayne who attacked a refugee block house in July last year coming back with nothing but livestock which he at least had the presence of mind to drive back to the American side.

"Yet Bergen cows still ruminate, Unconscious in the stall,
What mighty means were used to get, And loose them after all.

For many heroes bold and brave, From Newbridge and Tappan,

And those that drink Passaic's wave, And those who eat supaun;"

By now, several loyalists were laughing and wiping tears from their eyes while their Whig guests sat in stony silence at Andre's biting satire.

Sally ate her syllabub and listened with half an ear as the poem progressed until he came to words, she recalled reading recently. He was arriving at the end of the ditty. Laugher rang out. Sally squeezed her spoon in her hand and choked down her syllabub.

Relentless, Andre continued.

"His horse that carried all his prog, His military speeches.
His corn-stock whiskey for his grog,
Blue stockings and brown breeches."

He stopped and once again took in the table at large.

"This last stanza I completed only a few days ago and will appear in Mr. Rivington's Gazette at the end of the month." Taking a deep breath, Andre continued.

"And now I've clos'd my epic strain, I tremble as I show it,
Lest this same warrior-drover, Wayne, Should ever catch the poet."

With a flourish, Andre finished his poem and made a courtly bow before returning to his seat.

Sally laughed as loudly as the rest but inside, she burned.

After dinner, the party moved outside, and Sally and her two sisters did their best rendition of the three hags in Macbeth.

"Double, double, toil and trouble," she said, feigning a witch's cackle and waving her hands in a dramatic fashion over a copper pot hanging above an imaginary fire. "Fire burn and cauldron bubble!"

Their guests laughed and clapped over their rendition of the play. When the sun began its descent, the party broke up and their guests returned home.

Mr. and Mrs. Townsend, allow me to thank you for your wonderful hospitality and for the lovely tea party."

Andre kissed Mother's hand as he bade farewell to the Townsend family. He turned to shake Father's hand and as he did so, he caught Sally's eye. She stood behind Audrey in the front hallway.

Sally always hated saying farewell to him. His comings and goings were always so unpredictable, she never anticipated when he would breeze back into their lives. This time, she couldn't help a sense if he left their home today, he might be gone forever. Her heart pinged with sadness at the prospect and felt ridiculous. He said yesterday he planned to return in a fortnight, or next month if all went well.

He stepped up and took her hands in his. "My dear, why such sadness?"

Sally did her best to smile. "Must be I have Mr. Shakespeare on my mind, for the words 'parting is such sweet sorrow' fills my heart to overflow at your departure."

Andre's blue eyes softened, and genuine affection shone from his gaze. Raising her hand, he pressed his lips to her knuckles, then he kissed her cheek before whispering in her ear. "You are my dearest friend. Simcoe has found a gem in you, my dear."

He straightened and though he meant his words to soothe, tears filled her eyes and she blinked. Words failed her.

"Well," he said, spinning around and putting on a bright air, "I must take my leave, but I assure you all, look for me after a fortnight when I shall return. You have all been most generous in your hospitality and kindness toward me. Thank you so much. I shall miss you when I'm gone."

He smiled at each person until John appeared at the sitting

room door.

"Colonel Simcoe, escort me to the front walk," Andre held out his arm to indicate the front door.

"Of course, Andre," John said with a smile. "I shall be happy to."

Sally stood at the front door as the two men moved toward the waiting horses. They spoke, heads close, and from where she stood, Sally sensed the intensity in their conversation. Something was going on, but what and how West Point factored in, she had no idea, so she left it to Robert to figure out.

As if with Andre's departure extended summer went with him. Sally woke to cold, blustery northwest winds and heavy rain. Rather than the light linen frock she intended to wear, she pulled on her woolen petticoat and heavy woolen skirt and donned a shawl. She had the last of the linen to weave before David and Father restrung the loom for the wool.

Of all her tasks, Sally liked weaving the best. Alone in the weaving room, she let her mind wander, taking pleasure in a small bit of cloth growing into a bolt. This sense of accomplishment she did not receive from the never-ending task of spinning.

Finding a rhythm with her feet and hands, Sally's mind wandered. Despite John's dual personality, showing her the side of him he wanted her to love and keeping hidden his darker nature, she grew fond of him as a friend.

Was that enough to parlay into a marriage? Mother told her she didn't have to accept him, and she clung to the knowledge, but also feared what would happen to her or her family if she refused him.

A knock on the door startled her out of her musings.

"Enter."

She expected to find her father or mother appearing to discover her progress. Instead, John entered and stopped inside the door. Sally waited for him to speak but when he continued to stare, she let go of the batten and gave him her full attention.

"Did you need something, John?"

"The sound of your loom attracted me, and I wished to behold you at your task."

"Oh," she said with a smile and reached again for the batten. "I should think such work would bore you." She threw the shuttlecock and pulled the batten arm, which came down with a thwack-thwack. She shifted her feet, changing the warp to the weft, and threw the shuttlecock back. Down thwacked the batten arm.

"You don't become bored or lonely in here?"

She shook her head. "I like weaving. I find solitude here. A chance to be alone with my thoughts."

"And what are your thoughts? If you tell me yours, I'll tell you mine."

She smiled but didn't answer. How could she tell him what she'd been thinking?

"All right," he said, smiling. "I shall tell you mine." He took one more step inside the room. "Shall no fair maid with equal fire awake the flames of soft desire: My bosom born, for transport, burn and raise my thoughts from Delia's urn? Fond Youth, the God of Love replies, your answer take from Sarah's eyes."

He stepped forward again.

Sally tilted her head. He was giving her a message and she trembled.

"Maybe I will speak again this year," he said, and his expression suggested he expected success to come swiftly.

This year? Would the war end this year? Her brain flew back to the note addressed to James Anderson. Was that meant for him, and Andre took it knowing? Had Andre delivered it to John?

"John," she said, but he raised a hand and she stopped.

"Say nothing, for now, Sally. I simply wish to make clear my intentions. I must await events for now. But please, I must have an answer. Do I have reason to believe a discussion with your father would prove to my happiness?"

A knot of fear twisted her heart. To marry him would mean leaving here. Living in England. Hannah had no problem leaving her family, but Sally was different. She didn't have an adventurous spirit like Hannah's. She also didn't have a mother like Hannah's.

"I...I... don't...I can't say, John. We don't know when the war will end."

She studied his face, which darkened over her reluctance, and arched a brow. "Do we?"

John drew in a deep breath through his nose and the sound of his exhale reached her ears.

"Come to the training ground with me?"

"Right now?"

He nodded.

He hadn't invited her there in a long time, but he'd been gone for eleven months, and she tended to forget he'd been home only a few short weeks, so comfortable she'd become with his presence. If only he'd stop pestering her about asking Father to marry her.

At the training ground, John took her hand to help her from the saddle.

"Back at home," he said, lowering her to her feet. "What were you thinking about while at your task?"

"I was thinking about you," she said before quickly averting her gaze.

"Truly?" His eyebrows shot up. "What were you thinking of, if I may ask." Taking firm hold of her hand, he helped her ascend the hill to the training ground.

"I was thinking of our successful tea. I do hope Andre enjoyed himself. He said he did, but sometimes one can never tell with him."

John chuckled. "Oh, don't worry about Andre. What you see with him, is what you get."

"Oh, I don't think that's true," she said. "Andre strikes me as a man who never jests, teases, or engages in idle or pointless conversation."

That surprised him. Sally was observant but she was far keener than she'd ever let on before. He studied her, but she only offered a half smile and raised eyebrows.

He decided not to pursue the subject for now. "You seemed overly sad at his leaving," John said, trying hard to mask the jealousy in his voice, but Sally's sharp glance said otherwise.

"I like Andre. He's become a good friend, and since we can never anticipate when we'll greet him again, yes, I was sad," she said. "What did you and he talk about before you left? You were engrossed in conversation."

"Oh," John said with a negligent shrug of one shoulder. "He told me there is a big push planned and wanted the Rangers to take part. Which is why we're training and why we were so deep in conversation."

They reached the top of the hill and John puffed up at the sight of his men working hard.

"I realize we angered you with our single-minded focus, and I apologize, but we were making necessary preparations. I honestly didn't think you would be interested in listening to us discuss military matters ad nauseam."

When Sally didn't answer, he turned to find her studying him with her keen hazel-eyed stare. Did she doubt him? He decided the best response was to meet her gaze full. Besides, John loved staring into her eyes. Until the day he died, he would always have an affinity for hazel-eyed girls. Under his scrutiny, a red stain moved up her neck and into her face and she turned away.

"So," she said. "Tell me what mischief your men are up to."

Again, John puffed up. He couldn't help himself. If all went off as planned, the war would soon be over. This conflict was tedious, and John feared there was no end in sight, but now, with Andre setting things in motion, his fear abated.

"John," Sally pointed to a group of men scaling a makeshift wall in groups of two, one to stay at the bottom holding weapons and equipment while the other climbed to the top before reaching down to take the accouterments allowing their companion to climb. "What are they doing?"

"We're practicing a new technique for my men," he told her, again his chest puffing out. "All too often men are killed storming a stronghold so I'm teaching them to sneak up on an obstruction, climb over and surprise the enemy from within."

As he spoke, he prayed he didn't give away too much information. Sally was a quick study and had a way of making astonishing intuitive leaps often leaving him fearing he'd said too much. But nothing ever came from the things he told her, and he assured himself since she was only a woman, whatever he told her was safe. Nevertheless, he studied her while she took in the activity, and wished he had an idea of what she was thinking.

"Are you saying your next campaign will involve climbing walls?" She gawked at him. "Wouldn't it be easier to knock on the door?"

He couldn't help a chuckle. Of course, she wouldn't understand the significance of scaling walls.

"So, you are leaving again. I feared as much. So late in the season. How long will you be gone this time?"

He smiled at her concern. "We're not leaving yet, though plans are to head north as soon as I receive orders."

Her lovely brow furrowed. "You will be careful, this time, John, and not be captured again?"

He stepped close to her and using his body as a shield, he took her hand in his. "I will be at my most cautious, my dear. My love," he said in a whisper.

She shifted her feet and John let go of her hand. He half turned his body toward his men.

"Sally," he said, glancing at her from beneath his lashes and scuffing a toe in the dirt. "May I have permission now to ask your father? If what we plan is successful, I can tell you the war will end within the next few months and I will most definitely be out of harm's way when it does, so you needn't worry about widowhood."

He turned fully to her. "Please, Sally, might I have permission to ask to court you?"

Sally gazed at him with shining hazel eyes. Were they tears of joy or sorrow? John held his breath, terrified they were the latter.

Her lips parted as though she meant to speak but instead, she closed her mouth and shrugged.

"You may ask Father for permission, John," she said, casting her gaze to the ground.

In his elation at her final acquiescence, he missed how her shoulders slumped and she kept her gaze focused on her slippers.

46

"Sally." Father stopped inside the sitting room door. She was in the chair by the west window working on her quilt blocks, which she lowered to her lap. He peered through the sitting room to John's closed bedroom door before returning his blue-eyed gaze to her. "Come into the parlor, Poppet, I wish a word."

Laying her sewing down, she approached. Father let her precede him into the room across the hall. As he shut the doors, her heart stuttered in her chest, fearing she might have done something to deserve reprimand, though she couldn't think what.

He pulled a chair out for her. "Have a seat, my dear,"

Sally lowered herself and lacing her fingers together, placed her hands on the table. He sat at the head of the table and arranged the tails of his coat, so he didn't sit on them. Then, he adjusted his cravat before leaning close.

"Colonel Simcoe has declared his feelings for you, which should come as no surprise to either of us."

She nodded.

He leveled steely-blue eyes on her. "Have you changed your mind about him? Are you of a mind to accept his proposal?"

Sally opened her mouth but only a choked sound emerged. She

closed her mouth again.

He dropped his gaze to her hands and reached out a finger, drawing the tip along the knuckles of her hand.

"Sally, my dear, I must warn you of one thing. I am aware of your activities. You understand this to be true."

Again, he raised his eyes and stared into hers. "Whether or not the British win, if you marry Simcoe and he ever learns of your activities...well..." He sat back. "I fear what would become of you."

"I can't marry him, Father. But when he asked again for permission to speak with you, I ran out of excuses and couldn't think of one fast enough, so I agreed."

She clasped his hand. "I don't dare tell him no. I'm afraid of what he'll do to you or Mother or..." She broke off, not wanting to say more.

"Leave him to me," Father said, leaning forward. "I will tell him no for you and he cannot exact his revenge upon you."

"But he might upon you."

"Why? I am your father. It's within my rights as your parent to safeguard your life and if my answer is no, John Simcoe understands he must abide by my decision."

Sally studied him and found in his warm, steady gaze, security and safety. She smiled and squeezed his hands.

"Thank you, Father. I must confess, I told him he could speak to you with a heavy heart, and I feared you would give him permission. I'm sorry for doubting you."

He reassured her of her safety and lighthearted, Sally returned to her sewing.

Four days passed in which Sally waited for retribution from John to fall on her head. When it didn't, she sought out Father. He was in the new orchard, pruning the saplings, and preparing them to survive their first full winter in North America.

If not for John, they would be picking apples now instead of nursing along trees which would take another seven years to bear fruit.

"Father," Sally said, stopping next to the knee-high sapling. "May I speak to you?"

Father straightened and wiped his brow with his sleeve. "Is this a private conversation?" He asked, glancing around and she knew he was assessing whether to stop work for so long.

She reassured him. "I wondered if you'd had a chance to speak with John about...well...you know."

He smiled. "I do and no I have not. He's not made his presence felt in the past few days and made abundantly clear he and Andre are on a secret mission to end the war singlehandedly."

Sally chuckled at his sarcasm. Since their talk on Sunday, she'd become more aware of her father's dislike of both John and Andre and marveled at how well he'd hidden his feelings.

"Do you dislike them both so much?"

He shook his head. "'Tis against God's law to dislike people, so no, I do not dislike them. Quite honestly, if the circumstances had been different, I might have called them both great friends despite our age gaps. But I do dislike what they stand for and so therein lies my struggle."

Sally nodded and let her gaze roam over the orchard. "We should be picking now."

"Let it be, Poppet. He did what he had to do."

"It still angers me."

"It angers me too," he said. "But let it go."

Sally's gaze returned to him, and she wondered at the range of emotions in his eyes. Love, sorrow, sympathy, regret, and relief. She slid an arm around his waist and hugged him.

"I'll let you go back to work now."

Sally returned to the house with a lighter step. Father hadn't seen John to speak to him, which was why she'd received nothing but silence.

She entered the house through the front door intending to return to her quilt blocks.

"There you are, Sally," Mother said approaching from the kitchen. "I've been searching everywhere for you."

"I was in the orchard with Father."

Mother nodded as if that was unimportant. "I need you to go to Susannah's. She sent a note. Apparently, the weaver couldn't take all of her wool and she asks if you are able to weave the surplus."

"Of course."

"Good. David is waiting out back with Farmer Girl saddled."

"David needn't escort me, Mother. He has much to do with the flax still, doesn't he?"

A look of relief crossed her features. "He does. And I thank you for being so thoughtful."

Yesterday's foul weather cleared, though gray clouds scudded across the sky, occasionally darkening the landscape. A shadow chased across a wheatfield as men swung scythes. Women and children followed behind gathering in the sheaves. How much of the wheat the ravenous wolves in red coats would take was anybody's guess, but many families would starve this winter.

Once at the Youngs' Susannah once again bade her sit, this time in the front room where a cheery fire snapped and crackled in the hearth. A cup of cider and donuts sat beside Sally's chair. At her feet were six bags stuffed full of wool.

"I do thank you, Sally, for taking this on for me. There are several women in town I might ask, but no one takes better care when weaving than you do."

"Thank you, Susannah. I'll do my best with such praise ringing in my ears."

They laughed together and talked for a quarter of an hour before Daniel sauntered in.

He waved a hand at the overstuffed burlap sacks. "Good afternoon, Sally, dear. I see you've agreed to take on Susannah's task."

"I'm happy too, Daniel. Anything for a friend. Though you outdid yourself with spinning this year, Susannah."

Susannah and Daniel exchanged a significant glance. She'd seen them do so on any number of occasions and something in her now snapped.

"All right, you two. Many times, I've said something, and you've given each other that look. Explain."

She tried to sound as if she teased, praying they would tell her.

"The wool isn't for us," Susannah said lacing her fingers together in her lap. "The wool, if you still want the work, is for the continentals. I spin far more wool than I need and find people who will weave the cloth so the soldiers can clothe themselves."

Daniel sat down next to his wife. "She provides the cloth they need for clothing, while I..."

He stopped and she realized he didn't want to disclose anything about himself.

333

But Sally studied his face and suddenly everything made sense. "You're working with Robert," she said in an awed whisper. Her fingers flew to her lips and her eyes widened. "You're working with Robert," she said again this time with utter certainty.

Daniel nodded.

"No!" She stared, trying to absorb the enormity of the truth. "Robert told me if ever I needed to get him information fast, I need only come to you."

Daniel smiled and Susannah looked relieved.

"So, every time John went out on foraging raids, he often came back empty-handed because you were moving the food away, weren't you?"

Daniel tilted his head. "Not so much moving the food away as dropping a few well-placed suggestions to a farmer or two and letting them handle the situation as they decided."

He leaned forward and studied her with an intensity in his eyes. "Sally dear," he said, leaning forward. "You've been one of our dearest friends as well, and the hardest thing we ever had to do was keep you ignorant of our actions. I do hope you realize why it was necessary."

"Of course, I do. If anything happened..." She broke off not needing to say what she was thinking.

Daniel rose. "I received a dispatch today that I think you might find interesting." He went to his study and returned almost immediately, handing her the note.

Sally read aloud.

Oyster Bay, 14th September 1780
Sir:
By order of Colonel Simcoe am directed to desire you to furnish seven wagons or ox teams upon the next advice sent of the regiment moving. These wagons will be discharged the first post the regt. halts at. This is only to intimate to you to have the teams in readiness upon the first notice that the baggage stores, etc. of the Regt. may not suffer by the delay when the march is ordered.
Robert Gardner, Sergt. Complied with, Quarter Master, QR."

Sally handed back the note. "So, this means the Queen's Rangers will be on the move again."

She peered up at Daniel. "Any idea where they're going?"

He shook his head. "I was hoping you might find out."

The days were growing shorter and now candles glowed in the sitting room and a lively fire snapped in the hearth.

Sally spun flax while John and her father chatted of idle things. He wanted an answer from the man, but with Sally present, he lost his nerve and couldn't find a way to open the line of discussion. Sipping his port John racked his brain but his heart pounded so hard in his chest, he was certain Sally heard the thumps from her position at her spinning wheel.

Mr. Townsend sipped his port. Shadows from the fire and candles danced in the growing darkness, but John didn't miss the significant glance he directed at Sally.

"We might have to leave in a few days," John said. "I received a dispatch from General Clinton."

"We'll be sorry to see you go," Mr. Townsend said not sounding particularly sorry.

Something in Mr. Townsend's words made John wonder if he spoke the truth.

"Sally," Mr. Townsend turned his gaze upon her. "Would you please excuse John and me? We must speak privately."

In a lithe move, Sally rose from the spinning wheel, as if she'd been waiting. She shot John a nervous glance, clearly aware of what her father wanted to say.

"I'll say good night," she said kissing Father's cheek before leaving the room.

John waited, listening to her footfalls on the stairs and holding his breath while making sure to meet Mr. Townsend's piercing blue gaze.

"I've been waiting for a chance to find you alone, Colonel so we might talk."

Colonel. Usually, Mr. Townsend called him John, or son. He sighed but straightened his shoulders and sat up tall in his chair. He'd dealt with disappointment before in this God-forsaken country.

"You are refusing me permission, Mr. Townsend," he said, forcing the words from his mouth.

"Yes, I am. It's nice to anticipate what might happen, but none of us can truly comprehend the outcome of anything until it is accomplished."

John squeezed his lips between his teeth. "Sally said much the same thing to me over the past several months. I understand where she gets her wisdom from."

He turned his body in the chair and forced a pleasant smile. "Mr. Townsend, if the war should end in the King's favor, would you still deny me permission to court and eventually marry Sally?"

Mr. Townsend's eyes widened as though surprised by his tenacity. John was tenacious. He loved her more than life itself and he refused to be denied her.

Mr. Townsend raised his glass to his mouth and drained the contents, then with slow deliberation, he set the glass down.

"Let us not count our chickens, before they hatch," he said, and rising bid John a good night.

47

When Mr. Townsend proved implacable, John spent his time preparing for departure while Sally spent most of her time weaving the wool Mrs. Youngs asked for.

He was in his room, studying his last note from General Clinton. Andre had left for West Point more than a week ago. And hadn't been heard from since.

He was to meet with Benedict Arnold on Monday last. John was to head north days ago. Andre's silence was ominous. Something went wrong. That was the only thing that made any sense.

Anxiety gripped him making his legs wobble. He grabbed the back of his chair to sit. Snatching his quill and a piece of parchment, he dipped his quill in the ink.

"Israel" John's shout rang through the house. When the man failed to materialize out of thin air, he shouted again. "Israel!"

"Yes, sir," Israel said standing in the doorway.

"Where've you been? Dammit man, leave the wench alone. When I call you, I expect immediate obedience, do I make myself clear?"

When his aide didn't answer, he glanced up. The young

diffident boy had grown into a confident man standing at attention, hands rigid at his sides, his expression unreadable.

John sighed, releasing his distress-filled anger. "Forgive me, Israel. I am beset with worry."

"Yes, sir."

"I'm going to the training field," John said, finishing his note. "If I sit idle another moment, I will not be responsible for my actions."

He sanded the note and handed it to Israel. "Find a courier for my dispatch and tell him not to come back without an answer."

Israel took the note. "Yes, sir," he said and left.

John rose donned his coat and headed out the door after his aide.

Captain Youngs had found seven wagons, which pleased John. They waited on the far side of the ground, waiting, as was he. As John approached, he waved his arms to gather his men close. He couldn't stay in Oyster Bay any longer. With each passing day of Andre's silence, an impending doom fell over him until he was now certain something happened.

As the men gathered around, John began his speech. "Gentleman, be ready to move out at first light. We are returning to Manhattan City to await further orders from there."

"But sir," Lieutenant McNab spoke up. "If we move to Manhattan, won't we further delay if the adjutant general's orders come here first?"

"They won't. Andre will send word to headquarters first and they will direct a message to me. If we're in Manhattan we remove a fifty-mile trip, thus shortening our reaction time."

McNab nodded. "Very good, sir."

John searched each man's face. "All right, you have your orders. I want us ready to depart by sunup."

Spinning on his heel he stormed back to his horse and returned to the Townsend's. As he rode up, he found a dispatch rider waiting by the front gate. "You have messages for me?"

He handed over a note from General Clinton. John thanked him and went inside, walking slowly down the hall as he read the note.

"Is everything all right, John?"

He glanced up to find Audrey coming down the stairs. "You appear at once perplexed and relieved by what you're reading."

He smiled. "Everything is fine, Miss Audrey. I've been waiting on pins and needles for information," he said, flapping the note in the air. "Which has now arrived."

Audrey smiled. "I'm happy. You received good news, I trust?"

He pursed his lips. "Not good, but not as bad as I suspected. The mission Andre and I have been working on has been delayed a few days."

"I see."

She came down the last few steps and stopped in front of him. "Well, I pray all works out for you. And remember to be patient with those around you. They are here to serve."

John reddened. "Did you overhear me shouting at Israel earlier?"

Audrey's smile was at once understanding and reproachful. She lay a gentle hand on his sleeve. "Well," she said. "Who could not." With a soft smile she went to the back of the house.

John watched her leave. She was a lovely woman, but she didn't have the same fiery spirit as her sister. As he returned to his note, all thoughts of the Townsend girls disappeared from his mind.

According to the note, Andre had been delayed because his ship had been spotted by the enemy and fired upon, forcing them to retreat downriver. His heart thumped with the knowledge his dear friend was now trapped behind enemy lines until Wednesday when another attempt would be made to retrieve him. The information, having taken so long to find him, proved his point and he was glad he ordered his men to Manhattan where he might receive information about Andre's progress without waiting for dispatch riders.

Sally wove Susannah's cloth. Knowing the bolts of wool would eventually become uniforms for American soldiers made the work go faster and she hummed the tune Yankee Doodle.

Though Andre used the tune for his insulting poem, "The Cow Chace," at the tea party, Sally quietly sang the original words.

A British Officer wrote the song as an insult to Sally's countrymen, but as the war dragged on, the Americans took up the song with pride, turning the insult into a banner of honor.

A knock on the door stopped her song and weaving.

"Enter."

John opened the door and stood inside giving Sally a sense of Deja Vu.

She stopped her work. "John. What can I do for you?"

"I came to tell you I'm leaving in the morning. Back to Manhattan City."

"Oh," she said as disappointment and dread rushed her. "How long will you be gone this time?"

"Not long, I dare hope." He took a step further. "It's clear my work will be better served from headquarters. For the time being."

"So, you're not going on a late campaign as you did last year."

His sudden glare made her tremble. "What makes you say such a thing?" he asked in a sharp tone and Sally recoiled from the venom in his words.

"I... I, you just said your work will be better served at headquarters, so I deduce you're not going on a campaign like you did last year and were taken captive. When you came back almost a year later you were terribly ill."

He visibly relaxed. "I'm sorry," he said with a wave of a hand. "I've been on edge these past days. Forgive me."

A glance askance accompanied a wry grin. "I've noticed."

"What are you working on?" John's gaze fell to the cloth stretched on the loom.

"This is Susannah's wool. I want to finish so I can weave ours."

He offered an apologetic grimace. "I'm sorry for my irritability. I have pressing worries."

"Do you wish to share them? Sometimes talking through a situation helps one to solve the problem."

He studied her so long, Sally wondered if he suspected her role in the note about James Anderson or that she sent a warning to the Americans through Robert. Perhaps he discovered she'd been communicating with her brother for a year and a half regarding his actions. That the raid on Lloyd's Neck was successful because of her. A tremble started in her core and spread to her arms and legs.

She kept her hands firmly on her work so she wouldn't give herself away.

John lowered his gaze and spoke to his boots. "Andre left two weeks ago to embark on a mission for General Clinton. I should have had word by now of when to commence my part. His silence is worrying." He held up the dispatch. "But General Clinton sent word explaining the delay. However, if I go to Manhattan, I'll be in a better position to obtain necessary information as to my next move."

"I understand," Sally said, realizing how deeply he had worried about Andre. In his personal feelings, John was a tight lipped, private man, so his comment helped Sally understand the depths of his feelings for his friend.

"How long will you be gone?"

Again, he shrugged. "As long as needed."

"John," she slid off the loom bench and moved to him. Placing a hand on the woolen sleeve of his green coat, she peered up at him. "If you receive word of Andre, please, will you send it? He's become a great friend and if he's in distress, I should like to pray for him."

A smile pulled his lips and the worry in his blue eyes changed to gratitude. "I shall send word the moment I receive it."

"Thank you."

They drowned in each other's eyes until she became conscious John was ever so slowly lowering his head to hers.

Pull away! Step back. Sally should have heeded the warning in her brain, but she didn't. Instead, she allowed John's lips to touch hers. They were warm and surprisingly soft for a mouth she often thought of as harsh. His breath was minty, and his kiss was light as butterfly wings and lasted no more than two or three seconds before he pulled back.

"Sally," he said in a whisper, his breath brushing her cheek. His eyes were closed, and he moved to kiss her again but this time she heeded the warning and stepped back.

John opened his eyes and she saw a flash of anger, replaced quickly by regret and embarrassment.

He straightened. "Forgive me," he said pulling on the edges of his coat. "I don't know what came over me."

"That's all right," she said, unsure what to say or do, so she returned to the loom bench.

"Well," he said after a moment of silence, "I shall leave you to your task. I simply wanted you to be aware of our plan."

"Thank you," she said. "Give Andre my best."

"I will."

John turned to leave and Sally almost called out. Something told her if he left her now, he would never come back. Instead, she peered through the open door while he made his way across the yard to the house. When he disappeared inside, she resumed her work.

48

September eighteen dawned blustery and cold and a strong north wind blew dark clouds over Long Island. Rain scudded across the yard as the Queen's Rangers waited in the street for John to appear and mount up.

He stood with Sally at the front door saying his goodbyes. "Be well, Sally," he said. "I shall miss you."

She reached up and tugged at his collar. "And I shall miss you, John. Be well, don't get yourself captured."

He smiled at the teasing glint in her hazel eyes.

John leaned close and kissed her cheek, then straightened with a swift sudden movement he jerked the front door open and strode down the walk pulling at his collar against the weather. He didn't look back. At the gate, he mounted Hercules, and gave the word for the Queen's Rangers to ride out of town.

As they rode, he went over their plans for the millionth time, understanding the best-laid military plans always went wrong the minute they were executed, so he needn't worry because The Vulture had been fired upon from shore, forcing them back downriver.

But if they couldn't sail past, how was Andre going to return?

What was the next step? This was why he had to be in Manhattan. He had to be in on the planning.

These mental gyrations would accomplish nothing, but he couldn't help himself. This mission was of utmost importance. They had to succeed. They had to demoralize the American Army if they wanted the war to end sometime.

Once at Jamaica, the Rangers turned west. By midday, they would be back on Staten Island where they'd be able to prepare for their part in capturing West Point.

They'd been on Staten Island for a week, enduring cold rain and wind. By Saturday morning, the weather cleared, leaving in its wake a cold, blustery northwest breeze. Gray and silver clouds scudded across an otherwise azure sky, and though the sun shone, he could derive little warmth from the fireball. John wondered, not for the first time if this didn't portend disaster.

The grass, where the sun had not yet touched, glistened with a layer of frost and he dreaded spending another winter in this land. This would make his fifth. He couldn't stand winter's bitter temperatures and deep snows. The thought of the coming season sent a shiver through his body. Where was Andre?

Israel brought a tray of tea and food.

John's stomach grumbled at the sight of breakfast. "Thank you, Israel. Any word?"

Israel shook his head. "No, sir, I'll bring word as soon as I can." He set the tray on the camp table and stepped back. "Will that be all, Colonel?"

John nodded and sat down, but Israel planted his feet shoulder-width and placed his hands behind his back at-rest.

"Do you need something?"

"Yes, sir," Israel said and cleared his throat.

"Well, man speak out!"

"It's about Liss, sir."

John stiffened. Trying to keep the annoyance out of his voice, he studied his aide. "What of her," he said in a cautious tone.

"We wish to marry. Sir."

John sighed. "You realize that's not possible. She belongs to Mr. Townsend for better or worse."

Israel said nothing. He stared at John as if expecting him to fix the problem. John sighed again.

"I'm sorry, Israel but I have to say no. The British army cannot be purchasing women so their soldiers can marry," he said, cringing at his harsh tone. He was sorry for it, but rules were rules.

Israel stared at him for a few minutes, sullen and angry, but he drew himself to the position of attention. "What if..." He broke off and for the first time since he joined with John, fear filled his eyes.

"What if what?"

"What if she were to...run away...To come with us."

Horror ripped John's gut. "Do you mean to say the wench came with us? Did you sneak her away?"

Israel said nothing. He remained at attention and stared at a spot somewhere behind John's right shoulder.

John threw his fork down. It clattered on his plate. "Dammit man!"

"We wish to marry. They's a minister here said he'd do it."

John held up a hand forestalling any more words from his aide. With a murderous sideways glance, he said, "the less I know, the better for you."

His aide waited his gaze flicking between John's face and the spot on the canvas behind him. As John considered the repercussions of what the couple had done, he could hear Israel's strained breathing.

His breath exploded from his own body and John flicked a dismissive hand. "Go. Marry your lady and return here by this afternoon. I shall need your services. I suppose she can work as well since she's here."

Israel's face lit in a huge grin. He gave a swift salute and spinning on his heel he headed for the tent flap as fast as he could go presumably before John could change his mind.

As he left, John shook his head. Too bad he didn't have that kind of courage of his conviction. Perhaps he should have stolen Sally away and married her against her family's wishes. What would have happened then?

While John resumed his breakfast, he stared out his open tent flap. In the ocean, humpbacked whales, swimming south, breached and splashed in the Atlantic. Once upon a time, John would have beheld their majesty, fascinated by the leviathans, but his mind was taken up with worry and he barely registered the beasts as they capered offshore.

"General, my men are ready and on alert. What are your orders?"

General Clinton glanced up from his map and absentmindedly returned John's salute. "Stand down, Colonel. We have no information as to his whereabouts at the moment."

"Sir, do we know if he made contact with Mr. Arnold?"

"He managed to have his meeting with the so-called gentleman on Wednesday. This we obtained from the Captain of the Vulture, which dropped him off. However, the Vulture was discovered in the Hudson waiting for Andre's return. They were fired upon, compelling them to move downstream, and now Andre is trapped behind enemy lines."

John nodded. Clinton had already said as much in his dispatches. "Andre insisted on going under a flag of truce," John said. "The Americans will turn him over to Mr. Washington who will release him. At worst Andre will be a prisoner, and an exchange can easily be made. In either case, they will bring him to Philadelphia." John tried to sound confident in the hopes Clinton would be agreeable to his next idea.

"Sir, let me send a party out. My men can scour the roads and perhaps rescue Andre."

General Clinton shook his head. "We don't know his location, Colonel. No. We must await events."

"But sir—,"

"No! Colonel."

John clamped his mouth closed. It would do no good to try to persuade Clinton until he took his time assessing all contingencies. He drew a deep breath and tried not to exhale his frustration too loudly.

General Howe had had his shortcomings, but he was decisive, unlike Clinton.

John liked Clinton far more than he liked Howe, but he was damnably slow in making decisions. He turned away, moved to the hearth, and warmed his hands.

"If you pull a party together," Clinton said musing, "how long before you could be ready to depart?"

"Within the hour."

Clinton nodded and went back to studying his map. "Go back to camp and await my orders. Most likely Andre is on his way back with no way to communicate with us."

John saluted. "Yes sir," he said. Picking up his cap he walked from the room, but dread settled in his breast. Something happened and he wished he was with his friend.

49

Hours after the Rangers left town, pandemonium broke out in the Townsend home. Liss was missing. Mother sent Sally to the servant's quarters and Patty went with her to identify anything of Liss's left behind. Patty showed her where Liss's room was, and they entered to find she'd swept the area clean.

The ceiling sloped sharply up here, and bare walls allowed the cold to seep into the room. Though Sally had head room, she couldn't help feeling the need to duck as she moved about. She'd never been up here before, and the stark difference between the bare necessity in this space and the comparative opulence below struck her. Hard. For the first time in her life, Sally was uncomfortable in Patty's presence. She glanced at her from the corner of her eye. Did the older woman resent her? Did she and Hiram live like this too?

Pushing away her discomforting embarrassment, she searched the room. Nothing of the girl's remained. The bed was stripped, and clean linen folded and neatly placed at the foot of the overstuffed mattress tick.

Patty tsked. "That girl. What's she gone and done now?"

"I think that's rather clear," Sally said. "John never discouraged their relationship. Liss told me he'd known about it for months and only told them not to get caught." She sighed and turned to the older woman.

"I'm sorry, Patty. I should have listened to you, but the idea of a romance was sweet. I thought the same could be had for John and I and..." she stopped. "I should have listened to you the night of the holiday tea."

"It ain't your fault child." Patty took hold of Sally's elbows and squeezed. "I suspect no matter who said what to who, this would have been the outcome. Love hits and when it does, it's a powerful force." She glanced around the room. "Well, there's no help for it. We have to go downstairs and report she's gone for good."

"How did they do it?" Sally asked. "How did she sneak out of here unseen?"

"Probably stole away in the night," Patty said. "Good riddance to bad rubbish if you ask me. I had enough of that girl's sullenness and lack of respect and her lazy ways. She can be the Rangers problem from here on out."

Downstairs, Father vowed he'd get revenge on both Israel and John. Sally prayed he never got the chance to carry out his rage. She didn't want to see him in Wallabout Bay.

Strangely, none of the other servants appeared sorry to see her go. Father clamped down hard on the rest of them and as the days passed, a dark tension filled the household that Sally had never experienced before. It became so bad she used the excuse of needing to finish the weaving to avoid being in the house. As she worked, she thought about Liss and Israel. Didn't they deserve to live their lives free of the dictates of others? Free of oppression? Wasn't that what this war was about? Didn't Mr. Adams, Mr. Jefferson, even General Washington clamor about freedom and oppression? Didn't the Declaration of Independence say all men are created equal? If so, then what of men like Israel? Were only white men created equal?

Freedom and Liberty. That was what the war was about. Freedom and Liberty. If they were held in reserve for just one group of Americans, then she feared the stain of hypocrisy might never wash out.

Sally stopped the loom and leaning her head on her hands, she wept.

After a week, life settled back to comparative normal. Father was still furious at Liss's disappearance, but he no longer took his rage out on the rest of the servants, and in fact, apologized to each personally.

This morning, Sally and Phebe were in the sitting room. Sally read aloud from the Rivington Gazette the final stanza from the Cow Chace as written by Major John Andre, Adjutant General and aide to General Clinton.

Phebe sat next to her knitting woolen stockings for winter listening to Sally read.

"And now I've closed my epic strain, I tremble as I shew it. Lest this same warrior-drover Wayne, should ever catch the poet. Finis."

Phebe clapped her hands and laughed. "I do so love his poem and the droll way Andre depicts it."

"He is indeed a witty man."

Sally scanned the paper for Robert's articles. On the third page halfway down, she found one about Lieutenant McNab of the Queen's Rangers. Sally read with interest the personal information about the lieutenant. Where in England he came from, his family, and his ambitions once he left the army, as well as a short paragraph about what regiment he was in, what action they'd recently seen, and the lieutenant's speculation they were to go next. North. West Point?

"...when will John return?"

Sally jerked her head up. "I'm sorry, Phebe."

"I said I wonder when John and the Queen's Rangers will return. Did he say?"

"No."

She returned to the article, but through the open window, a commotion of horses and men shouting caught their attention.

Before they could react, the front door flew open, and John strode in.

They jumped from their seats. "John!" Surprise made Sally and Phebe exclaim at the same time.

"You're back! Sally said.

"Only for a few hours." He headed for his room.

Sally followed him as he passed by her without so much as a glance her way. "John I must speak with you. It's about Liss."

"Not now, Sally," he said and tried to shut the door on her, but she put her foot in the door.

Pain shot through her toes, but she refused to yield. "Yes, now. She's disappeared and we fear she may be with Israel. She needs to return home where she belongs."

He stared at her for such a long moment her scalp tightened, but she held his gaze.

"Yes, she is with Israel. She is his wife."

Did she see condemnation in his face? Did he allow them to marry to get revenge on her or Father for refusing him? If so, that was a level of petty she never thought possible in him.

Sally sucked in her breath as behind her, Phebe squealed.

This situation was out of her league. She didn't have the capacity to fight him on this and so she withdrew. A strategic withdrawal, as John would put it. Crossing her arms, she stepped back. "Be assured I will be informing Father of this."

"Be informed, I don't much care. They love each other. Slavery is an abomination and your family—," he broke off but straightened his shoulders and glared at her.

"My family what? Is an abomination? I'm an abomination?"

"I have work, Sally," he said and slammed the door in her face.

An hour later, he emerged from his room, saddlebags slung over his right shoulder, bulging with items. Sally rose from her seat where she'd taken up her knitting needles. "Are you leaving now?"

"I am."

"And you have no idea when you'll return."

"No."

A sharp rap on the front door made her jump. Phebe answered and a dispatch rider entered.

"I have messages for—," he stopped when he saw John and held them out. When John took them, he saluted and left.

"A dispatch from General Clinton," he said.

Sally waited, breathless, as his eyes quickly scan the parchment.

"The devil!"

She and Phebe exchanged startled glances. "What's wrong?"

He didn't answer, but ashen faced, read the note again.

"John, what's happened?"

"Andre has been taken prisoner by those...those scoundrels!

351

Now we're to remain here to await further developments."

Sally's breath caught in her throat, and, for a moment, she thought she might faint.

"Well, that's not so bad. After all, you became a prisoner and were exchanged, so perhaps will he."

John dropped his hand to his side and covered his eyes with his other hand. In a swift movement making Sally jump, he spun on his heel and stormed back to his room.

"I must write to the General. I can send out a search party for him. No doubt they'll take him back to Philadelphia. I can have men on the roads waiting to ambush the party and rescue him."

"John stop!"

He spun back around a murderous glare in his blue eyes. He advanced on her, finger out and in her face in a blink of an eye. He scared her, but she refused to back down.

He shouted at her. "Don't you dare tell me what to do!"

Phebe gasped and fled, but Sally held her ground.

Not knowing how she dared, she placed a gentle hand on his arm. "I only mean if he's been taken prisoner why the rush to send out a party to rescue him? He'll be kept for a month or two as you were and released for some other prisoner. Like you were. Don't get yourself in trouble or cause Andre more distress by doing something foolish."

He drew in a deep breath through his nose and slowly exhaled and Sally dared hope he was listening to her. Chewing his lower lip, he shifted his now calm gaze to his boot tops.

"You are correct, my dear. I'm sorry I snapped, it's just...Andre is one of my dearest friends and I don't claim many people as dear friends."

"I understand," she said fighting a sudden guilty urge to cry. Did she have something to do with Andre's predicament? She only told Robert what she found. John Andre was a grown man capable of making his own decisions.

"Give Andre time. I'm sure he'll return soon."

He offered her a strangled smile. "I'm sure you're right, however, I am still going to write a note to General Clinton making him aware we are ready should he need us."

"That's a fine idea."

John stalked back to his room and Sally let him go. Logic told her Andre was taken captive and would return in a few months or a year. Intuition told her she was dead wrong.

Father knocked on John's door.

"Not now, Sally," John said, barely squelching his annoyance. He had no time for her anger over Israel and Liss, whom he wisely left behind on Staten Island.

"Colonel Simcoe open this door."

John snapped his head up. He rose from his chair and opened the door to Mr. Townsend's thunderclap expression. He backed up as Mr. Townsend advanced into the room and closed the door.

"You have something that belongs here," he said. "And I want her back."

"Why?"

"You know why. She had no right to run off. If she had come to me and explained her situation. If Israel had come to me and expressed his feelings for her, I might have been willing to listen and perhaps grant her freedom so she could live as she wanted."

Mr. Townsend took one more step forward. "I am not ignorant to the arguments for and against slavery, Colonel, but a homestead this big needs many hands. I don't engage in the business of slavery. I do not buy and sell men or women for profit. If I need an extra pair of hands, I acquire them. But then they become part of my family. As was Liss."

"A part of your family that doesn't have the right to come and go as they please? Clearly that was how Liss saw it, or she would have come to you. Don't you think?"

"If anyone else here wants to leave, then they will be granted their freedom. Until then, you must return her to me."

"I must not do anything of the sort. She has been granted her freedom and is now Israel's wife."

"No one can grant her freedom but me!" Mr. Townsend shouted and for the first time since entering this house, John feared the older man and doubted the wisdom of his actions in granting Liss her freedom. Still, he squared his shoulders and met Mr. Townsend's wrath head on.

"The British government has granted her freedom and there is nothing you can do about that."

Mr. Townsend glared at him. "We'll see about that," he said.

"Where is she? I wish to speak with her."

"Israel had work to do at camp. I left him there to perform his duties."

"Very wise of you, son, to deny me an opportunity to speak with my servant." Mr. Townsend poked a finger into John's chest. This isn't over, Colonel Simcoe." He turned and left, slamming the door behind him.

When he'd gone, John resumed his seat and struggled to get his breathing under control. He picked up his quill to get back to work but his hands shook so, he had to put it back down. It was several moments before he pulled himself together and got back to business.

50

The next morning, a dispatch rider from General Clinton's headquarters arrived with a note stating that Clinton believed the enemy would deal with Andre from Tappan where he'd been captured, rather than go to the trouble of moving him south.

In his reply, John told him he would remain in place and await orders, but reiterated he was prepared to send scouts to patrol roads to Philadelphia. He didn't believe they would keep him in Tappan. Andre was too big a prize.

For the next week, he stayed clear of the Townsend's, especially the patriarch who glowered at John and no longer tried to be civil to him. Only Sally remained by his side, a silent witness to his constant pacing and mumbling of actions to take if only General Clinton would give the word.

She said little, not daring to incur his wrath. John was aware he was being difficult, but he couldn't help himself. He wanted his friend back and somewhere in the back of his mind he began to suspect someone alerted the enemy as to their movements and actions.

He paced the sitting room until Sally glanced up from her knitting. "May I make you some tea, John?"

He glared. "Tea? Just like a woman to think the world's problems can be solved with a cup of tea."

He resumed pacing, turning away from her reddening face and the anger flaring in her hazel eyes.

With slow deliberate movements, she set down her knitting needles. "I'll make some anyway in case you change your mind."

With a stiff back and stilted gait, she left the room.

John chastised himself. She was only trying to ease his mind, to relieve his burdens. He needn't snap at her.

Several moments passed before Sally returned, carrying a tray with a teapot, two cups, and some biscuits, which she placed on the small table at the front window. Good thinking. He'd sit, enjoy his tea and keep an eye out for dispatch riders.

"Thank you, Sally dear," he said, pulling out a chair for her. "Please forgive my rudeness. I'm being terribly boorish snapping at you."

"If I didn't know how much you care about Andre, I would be most offended, John, but I understand you're worried, and worry makes us all do and say things we regret."

"You're being more than kind," he said, taking a seat across from her as she poured.

The door knocker rattled, and John nearly overturned the table in his haste to answer the summons. He returned opening a note.

Sally put down the pot and lifted her cup to her mouth. "I do hope you have good news," she said, then sipped.

John stood frozen on the spot. This wasn't good news. It was the worst news anyone might deliver. He lifted his gaze from the dispatch and stared horror struck at her. He was nauseous and his eyes burned as he blinked back sudden tears.

His voice sounded flat to his ears. "Andre won't be released. He's being held as a spy."

"What? How? Why?"

He shook the paper, which wasn't hard. His hand shook so hard anyway, the parchment naturally rattled. "This is a reply from General Harry Lee. In his last letter, he assured me Andre would be released to his own countrymen, exchanged for a major or some such, but now he says the situation changed and he can do nothing. Andre will be treated as a spy and hung."

Slowly he lowered himself back to his seat and leaned his

elbows on the table. Cradling his head in his hands, he ran his palms over his hair, mussing his dark curls, before covering his face to hide the wetness streaming down his cheeks.

Abruptly he dropped his hands to the table with a thump. "But he can't be charged as a spy. He was in uniform. That means they must treat him as an officer traveling under a flag of truce. Andre insisted on traveling under a flag of truce."

He glanced at Sally, who stared at him in wide-eyed, fearful silence, her face white as a sheet as tears pooled in her eyes.

"Oh, John," she said, her voice choked from anguish. "Surely not. They will treat him as an officer and a gentleman. He will not be harmed. He will be exchanged soon."

"This note is dated October the second. Yesterday. I can still do something before they hang him. Excuse me, Sally. Thank you for the tea, but I must write to General Clinton immediately."

"Of course," she said, letting him go.

Sally remained at the table long after John left. A spy! Not Andre. He was too smart for that. He would never put himself in such a position. The only man she recalled hung as a spy was the young Nathan Hale, at the beginning of the war. He'd foolishly told Robert Rogers, at the time the leader of the Queen's Rangers, he was to gain information on the British and was duly hung.

"'I only regret that I have but one life to lose for my country.'"

Sally recalled reading those famous last words and now they came back to indict her for her actions.

Though John didn't say so, she understood with unerring certainty Andre went to West Point. She listened to their conversations from upstairs, found the note addressed to James Anderson, and informed Robert of everything. If Andre was hung for espionage, his blood would be on her hands.

How would she live with herself?

She needed to talk with Father. Sally jumped from her seat and left the tea fixings where they were as she ran to the back of the house and out the back door.

She found him working in the fields, helping with the harvest.

"There you are, Poppet. We need every hand. Help us gather in the pumpkins."

"Father!"

357

Her voice choked and she had to stop. He straightened at the strangled sound and stopped his work to peer closely at her before wiping his forehead with the sleeve of his linen shirt.

"Father, I need to speak to you. Urgently. Something terrible happened."

"Let's go back to the house," he said coming toward her.

"No!" She held up both hands. "Not in the house. John might overhear."

"The weaving room, then."

Once in the weaving room, a scowl crossed Father's face as he excused Hiram and Patty who were preparing the loom for the next round of wool. She didn't need to ask what he was thinking: If Liss were here, Hiram could be helping with the harvest.

When they left, he guided Sally to the bench.

"Now," he said, placing a gentle hand on the top of her head. "What's distressing you, Sally."

She drew a deep breath and started talking, telling him everything going back to the day before the tea party when she found the note addressed to James Anderson.

"I listened in Solomon and Samuel's room through the grate. They planned somehow to take over West Point. I sent a packet to Robert the same day outlining everything I learned, including the information about the note. Of course, I have no knowledge of what happened after, just that Andre has not only been taken captive, but he is being treated as a spy."

She gasped and clung to his arms. "Father, the last person to be treated as a spy was young Mr. Hale. What if they hang Andre? It will be my fault!"

"No, Sally. If they hang Andre, and I will be most sorry if they do, it will be because of his own actions. You are incidental to this business."

She shook her head. "No. If I hadn't given Robert the information, he couldn't act on it and Andre wouldn't have been captured."

Father straightened and peered down at her. "Do you have specific knowledge your information contributed to his capture? Did Simcoe tell you so?"

"No."

"In that case, you may not have had anything to do

with anything. It's possible Andre made a fatal mistake having nothing to do with you."

She studied his blue eyes, his hair which at the beginning of the war showed streaks of white mixed with auburn was now completely white, tied back into a queue with a blue ribbon. "Do you think that most likely?"

He leaned down placing his hands on his knees to meet her eyes. "I have no idea. But that is exactly what I want you to put in your head. Tell yourself those words until you are convinced so if John does suspect something, he won't suspect you."

Father straightened. "Thank you for telling me all of this." He started to leave but turned back.

"Be wary of John, Sally," Father said. "He's a dangerous man right now."

51

For two days, Sally walked on eggshells around John, keeping at the top of her mind the advice Father gave her. She had nothing to do with Andre's predicament. The situation would work itself out and he would be restored or not, according to God's plan.

Then came more explosive news. General Arnold had defected to the British and intended to hand over West Point to them. Oyster Bay reacted with varying degrees of shock and disbelief.

Still primarily a Tory town, many in Oyster Bay rejoiced at the fact. But for Sally and a growing number of many like her, the news was received with fury.

Calls immediately went out for the exchange of Arnold for Andre so the proper turncoat could be punished.

Sally prayed this may still happen. Father stayed close to her since their talk, and he now worked in the sitting room while she knitted. As per usual, John paced up and down muttering dire threats if anything happened to Andre.

"What say you to the news of your much beloved and praised General Arnold now, Mr. Townsend? Wounded twice in the left leg, he's been hailed as the hero of the so-called American cause."

Ever so slowly Fathered lowered his quill as he deliberated his answer. "I think," Father said, glaring at John, "we should cut off his left leg and give it a proper Christian burial, then hang the rest of him." He rose from his seat, bowed to John, and left the room.

Sally turned an astonished gaze to John, who stared back with equal aplomb. Never, since the start of the war, had Father expressed himself so openly. The rattle of the door knocker brought them back to reality.

John answered the door and returned to the sitting room accompanied by a young man Sally had never met but whom John knew well.

"Peter," he said, placing a solicitous arm around the young man's shoulder. "What brings you here?"

A request from my master," he said, acknowledging Sally with a curt, "Miss."

Sally rose. "I'll leave you two to talk."

"Are you by chance Miss Sarah Townsend?"

"I am," she said with a confused glance at John, who appeared as perplexed.

"Please stay, madam, for what I have to say concerns you as well."

David appeared in the doorway. Suspecting Father sent him as a protector. She beckoned him in.

"This is my brother, David. If you don't mind, I'd like him present for your message."

Peter shrugged as if he didn't care and wiped his face with the palm of his hand.

John grew impatient. "You come with good news I trust. When will Andre be released? How soon can I speak with him?"

"The major is dead."

Peter began to cry but pulled himself together with effort. "He met his fate two days ago. I brought him his regimentals, so he at least died dressed like an officer, but the low-down, dirty...." He broke off as if not wanting to insult sensibilities. "They wouldn't let him die by firing squad. They hung him like a thief."

David moved close to her, and Sally clung to his hands. Disbelief shredded her mind and rendered her mute.

Peter turned to John. "When they drove him to the site of his death and he found only a gibbet, he addressed the crowd and said, 'All I request of you, gentleman, is that you will bear witness to the world that I died like a brave man.' And then he turned to me and said, "'it will be but a momentary pang.'"

Sally's heart dropped into her stomach. She never believed Andre would suffer. The British would trade him for Arnold, the real criminal, or exchange him for a minor officer. John would somehow come up with a plan Clinton would approve, but not this. Not death. He was too young. Too vibrant a man, too wonderful to die such a death.

She couldn't contain her grief any longer and fled, pounding up the stairs to her room where she flung herself on the bed and wept bitter tears.

Sally noted a shift in her relationship with John, over which her guilt and shame rendered her paralyzed.

For his part, he stayed away from the house for long periods of time and when they did speak, they were stilted, or angry words exchanged. Sometimes, he reacted to her with instant anger or bitterness such that many times she came to the brink of confessing her heart.

He'd had the Rangers add black feathers to their caps in mourning and when she tried to compliment his thoughtfulness, he glared at her as if he blamed her for the necessity.

"If I catch the culprit responsible..." he muttered, pacing the floor of the sitting room on a rare day home.

Sally spun wool and remained silent, not wanting to bring his wrath down on her head. It had happened far too frequently these days to the point where she was starting to fear him.

"I'll find out who did it," he turned and headed back her way. His gaze fell on her, and he wagged his finger at her. "You mark my words, Sally. My enemies will feel my wrath. I won't stop until every single person calling themselves Americans feels the point of my bayonet."

Her wheel stopped and she stared at him in utter astonishment. That was the first time, in her presence anyway, that he referred to Whigs as enemies and not as misguided Englishmen who would one day understand the error of their ways and return to the King's fold.

"John, surely you don't mean that," she said, but his venomous glare silenced her.

"I most certainly do. Mr. Washington is nothing but a barbarous and ungenerous fool. I know who is really responsible for Andre being hung at any rate and that is that nasty General Lafayette. He was on the court-martial board. If not for him, Andre might not have met such an ignominious death."

Not knowing what to say, she returned to her spinning and tried not to weep.

He sat in a chair and picked up a book to read. He seemed not to have much to do today with the Rangers. Either that or he had lost interest in them for the time being. He put the book down and looked at her.

"I read an interesting piece this afternoon from Dr. Samuel Johnson. Are you familiar with him?"

Sally glanced up but only nodded, not daring to speak, but he continued as though unconcerned by her silence.

"He wrote regarding Andre's murder denouncing all Americans, writing thus, 'I am willing to love all mankind, except an American.'" He laughed. "I quite agree with the sentiment. Don't you?"

Sally's back stiffened and she raised her sad gaze. "Does..." She had to clear her throat. "Does Mr. Johnson's sentiment include me, John? My family? Do you consider me unworthy of love now? An unworthy foe?" She couldn't resist throwing that at him, gratified that he at least had the grace to appear embarrassed.

"No, Sally, of course not," he said, his tone sounding as if he addressed a small child, and he kept his gaze on his lap.

The whirring of her wheel started up again. She'd had an insight the day before the tea that John wouldn't have the grace to handle tragedy the way Andre did and now, he proved her correct. The idea saddened her, but in a detached way like an interestingly shaped puddle in the road.

Near dawn, Sally was awakened by an uproar in the house. Throwing on her clothes she ran downstairs to find out what was amiss. The Queen's Rangers were leaving. So early in the morning? Why?

Taking a candle, Sally went to John's room, but his door was open. She gazed into his room, finding it empty. No, not empty. Empty would imply he left for the day. The room was deserted, though he'd left a candle burning on the night stand next to the bed. He'd packed his belongings except for one item, lying on the pillow.

She entered, her heart pounding as it often did when he was here. It was now an automatic response, the sense she had no right to be in a room of her own home.

She picked up the page and studied it in the light of her candle. It was the silhouette Andre cut of her. She noted The curl that fell upon her forehead, her hair in a utilitarian bun on the crown of her head, her soft lips, and small nose. He even caught the ribbon which closed her chemise.

Sally burst into tears. This was a message from John. He blamed her for Andre's plight. She sank onto the mattress and wept, her guilt and sadness. She never meant for Andre to die, and she never meant for John to hate her.

As the sun rose, Sally arrived at the training ground, dressed in a woolen skirt and her camlet cloak. She held the silhouette in one hand and had to dodge this way and that to avoid men preparing for action. For war against their fellow countrymen. She stopped to look for John. He shouldn't be hard to spot, he stood head and shoulders above most of his men.

Buffeted by passing men, who barely acknowledged her, she found John by the wagons Daniel procured.

"John," she called out. He turned and watched her approach and when she drew close, she held up the drawing. "So this is goodbye?"

"Not now, Sally," he said and tried to move past her.

"Yes now!" Her shout froze and silenced the men around them. "Such a brave soldier you are, John, but you don't have the courage to say goodbye to my face?"

He said nothing but his face reddened in a way that had nothing to do with the cold.

"What would you have me say?" He snarled, drawing close to her face, but she was too angry to be intimidated by him.

"I know someone in your house did it. I know someone found out what we planned. I don't know how they found out but when I discover the means and the culprit, believe me, Sally they will pay with their life."

Appearing as if he'd decided he'd said enough, he turned and stalked off.

She wasn't done and hollered after him. "Where are you going?"

He glared at her violence in his eyes. When he advanced on her, she retreated a step.

"I am going," he snarled, "to complete this bloody war, and when we win, and we will win, I will come back here and exact my revenge upon everyone responsible for my friend's murder."

She gawked at him. For the first time since knowing him, she was truly frightened of John Simcoe.

"He was my friend, too, John," she managed to squeeze out.

"Go home, Sally!" He said and his shout echoed across the training ground. Soldiers stopped their work and eyed them with varying degrees of concern. He flapped an angry arm at her. "Go home! I have a war to win." He turned and stalked away, shouting at his gawking men.

Sally let him go. She had a war to win as well. On the way back to the house, she recalled her conversation with Liss.

She'd said Israel loved her and she loved him. Perhaps someday, Sally would find a man to love. A man who would possess her to give up everything she knew for him. As Liss obviously did.

She had wanted Israel. She had wanted freedom. Was that so bad a thing? As though a living being separate from her body, Sally's heart shifted. She would not have love. John said he loved her, but she saw now his love was conditional upon their success in the war. Father had warned her he was too ambitious a man to take an American as a wife, especially if the Americans won the war and with the French now aiding them, most people had begun to accept the inevitable. The Americans would win because the French wished it.

True Sally entertained the idea that she loved John but had known for some time that she did not. But that didn't mean Liss couldn't have her happiness and her liberty. After all, wasn't that what this war was about?

On that Christmas night, Sally had been called upon to declare her loyalties. Though she didn't comprehend it at the time, when Robert gave her the code book, she'd declared herself. Sally Townsend would be a patriot.

HISTORICAL NOTES

The Belle of Oyster Bay is first, a work of fiction. If you, dear reader, watched the AMC series Turn, then forget everything you think you know about John Graves Simcoe. By all accounts, John Simcoe was a brilliant, if sometimes ruthless soldier, but he never killed for sport. He was a gifted builder and politician. After the war, he married Elizabeth Gwillum who was the ward of a friend of his father.

John went on to found the city of York, in southern Ontario, Canada, now known as Toronto. He laid out the streets and set up the government. He worked for years as a member of Parliament and was on his way to India to take the position of Governor General when he died on board ship.

John Simcoe's father died when he was eight years old, but there is no evidence his grandfather was alive. However, I needed a place for him to grow up and so invented one.

Sally Townsend never married. She lived the rest of her life in her home with Robert and her two sisters. There is no evidence she became involved in the Culper Spy Ring just as there is no evidence of any woman being designated 355, the code for "lady." Most scholars today believe it was just that. A coded designation. However, with John Simcoe living in their home and this being a work of fiction, a little "what if" was not out of line.

Robert Townsend was the number two man in the Culper Spy Ring, designated as Culper Jr. Spying in those days was considered beneath a gentleman's dignity, Robert did not want his identity ever discovered. Therefore, Robert was so private about his wartime activities that it felt reasonable that if he got Sally involved, he would keep her identity as private as his. The only other person who knew his true identity was Benjamin Tallmadge, who recruited him and went by the name of John Bolton. You'll see that name in the codebook Robert gave Sally. Robert made Tallmadge promise to take his involvement to the grave, and it seems Tallmadge did. Not even George Washington knew the true identity of Culper Jr. and when he traveled through Long Island after the war, he stayed with the Woodhull's, visited the Youngs' and several other families, but never stopped at the Townsends. It wasn't until the nineteen thirties that handwriting analysis identified Robert Townsend as Culper Jr.

The Townsend's were not Quakers. This is most evident in the fact that they owned slaves. Forgotten through history, is the fact that New York was a slave owning colony, and the Townsends had several. Many of the names are made up in my story, but Liss was a real slave owned by the family. According to the director of the Raynham Hall Museum, once the home of Sally and her family, Liss ran away from the Townsend's around the time the Queen's Rangers left Long Island for good, so I invented Israel, with whom Liss falls in love and runs away. Also, in my own poor way, I tried to juxtapose the hypocrisy of white freedom and liberty against the institution of slavery and the reverberations of racism still felt today. I do hope, dear reader that you will forgive me for my weak efforts at doing so.

Angela Moody

CPSIA information can be obtained
at www.ICGtesting.com
Printed in the USA
JSHW020343190123
36307JS00004B/15